TALKING OSCARS

Like the pistol shot that sets the sprinter running, 'Action' is the switch that turns the actor on. It is the mantra that launches him. For a split second he's suspended in a vacuum where he dies and comes alive again, like a high diver frozen in flight. The pulse races, the nerves are stifled, the senses rev up . . . and splash, he arrives in fiction.

There are two things that are notoriously difficult to fake for the camera: a slap in the face and a kiss on the mouth: and they seldom are. Nevertheless Paddy was surprised by the gusto of Jemma's kissing. It was fierce and soft and she tasted of mint or cloves or something outdoors and summery. Her tongue flicked an invitation at him. With their mouths locked they parried and thrusted like blind duellists. Were they fooling themselves or each other or just the camera – that greedy voyeur that gobbled up their intimacy at thirty-two frames per second? . . . All in a day's work.

'Cut.'

SIMON WILLIAMS

Talking Oscars

A Mandarin Paperback

TALKING OSCARS

First published in Great Britain 1986
by William Heinemann Ltd
This edition published 1989
by Mandarin Paperbacks
an imprint of Reed Consumer Books Ltd
Michelin House, 81 Fulham Road, London SW3 6RB
and Auckland, Melbourne, Singapore and Toronto

Reprinted 1994

Copyright © by Simon Williams 1988

A CIP catalogue record for this title
is available from the British Library

ISBN 0 7493 0145 7

Printed and bound in Great Britain
by Cox & Wyman Ltd, Reading, Berks

Love and thanks
to my mother,
my brother
and my wife

1 'That is one hell of a book,' said Fernando Cass as he closed his hardback copy of *Stratagems and Spoils*. He studied the dust-jacket, reluctant to withdraw from the fiction inside. He seldom read books these days and was unaccustomed to the feeling of disorientation that he was left with. His own reality seemed somehow in question.

Certainly the story had intrigued him and the outcome had taken him quite unawares, but what had really struck a chord in his actor's psyche was the central character. Fernando understood everything about Eliot Blandford, could visualise him in every detail and was instantly determined to have the role and create Blandford in his own image. The actor's urge to transmogrify can be quite as fierce as love at first sight.

Fernando plucked some ash from the gold hairs round his navel and flicked the butt of his cigar into the ocean. There was no wind and the sea was calm like milk before it boils. The tapping in the rigging had lost its tempo and Fernando hoped there would be a storm that evening. He felt like danger, 'FERNANDO CASS IN OCEAN DRAMA'. He had an *alter ego* who lived in headlines.

'That is one hell of a book,' said Fernando. Irving Barstow hated the sun, and was sitting a little way off in the shade, with his freckled skin swathed in Paisley. He even wore a panama hat as though to endorse his Britishness. Irving sipped his Campari judiciously in the manner of a literary man and said, 'Yes it is a good book, one of his best.' It had in fact earned for G.P. Conran enormous posthumous acclaim and had won the Webster Prize.

'I liked it a lot,' proclaimed Fernando scanning the horizon through half-closed eyes. Scanning the horizon through half-closed eyes was one of his most notable traits. In all his films he did a bit of horizon scanning (in close-up of course). 'I never read anything like it before,' he went on. 'It was full of surprises, you know, great descriptions and stuff. A lot of mood. A lot of suspense. Terrific.'

It was rare for Fernando to wax so lucid, and Irving sat up to polish his sunglasses. 'Yes, Conran has always had a good

1

eye for treachery and of course there's a lot of muscle in his prose – pace, wit. An understated *je ne sais quoi . . .*'

Irving squinted through his amber lenses at the hazy coastline. 'There's something of Le Carré in his style . . . he's almost in the league of Graham Greene in terms of narrative finesse. A good book.'

'Yeah,' concurred Cass. He respected Irving's intellect, even if he did not quite understand his meaning. A literary adviser was an asset on a film set. Producers reckoned Irving had class, even if in their hearts they knew there was precious little that Irving could do to enhance lines like, 'I want you out of town by noon tomorrow'.

It had only recently occurred to Fernando that he hardly had to use his brain at all nowadays. Did he not have a host of managers, consultants, agents and accountants on the payroll to do his thinking for him? They were supposed to be a buffer for him; they took the blame and he took the credit. But Fernando sometimes thought he had been robbed of purpose. What had happened to the young Cass who had wowed the critics off-off-Broadway and hiked west to Hollywood? Fernando was nostalgic for his earlier life, he felt irked by a sense of atrophy. Even his films were tailor-made to confine him to a popular formula, his instinct had perhaps been dulled by years of foolproof roles. Fernando felt suddenly determined; he could damn well show Al Pacino a thing or two.

'Do you think it would make a movie?' he asked.

'That depends,' answered Irving safely.

'I think it would make one hell of a movie.'

'Yeah, I think you're right it would make a hell of a movie.' Irving was never slow to follow suit, and he knew which side his toast was caviared.

'With Joss Dixon directing, it would be great. It's just his ticket. I mean look at *Limited Use* . . . beautiful film, a touch of the Goddards . . . Even Nigel Havers got nominated for Christ's sake and poor old Rachel got raves . . . it could be a winner.' He spun the ice round his empty glass.

Fernando regarded Irving as the eunuch of his entourage. In general, the idea of Englishmen screwing was hard to imagine, but the thought of Irving in particular in any kind of *flagrante* was absurd.

'It's not what you'd call an action movie,' Fernando said.

'No.'

'Not my usual kind of part.'

'No.' Irving began to realise that his employer was seriously contemplating the role of Blandford. It would be a calamity of course, the ruination of a good novel. 'Look on it as a challenge. You could be great in it.'

'The guy is supposed to be British for God's sake.' Fernando was inviting his objection to be quashed.

'It's not an unsurmountable problem,' Irving obliged. 'It's a question of essence.'

'That's right,' Fernando agreed, watching the gulls swoop low over the sea. 'I mean damn it all, I can't play him English can I?' He aped the accent and amused himself.

'No,' said Irving. 'Well perhaps it could be altered ... possibly Blandford's mother was American. Or maybe he went to Yale? They can fix it.'

'Right,' Fernando said, taking the persuasion easily. 'He could simply be British but sound American.'

'It could even add a dimension,' Irving continued. 'It would certainly broaden its appeal. I think it's a great idea.' The thought of filming in England appealed to Irving, he missed his flat in Highgate, and his flatmate too.

'You think I could play it, huh?' Fernando asked.

'Blandford? Sure.' On $2,000 a week who was he to gainsay his boss?

'It's not my usual bag you know. You don't think maybe I should play safe and do *Life Sanction III* instead?'

'I think you should go for it. Take a chance. Do it,' Irving goaded. 'The *Life Sanction* deal can hold. You can do that any time.'

'You don't think it's too tame? There's not that much violence. Menace, yes, but not violence ... people go to see my movies, they want action you know.'

Fernando was looking at the two girls sprawled on the foredeck. They seemed frozen in a still life. Bright drinks and magazines were scattered around their raftans and their four oily nipples pointed listlessly to the sky. Fernando had had them both, individually and together. It had been a joyless ménage that had left all three of them with an overwhelming feeling of indifference and Fernando with a nasty bruise on his shin. 'Superstud in sex trio saga'.

Fernando liked his sex brutal and dirty. He wanted protest

and then to conquer it. Acquiescence rather spoilt his game. Women who had been to bed with him agreed that it was not much fun, but his macho reputation somehow remained intact.

'There's not that much sex in it either. The book is very short on sex ... only straight romantic stuff. No big turn on ...'

'No,' said Irving Barstow, who actually loved G.P. Conran's understated way of handling the romantic storyline.

'In the screenplay we'll have to get it made a bit ... fruitier you know. Explicit.' Fernando grinned. Fruitifying scripts was another of his traits.

Irving was suddenly caught in a spasm of indignation; his whole life seemed futile. His knowledge, his integrity, his energy were being squandered. What was he doing sacrificing his honours degree in English Literature to this pig-witted baboon? For an instant he felt a surge of adrenalin pushing him to revolt. He nearly stood up and shouted, 'You stupid, self-centred slob – you're nothing but a stinking great ham. Your acting makes Burt Reynolds look like John Gielgud. So stuff it up your arse.' But the moment passed and what he said was: 'Fernando – go for it. You could be great in the part. I mean it, really great. It's an opportunity you should take with both hands and if you don't get an Oscar nomination, at least, I'll eat my hat.'

Fernando nodded in the way that one sage acknowledges another, and brooded awhile. 'FERNANDO CASS IN OSCAR BID SENSATION.' The two girls were giggling at something in a magazine. 'Well I'm sure as hell not going to shoot it in England,' he said. 'Lousy showers. Lousy beef.' Irving felt numb with loathing. He pined for the trim rare beef of Simpsons. And what was wrong with a good hot bath? 'Where would you film it then?' he asked, curtly.

'North Carolina – and Philadelphia. Philadelphia looks pretty much like London in places, kind of old and shabby.'

'Regency and Victorian,' muttered Irving.

'Yeah, whatever. Well I'm going to call Bud Schwartz and tell him to proceed. Get it set up.' Irving handed Fernando the cordless telephone and he began to dial Los Angeles.

Unlike a lot of agents Bud Schwartz only had two telephones

on his leather-topped desk, black and gold. The black was for riff-raff – starlets, has-beens and B-league directors whose calls came through the switchboard. The other telephone was a direct line reserved for the clients and producers who between them had made him a millionaire. It was the gold line.

Although Bud was chewing a Nicoret he held an unlit Havana cigar in his hand just in case of an emergency. He was listening to Kiki Grainger, on the black telephone, berating him about the inadequacies of her mobile dressing-room out in Arizona, and 'furthermore' she squealed that she was not that happy about the way this Polish director was treating her.

'Does he think I'm dumb or what?' Her question was rhetorical.

Bud spent most of his day smoothing the ruffled feathers of his actors and actresses. He could flatter and cajole effortlessly and rather enjoyed his avuncular role. He was happy to let Kiki get whatever it was off her ample chest. He listened patiently and set the executive toy on his desk in motion. Six balls suspended in a row swinging back and forth. Click. Click. Click. He figured in another half-hour his chauffeur would be speeding him home to a large Martini in Belair.

'I mean what am I? A fucking star of this shit film or what?' Kiki concluded sweetly.

'Sweetheart . . . of course you're a star, an artist. Now I don't want you getting all steamed up, baby, so you leave it to me. Leave it to Bud. I'll talk to them . . . It's diabolical . . . I'll fix it first thing . . .'

Bud was interrupted by the ring of his gold telepone. 'Talk to you tomorrow, sweetheart.' He disconnected Kiki in mid-squawk from Arizona. He plucked up the gold receiver.

'Bud Schwartz,' he murmured.

'Hi, Bud, it's Fernando,' Cass's voice was blurred by static.

'Fernando. How are you? I was about to call you,' he lied. 'How's the Bahamas?'

'So-so.'

How could life on a yacht with two gorgeous broads be so-so, Bud wondered. He said, 'Have you had any thoughts about *Life Sanction III*? Hoffman wants to tie us up. Do you want to work or what?' There was a pause.

5

'I've been thinking,' said Fernando. Bud's heart sank.

'Yeah?' he said.

'You know that book the guy sent over, *Stratagems and Spoils*? I've been reading it.'

'How was it, Fernando?' asked Bud.

'It was good. I liked it. I want to do it.'

'Wait a minute now, Fernando. You're talking about *Stratagems and Spoils* by that English guy, right? The one that died . . . something Conran. You liked it, huh?'

'Yeah. It's a good book. Well written, a lot of muscle in the prose. A bit like Graham Greene and that other French guy. I want to do it.' Cass was shouting above the static but Bud heard him clearly. He stopped the balls swinging and reached for the lighter. He sucked in a plume of blue smoke. This was the price you paid for hiring smart-ass British literary advisers. Bud wished Irving Barstow would rot in hell.

'Bud,' Fernando called.

'I'm here. I'm here. . . You're right, it is a good book. Very good. I liked it too.' Bud supposed he would now have to read the damn thing.

'Who's the producer again?' Fernando asked.

'Man by the name of. . .' Bud searched through his memo pad, 'by the name of Lefrak, Lewis Lefrak. He's new to the game, from Chicago.' He did not add that Lefrak had struck him as being sharp and sly, the kind of producer with whom Bud would not relish joining battle.

'Fernando, listen, this was a little while back; a couple of months?'

'What are you saying?'

'It's been a long time since you were sent the book . . . a couple of months . . . what are you, a slow reader?' Bud always chuckled in the face of disaster.

Fernando said, 'So?'

'What I'm saying is, I have an idea the project is now under way . . . it's too late . . . I may be wrong . . . I'll check it out.'

'I want to do it, Bud.' Fernando sounded peevish like a child.

'OK, OK.' Bud was suddenly in the time-honoured no-win situation in which an agent spends his working life. On the one hand he knew the film in question was in production in Britain somewhere, and on the other he had already pretty well committed his most treasured client elsewhere. He'd have trouble coming out of this with the smell of roses. 'Listen what's your thinking on the *Sanction III* deal ... Frank Hoffman's pushing to finalise.'

'Put it on hold,' said Fernando. 'Tell Hoffman we'll shoot it next year, OK?' Asking Bud Schwartz to put a twenty million dollar film on hold was like asking a child to shoot Santa Claus.

'OK, I'll tell him,' said Bud. The prospect appalled him.

'You know, I reckon this could be good for me, Bud. I mean it's really different, it's got a lot of acting in it. Mood. Something I get my teeth into ... It could be the big one you know.'

'Sure, sure.' Bud was forever chastened by the memory of having once rejected Sylvester Stallone. 'I'll talk to Lefrak and get back to you. OK?'

'OK. How's Thelma?' asked Fernando.

'Phyllis. Phyllis is fine.' To Bud there was a world of difference in his wives but to his friends and clients the four of them merged into one plump blonde composite. 'I'll get back to you, then,' he said, concluding the social niceties.

'I am serious you know,' said Fernando, as if it were in doubt. 'This *Stratagems and Spoils* could be one hell of a picture. Buddy, I mean, we could be talking Oscars, right?'

'Right,' said Bud. 'Sure thing. Bye now.'

He hung up his gold telephone ... and Liberace died of food poisoning, he thought.

2 On a clear day, and there are not many in Los Angeles, you can see the boats round Catalina Island from the small offices of Mediavision Inc., but Lewis Lefrak was not concerned with the view as he stood by the window. He was not taking in the yellow-pink splendour of the setting sun; he was gazing at something he much preferred, his own reflection in the glass. He met his own ruthless inspection unswervingly as if to outstare himself.

The face of Lefrak was pallid and yet swarthy and altogether narrow. His eyes were close together under a shallow forehead. They were pushed in, it seemed, by the sideburns that flanked his cheeks. His finely sculpted nose was not the Lefrak original. It was the work of a cosmetic surgeon in Chicago. The job had cost him three weeks' salary and had caused a furious dispute in his family. He had his nose cut off despite his father. His chin was thrusting and his lips had a cunning slant, but Lewis liked his face. It was the face of his hero.

The telephone rang in the outer office and Nancy answered it. Her gold-clad hand slid the receiver under her red hair.

'Mediavision, good afternoon,' she purred. 'Can I help you?' She listened. 'One moment, I'll put you through.' She put the call on hold, and scuttled into Lefrak's office.

'It's Bud Schwartz on the line from Renowned Artists,' she announced. Nancy knew this was a call her boss had long awaited and imagined that he might find her attractive as the harbinger of the good news.

'Put him on,' said Lewis, masking his excitement with the cool of Paul Newman. He wondered what the agent of the great Fernando Cass had to say to him and his mind was racing with possibilities.

'Hi, Bud, what's new?' he asked. They had not actually met but both of them were comfortable dealing in familiarities. The film business is no less lethal for its informality.

Lewis listened keenly to the glad tidings that Fernando was showing interest in *Stratagems and Spoils*. Since he had arrived on the coast Lefrak had been producing commercials and short documentaries. They paid the rent, but he longed for the chance to make a proper feature film. His desk was piled high with projects and scripts waiting for the endorsement of a star name to make them viable. As a producer he reckoned to keep his eggs very much in separate baskets. Only God and Nancy knew how urgently he needed one to hatch. And this could be it. He was sick of being treated like a novice. He would show them. He would show his father. Fernando Cass in *Stratagems and Spoils* produced by Lewis Lefrak . . . The dream was soon grounded.

'Now what about the rights to the property?' asked Bud. 'Didn't I hear there was some British production?'

Lefrak did not own the film rights and knew full well that the British production was already under way. He had a momentary feeling of nausea – he would not accept that the egg he was trying to hatch was infertile.

'Look, there's no problem,' he said. 'We're not talking about an itty-bitty domestic television show. We're talking about movies, right? International movies with international stars. There's no problem.'

Lefrak paused. He was puzzled to hear the sound of a faint click-click-click on the other end of the line. For a moment he imagined that the conversation was being recorded. He had no use for executive toys and failed to recognise the innocent sound of Bud's balls.

'I've got it all tied up OK . . . I mean Fernando is going to be just great in this movie. Just great.'

'We could be talking nominations,' said Bud.

'Sure thing. The part could have been written for him,' agreed Lewis.

'It will be,' said Bud. 'Who's doing the screenplay?'

'The screenplay? Who's doing the screenplay?' Lefrak gave the impression the line was at fault. 'Hank Zimmerman is doing the screenplay.' It was not just his modesty that prevented Lewis mentioning that Hank Zimmerman was his own *nom de plume*.

'Oh yeah. Hank Zimmerman. That's good,' Bud bluffed. 'And Joss Dixon will direct?'

'Yes, Joss will direct it.' Lefrak spoke loud and clear. He knew that lies need a positive emphasis to speed them on their way.

'And we'll shoot it over at Global.' They discussed publicity and agreed, for quite different reasons, to keep the project under wraps for the moment. They agreed to lunch in the near future and disconnected.

Lefrak sat back in his leather chair. 'Nance, we could be in business. Big business,' he said.

'Hot shit,' she answered with true Texan eloquence.

'But there are one or two problems to be sorted out.'

'Nothing we can't handle, honey,' said Nancy. Lefrak smiled a thin smile that thrilled its victim.

'See if you can get me Marty Clanger in New York will you,' Lewis asked. In her day-to-day fantasy Nancy was Jane Russell but she left the room with a hint of Rita Hayworth.

Lewis returned to his reflection in the LA gloaming. He felt fiercely possessive about *Stratagems and Spoils*. It was his brainchild and he saw it as belonging to him by right, if not by copyright. He had been thwarted in his efforts to buy it properly so he would now seek ownership by other means. As his mother said, there were more ways than one to cook a goose.

'I've got some good news and some bad news,' Lewis told Marty Clanger who listened to both without interruption. The two of them had been blood brothers since the fifth grade way back in Chicago. Together they were greedy rebels pledged to conquer the world they hated. Together they had skived and cheated and bullied their way through high school. They had shared everything, money, girls, cars, dope, ambition. As sophomores they had together made an illicit fortune in pirate videos, had dropped out and eventually gone their separate ways. Marty east to make money in New York, and Lewis west to make movies in Los Angeles. But they were still a team of two, ruthless and greedy; blood brothers.

'What's to be done, kid?' asked Marty when Lefrak had finished.

'Remember you told me you thought it would not be too difficult to pull the plug on this British outfit?'

Marty remembered.

'Pull it,' said Lefrak.

Two days later in the back yard of a pretty Georgian farmhouse in Oxfordshire a cock crowed. The raucous impatience of the sound echoed from the barn roofs and seemed to summon rather than announce the dawn. In the grey darkness a dog barked without purpose, and a short while later, upstairs in the main bedroom, Radio Oxford sprang to life on the radio alarm.

Paddy woke to the price of vegetables and fruit; in his semi-consciousness he learnt that leeks were scarce but bananas were holding their own. He knew that to move would be to activate the familiar symptoms of another hangover. Therefore he lay still. He was reluctant to leave the cocoon of his dreaming world where his half-buried notions were distorted by the rosiness of hindsight. His dreams were like cul-de-sacs that he could not help turning down again and again; each time they forced him back to reality with their dead-ends.

By rote he showered, shaved, made coffee, fed animals and ate muesli. He wrote a note to Mrs Goodall to the effect that he had enjoyed her casserole and could she change his sheets. PS Of course she was welcome to any eggs she could find in the barn. PPS Perhaps she could make one of her lovely haddock-in-cream-sauce dishes for tonight? He turned on the answering machine and gathered together his script, his filofax, and a pile of mail, then, pausing like a man with a half-forgotten thought, he fetched a small bottle of Smirnoff and packed it into his briefcase with the rest. He told himself he wouldn't necessarily need a drink – it was simply a contingency measure.

Paddy threw some Layers' Mash into the hopper for the hens and noticed as he left that the magnolia was budding, perhaps too soon. His thoughts turned to Hannah (didn't they always?) and how much she had loved the tree; he'd have to ask her when to prune it. As he slalomed round the pot-holes in his drive he thought again how different things had been five years ago when he and Hannah had first moved into the farm.

In those days when he was filming he would set the alarm earlier than he needed, and he would make love to Hannah before leaving. Her passion would be like part of a dream, sleepy and fierce; her body taking flight while her mind slept on. Paddy would then sneak away like a cat-thief in the dawn, and go to work feeling like a million dollars, the flavour of her still with him.

Without Hannah the farm seemed filleted. Without her

there was no pleasure or purpose in it. For Paddy it had become just a point of departure and return with no identity of its own during his absence. It was a house not a home in the way that a corpse is not a person, it's just a corpse. Paddy knew that the time would soon come to sell the house – he was too young to be playing Miss Havisham.

Paddy weaved along the base of the Chilterns to join the motorway. Pale sunlight angled through the leafless trees and gave the cows long shadows on the hillside. He pushed a cassette into the dashboard and listened to his own voice repeating the lines of the scene he was to film that day. Some actors are happy with a sketchy knowledge of the text. They feel it gives them an edge of spontaneity. But Paddy liked to be completely fluent with the lines by the time he went on the set. He liked precision in his work and spontaneity was not something to be left to chance. Paddy glimpsed a family of gypsies burning door panels on a bonfire by the road and hugging mugs of tea – their still life looked simple and he envied them. Whatever happened to simple? He rewound the tape and began again.

In times of trouble an actor is often at his best – his faculties are eager to take refuge from reality. His mind is happy to be transported to the safety of fiction with its predetermined outcome. And so it was with Paddy; for him *Stratagems and Spoils* was a panacea. He looked forward to his work, felt an affinity with the role he was playing. Eliot Blandford demanded a lot of his energy and imagination and Paddy was pleased to be giving them, at the moment he had no other use for them.

Frank Hoffman Junior was not a happy vegetarian. He hated meat and he hated carnivores. Above all he hated carnivores who smoked cigars, like Bud Schwartz who was sitting opposite him. For Frank, life was a running battle for longevity. He was panicked by pollution and haunted by cholesterol; his preoccupation with good health made him sick with anxiety. His blockbusting aptitude for horrific violence and the success of the *Life Sanction* films never ceased to disturb him. He made his living making movies but germs and microbes would be the death of him.

Once in the early days of their long marriage, Mrs

Hoffman, a nice woman who believed in moderation in all things including cleanliness, had found her husband abluting himself in disinfectant after coitus. Their sex life had never burgeoned, and the sole outcome of their endeavours was a daughter who delighted in squalor of all kinds.

Frank slipped an antacid tablet under his tongue; he really didn't like the plume of blue smoke from Bud Schwartz's cigar that was wafting towards him across the dinner table. Even less did he like what Bud Schwartz was telling him.

'I thought we had an understanding – a commitment,' said Frank ruefully. 'I'm desolate.'

'Believe me, I'm sorry, Frank, but there it is.' Bud had taken no pleasure in the meal either. Teetotal vegetarians were not his notion of good company; on top of which he hated apologising.

'How did it happen? How did Fernando come by this project? It must have come through you.'

'Indirectly, it was a long while back. It takes him for ever to read anything. Then, out of the blue, he calls me to say he wants to do it.'

'But we had a firm agreement.'

'We had a loose understanding.' Bud knew he was on dodgy ground. If only Hoffman had a better nature he would appeal to it, for diplomacy was his only hope.

'As I said, I am desolate,' said Hoffman sipping his decaffeinated coffee.

'It may come to nothing for Christ sake's.'

'What is it? This "Stratagems" and what is it? Who's doing it?'

'"Spoils". *Stratagems and Spoils*. It's an English novel by G.P. Conran,' Bud told him.

'Oh yeah, Conran.' Frank often wondered why he had resisted following in his father's footsteps. He would have been happier in pharmaceuticals. Instead he made films – crude, violent, popular films. Initially he owed his wealth to martial arts movies and was now doubling his fortune with the profits from *Life Sanction I* and *II*.

'And who is producing it?' Frank asked.

'A guy called Lewis Lefrak.'

'Never heard of him.'

'Like I say, Frank, it may not come to anything, but Fernando feels it's an opportunity he's got to take. He wants to stretch himself. He's an artist.'

13

'He's an asshole.'

'Look, all I'm saying is we want to postpone, not cancel, just postpone *Sanction III*; that's all, huh? I mean what's the problem? We can shoot it next year ... This *Stratagems* picture would be good for Fernando ... I mean we could be talking Oscars and think what that would do for *Sanction III*.'

'I want to start filming in six weeks.' Hoffman's tone was flat like cream.

'No can do.' Bud shrugged. He could find no common ground with Frank; he felt disadvantaged by his virtues. A man who didn't drink, or smoke or screw around had no business being a movie producer. 'If it was down to me, Frank,' Bud went on pleasantly, 'we'd be there. But Fernando Cass is his own man. He's made up his mind. You'll have to wait a while. I'm sorry, but there it is.'

'I tell you we had a firm agreement, you and I, to shoot this spring,' said Hoffman. Bud knew that it was true, he had perhaps been a little previous in the matter. He should have consulted his esteemed client before committing him to a third *Life Sanction* project; equally Fernando should not have taken so long to read the damn Conran novel and get himself worked up. All in all Bud had a feeling that the buck looked like stopping too close for comfort.

'We have no contract ...'

'Our conversations are recorded, and I reckon Fernando Cass has an obligation to me.' Frank took a deep breath, as instructed by his guru, to avoid stress. He went on, 'We're talking about seventy million dollars plus. Seventy million. Not some arty-crafty two bit load of horse-shit.' He was not a man blessed with the love of beauty or culture; indeed he felt somehow threatened by them.

'What can I do, Frank? He's my client, my friend.' A client he could not afford to lose. Without Fernando Cass on his books the Bud Schwartz pension fund would fall a long way short of the Bahamas. Bud launched another cloud of smoke into Hoffman's airspace.

'He was nothing before *Life Sanction*. He was on the scrap heap, a wash-out, a has-been. It was me who was responsible for his renaissance. And I tell you he owes me for that.' There was in his voice the cool anger of a scorned benefactor. 'And so do you. Your ass is on the line.' Bud hated being told his ass was on the line.

'God knows, I am not a vindictive man,' said Frank. 'But I have to protect myself. My attorney has advised me . . .'

'Steady, steady now. Don't let's get this thing out of proportion.' Bud was further alarmed by this mention of attorneys. 'My client has maybe been a little hasty in his decision; I'll talk to him.' Bud's loyalty could be quite flexible when it came to saving his own skin. 'We can work it out, Frank, we can resolve things.'

'I have worked it out,' said Hoffman coldly and folded his napkin four square to conclude things. It was past his bedtime.

'Look for goodness sake, Frank, we must not let this come between us. I respect you. I like you.' Bud leant forward and touched Frank's arm and smiled. He felt quite weak with disdain for this polyunsaturated man. 'Look I'll talk with Fernando. It'll be OK, OK?'

As he drove home that evening the consolation for Bud Schwartz was that the dinner hadn't cost him much, and he'd be back in time for the Johnny Carson show. However, the problem of removing his ass from the line was still unresolved.

3 During a ten hour day a film crew can produce approximately four minutes of eventual screen time, on a good day. So in order to produce the goods on camera, an actor has to pace himself. He has to learn when to conserve his energy, how to ration his adrenalin.

Paddy Brummel, having heard, 'It's a print, gate's clear,' meaning the take he had just completed had got its final sanction from the camera crew, stepped off the set across the spaghetti of cabling and slumped into his canvas chair in the corner.

It had been a tricky emotional scene between Eliot Blandford and his estranged wife. Normally Paddy might have loitered on the set to exchange small talk with his leading lady. It was Jemma Culver's first day on the film and it would have been courteous at least to make her welcome. Later Paddy would ponder why it was that he felt threatened by her vulnerability and her huge green eyes.

There was nothing more soothing to Paddy at these moments than *The Times* crossword. He found relaxation in the mental contortions of it and was oblivious to the background noise of the studio. His dresser brought him coffee and tucked tissues in his collar to prevent make-up marking the shirt.

'How's it going Mr B?'

'Fine, it's going well. Thank you, FQ,' answered Paddy. The name of the dresser was in fact Bernard, but he had long ago abandoned it in favour of FQ which stood for Frock Queen. As a name it neatly encapsulated both his working function and his private leaning. And anyway 'Bernard' simply wasn't him.

'Any quotes this morning?' FQ asked. He liked to help with the crossword. Anagrams were beyond him but he knew his Shakespeare and a bit of Milton although his Homer was scant.

'Yeah,' said Paddy without looking up. '"For now hath time made me his – Blank – clock." Nine letters, Richard the Second.'

'Oh lor. Let me see.' FQ stood with his arms akimbo and his right knee sagging. 'I can only think of Ian McKellen. Bless him.'

Electricians, carpenters, propmen, sound men, cameramen filled the studio with the noise of industry. They were working well and fast. Henry Gorringe, the director, had a knack of involving everyone and firing their imagination. The crew could certainly make more money working on a glossy international movie but *Stratagems and Spoils* appealed to their patriotism. It was a home-grown enterprise: British writer, British director, British actors and, most importantly, British financing. The feeling was that all too often it was British talent that won the Emmys and the Oscars while the Americans made all the profit. So the crew were keen; they'd show Steven Spielberg a thing or two. This was the second week of a fourteen week schedule, morale was high and the work and the wit on the studio floor were fast.

Henry Gorringe and Heime Chadwick, the producer, were both tacitly optimistic. The rushes looked good. The footage so far seemed to vindicate their controversial decision to shoot the entire film in black and white. It had been argued that it would look skimpy and that people had lived too long with colour on their screens to be thrust back to monochrome; but there was a fine tension in it. The film had that sharp texture of verité.

After five years in the popular TV series *The Declancey Inheritance*, there had been some worry that Paddy might have trouble finding the proper depth of character, but from the beginning his performance had an edge, sure-footed but subtle. On the surface his character had intelligence and charm but underneath the camera was finding an anger that was riveting. He took risks in his acting and gave off danger.

Paddy had not normally been known to be an ambitious man, but when he had first read the novel in proof form he had decided he would have the role of Eliot Blandford at all cost. And now it was his he knew, with the precision of an expert, exactly the impact he could make with it.

For the moment, however, Paddy was conserving his energy, engrossed in the cryptic problems of *The Times*, while FQ was lost in wonder at the thought of Ian McKellen's voice, among other things.

'Ooh, I nearly forgot,' he said. 'Mr Chadwick wants to see you in his office before lunch. He seemed to me to be in a bit of a five-and-eight.' FQ thought it cutely butch to use rhyming slang from time to time.

'Right,' said Paddy.

'Well, idle hands,' said FQ moving off. He turned back, suddenly hit by recall. 'I know, it's "Now hath time made me his numbering clock". "Numbering clock", that's it.'

'Good. Yes. Thanks,' said Paddy. FQ minced off thrilled with himself. He wasn't just a pretty face. Paddy wondered what it was that could have flapped the unflappable Heime Chadwick.

After the noisy labyrinth of linoleum corridors that led from the studio, Heime's office had a subdued atmosphere. Heime was sitting at his desk immobile in thought with the light behind him, like a portrait.

With no greeting and no eye contact Heime offered Paddy a drink. 'No thanks.' Paddy confined his drinking to the solitary hours of his own time where it helped to suspend him from reality and foreshorten the time before he could escape into his fictional persona. In that world when things went wrong, 'Cut' would halt it all and his mistakes could be reshot.

'Have a drink.' Heime repeated his invitation without a question mark. Paddy declined again sensing he'd need one in a minute though. He paused, expecting that the silence would elicit from Heime the substance of his gloom. Paddy had changed into a dressing-gown and now felt like a patient with a fatal diagnosis pending.

'What's up?' he asked.

'It's off.'

'What?'

'It's off. The film is off.'

What did he feel? What did he feel at that moment? Paddy was forever trying to recall what his first reactions to things had been; he was so preoccupied with masking them from the world he often forgot what they were. It was only in retrospect he could freeze frame and examine moments of impact.

The film was cancelled. *Stratagems and Spoils* was off. This was no joke. It was real, for sure. So, what did he feel? Anger. He felt angry. The pulse was banging in his neck and his scalp was scorching. What he felt was furious, he must remember that.

'What do you mean?' he asked stupidly. The notion of a vodka took his fancy.

'The studio have cancelled it. Matthew and I were called in to the head of programmes this morning. He was, of course, very embarrassed but he said there was nothing he could do. It was a Board decision.'

'Why?'

'Christ knows. Matthew is trying to find out.'

'We're not over budget. We're on schedule. I thought everyone was pleased with what we've shot.' Paddy found himself pouring a drink.

'So did I. They all seemed thrilled.' Heime looked pale and defeated.

When Paddy had heard there was a new G.P. Conran novel in the pipeline he had telephoned the reclusive old writer and enveigled from him an invitation to lunch at his home on the edge of the Ashdown Forest. He had so impressed the old author that he had readily agreed to let Paddy read a proof copy of *Stratagems and Spoils*. Conran's wife, Celia, had been a devotee of the much lauded and repeated *Declancey Inheritance* and was a personal admirer of Paddy's. It was she who had helped persuade her husband that Paddy would be perfect in the central role.

So, against the better judgement of his agent, who favoured a more obvious and lucrative Hollywood deal, George Conran had agreed to give Paddy a film option on what was to be his last novel. He had been repeatedly disillusioned by the way his earlier novels had been vandalised: 'Slashed to bits by the Technicolor scalpel,' the old boy said. Paddy had promised to do justice to *Stratagems and Spoils*.

There had been much gnashing of movie moguls' teeth; Paddy had snatched a prize morsel from under their noses. American producers had at first tried to coerce him into co-production with large sums of money and then with oblique threats. But Paddy knew that selling out would mean the sacrifice of his treasured role of Blandford to some Hollywood megastar (like Clint or Burt or Fernando, God forbid).

'Who's a clever boy then?' Heime had chuckled when Paddy dropped the juicy bone in his lap. 'It'll win you an Oscar, of course.' There was never any question that Heime would be the producer; he had taste and integrity, a rare combination in the movie game and he was Paddy's oldest friend.

'We'll get Henry Gorringe to direct – he'd be perfect.' And they did.

'And I think we could do worse than get young Matthew Goddard to be the executive producer. He's Sir Toby's blue-eyed nephew, keen as mustard and dead sharp. I think we should give him a break.' And they did.

With the glee of truant children at a picnic they had lunched on champagne and oysters. A giggly celebration of their partnership, they were invincible and their success was a foregone conclusion. They couldn't fail. All they had to do was get the cameras rolling. Easy.

'Another bottle of Krug.' It had been a good beginning.

The sharpness of vodka loitered in his mouth and Paddy could hear the wail of a police siren far off and wondered what other crisis was afoot.

'Then why, for Christ's sake are they cancelling it?' Perhaps this kind of thing was a habitual hazard of film production like wagon wheels going backwards.

'I've no idea.'

'Can they do it? I mean do they have the right?'

'Yes. They hold the purse strings so they have control . . . There's nothing to be done.'

'It doesn't make any fucking sense. It's crazy . . . They'll have to pay everybody off . . . I mean – why?' Paddy's mind was blank and his glass was empty. 'What can we do?' he asked.

'I don't know. Nothing. I said we'd meet Matt for lunch, he may know something.' Heime sounded resigned. He was an honourable man who liked to meet disaster with the same dignity as that other twin imposter. Over the years he had established a reputation for producing stylish and ambitious drama for television. His programmes didn't always make the ratings in England but they always won acclaim around the world. It was Heime who had first cast Paddy in a major role years ago, and their trust in each other was absolute.

'Surely we can just postpone for a while? Fix up some other deal?' Paddy was set on playing the optimist. He smiled and for a moment the distress in Heime's face lifted as he smiled back. It was an honest, healthy face whose features were elegantly surrendering to his fifty-odd years. Deep lines furrowed his dark skin and wings of grey hair swept back from his temples; his eyes had an unflinching quality and a warmth.

'It's not that easy,' he answered.

'There must be some other way . . . I mean we're not going to stop. It's not final.'

'It rather looks that way at the moment. You don't understand.'

Paddy understood that there was no way he would let the plug be pulled on him that easily.

In the midst of this first crisis of his career as executive producer there was no evidence of pessimism or despair in Matthew Goddard. Rather he displayed only ebullience and his usual huge appetite. In fact, the vigour with which Matthew was setting about his salad inspired confidence. Heime, Paddy and Henry had finished eating and were focused on Matthew who could eat and talk at the same time without diminishing either function.

'It's quite fishy really,' he said. He had spent the morning in the administration offices of the main television studios of Capitol and was glad to be back among friends. 'They were all extremely sorry and sympathetic and embarrassed and so forth, but quite unable to give the smallest explanation. James Morrison, who as you know has only been head of programming for two years, is furious. He's never known anything like it. He wasn't even consulted and he was only told this morning that the Board had decided to cancel. A lot of chat about having a dog and barking yourself . . . a very miffed man indeed. He says there's no point in pursuing it with the Board – they don't want to discuss the matter and that's that.'

'What about your uncle? Did you talk to him?' asked the laconic Gorringe with a Gauloise to his lips. Matthew's uncle was Sir Toby Goddard, chairman of the Board of Capitol TV. Everyone was so mindful of the universal distaste for nepotism that they hadn't liked to mention it, but not Gorringe who had a healthy contempt for the old boy network. 'I mean did you ask him what the bloody hell was going on?'

'Of course I did.' Matthew looked a trifle cowed munching

on his coleslaw – quite like a nephew. 'I was coming to that. He was particularly unkeen to see me. He said he owed me no explanation. How Board decisions were made was entirely privy and he had no obligation to me either as an executive producer or a nephew. All in all it was very much the less acceptable face of nepotism. I simply couldn't get anything out of him.' The blueness of Matthew's eyes could do the trick if anything could. 'We must assume that as far as Capitol TV is concerned we are, for unknown reasons, up shit creek without a paddle.'

'They hold all the purse strings? It's just them?' Gorringe asked. He had no interest in finance although he liked money.

'Yeah,' Matthew nodded. 'Heime and I considered spreading the load, but Capitol made us such a good offer in terms of co-production and so forth that we saw no harm in having all our eggs in one basket. Little did we know . . .'

Out of the window Paddy was watching three scene shifters manoeuvring a large papier mâché statue of Henry VIII out of the studio on to a trailer. 'So what can we do?' he asked.

'We've just got to find three million pounds or thereabouts, that's all. Quite fast,' Matthew grinned.

'Did you ask them if they would reconsider in the event of our coming up with a new partner?' Heime had every faith in Matthew who was his protégé, 'To share the financial load?'

'Yes. No. I suggested it to James and he called me back to say he was sorry, but it seemed they could not accommodate us on that.'

'Bastards,' said Gorringe. For him the only thing that mattered in filming was filming. 'So we're out of a job, as of when?'

'Tomorrow. I'll have to make an announcement at the end of shooting today,' said Heime.

'For Christ's sake it doesn't make any bloody sense. They'll lose a packet if they wrap it up. It's crazy.' Paddy was bubbling with indignation.

'Not our problem, Paddy,' Matthew seemed indomitably calm.

'But why for God's sake? What the hell are they doing this for? I mean, am I losing my reason or is this not going to be a very, very good film.' Paddy spoke slowly but with an icy emphasis. They all nodded, seldom had any of them seen him so animated. 'Well what in the name of fuck is going on?'

There was a pause. None of them had any cogent theory about what in the name of fuck was going on.

'It's bloody fishy,' said Gorringe. His CND badge was lopsided on his corduroy lapel. 'Bloody fishy ... I don't understand it.'

'Look there's no point in wasting time worrying about why.' Matthew was the youngest man at the table by ten years, but was the natural captain. 'What we have to do is sort out our options which are as follows: We can fold the whole thing lock, stock and barrel ...'

With one voice the first option was eliminated.

'Or ...' Matthew went on, 'we can carry on, right?'

'Right.'

'Right.'

'Is that possible?' said Gorringe.

'Oh yes. We still own the rights and, as Paddy said, it's still going to be a very, very good film. Our only problem is this question of the money.' Matthew made it sound easy.

'To be realistic though,' began Heime who found himself in the gloomy role of *loco parentis*, 'it's very rare that a salvage job ever works on a movie. They all cry, "sinking ship", no one wants a project second hand, that's the trouble.'

'Also, technically speaking, Capitol own everything we've shot. And on present form it's not unlikely that they would choose to withhold it. We'd have to start again.' There was no hint of pessimism in Matthew's voice. He had trained as an offshore accountant before going to serve an apprenticeship in the film industry. He knew how greedy and vicious people could be and he had learnt not to take treachery too personally. He cheerfully anticipated the worst in people and was seldom disappointed. There remained about him, however, the naïve look of a cherub.

'Can't you get it pre-sold; world rights and all that.' Gorringe was picking his teeth.

'We agreed at the outset not to do that,' Heime answered. He was an expert in marketing overseas. 'If you pre-sell, you undersell. We committed ourselves to making the film as well as possible and then trusting the open market. We didn't want to mortgage our profit potential, and I don't see any point in changing that opinion now.'

It was raining and Henry VIII looked forlorn standing full square on the low loader. Life hadn't been that easy for him either, Paddy supposed. He said, 'What are our chances then, do you reckon, of getting the funds together?'

'Good. I think we can manage it. The question is on what terms,' said Matthew. 'Time is not on our side I'm afraid.'

'How do you mean?' Paddy asked.

'Today is Thursday. If we're going to continue filming on Monday we'll have to notify the work-force tomorrow. That gives me less than twenty-four hours to rustle up the readies, it's not impossible . . .'

'It's crazy. It can't be done,' Heime's voice was sharper than he intended. 'The only sensible course of action is to suspend shooting altogether. Give ourselves time to regroup . . . let the dust settle.'

'The only danger with that is that we may not be able to gather everyone together again. People would be under no obligation to keep themselves available. The thing could fall apart.' Matthew sank his teeth into an apple. Henry Gorringe stubbed his cigarette and said, 'Yeah, well I'm afraid – much as I'm devoted to *Stratagems*, if it came to the crunch I'd have to . . .'

'Look around,' Heime prompted. 'Sure, exactly, we understand.' Unlike the others, Henry had elected not to be a partner in the enterprise. He did his work behind a camera, not a desk.

'How much would it cost to keep going?' asked Paddy.

'Difficult to say,' for most people, but not for Matthew. 'Approximately £30,000 a day.'

'I'll pay for the next week,' said Paddy. He didn't care what the hell it cost, he was sick of life backfiring on him. His voice was positive but the focus of his eyes was stuck on the poor wet king in the courtyard.

4 Intelligence of all that had been discussed at that lunch in the Capitol studio canteen was shortly to be relayed to the master bedroom on the thirty-seventh floor of a brownstone apartment block on the Lower West Side of Central Park, New York, New York, where a renowned nymphomaniac called Gloria lay contemplating the sleeping profile of her recent conquest by the pale light of the city dawn.

He had the irresistibly wholesome look of a real rogue; blonde and sleek. Beneath the untroubled skin of a financial whiz-kid, Gloria knew there lay the cruel nature of a bully. She liked what she saw and resolved to have him again, forthwith.

Pressing her belly against his flank she slipped her leg between his thighs, and shifted softly against him in a way he could think was simply for the sake of cosiness. (She revered the male initiative.) Her subject grunted in his sleep; Gloria draped her chestnut hair across his chest and muzzled at his neck. Surely he must be awake – the look on his face said not but there was hard evidence in her hand that told a different story. With the stealth of a lizard, she slid down him and took him in her mouth. To her this was home territory. She loved the feeling of power it gave her. . .

What actually brought Marty Clanger to full wakefulness from his pleasant slumber on that windy Thursday morning was the sharp ring of his bedside telephone. He felt a little scandalised at finding himself unwittingly *in flagrante delicto*, and at the same time irritated by the interruption of it.

Despite the dilemma, he was not a man to leave a telephone unanswered and by the fifth ring he had disengaged himself from (for Christ's sake who was it down there?) and picked up the receiver.

Marty's first lie of the day was 'no' when asked if the call had woken him. It wouldn't be his last. He listened to the clear-cut English voice and was not altogether pleased with what he heard.

'Who is he? This Paddy Brummel – some kind of nut . . . ?' Marty Clanger was speaking like a man who was fully

dressed and sitting at a desk. 'Look we don't have time . . .
You must stop him . . . with money . . . Yes . . . No, don't let's
be too hasty . . . Right . . . Right . . . do it. Fast. OK. Bye.'

Later he would call his old friend and ally, Lewis Lefrak,
who would no doubt be impatient at his progress. Meanwhile
there was other unfinished business closer to hand.

The atmosphere on the studio floor was one of mute
efficiency; there was crisis in the air and jokes were out. To
compensate, Henry was brisk and cool, which only served to
flame the crew's suspicion that all was not well. He kept
them busy though – his hallmark was speed; he shot fast and
tight. The camera never lingered in a Görringe film – it
panned and tracked and zoomed and snuck in crafty angles.
For technicians Henry could be dictatorial and demanding
but with his actors he was as gentle as a chef with velouté
sauce.

The scene they were preparing was between Blandford and
his former wife. It was a tricky confrontation, rife with
innuendo, and ending with a rather ambiguous kiss which
Henry saw as somehow more cruel than passionate; a kiss
wherein both parties call the other's bluff; a disclaimer not a
claimer of a kiss. In the cause of spontaneity they agreed to
leave it unrehearsed . . . It was to be what Henry called 'a
free-range job'.

Wardrobe and make-up and continuity went about their
final checks – powdering, dusting, adjusting – preening the
two actors like proud owners at Crufts. Filling Paddy's mind
was the new problem of his daily need for £30,000. Where
would it come from? Where did it go for God's sake? Was he
as mad as the others seemed to think? He felt unreal and
calm with the resolution of a kamikaze pilot. Paddy and
Jemma were ready.

'Absolute silence, please – we're going for a take.'
'Stand by.'
'I said QUIET.'
'Turn over. Go, sound.'
'Speed.'
'Sound running.'
'Mark it.'
'137 take 1.'

'ACTION.'

Like the pistol shot that sets the sprinter running, 'Action' is the switch that turns the actor on. It is the mantra that launches him. For a split second he's suspended in a vacuum where he dies and comes alive again, like a high diver frozen in flight. The pulse races, the nerves are stifled, the senses rev up . . . and splash, he arrives in fiction.

There are two things that are notoriously difficult to fake for the camera: a slap in the face and a kiss on the mouth; and they seldom are. Nevertheless Paddy was surprised by the gusto of Jemma's kissing. It was fierce and soft and she tasted of mint or cloves or something outdoors and summery. Her tongue flicked an invitation at him. With their mouths locked they parried and thrusted like blind duellists. Were they fooling themselves or each other or just the camera – that greedy voyeur that gobbled up their intimacy at thirty-two frames per second? . . . All in a day's work.

'Cut.'

Henry was pleased. The dialogue had gone well and the kiss was great. The camera was checked and a tea break taken. Paddy hurried off to his dressing-room to meet Heime who had news of a curious development.

G. P. Conran's literary agent had called Heime to ask if the rumour of collapse was true. And if so, could he enter into negotiations with another party who was interested in acquiring the rights of *Stratagems and Spoils*.

'Who was it?' Paddy asked.

'He wouldn't say.' An anonymous vulture who liked his meat fresh.

'You said no?'

'I said we'd think about it.'

'How the hell did they get to hear about it?'

'I've no idea.' Heime sounded impatient. FQ was making the tea and doing his impersonation of a trusty servant who knows his place, but his mouth got the better of him.

'Everyone knows.'

'What?' said Paddy.

'The company has gone broke. It's common knowledge,' he said, swishing an Earl Grey tea-bag round the pot.

'How can it be?' Paddy asked.

'Mind you, Toady Griffin is not a man I'd trust further than I could throw him.'

'Who is he? What do you mean?'

'Electrician. Always in the know. It started with him, said he'd heard from a friend in admin last night . . .'

'Anway,' Heime began in the tone that retrieves conversation from a side track, 'what we have to consider is whether or not this offer is worth pursuing.'

'No. What we have to consider is how to refinance our own production, not how to sell it off.'

Paddy felt indignant that Heime should be so unstalwart. Normally he was known to be a fiercely uncompromising producer – a renegade even in the style of his distaff Spanish blood. His father had been a farmer who, against all advice, had married a flamenco-crazed marquesa, and they had lived compatibly ever after. Their sole progeny benefited from a fair blend of Suffolk and Seville; a British phlegm and a Spanish charm combining in a determination that won Heime his way – usually.

'Paddy, look, I don't want to sound patronising or craven but one of the great virtues in life is knowing when to quit.' To Paddy he sounded patronising and craven.

'Of course I admire, we all admire, your notion of putting up the money and saving this film. It's very heroic . . . noble; but foolhardy. Foolhardy. You simply can't afford it; £150,000. And that's just for starters. Nobody can. You'll just bankrupt yourself and nobody will give a damn. I know it's impossible to be objective . . . but it is just another film.'

'No, it isn't.' Paddy felt like a petulant son in the face of this paternal wisdom. Was he being foolhardy – perhaps obsessive about the project? Was he wrong to cling on? Was not the whole thing fishy though? 'I'm sorry,' he smiled at Heime, 'I can't explain but there it is.' FQ was sipping his tea behind the arras and kept his counsel. Paddy continued, 'We must carry on. Mm? I mean, what is happening to us? We can't let these people . . . do this to us.' Later he realised the word he had been looking for was sabotage.

Of four telephone calls, which would each perplex their recipients, the first was to Mr Fothergill, the friendly manager at Coutts Bank. He was surprised that the prudent Paddy Brummel should be undertaking such a commitment, but it was the very prudence of the man that

28

persuaded him to agree to a loan of £200,000. And anyway Mrs Fothergill would be pleased as she thought Paddy was the cat's whiskers.

The second call was received by the young director of an advertising firm. He was surprised to hear from Paddy Brummel's agent that, for unknown reasons, the elusive star had changed his mind and would now be only too pleased to accept the offer of six commercials for a new instant mashed potato. However, the fee that Mr Brummel wanted for his services made him wince. A lot of potatoes.

The third call was to the offices of Bentley and Harmer of High Wycombe, where Nigel was in charge for the afternoon while his father, Ronald Harmer, was detained at a managerial consultation. (He was in fact in bed with a divorcee in Maidenhead.) Nigel's chin was landscaped with acne even though this was, technically, his last year as a Young Conservative. He was perhaps too mild a man to be a first-rate estate agent. He had the ruth his father lacked. But he was a sincere lad and sincerity has its uses.

Surprisingly Paddy Brummel (*the* Paddy Brummel) was on the telephone seeking a quick sale for his farmhouse. It was a property that Ronald rated highly in terms of development potential; tastefully converted barns with inglenooks and rustic beams were his forte. And with his contacts in the Rotary Club he could probably swing a bungalow or two in the paddock.

Nigel was overcome with a feeling of triumph. Daddy would be pleased. He assured his caller that a quick sale would be no problem, regretted he was unable to estimate the price himself, thanked Paddy profusely and hung up. He hadn't felt so elated since he had got to the final of the Amersham Junior Badminton Tournament. Alas, he was a runner-up.

The fourth surprise call was taken by Hugo Cavendish, a devious old Harrovian journalist who had done more than most over the years to lower the tone of popular journalism. He had never imagined that Paddy Brummel of all people would volunteer a personal interview. He braced himself with a substantial swig of gin before going to inform his editor of his scoop and its breathtaking price.

FQ was half delighted and half appalled at the instructions his master's voice had been giving on the telephone during the last hour. He had heard Paddy lose his house, his integrity and his privacy. His marbles, too, FQ didn't wonder.

'Why is Toady Griffin called Toady Griffin?' asked Paddy, on the spur of an earlier thought.

'Well, I suppose,' FQ swung his weight onto the other hip, 'it's because he's such a creep, a sycophant. He's always toadying to the bosses, you know, towing the management line, etcetera.'

'I see.' Although Paddy looked tired, there was, FQ fancied, a certain lustre in his mien. Here was a man who would go down fighting. Ever so British.

There was a knock at the door and both Paddy and his dresser were surprised to see Jemma Culver. She had an air of apprehension as she came in. Her head was up but her eyes were down.

'I wonder if I could have a word with you?' she asked.

'Sure.' Paddy had risen.

'Alone.' Jemma indicated FQ who indicated a mute well-if-that's-how-you-feel-I'm-off expression and left.

'Would you like some tea?' Paddy asked.

'No thank you.' She sounded crisp. He offered a chair which was also declined. Paddy suddenly realised with a hideous clarity that he was wrong in thinking his visitor was nervous. Jemma was angry.

'Look,' she began quietly, 'I'm sorry to barge in like this but I'd just like to know what the hell is going on.' She swallowed. Why did her mouth never have the right amount of saliva? It was either too dry or so full of spit she was forced to punctuate her speech with unscheduled gulps. She went on. 'I haven't done much filming. I'm a stage actress basically so I don't give a monkey's toss what you think of my work but I do think I am entitled to a bit of common courtesy. That's what I'm used to. I can't work like this, I'm sorry but there it is. I think you're the rudest actor I've ever worked with. Ever.' This emphatic repetition stopped her in her tracks. She felt winded and needed a prompt.

'Go on,' Paddy said. He was leaning on a chair looking oddly sad. Jemma wondered if she had misjudged the whole thing; had simply been tricked by that old hobgoblin, paranoia.

'Well, um . . . that's all really. I just wanted to say that if you don't like what I'm doing . . . that is, how I'm playing the part, that's fine. Why can't you say so? Discuss it. Sack me even. I don't care – but let's do it nicely. I mean manners. You haven't spoken two words to me all day. As soon as we finish a scene you rush off . . . I don't want a great heap of flattery and attention but I won't be ignored either . . . it's not how one actor should treat another. It's not friendly,' Jemma concluded, and swallowed.

Paddy turned and walked over to the window. He felt like Goliath, struck between the eyes by the truth of what she said. What an oaf he was not to have realised Jemma must be the only person in the studio who had not heard the rumours, was unaware that the feeling of unease was not to do with her. His mouth was dry with contrition, he was appalled to find himself guilty of such ghastly offences. He had been unkind, unprofessional and the rudest man this girl with green outrage in her eyes had ever met. Ever. Could the day get any worse? He wondered. And how did one set about enlisting as a Trappist monk?

'I am very sorry.' He watched a jumbo jet clawing through the damp orange miasma of West London. Wanted to be on it flying away from his embarrassment . . . He turned. 'You're going to be very good in the part. Excellent . . . you don't need me to tell you that . . .' She was standing very still with her arms folded like someone waiting for a bus, or an explanation. Paddy suddenly remembered the kiss and the taste of her mouth. The thought did nothing to relieve his guilt.

'It's been rather a difficult day,' he said inadequately. There was no excuse, but he wanted her to know the situation. 'Are you sure you won't have some tea?' She shook her head.

'Everyone on the set, please, Mr Brummel,' FQ shouted through the door.

'I am sorry,' Paddy repeated, as they left. Jemma shrugged a fraction of remission.

5 'Ladies and gentlemen.' The assistant director clapped his hands for attention. 'Before we wrap for the day Mr Chadwick wants to say a few words.'

The thirty or so members of the film unit gathered round – solemn as church-goers. Heime emerged from the shadows on to the set, looking tense and blinking under the lights. He held a page of notes in his hand but spoke without reference to them.

'As some of you may have been aware, we have today hit something of a crisis. Due to unforeseen circumstances Capitol TV are having to withdraw their financial support for our film. This means that we should technically speaking suspend filming forthwith.' Paddy was standing with Jemma at the side of the listening group and could see a pearl of sweat swerving down Heime's jaw. 'However, we feel, that is, Henry, Paddy, Matthew Goddard and myself that what we have here is Something Good. Very good. And I'd like to thank you all for your excellent work and enthusiasm . . . On the strength of what we've shot so far we feel it's worth persevering. So we are going to try and carry on . . . Paddy perhaps you would like to try and explain.'

What? Paddy was aghast. This unsolicited invitation to speak came as rather a shock. His thoughts were quite unmarshalled and nowhere near ready to be harvested for speech.

It is a popular misconception that an actor can cope without a script; the truth is that the very nature of his job renders him especially naked without a written text to hide behind. Actors like to camouflage themselves with their dramatic personae. In public they need that licence to be someone else. Someone better maybe. Like masked dancers at a ball, they guard a certain secret.

'I don't know what you think about *Stratagems* but I think it's going to be terrific. Bloody marvellous. And it means a great deal to me.' The studio seemed quieter than Paddy had ever known it. He had taken off his tie and his eyes were earnestly focused on it as he wound it neatly round his fingers. 'And it seems to me to be utterly pointless to abandon it. So, I have arranged some alternative funding . . . of my

32

own, on an interim basis, which means we should be able to work for a week or two, while Heime Chadwick and Matthew Goddard look for some other backers.' The tie fell loose from its coil. Paddy looked up and by chance got caught in the intent green stare of Jemma Culver. She seemed to nod, Paddy thought, as he once again began rewinding. 'There is of course no guarantee they'll succeed but I suppose I think it's worth a try. I hope you do too . . . Er . . . Perhaps you'd all like to join me for a drink in the bar – while I can still afford it. Thank you.'

At the back of the gathering a famously disgruntled chippie called Mervyn clapped his hands together quite slowly, as if to lead the others. The applause immediately took off and Paddy put the tie back in his pocket at last.

The walls of the studio bar were adorned with photographs of actors and actresses, row upon row. An ageing collage of familiar faces, head on, over the shoulder, into the camera, at the middle distance, smiling, scowling, pouting, leering . . . younger. Each one bore a personal message to Betty who had run the place since before Technicolor. She was as amiable as an old labrador and believed thespians were all children who needed a little love and alcohol. And who should contradict her?

Older actors could recall that she had once had a figure that rivalled Jayne Mansfield but now gravity had taken its toll. She was arguably one of the most talkative women who ever drew corks, but she ran a friendly bar with clean glasses and ample measures. Her heart was in the right place even if her bosom wasn't.

Betty was teetering about collecting glasses among the remaining dozen of Paddy's party (nobody pinched her bottom nowadays). It had all been ever so jolly, and earlier she had been surprised to hear that nice Paddy Brummel telling quite a rude joke at the bar. Such a quiet man normally – well no wonder after all he'd been through.

In the corner Matthew was telling Paddy that he had had no luck in tracing the mystery caller who had sought to buy the film rights from G.P. Conran's agent.

'If we knew who it was,' Paddy said 'we might be able to get some idea of what's going on at Capitol, why they've pulled out.'

'We might, but it wouldn't help us. Anyway we don't know there's a connection. We're only guessing.' Matthew was munching crisps with zest. 'If my uncle and the Board choose to renege on us, which they are legally entitled to do, our problem is not to reason why. We simply have to get our act together and find some other money – it would just be a waste of time trying to find out what their hang-up is. The fact that I hope dear Uncle Toby rots in hell is neither here nor there.' Munch. Munch. 'No, what worries me is the idea of you putting yourself in hock for a quarter of a million pounds. That really could be a bit of a ball breaker.'

'I suppose so,' said Paddy. He had a fleeting image of his genitals in a meat grinder with a wad of money. 'Heime thinks I'm crazy.'

'So do I,' Matthew laughed, his white teeth flecked with crisps. 'But for Christ's sake that's what life's about. You've got to go for it.'

'He thinks we should pack it in.'

'Not really he doesn't. He knows how good this film is going to be – he's just worried about you. I tell you it's down to me to find the loot, that's all.'

Across the room Jemma was laughing at something Henry had said. It was a rippling sound that might have been bottled up for ages, dirty and pure at the same time. Her hair was scraped back and her skin shone with moisturiser. On the wall behind her Norman Wisdom was laughing too.

'Any luck?' Paddy asked.

'Not yet. I'm seeing some bankers tomorrow morning. If need be what I'll do is form a consortium of backers, each in for, say, half a million. It'll be OK.' Matthew was brimming with confidence, throwing peanuts at his mouth with a practised flick. Was his appetite limitless? 'I tell you, Paddy, if I had any capital I'd be right in there with you.'

'Would you really?' Paddy liked Matthew, although when they had first met he had struck him as being a cocky little bugger. 'Thanks,' he said.

'I reckon Gorringe might be your problem,' said Matthew, about to move off. 'I know he's a good director and all that but he's a commercial animal at heart . . . he could be the one to cry sinking ship.'

Stan, the sound man, was doing an impersonation of Heime, who had left earlier, looking immaculate after three large gins, but with the tell-tale walk of a man ascending invisible stairs. Everyone was laughing. Paddy sensed an atmosphere of gleeful defiance in the face of the production's adversity, and wondered if it would translate into the co-operation that was needed . . . sinking ships he didn't like.

Paddy was on the point of rejoining the party when he was intercepted by an earnest young actor with a red beard and outstretched hand.

'Dennis Hills,' he announced with the confidentiality of a password. Paddy shook the hand, glad to have been reminded of its owner's name.

'Hallo Dennis. How are you?' he said.

'Well the thing is, I was wondering if you had heard about this repeat fee row that's been going on. Another bloody case of exploitation of the work-force.'

Paddy remembered him now. They had done a production of *The Importance of Being Earnest* together at Leatherhead. He was a dullish actor who always seemed to have a political axe to grind. On that occasion, Dennis had sought to introduce a subtext to the play wherein Algy turned out to be a militant Marxist. An exercise that would have had both Oscar and Karl spinning in their graves.

'What row is that?' Paddy asked with the caution of a closet Liberal.

'Well, there's quite a high level investigation going on about it with the Union.' British Actors' Equity being what it was, Paddy reckoned this meant that two old actors were talking it over in the Garrick Club. 'As usual, the employers are trying to rip us off.' Dennis was standing too close, the way all zealots do, and Paddy found that his breath was sweet with nicotine and fried food.

'How's that?' he asked.

'Well that's what we're trying to find out. It's the royalties, you see, all looks perfectly kosher but it seems that a couple of the big independent telly companies, including Capitol, have been operating a bit of a con.'

'In what way?' Paddy asked. Alcohol was staving off his tiredness and he felt alert, lightheaded even. He wondered what Dennis was doing here, he had nothing to do with *Stratagems and Spoils*.

'Well look at it this way. How can it be that in America, all we got of our original fee is 15 fucking per cent. Fifteen per cent for the whole of America. And that's for three showings. Five per cent a go. It's peanuts. Bloody pathetic. I mean look at the size of America. It's fucking huge.' Paddy could see there was no arguing with the size of America and now he came to think of it, his royalties from *The Declancey Inheritance* had not been that impressive.

'I was told it was only a syndicated sale not networked,' Paddy said. He regarded repeat fees as a bonus and banked whatever he got gratefully. 'Apparently the audience is really quite small.'

'Not smaller than bloody Gibraltar, mate.' Dennis seemed obsessed with acreage. 'You get 6 or 7 per cent for Gibraltar. No, that's what they always say, about it only being syndicated. But, you see, what happens is Capitol and Northern TV have formed this company called Transworld Telly Sales and they market all their programmes abroad through them. It's supposedly an independent set-up but wouldn't you know it, of course, Sir Toby kiss-my-arse Goddard is one of its leading lights. Surprise. Surprise.'

'There's not necessarily anything wrong with that,' Paddy said. He was impatient to be gone.

'Oh no. The old pals act still rules OK. But it means they don't have the problem of accountability. They only have themselves to answer to.' Frothy missiles occasionally shot from Dennis's mouth.

'But if Equity are investigating them and their books aren't in order, it will all be resolved surely. And we'll get some back payments.' Paddy could certainly use them.

'No. No. Transworld Telly Sales are too clever for that. Their accounts are all pristine, as you'd expect. What I reckon is they've done some under-the-table deal – a trade-off against some fucking American programme or other. Who knows? The point is it's always us poor sods at the bottom of the dung heap that lose out. We're the ones who get exploited, as usual.' His beard seemed even redder with revolutionary fervour.

'What's to be done then?' asked Paddy.

'I'll give you a ring and you can come to our next meeting. And tell your agent not to sign any overseas sales agreement with Capitol. Boycott them right.' There's irony for you, thought Paddy.

'Come along now, boys,' Betty's voice was calling out, 'time for Betty to go bye-byes.'

'Thanks, Dennis, for putting me in the picture.' Paddy shook his hand again, and was suddenly aware that Jemma had gone. He was irritated at having wasted his time in conversation with this angry man – an opinion he would revise before long.

Paddy approached Betty to find out what he owed her. Thirty film workers drinking for two hours couldn't be cheap.

'No, love, it's all done,' she told him.

'What do you mean?' Paddy asked.

'It's all paid for.'

'It was my party. My tab.'

'I can't help that now Mr Brummel – they absolutely insisted,' Betty simpered, although her simpering days had long passed.

'Who?'

'All of them. The camera boys, the sound crew, the sparks, the chippies – the lot. Mervyn had a whip-round.'

'Oh.'

'Said to tell you that you could pay next week.'

'Oh, that's nice,' said Paddy. He hated words like heart-warming.

'However, you owe me six pounds and twenty-five pence, for four pints of lager and two whiskies.'

'Oh?'

'Chap with the red beard said you would pay.'

'Oh right,' said Paddy looking round for his guest. But the room was empty, Dennis had defected.

6 In order to be late Lewis Lefrak instructed his driver to pull off the highway at the Vue And Chew Saloon. To be early was to be eager and that was the last thing he wanted to be seen to be on his first encounter with Fernando Cass. They would meet as producer and star, not as new boy and headmaster. Above the doorway a neon light flashed feebly in the midday sun and as he entered Lewis was soothed by the cool darkness of the empty bar.

'Hi, man – I would sure like to be of service on this beautiful day,' said the barman, a bearded refugee from the flower kingdom of his youth. He had that seventies look of startled godliness. Lewis hated Northern California; it was full of folk singers and religious freaks – the drop-outs who couldn't make it in the civilised world of LA.

'Give me a beer,' he said in a tone that cut no Christian ice.

The day had started badly for Lewis. Firstly Marty Clanger had interrupted his work out by telephoning with the news that the British production of *Stratagems and Spoils* had not crumbled as planned. Despite the withdrawal of their finances, they were set on continuing the film using the private funds of the leading actor. Lewis had been forced to suggest that Marty should buy him off. A hundred thousand dollars seemed a high price to pay to prise this stubborn actor's fingers from the rights. Lefrak was not optimistic in this regard; the tenacity of the Brits could not be underestimated: to wit David Puttnam and Margaret Thatcher.

Secondly the *Hollywood Inquirer* carried a headline: 'CASS DUMPS SANCTION DEAL' which prompted an early call from Bud Schwartz (whose nubile secretary it probably was who leaked the story) to say that in view of this regrettable and mysterious leak, he was keen to negotiate terms for his client as soon as possible to avoid further speculation.

Thirdly the secretary of Fernando Cass had telephoned Lefrak to say that the star himself would like to see him for lunch today, to discuss the screenplay which he had just read. It had been a summons more than an invitation but Lewis had readily agreed. An hour later he had found himself reluctantly flying north to Sacramento.

Lewis looked down into his beer and reflected on his plight. He was fast becoming committed to producing a film to which he had not the slightest legal entitlement. Lefrak was used to flying by the seat of his pants but this was a jumbo jet and he was out of his league.

To cap it all the barman was now singing along with Willie Nelson on the juke-box while he polished the glasses ... 'Rings on her fingers and time on her hands.' Lewis loathed Willie Nelson. He finished his drink and walked out of the bar with the swagger of a cowboy going to a shoot-out. Before continuing his journey he called Nancy at the office to learn that Frank Hoffman had telephoned to invite him to lunch. What did this sly man have in mind, Lewis wondered uneasily like a new leopard in the jungle.

As they approached the first set of electric gates, they were scrutinised by a closed circuit camera. A disembodied voice asked Lewis his name then bade him 'Welcome to the Cass ranch', and told him 'to proceed'. Speeding up the endless drive he already felt overawed by the opulence. He braced himself against his old bogey – the feeling of inferiority. He wished he was meeting the great star on neutral territory – at someone's office or a dim restaurant in Beverly Hills. They drove through oceans of pale crops lolling in the light breeze and nearer the ranch itself they passed corrals of palomino horses – ash blondes against the sepia hills.

The house was surrounded by cultivated trees and was itself made of a reddish timber with a low Spanish roof. A pretty Mexican boy who sounded Chinese greeted Lefrak and led him to the pool area. He had seen it all before, of course, in the movie magazines, but he was unprepared for the shocking brilliance of the turquoise water set in a lawn of the greenest grass. For a moment he wondered if his dark glasses had lost their tint.

'Welcome, Lewis, welcome, I am so glad you could be here,' said the approaching Fernando Cass with his hand outstretched, 'pleased to meet you.'

Lewis shook his hand – the hand of Fernando Cass. He had come a long way from downtown Chicago. He was dazzled, again, by the whiteness of the Cass teeth and was surprised by how big he was. Why were stars never the size you expected?

His face had a neolithic power with deep-set eyes the

colour of American Express. The two other guests were a languid black actress called Candida Pink and the very white Irving Barstow who was sitting in the shade rereading *Vile Bodies*. Nobody seemed to have noticed Lewis was late, damn it. The informality nonplussed him; he had imagined the meeting would be round a table with perfect air conditioning, not round a pool in this searing heat. He felt ill at ease in his lightweight Dior suit and was soon forced to shed it, like the others, in favour of a pair of baggy borrowed trunks.

'I liked the screenplay,' said Cass later as they sat under a fig tree. 'Isn't that right, Irv?'

'Yes, you did. We all did,' said Irving with hardly any sincerity in his voice. Small Mexicans were clearing away lunch.

'I read it through last night. I liked it a lot,' said Cass. If only you had read the book with the same speed, I wouldn't be in my present predicament, thought Lefrak. 'Zimmerman has done a great job.'

'Yes. I think so, it's a fine adaptation,' Lefrak agreed. Now was not the moment to reveal his *nom de plume*.

'I thought it was terrific, really terrific,' said Candida flashing a smile at Lefrak.

Under his panama hat Irving felt like a traitor. For the ten thousandth time he contemplated removing himself from the back of this idiotic tiger and regaining his self-esteem in Highgate. He feared for his soul even though the night before his flesh had been thrillingly sated by the houseboy.

'There's still a lot of work to be done, of course,' said Cass. 'I mean Blandford has got to be Americanised and so on.'

'No problem at all,' said Lefrak.

'It's going to be one hell of a movie.' The smoke from Fernando's cigar was souring the sweet smell of the fig tree. 'It's got a lot of scope. It's a great role, Lewis, I mean, meaty. I tell you Blandford is going to be good for me – I'm going to tear the balls off it.'

'That's what I figured,' said Lefrak sipping his tequila.

'And I've had this great idea,' said Cass fondling himself round the left nipple. 'Candida is going to play Blandford's ex-wife, Helen.'

Irving's mouth had been full of coffee but at this news his epiglottis went into spasm forcing it up into his nasal tract.

'What about that?' beamed Fernando. He leant forward

and stroked Candida's thigh. It was like polished mahogany. She smiled modestly as though it had been announced she was having a baby.

Lewis gulped. Tequila scorched his throat and he could smell his Givenchy aftershave evaporating in the heat.

'I must admit I hadn't thought of it . . . being played that way. It hadn't occurred to me,' he said, masking his apprehension with a look of shrewd deliberation.

'Wouldn't that just make it?' enthused Cass. 'I mean wouldn't that add something?'

'It could be interesting,' said Lefrak. Was this a dream? 'Very interesting.'

'What do you think, Irv? Wouldn't that give it an extra dimension?'

'It certainly would,' said Irving. The coffee was still stinging his adenoids. 'It could make quite an impact . . . very dramatic.'

'Wouldn't it just give that *Je ne say coit* you were talking about?'

'I think it might,' Irving nodded. The previous night the sound of Cass and Candida coupling had awoken the entire household. Even the coyotes in the woodland behind the house had answered with a howl. It was an atrocious piece of casting – but this was the way the world wagged, Irving concluded.

'How do you feel about it, Candida?' he asked.

'I think it's kind of crazy but what the hell,' she shrugged. 'It's a good part, but I guess I'll need a voice coach to get the accent.'

'Yeah. Well she's supposed to be the daughter of a conservative politician. Right?'

'Yeah. That's right,' said Lefrak groping his way to an escape route. 'But what worries me is . . . that I saw the character of Helen as . . .'

Irving held his breath.

'Older.'

They drank more wine and discussed rewrites, schedules and locations. Fernando, it seemed, was keen to start work as soon as possible which did nothing to soothe Lefrak's anxiety about his ownership of the film rights. The idea of filming it in Philadelphia was the least worry. Lewis had the feeling that there was some further business that his cordial host was holding back. Stay cool, Lefrak. Keep your powder dry.

Fernando had had an acrimonious conversation on the telephone with Frank Hoffman, that morning. The aggrieved producer of the *Life Sanction* films had been in turn peevish, aggressive, conspiratorial and then conciliatory. Litigation, however, seemed inevitable. One of the conclusions of their discussion was that the best arse to be on the line was that of Bud Schwartz. The other was that Fernando had agreed to spend a week in London promoting *Life Sanction II* and attending the British première.

'Let's take a swim, Lewis,' said Fernando. He liked Lefrak. He had the makings of a good producer too, flexible and amenable, unlike Hoffman. They could do business together.

'Sure,' said Lefrak. He took the invitation to be a token of friendship and was only a little worried that his borrowed trunks would stay on as he dived into the water after the star.

To outpace his host, Lefrak thought, might be unwise, so they swam abreast for a dozen lengths before sprawling in the shallow end.

'You're in pretty good shape,' said Cass.

'So-so,' Lewis answered modestly. His own body was a source of constant pleasure to him. 'You too.'

'I'm OK,' said Cass swishing back his golden hair. 'Pretty fit. I'm forty-eight, you know.' And he had been for ten years.

'Now here's the thing,' began Fernando. Lefrak tensed himself for something he might not want to hear.

'I'm in a kind of an awkward situation ... with regard to my personal representation, that is Renowned Artists Incorporated. It's like this, Lewis, I'm not happy with the way Bud Schwartz has been handling things. He keeps fucking up. And an agent who fucks up ain't no use. Right?'

'Right.' It was the plain truth.

'I mean who needs an agent who fucks up the whole time. I need that the way the Pope needs testicles, right?'

'Right.' It was a fair analogy.

'So I've got to fire him, see. He's screwed me up, you understand, in this matter of the *Life Sanction* deal. He gave a commitment to Hoffman which he didn't ought to have done. He goofed up. Right?'

'Right.' It was Fernando's view.

'I want to do your picture, understand, I'm keen, very keen

– it's going to be great. Between you and me, we could be talking prizes ... Bud Schwartz goofed up with Hoffman and it seems like someone is going to have their buns busted. Right?'

'Right.' It was the inevitable price.

'So what I have to do is disassociate myself from him.' This had been the advice of Fernando's personal attorney that morning. 'If Hoffman is suing Schwartz, I want out.' What it lacked in loyalty it made up for in logic.

'Are you not under contract to Renowned Artists?' asked Lefrak.

'Sure I'm under contract to Renowned Artists. No problem. I'm suing them for malpractice. If Hoffman sues Schwartz then I sue Schwartz. I'm off the hook, see, Schwartz carries the can. It shifts the liability, so to speak. Makes sense huh?'

'Yes,' said Lefrak. Here, indeed, was a kindred spirit. 'Do you have a case?'

'Course I have a case. The screwball fixed for me to do *Sanction III* with Hoffman without consulting me. He knew all along I wanted to do this *Stratagems and Spoils* movie with you guys.'

'I see,' said Lefrak remembering that Fernando's enthusiasm for the project was in fact less than a week old. Schwartz was going to pay the price of Fernando's change of mind. On the grass at the other end of the pool Candida had prevailed on the reluctant Irving to rub sun oil on her back. Disdain was thinly hidden on his angular face, her brown breasts rocked gently with the motion and there was an amused smile on her face. She knew it was her sex not her colour that was making the British wimp squirm.

'So what I want is for you to bear in mind that we had an understanding. You and me.'

Lewis was beginning to see the light.

'It might even be,' Cass went on 'that you will be able to make it clear to my legal representatives that it has been my intention to do your movie ... for some time.'

'Sure. Since when?' He knew what he was being asked and he knew what side his conspiratorial bread was buttered.

'Say, six weeks.'

'No problem.'

'It must have slipped Bud's mind. I sure as hell told him about it.' Fernando shook his head sadly.

'He's not a young man, I don't suppose,' said Lewis.

Poor old Bud.

Lefrak would have to relay the new urgency of the situation to Marty Clanger with all speed.

'Good. That's fine,' said Cass. 'Come on inside; I want to play you a new tape I just got. Tell me Lewis, do you like Willie Nelson?'

'Sure thing, Fernando.'

7 Normally Paddy would set out for Oxfordshire as soon as he finished filming. He would listen to a Brandenburg Concerto on cassette followed by *The Archers* on Radio Four and would be home by seven-thirty to eat whatever supper Mrs Goodall had left him. But although his ordered life had been shot to pieces, it was not to be an altogether luckless day for Paddy.

In the studio car-park, as he went to leave, he found Jemma stooped under the bonnet of her Morris Minor.

'Bloody thing won't start,' she told him, obviously. 'You haven't got any jump leads have you?'

'I'm afraid not,' he answered. He was no use to her at all that day. 'Do you want a push?'

Jemma was furious with her ex-husband. It was typical of him to return the car with a flat battery and she loathed being forced into the role of woman in distress, especially in front of Paddy who could hardly feel disposed to help her after the way she had behaved that afternoon. Furthermore she had promised the bolshie baby-sitter she would be home an hour ago.

They pushed the sick Morris back and forth in the light drizzle to no avail, and eventually Jemma was forced to accept Paddy's offer of a lift home to Battersea. It was a journey that brought forth a glut of apologies on both sides: she apologised for her tirade, he for his rudeness; she was sorry not to have realised what was going on – he for not having explained; she excused her car and he his lack of jump leads. By the time they reached the Embankment they were sated with contrition and they drove in silence.

'Would you like to have dinner with me?' Paddy found himself asking. Sometimes he felt like a ventriloquist's dummy with a mischievous hand operating his mouth against his better judgement. Perhaps he was drunk or in shock.

'I can't, I'm afraid. I've got to get Kelly to bed. Thanks all the same.' She didn't like pleading single parenthood in the face of this olive branch. 'Why don't you take pot-luck at my place – I must have something in the freezer.' Was she mad? She had planned a cup of soup in bed learning her lines.

Paddy imagined his mouth was going to say, 'No thank you,' but it said instead, 'Why not – that would be lovely.' He was just a dummy. They stopped and bought some wine. Paddy reflected that his cats would be only too glad of Mrs Goodall's haddock in cream sauce.

As they walked into Jemma's terraced house they were greeted by Kelly who was bubbling over with way-past-bedtime euphoria. The Australian baby-sitter was dispatched and Jemma went into overdrive; stashing Lego and dolls and plumping cushions with a ceaseless apology for the mess. Paddy liked mess, preferred it to the spick-and-span bleakness at home.

It was a cosy room that abounded in Laura Ashley. The walls were decked in Victoriana and in the corner there was a weary piano with Kelly's exercises on the music rest.

Paddy was given a glass of wine and was soon commandeered by Kelly on the sofa. Her mother's green eyes shone out from a profusion of freckles – she seemed to lack any inhibition and most of her front teeth. Did he like horses? Dolls? Michael Jackson? Was he famous? Was he married? Did he have a dog? A cat? . . . Hens golly!! Did he believe in fairies? Ghosts? . . . Burglars? . . . Would he put her to bed? Paddy said it would cost her half a million pounds; she agreed to pay but he would have to give her a piggy-back upstairs and tell her a story.

While Jemma willed prawns to defrost in the kitchen Paddy allowed himself to be hijacked by her garrulous daughter. Whether it was men in general, or himself in particular that struck a chord in this little girl, Paddy didn't quite know. Who ever does? He told her a story about a giant and a freckled Brownie with a catapult, and by the time he had finished the sandman had almost bagged her. He watched her for a while drowsily sucking her thumb, but the pang of the smell of Johnson's baby talc soon sent him scurrying downstairs to refill his glass and stifle the memory.

'I'm afraid she can be rather overpowering,' Jemma said. She had chosen Vivaldi to cook to. 'She doesn't see much of her father, so men are rather a rarity in her life.'

'She's sweet. I enjoyed it.' Paddy smiled. Change the subject – keep off children, she thought. Jemma couldn't imagine what he felt. Didn't want to. She suggested he light the coal fire.

'I hope you don't mind pasta?' she asked.

'Lovely,' answered Paddy and set about his task. Twisting old pages of the *Guardian* into kindling he wondered if reality was returning at last. He felt like a passenger on a mystery tour; helpless and curious. Events were overcoming him but he was surprised by the vigour of his own response. It occurred to him that, perhaps, he should actually welcome this kick up the arse that the day had brought forth. Maybe the time had come for him to stop leading the life of a self-centred recluse sulking at the world. Foolhardiness notwithstanding, Paddy felt a flicker of excitement as the twigs and coal sprang into fire.

There was a smell of basil in the kitchen and Paddy watched Jemma moving fluently about her home territory – grinding, whisking, chopping, stirring. He had always enjoyed watching cooks at work brandishing their expertise like conjurors. The swift metamorphosis they inflicted on food fascinated him. He remembered how it had puzzled him as a child that his mother wore a frown for beating eggs and a smile for rolling pastry. He didn't reckon it was male chauvinism, he just liked the sight of a woman preparing a meal. It whetted his appetite.

Before eating he rang home to activate his answering machine. His first message was from Celia Conran who was clearly ill at ease with the device. 'Just to say I've heard what's happened . . . and what you're trying to do . . . You're a dear man . . . ,' her frail voice was shouting . . . 'That's all . . . call me sometime, goodbye.' The second was the usual call from Sister Wordsworth at the nursing home to say all was well and Mrs Brummel was fine; which meant no change. Oh, Hannah. Like someone who is used to permanent pain Paddy had developed a quick process for shutting out the image of his listless wife, drifting in oblivion. A small, lost dinghy on a flat sea. The third call came from an anonymous lout. 'You're wasting your time on *Stratagems and Spoils*. Leave it alone, Brummel, or someone may get hurt.' It wasn't so much the message that chilled Paddy as the flat cold voice of its harbinger. It was a voice with the flavour of cauliflower ears. But who could it be? And why? On whose toes had he trodden? Someone at the studio perhaps who didn't trust Paddy's proposal and felt somehow threatened . . . curiouser and curiouser.

Jemma and Paddy ate their *tagliatelle vongole* with a certain formality — each of them self-conscious and wondering how it had come about that they were eating together. They spoke of distant things, nothing personal, and kept their eyes down as if the candlelight was booby-trapped. They were like dancers at arm's length.

'What was Dennis on about?' she asked, making coffee.

'Dennis?'

'Hills. Dennis Hills, you were talking to him in the bar, or rather he seemed to be talking at you.'

'Oh yeah.' Paddy recalled the furious red beard thrusting at him. 'There's some question about repeat fees that Equity is looking into. He reckons there's been some great swindle. So who knows we may get some more money ... I wasn't really listening I'm afraid. He seemed quite concerned ... not to say overwrought.'

'Mm. He's like that,' she nodded.

'Do you know him then?'

'Not that well. We were only married for four years.'

'Oh I see.' What an extraordinary thing ... 'Well he seems ... pretty conscientious.'

'He's a bastard,' Jemma laughed. The attraction of opposites was one of the biological quirks that eluded Paddy's understanding. He and Hannah had often been taken for brother and sister. 'A rotten husband and a lousy father,' she said without rancour. 'I suppose I was rather dazzled by all that revolutionary fire.'

'He's Kelly's father then?' Paddy failed to conceal the amazement in his voice. Perhaps the beard was recent and there was a spectacular chin underneath.

'Yes,' smiled Jemma, 'not that you'd notice.' The effort to be flip failed and a shard of bitterness caught the light. She wasn't as tough as she'd like you to believe. She was hurt like any other casualty of the marriage tumbril.

'What was he doing at the studio?' Paddy asked.

'He came to return my car. He's been filming in Wales, he borrowed it. Could have warned me the battery was flat. The pig.' The coffee grinder howled in agreement.

'He's a political sort of man, I gather.'

'Oh yeah. Up the workers. Screw the management ... I'm surprised he ever works, he's always agitating ... sit-ins and marches and things. Once he sold a lovely necklace that my gran had left me to finance a demonstration. I could have killed him.'

Paddy should have gone home but they left the washing-up and took coffee by the fire. He told her about the menace of the recorded message.

'It must mean an awful lot to you – this film?'

'I suppose it does.'

'You can't let go?'

'No. Do you think I'm crazy?' Paddy asked. He wanted support.

'No, I think what you're doing is fine ... very defiant ... heroic even ... and yes, crazy. I mean here you are bankrupting yourself practically, and threatened with violence ... who needs it? It's a sad fact of life that films get cancelled – it's par for the course. The actor's lot is not a happy one ... we have to accept it ... don't we?'

'No. We don't. Not with this one.'

Paddy tried to explain to her why *Stratagems and Spoils* was important to him; how he had loved the book, how he had courted George and Celia Conran and promised them that this would be a film to be proud of. The fact that it would now be an epitaph increased that responsibility. Paddy's mind was suddenly overflowing with things he had left unsaid for too long ... things that were tumbling out desperate to be heard.

He wanted her to understand ... 'The point is, you see – I used to love acting. It was all I wanted – I just loved the theatre – films and telly and all that too, but the theatre mainly. The theatre was just the only place I wanted to be – I liked the idea of it, the look of it, the smell of it. I didn't care what theatre, I just wanted to be there ... all day, all night. Work, work, work, that's all I could think about ... Any part, anywhere. I was going to be the greatest Hamlet since Gielgud, the best Mercutio since Olivier... Very happy times ... well I suppose I got side-tracked ... Shakespeare is all very well but it doesn't pay the rent ... I've been very lucky. I've done a huge amount of very popular telly ... and that's fine, but just standing there speaking your lines week after week, the business of acting becomes rather ordinary – a lot of it is rubbish ... banal ... no buzz – good fat pay cheques but no buzz ... Rich actors get lazy, you know, flabby. I don't want that. I want it to be exciting again, that's all.'

The coffee was good. Jemma was staring in the fire.

'And this book,' Paddy went on, 'this extraordinary book of George Conran's is . . . is . . . what I want to do. It's all I want to do, and I don't care really, if it does ruin me . . . it's worth it to me. There's nothing else I . . . I'm probably being far too emotional about it but I can't help it – I am not going to let those bastards at Capitol just . . . squash it, for whatever reason. I will not be squashed by them because I care about this film . . . I haven't cared about anything, work I mean, for years . . . I've been too busy with . . . other things . . . the farm and . . . other things.'

It was 'other things' that brought him to a halt. 'I am sorry.' Paddy was appalled at having jabbered on. 'I'm being extremely boring.'

'No,' said Jemma after a pause. 'I quite understand.' And she did. His incoherence had made his meaning clear. Jemma sympathised for she knew how elusive ideals could be; had sat stranded like Canute while her own were beached behind her. She studied his face and saw no trace of the actor's usual bag of tricks – the weary arrogance, the sardonic amusement, the smouldering, etc, etc. Here was simply a tired, frustrated man who had had too much to drink. When it came to men, she was a girl who had always had a weakness for vulnerability.

'The point is I just don't care if it does break me. My problem is how to raise the money that's all.'

'Yes I see that, but I'm not sure you're right.'

'How do you mean?'

'Well I can see that finding the finance is obviously your first priority – to keep things going, but I think it's equally important to find out what the hell is going on: why Capitol have pulled out. Who tried to buy the copyright? Who threatened you? I mean there's no point in getting a lot of new investment together if the whole house of cards is liable to crash again.'

'I see what you mean,' he said. It hadn't occurred to him – he was trying to find a remedy without diagnosing the ailment.

'Why is this production being stopped – that's the question.' It was indeed. Jemma wasn't just a good *tagliatelle vongole* cook. She went on: 'Either there must be some good reason for Capitol to pull out, which we are not aware of – or someone else has another production in mind. My feeling is that it's a bit of both.'

Paddy poured some more Chablis for them both while he digested the simplicity of what she said. He hadn't made the obvious connection between the events and saw immediately the wisdom of it — he must investigate.

'You're not telling me that Capitol would just pull out of a major film commitment without good cause,' Jemma continued. 'They're certainly not short of a bob or two — it doesn't make sense them pulling out.' Unless, of course, they simply didn't like the way the film was looking, thought Paddy. Insecurity is an actor's Achilles heel — of all the arts his is the one that falls prey to subjectivity most readily. The actor himself is horrifically integral to his work — it is his face, voice, essence that are involved up there on that vast screen. In close-up each eye can be the size of a washing-up bowl and it's not easy to be detached looking oneself in the eye on that scale.

But Paddy knew, was more certain than he had ever been that *Stratagems and Spoils* was good. Very good. It was the film that George had approved, and would have approved of. He trusted Henry Gorringe and he trusted what he had seen in rushes. And further, he had a sneaking confidence that he himself had never been better. If it was not the quality of the film they had shot so far that was the cause of Capitol's intransigence — what was?

'We own the rights,' Paddy said, 'and as long as we own them, they can't stop us.'

'Who is we?' she asked.

'Heime, Matthew and me.' Paddy went on to explain how the three of them had conjoined and formed Fledgling Productions as equal partners.

'Not Henry?' she asked.

'No. He likes to keep his freelance status, but that doesn't mean he's any less committed.'

'And you're all in agreement that the show must go on?' Jemma used the cliché with a grimace.

'Absolutely,' said Paddy although he sensed that Heime's inclination was to take the line of least resistance. 'Somehow or other we'll finish the bloody thing.'

'Good, if there's anything I can do — let me know.' She said it lightly but meant it. Her gaze was lost in the fire — a wide-eyed focus on infinity. Paddy should have left an hour ago.

'Thanks,' he said. 'Do you play backgammon?' The question surprised them both; however, they played for an hour, as did Vivaldi – an ancient record of the 'Four Seasons'. What can be learnt, Paddy wondered, about a girl whose Autumn and Winter are fine but whose Spring and Summer are badly scratched?

Jemma beat him repeatedly without meaning to. They exchanged memories of their early working days, of provincial tours and monstrous landladies. They laughed together at time-honoured anecdotes and Paddy was reminded what confederacy there is in laughter. There's an acquiescence in it that binds people; makes lovers of them in its aftermath.

Paddy should have gone home two hours ago. He remembered a time when all this ritual had been so easy. He wanted to be twenty again; lighthearted and flip and in control, breaking promises and screwing around without a backward glance. Paddy contemplated kissing her and felt the fear of falling on his sword.

They had done the washing-up and Jemma was leaning against the sink. She went to speak, then didn't. Was she smirking?

'What?' Paddy prompted.

'I hope you're not going to . . .'

'What?'

'Try and take me to bed.'

Paddy was nonplusssed by this pre-emptive strike and smiled at the irony of it without answering.

'It's in your eyes,' she said. They were brown like toffee.

'Is it?' . . . Is it indeed.

'Yes . . . and it's just that I'd rather you didn't . . . oh dear, that sounds rude . . . well I can't cope. It's a simple as that.' She was wiping the kitchen table that was spotlessly clean – massaging her thoughts into the pine surface. Was she the same girl who had once been so nonchalant about the thin dividing line between comradeship and sex – had straddled it even. Had motherhood and a broken marriage taken away her frivolity; after all where was the threat? She went on: 'I mean I'd love to . . . but I can't. There it is. I'm afraid . . . I'm not terribly together – yet. I mean my togetherness count is pretty low. I can't explain – it's nothing to do with you. It's me ... the old having-fallen-off-a-bicycle syndrome. I'm not quite ready to be remounted.' She laughed half an octave and looked him in the face. 'Sorry.'

Like an eavesdropper, Paddy had felt powerless to interrupt; he wanted to staunch the flow of this unsolicited rejection, but couldn't. He was full of compassion for this wounded soldier from the age-old battlefield; a fellow victim more or less.

'Me too,' he said, imagining she might think it was only out of kindness. He wished he could reassure her with the truth, but his secret was locked in too deep. His impotence could not be given voice. He shrugged, 'No problem.' They stared at each other for a moment across the kitchen, their separate histories spinning between them. 'I think you're terrific,' he said.

'Good,' she said. Later, as she cleaned her teeth, it crossed her mind that she might have made a fool of herself. Perhaps she had misconstrued the look in his eyes and the bud she had nipped wasn't a bud at all.

'I must go home,' he said. As he kissed her on the cheek, Paddy had a memory of the taste of her mouth as Blandford had kissed her that afternoon.

'Let me rub your shoulders, honey,' said Nancy as Lefrak slumped forward on his desk. She had stayed late at Mediavision especially to be of service. She was eager to please him, mother him, smother him, utterly Mae West him. Nancy wanted to engulf him in her great roly-poly fantasy and did her best to insinuate her desire into the taut muscles of Lewis's shoulders.

Lefrak was exhausted. Fernando had wanted him to stop overnight, but keen though Lewis was to acquire the status of 'buddy', his threshold of endurance on the country-and-western front was limited. Furthermore Irving Barstow gave him the creeps. Lefrak had been glad to escape. Indeed, flying south he had felt a surprising sense of relief as he saw the spangled network of tinsel city come into view under its chiffon of yellow smog. It was home.

Nancy listened to the developments of the day and chuckled at the plight of Bud Schwartz. Sadly the innuendo of her fingers had not transmitted itself. She would suppress her passion though, with the dignity of Bette Davis.

'Well how are you going to get those crazy sons of British bitches to let go the darn thing?' she asked.

'The French have a saying,' he answered. '*Pour faire une omelette il faut casser des oeufs.*'

'So what's it mean?' she asked, hoping it might be dirty. 'It means,' he said with the smug tone of a guru, 'to make an omelette you have to break fucking eggs.'

'Cute.'

'Get me Clanger in new York,' he instructed.

To Lefrak, Marty didn't sound at all drunk; merely extremely impressed with the gravity of the situation. The answering service had eventually traced Marty to a friend's apartment on the Lower West Side, where the pressures of the day were being eased with Chablis and cocaine. Marty promised to call their London partner.

'Tell him to make this asshole an offer,' Lewis instructed. 'Let's get this Brummel guy the fuck out of the picture . . . or I'm in shit. I mean real shit.' There was no doubting the authenticity of the excrement in question.

'Sure thing, Lewis, stay cool,' he answered and they disconnected.

Marty knew exactly what was to be done. His mind was razor sharp with the liquid and the powder. He didn't care what the hell time it was in London and he was soon giving urgent instruction to his sleepy ally in Bayswater.

8 On the motorway Paddy's thoughts sped ahead of him locked in the beam of his headlights. He had the window down to chill his optimism and Mozart at full volume to warm it up again. It would have made sense for him to stay at his London flat but, as usual, Oxfordshire held its sway. Paddy did not notice the bottle-green Porsche parked at the end of his drive.

From his perch in the garage the old barn owl gave Paddy the look of a long-suffering concierge.

'OK, wise guy,' Paddy apologised and closed the car door quietly. As he crossed the yard he heard the sound of a foolish driver squandering his suspension on the pitted track. Whoever it was, he was in a hurry and there was a menace in the wild swerve of the headlamps as they arced through the trees.

Paddy should have hidden perhaps, but the events of the day had drained him of adrenalin – he felt inquisitive and immune to danger. He stood still and let himself be pinioned in the light of his visitor's car. It stopped ten yards away, the engine was cut but not the beam. Paddy stood transfixed. Somewhere in the house his dog was barking.

Anywhere in the world a trespasser can expect to be confronted with a show of aggressive bravura at least. Only among a nation of shopkeepers could he expect a greeting of, 'Can I help you?' Paddy regretted it immediately.

'Yes I think you can Mr Brummel.' The voice behind the glare was clipped and gentle.

'Do you want to come in?'

'No, thank you. Here's fine.' Beneath the cordial tone was a tacit order not to move. Paddy felt cold and disadvantaged, trapped like a coy calendar girl in the bright light.

'Well?' he said with continued patience.

'I represent certain parties in the US who are very keen to own the film rights of *Stratagems and Spoils*.'

'Oh yes.'

'Now apparently your production has met with difficulties and your backers have pulled out. What bad luck.'

'Thanks,' said Paddy, irked by the hollow sympathy.

'I gather you intend to persevere though, using private funds of your own?'

'Yes.'

'Very risky.'

'Maybe.'

'I am instructed to ask you to reconsider . . .'

'How much?' Paddy interrupted.

'Mr Brummel,' the silhouette gave a mock reproach followed by a pause. The night seemed very black beyond the brightness. 'One hundred thousand dollars.'

'In cash?' Paddy was amazed.

'If you like. No one need know. Your partners might not like it. We understand that.'

'One hundred thousand dollars,' Paddy repeated.

'That's it.'

'For me to change my mind?'

'Exactly.'

'So that as soon as I've officially backed out your parties can snaffle up the rights?'

'Yes.'

'To make another film of it?'

'I'm just a courier, Mr Brummel.' The voice oozed reason. Paddy tried to imagine the appearance of his would-be benefactor and could only summon up a vision of wide lapels and a Windsor knot.

'For whom?' Paddy asked.

'I can't tell you that.'

'Why not?'

'Don't ask questions, Mr Brummel. It's a handsome offer – accept it.'

Paddy's indignation was on a slow fuse but his own anger now took him unawares.

'Get out.'

'If you should reconsider . . .'

'GET OUT.' Paddy's shout ricocheted off the barn roofs.

The car door slammed. It was the solid sound of an expensive car. The engine started and Paddy's visitor left, reversing down the drive. The receding headlamps guarded the anonymity of his number plates.

The driver of the bottle-green Porsche was indeed wearing a tie with a Windsor knot which he now loosened as he considered the unsatisfactory outcome of his journey. He had known full well that it would take a stick and not a carrot to shift the arrogant Mr Brummel. Now perhaps his partners would listen to him, he thought as he headed for his home in Bayswater.

'We've had a late night have we?'

'Mmm.'

'We're looking a little jaded, aren't we?'

'Mmm.' Paddy was forced to agree. He was slumped in the make-up chair at the studio and too tired to object to Sally's verdict or even her use of the personal pronoun. After all it carried a homespun reassurance that Nanny would make it better.

The soft brushes and sponges danced about Paddy's physiognomy insinuating the hue and texture of a healthier man. The brilliant pain of Collier Bleu scorched the whiteness back into his eyes and Paddy knew that the outer man having been restored, the inner one would soon fall into line.

He had slept soundly albeit briefly and his mind was now struggling to repossess the catalogue of yesterday's events, and to reappraise them with today's perception. Seeing the story of his misfortune in the morning papers only served to endorse the reality of it all. The reports had only the bare bones of the matter but were generally sympathetic to Paddy and his bid to 'Go it Alone'. The *Courier* carried an old photograph of Paddy with the bleak caption 'AXED'. Next to it was one of Sir Toby Goddard grinning. No comment.

A friend of Paddy's had once worked on a film with Gregory Peck and had been puzzled to see that the star had pencilled the letters NAR in the top right-hand corner of a number of pages in his script. When asked the meaning of this mnemonic, Gregory had confided with a grin, 'No acting required'. For Paddy, that Friday was, relatively speaking, an NAR day. The shots for which he was required involved Blandford searching his house for a missing document, going from room to room, opening and shutting drawers and cupboards. A tricky day for the camera but one that would afford Paddy time to pursue his purpose. A list of priorities, possibilities, and questions was taking shape in his mind. So, too, was Jemma Culver.

As she arrived for work by taxi, Jemma had noticed, with dread, that a note had been stuck under the windscreen of her ailing Morris. It was from Paddy. 'Thank you for a lovely evening – please find small token of gratitude under the bonnet. Yours, Paddy.'

Now a brand new Exide twelve-volt battery may not trigger in many people the same *coup de foudre* as, say, a dozen roses, but in this case it dealt a severe blow to Jemma's recent resolve to be sensible.

'It's one of the nicest presents I've ever had,' she told Paddy in his dressing-room. She was wearing a red cloche hat and a huge grey military coat. She kissed him on both cheeks and in the corner FQ watched through half-closed eyes. Things were surely quite bad enough, without this whiff of romance in the air, he thought as he polished his master's boots.

'I'll see you on the set,' Paddy told Jemma. Was he tilting at windmills he asked himself as she left to get ready.

Before filming was due to start the unit had agreed to give their verdict on Paddy's proposal. After the warmth of feeling on the previous evening Paddy was confident of their support.

'It's Toady Griffin you've got to watch out for,' warned FQ.

'How do you mean?' asked Paddy.

'He's the rotten apple in your barrel,' said FQ with the gravity of a tricoteuse. 'He's been mongering about the canteen saying what a liberty it all is . . . and how can they trust you, etcetera.' Paddy thanked him and armed himself accordingly before going down on the set.

'Have you all had time to consider the situation?' asked Heime of the assembled group. They had, it seemed.

'Are there any questions anyone would like to ask? Any problems?' Behind a sea of shaking heads a hand was raised at the back of the meeting. It belonged, sure enough, to Ron Griffin aka Toady, a neat-looking little man whose face appeared to have an aptitude for frowning. He had the earnest look of an animal sniffing out danger in the wind.

'Yes, Ron?' asked Heime.

'I was only concerned as to what guarantees we could be given?' Toady spoke with a cutting nasal precision.

'As Paddy said last night – none,' answered Heime truthfully.

'What I mean is, what guarantee do we have that our salaries will be paid? How are we supposed to know whether Mr Brummel can honour his commitment? If, for example, he ran out of funds, what recourse would we, the work-force, have? I mean it's hardly regular is it?'

'May I?' asked Paddy. Heime nodded. 'Thank you, Mr Griffin. I'm glad someone has brought this up. It is, as you say, highly irregular and you're quite right to mention it. For the moment there is no guarantee I can offer – I wish there was. My bank, of course, could issue a letter of credit for you all to see, but perhaps a more obvious idea is for me to pay anybody who wishes a week's salary in advance. Or perhaps you'd like a fortnight Mr Griffin?' Paddy produced a fat wad of money with a grin and Toady frowned at the floor. 'You're very welcome – anyone who wants can have an advance. I'll leave word with the accountant.'

Toady muttered something about it being merely a hypothetical question; Heime thanked everybody and the meeting was over.

'Clever move. Well done,' said Heime later in his office. Paddy had come to tell him about the encounter he had had at the farm and the cash offer to withdraw from the film. Heime was amazed. Paddy went on to explain his theory that Capitol's intransigence and this rival interest in the project might be connected. Heime sucked air through his teeth to consider the possibility.

'No,' he said after a moment. 'It's out of the question. Sir Toby might be a hard man but he's straight. Straight as a die.'

'In the face of so many coincidences, I wonder,' said Paddy.

'Paddy, for Christ's sake, think what you're suggesting,' Heime exploded.

'A knighthood is not necessarily the hallmark of honesty. What he has done is at the very least unfair, and there's no reason why it shouldn't be actually crooked as well. The bastard won't see me, speak to me even.' Paddy had tried several times already that morning to reach the omnipotent man.

'Of course he won't. He's got nothing to say to you. It can't be that easy for him – put yourself in his place.' Heime looked weary, like a man whose stomach was not in the fight even if his heart was.

'He owes me some bloody explanation and somehow I'm going to get it.'

'Paddy,' Heime shook his head the way elders do confronted with hot-headed youthfulness, 'what good will it do?'

'What good will it do?' Paddy echoed. Was Heime being cynical or naïve? He couldn't figure which. 'Well for a start there's always the jolly old fair play angle to consider. And secondly we might just be able to get on and finish our fucking film. That's what good it will do.'

'Of course,' Heime relented. He was very fond of Paddy but this obsessiveness disturbed him. 'I'm sorry. You're right.' The smile he tried to give Paddy lost its impetus and ended up a grimace. 'Just go easy, that's all.'

'One other thing,' said Paddy, pausing at the door to give his question the appearance of an afterthought, 'What do you know about the repeat fee enquiry?'

'What?' said Heime, as though the question was in another language.

'I said, what do you know about the repeat fee enquiry. Apparently there's been an investigation.'

'Oh yes. Bloody waste of time. Everything was perfectly in order. Why do you ask?' Pale sunlight filtered through the plate-glass window throwing Heime's head into silhouette and obscuring his eyes.

'I was curious. Someone was telling me about it last night in the bar. It sounded quite serious.'

'One of those meddling left-wingers, I suppose?' Heime muttered.

'Yes.'

'They proved nothing. It was greed, plain and simple, a waste of time. I mean we'd all like to have a bigger slice of the cake, wouldn't we?'

'Were you involved?'

'In the enquiry?'

'Yes.'

'An independent panel was set up. They asked me to appear – which I did.'

'As a producer?'

'Yes, or an expert at any rate. I've sold a lot of programmes overseas, as you know.'

'For Capitol?'

'Among others. Yes.' Heime's tone was spiked with patience.

'It's mostly Capitol they're concerned with.'

'And Northern. Only because they export more than the other companies.'

'The implication was that the programmes had been somehow undersold. Is that possible? In some kind of trade off.'

'Yes. The usual mistrust of management, that's all.'

'But that would deprive the actors, directors and so forth . . .'

'And the producers,' interrupted Heime.

'Yes. And the producers . . . of their fair share of the profit right.' It was Paddy's turn to show patience.

'They didn't know what they were talking about. They couldn't prove anything.'

'There must have been some grounds for an investigation, or Equity would not have been involved.'

Heime studied his fingers which were interlocked as in prayer. He exhaled deeply – not quite a sigh. 'Look, what is this, Paddy?' he asked with a tired indignation.

'I want to know. Anything to do with Capitol may be of interest, to all of us . . . It may be relevant.'

Heime took the point.

'It's a separate department,' he explained. 'The marketing of programmes overseas is handled by an independent company, Transworld Telly Sales. Their job is to get the best price they can – there's no secret made of the figures. They are available for anyone to see. As you know everyone gets a prearranged percentage of their original salary, on a pro-rata basis. Perfectly simple and straightforward.'

'Let me get this clear,' said Paddy refusing to be soothed from his purpose. 'Transworld Telly Sales are simply brokers then?'

'Yes. They receive a commission – 5 per cent.'

'And who exactly are they? Transworld Telly. Who does it comprise?'

'It was set up three years ago by Capitol and Northern combined. Two directors from each.'

'Sir Toby and yourself from Capitol?'

'Yes.'

'Not that independent then?'

Paddy's question was rhetorical but it further martyred Heime.

'It was a way of pooling resources, Paddy, that's all. We were able to retain a full time representative in the US. It proved extremely effective. Sales have vastly improved.'

'Certainly,' agreed Paddy.

'Only in this particular case certain people chose to consider the sale price too low. They wanted more. Don't we all? As I said it's pure greed.'

'I see,' said Paddy. As an academic point the purity of greed hung in mind.

'Everyone bangs on about the geographic size of America. What they don't realise is how small the actual market is. It's tiny. Television stations are ten a penny over there, and certainly no one is going to get rich on the profits from a syndicated sale. It's peanuts; there's no room to negotiate. We do the best we can but it's very much a buyer's market.' Heime's hands were now flat on the table to denote his impotence in the matter.

'I see.'

'There's no way the books could be fiddled, as the panel established. They spent eight days going over the figures. The whole thing was a waste of time, honestly.' So Dennis was barking up the wrong tree.

'Oh well, thanks,' said Paddy.

The sun was overcast again now and he could see in Heime's eyes an oddly wistful look.

'Paddy,' Heime stopped him as he went to leave. 'Stick to acting.'

9 Paddy told himself that his reason for taking lunch in the canteen, instead of his usual solitary salad in the dressing-room, was good public relations. But his *alter ego* had another motive – a tryst with Jemma. However, the first person he encountered there was the effervescent Matthew who had had a luckless morning with the begging bowl. Enthusiasm for a half-made black and white British film with no international star name was not in abundance in the City it seemed. Paddy told him about the threat he had received – also the offer of a bribe.

'A hundred thousand dollars?' Matthew asked.

'Yes.'

'Well-spoken guy with a quiet voice?'

'Yes.'

'Me too. Same chap. I had him on the entryphone when I got home.'

'Said he represented some Americans.'

'Yeah.'

'What did you do?' asked Paddy.

'I told him to shove it up his arse,' said Matthew munching a Mars Bar. Paddy pondered this news a moment.

'It's curious,' he said, 'that they didn't approach Heime.'

'They must have reckoned he was too inscrutable.'

'Either that or they knew we only had to have a two-one vote to cancel,' suggested Paddy. Or they already knew that Heime's resolve was less than solid.

Henry Gorringe arrived with a glint of the Borgias in his eyes and a large manilla envelope under his arm.

'Look what the bastards have done,' he said brandishing a script. 'They offered me this heap of crap to start next week.'

'What? Who?'

'This abysmal thriller. Capitol want me to do it.'

'Capitol?' asked Paddy.

'Yeah.'

'That's a bit rich,' said Matthew.

'Exactly. Fab money though,' chuckled Henry.

'What did you say?' asked Paddy, him of little faith.

'I told them,' Henry pronounced with a degree of self-righteousness, 'that for the moment I was busy on another project, as they well knew.'

In the face of all the blatant sabotage, Paddy was touched by this spark of loyalty. He had no doubt that the withdrawal of Capitol's finance was far more positively motivated than they had thought at first. An investigation of Sir Toby was now uppermost in Paddy's strategy, but out of deference to Matthew and Heime he decided to keep his plan to himself.

Over lunch they were joined by Jemma. Her wig had been removed and her hair underneath was tightly netted; her eyes were huge with borrowed lashes giving her the look of a Pierrot. She had clearly been applying herself to the problem of the film's budget for she had several suggestions to make. There were a few scenes, she reckoned, that could be cut out and others that could easily be transposed from location to the studio without detriment to the overall film.

'And,' she went on, encouraged by their approval, 'there's no reason why the Munich scene couldn't be shot in, say, Coventry.' Here spoke a frugal housekeeper. 'And there are parts of Torquay that look quite like the South of France. I mean, at a pinch you could manage it, couldn't you Henry?'

'The way Henry works he could make Bognor Regis look like Shanghai, and vice versa,' said Matthew.

With a little cosmetic revamping a good set designer can camouflage practically anything. The camera's notoriety for the truth is a myth. It lies with the panache of an adulterer.

Paddy was called to the telephone in the corner of the canteen, and reflected as he went that the film might in the end stand or fall by just such thrift.

'It's me. I've been thinking,' shouted Celia Conran down the line. 'It's just too awful. How much do you need?' she asked in the tone of a lady settling her account at Harrods.

'Well it's very difficult to say exactly,' Paddy began quietly. He was keen to reduce the decibel count.

'What?'

'We don't really know . . . exactly . . . we're trying to work it out.' Paddy was confused by the kindness of this frail old lady. 'Look, I really don't think you should do this. It's wonderfully generous of you to offer but it might be rather . . . foolhardy.'

'What?'

Paddy shouted, 'Foolhardy,' and several heads turned. 'Anyway we may have a solution, so it may not be necessary,' he lied. The idea of dragging Celia into penury with him was appalling.

'Good. Good,' she answered. 'All the same, I want to help. I've told the agent I shall flatly refuse to sell the rights to anyone else.'

'That's great,' said Paddy.

'And I've instructed my brokers to sell off a few bits and pieces. I'll send you a cheque for £200,000 to begin with.'

'No, no. Don't do that. Not yet. It really may not be necessary, honestly.' Dishonestly.

'I don't believe you. George's agent said you'd find it impossible.'

'Yes, well it's not.' Paddy was desperate to divert her crazy generosity. 'Look, why don't I come down and see you next week? We could have dinner and talk it over; at Wheeler's in Brighton.' Paddy knew she loved oysters and it had been at Wheeler's that they had first celebrated when Heime and he had first bought the rights to *Stratagems and Spoils*.

'What a gorgeous idea,' said Celia, suddenly sounding half her age. 'I'd love that.'

'So would I. We'll fix it up next week, and meanwhile please don't do anything. Call your broker and tell him to hold fire for the moment OK?'

'All right,' she answered. 'But you mustn't worry about me, you know. I'm as old as the hills and rich as Croesus apparently. And I want to help.'

'I know.'

'And also, Paddy,' she sounded stern – the audio version of a stiff upper lip, 'it's what George would have wanted ... Hallo?'

'I'm here. Yes, I know.' Paddy swallowed. The taste of goulash was still in his mouth. 'I'll see you next week. Goodbye, Celia.' He hung up and disconnected the picture of Celia standing erect in her bay window staring defiantly out at the Downs. And the big bad world beyond.

Jemma was alone when he got back to the table and had ordered two coffees. Paddy told her about the call.

'Oh by the way, I meant to say earlier that of course I'll waive my salary ...' she volunteered lightly.

'No.'

'For the time being.'

'Certainly not.'

'It's called deferment.'

'Don't be crazy.'

'If I had realised that de fur meant so much,' she mimicked Schnozzle Durante, 'I'd have given the dame a mink.' They groaned and the dispute was left to be continued.

'You got back OK last night?' she asked.

'Yeah. Thanks again for supper. I'm sorry I stayed so late.'

'Not at all.' She intended to acknowledge the thanks.

'How's Kelly?'

'Full of beans. Wanted to know why you hadn't spent the night. I think she takes after her father. I shall have to watch her.' She grinned.

'Why don't you bring her down on Sunday,' Paddy heard himself suggesting, 'to see the animals?'

'That would be nice.'

They were interrupted by the arrival of Hugo Cavendish of the *Sunday Globe*. Paddy had forgotten they were due to have a preliminary interview that afternoon.

'Mind if I join you?' Hugo brandished a bottle of white wine and three glasses.

'Not at all,' Paddy fibbed and then introduced Jemma. Hugo's eyes had the look of a lurcher after game – frantic and eager under lazy lids. Altogether there was a grubby aura about him – he was a journalist who needed drycleaning.

'We've met before,' he beamed at Jemma. 'I did a piece about the split with your ex.'

'So you did,' said Jemma, getting up. 'If you'll excuse me, I have to get back to the set.' Exit a frosty Pierrot.

'Sensitive little creatures aren't they?' said Hugo adjusting his stained bow-tie with mock indignation.

Some time later FQ brought coffee to the corner of the studio where Paddy and Hugo were sitting.

'Now I hope we're not going to read anything unpleasant about Mr B.' FQ was using his Lady Bracknell tone as he tore open a sachet of sugar with his teeth.

'Heaven forbid,' said Hugo. FQ gave Paddy a new variation of an old-fashioned look and left.

'I'm really not the villain that people seem to think,' Hugo complained.

'Ah well, we all have a cross to bear.' Paddy's platitude sprang from nowhere like a useless mushroom. He would play the mongoose to Hugo's snake.

'Now, I thought I'd tell you a little of what I had in mind for the article, so we know where we are.'

'Fine.'

'The paper by the way is delighted that we've got you. Quite a coup. It's not often a recluse like you decides to open up. It's a real human interest story after all. I want to make it, you know, really sympathetic. I mean sympathetic with a capital "S".'

'I want to talk about the British film industry and in particular *Stratagems and Spoils* and the problems that we, that is Fledgling Productions, are having.'

Paddy's suggestion was like a lump of dough landing on a table. Hugo thought, softly, softly catchee monkey.

'Yes, of course,' he said. 'We want to discuss everything – work as well as the personal angle. You know what the *Globe* readers are like – and for a hundred grand it's got to be good, huh?' He made his point with a smile.

'Absolutely,' said Paddy. In the pit of his belly something churned – his integrity perhaps. He decided to take the actor's refuge and hide behind a role. He would act the part of a candid man revealing all. He could always retrieve his real privacy later.

'So, it's going to be a proper in-depth number you understand?' Hugo enthused.

'Sure,' Paddy enthused back. Who the fuck reads the *Sunday Globe* anyway? 'Fire away.'

Hugo had done his homework well; his research was so thorough that, for the most part, Paddy merely had to confirm the details. They covered his parents, childhood, schooldays and university, followed by his early years in repertory and his various dalliances with girls. Hadn't there been a Brazilian heiress? Was there any truth in the rumours that he nearly married that French actress? Paddy found himself being frank, and lighthearted even. It was somehow nothing to do with him – someone else's life, a different incarnation.

'How's it going?' Jemma asked. Paddy had been called to the set for a brief take.

'So far so good.'

'Do be careful – he's a bastard,' she warned. There was an urgency in her concern that made him want to explain his motive. He hated the idea of her thinking him cheap. He certainly wasn't that.

The camera rolled and cut and before returning to his

interviewer Paddy tried for the fifth time to reach Sir Toby's office on the telephone. The switchboard operator was polite but adamant; his call would not be taken.

'I'm ever so sorry.'

'That's not Monica is it?' Paddy asked. Having worked in the studio on and off for so long he knew a lot of the staff.

'Yeah.'

'How's your dad?' he asked. Monica's father had been a commissionaire at the studio who had been forced to retire after a stroke.

'Not so good. He seems so frustrated.'

'I'm sorry. Look . . . er, what time do you get off work?'

'About half-past five. Why?'

'Perhaps we could have a drink?'

'Great. I'll see you about five-forty-five then.' They arranged to meet in the King's Head round the back of the main TV studio. Paddy returned to his interrogation.

'Now,' said Hugo in a tone that heralded a change of gear – an assault on the nitty-gritty. 'Eight years ago you went on tour with a production of *The Recruiting Officer*?'

'Yes.'

'Also in the cast was an actress called Hannah Murray?'

'Yes.'

'You met and fell in love.'

'Yes.'

There was no denying that it had indeed been as simple and spontaneous as that. The past was catching up. Suddenly this was him, the Paddy he was now, a recent him that he could recognise. The distance had gone from the biography and Paddy could see Hannah now, her face pale against the pillow, the bed unruffled. White on white. Was he betraying her? The thought was sour in his mouth.

'When the tour ended the two of you set up a love nest?'

'We lived together in a damp basement in Holland Park.'

'Three years later you decided to get married?'

'Yes.'

'A magnificent white wedding?'

'Yes.'

'And then you moved out to the country?'

'Yes.'

'A dream home.'

'Yes.'

'By this time you were having quite a success with *The Declancey Inheritance* on the telly. Right?'

'Yes.'

'Chat shows, panel games, awards. Your name became a household word. You became a heart-throb – a star.'

'More or less,' Paddy shrugged. He was fully aware how inadequate he was being but felt powerless like someone in a dream.

'You must have been idyllically happy. You had everything going for you.' Hugo's voice was gentle as a dentist's – trying to lull nostalgia from him.

Paddy wanted to renege, to abort the whole interview and run away with his past intact. He hadn't really considered what it was he was undertaking, hadn't realised how fresh the salt would feel in the wounds. He wished he could shout at Hugo to leave with a capital 'F', but felt paralysed like a rabbit caught in the headlights of an advancing car. He said, 'Yes.'

'How would you describe your life at that time?' Hugo had the patience of an old fisherman. Paddy cleared his throat.

'Very nice,' he answered. Hugo let the pause ride. 'Looking back it's difficult to see things clearly. Time passed very quickly it seemed. Everything was very simple and pleasant. We liked the house; it was always full of noise – music, machines, animals and things.' Hannah had always given the impression of perpetual motion – filling the house with frantic industry. She would set about making things, dresses, shelves, bread, picture-frames, marmalade, curtains, pickles, with a childlike enthusiasm that soon waned, leaving every room strewn with her abandoned enterprises.

Once she had built a rabbit-hutch in the dining-room only to find when she had finished that it couldn't be got out through the door. Always there was music playing, she loved rock 'n' roll but somehow when Paddy got home there was always opera on.

'They were good times,' Paddy said as a matter of fact. 'Lovely really. Quite brief.'

'A happy home,' concluded Hugo scribbling on his pad. 'And in due course you decided to start a family?' Oh Christ. 'Is that right?' No. Stop this.

'Yes.' Was this the price of saving his film? Paddy tried to concentrate on the futility of the *Sunday Globe* and its mindless readers for whom this would be a blur of fact and fiction. Nothing mattered and yet it all did.

'I understand,' said Hugo warmly, sucking the blood from Paddy, 'that this must be painful for you to go through . . .'

A roar of laughter went up from the crew at the other end of the studio, no doubt at one of Mervyn's jokes. They might have been on another planet. Paddy was cooking up a hate for Hugo to help him through. Here was a man who spent his life scavenging for the unhappy scraps of other people's lives to make his daily bread – and relished it. From his blazer inwards he was an unclean man.

'Certainly it's painful. But that's OK. What do you want to know?'

'You were naturally thrilled when Camilla arrived then?'

'Yes. Yes, we were thrilled. She was lovely. She was a very lovely baby.' Paddy made the statement as flat and simple as he could, he would show none of the mawkish sentimentality that Hugo sought.

'It can't be easy to talk about it,' urged Hugo, his pen poised.

'It's no problem.' Talking about it is only a question of arranging words; when you choose to stop you close your mouth and that's that. It's the thinking you can't stop. The brain is not so easily silenced. 'You want to hear about the details, of a cot-death. The agony. The panic. The drama and detail. That's what you want isn't it?'

Hugo seemed to be able to write without looking down, as though his hands were disembodied. He didn't answer; he sensed it would be dangerous, it might spoil the flow.

'That's what you want to know isn't it? That's how I'm to earn my money? Well I tell you it is no problem. It's as old as time, man's fascination with the morbid, his curiosity in death, his neighbour's in particular. Well I'm here to oblige; firstly because I need the money, secondly because the Foundation for the Study of Infant Deaths, 15 Belgrave Square SW1, should you want any statistical details, is desperate for a platform from which to voice its outrage. Outrage at the present cut-backs in the funding of medical research into the mystery of 1,200 babies dying each year.'

Paddy was speaking with the quietness that holds a tight coil in check. Hugo's face was arranged in a semblance of compassion but his pen scratched on. It was a face that looked as if it had been somehow deflated, the flesh seemed to have lost its purpose. Only his eager eyes showed any sign of life. 'And thirdly,' Paddy continued, 'I don't mind talking about Camilla's death because I know that between us – you with your finest prose and me with whatever eloquence – we could not grasp one small fraction of 1 per cent of what it's like to hold your dead baby in your arms.'

Hugo had stopped taking notes and was silent. Paddy who had been a non-smoker for three years suddenly pined for a cigarette with a feeling not unlike the homesickness he had felt thirty years ago in his school dormitory.

'Excuse me, Mr Brummel,' FQ had materialised from nowhere. 'You're wanted on the telephone.' Paddy apologised to Hugo and followed his dresser out of the studio and into the wardrobe-room.

'Who is it?' Paddy asked.

'Nobody. I made it up. You looked as though you needed a break. I've made us a cup of tea.' Paddy smiled and nodded and remembered why he was so fond of FQ.

There was much to occupy Paddy's mind as he drove to his rendezvous with Monica. Each thought seemed trapped in the rhythm of the windscreen wipers – he couldn't break the spell. He had dispatched Hugo Cavendish having arranged to continue the interview the following week. Perhaps by then he could afford to break the deal and buy his secrets back . . . was that what he wanted?

Didn't he actually feel a sense of relief at having broken his silence albeit to that toad? How long was it, he asked himself, since he had said Camilla's name out loud? Was it possible that his introspection was turning stagnant on him? What was he hoping to achieve by it anyway? Maybe the time had come for him to have his floodgates breached. Paddy found the truth elusive, either couldn't find it or couldn't face it. He was reluctant to admit that the interview had lifted something from his private load – anger.

'What are you after then?' asked Monica as she sipped her second Pernod and lemonade. They had gossiped awhile but she was bright enough to know that it wasn't her company that Paddy was seeking, more was the pity.

'Well you know I'm working on this film *Stratagems and Spoils*,' he began.

'Oh, yeah. The one Capitol have just cancelled?' Monica chirped. The innocence of her face was camouflaged in a death-mask make-up. Her eyes and lips were etched in thick indigo and heavy shading failed to lend cheekbones to her round face.

'Exactly,' Paddy answered. 'Well that's what they are trying to do – but I want to find out why. It doesn't make sense you see, because apart from anything else it's going to be a bloody marvellous film.'

'So you want to carry on. Right?'

'Yes, but what I need to know is why Sir Toby decided to cancel it . . .'

'So you thought I might be able to tell you what he's been getting up to on the old dog-and-bone.' She grinned.

'Er, yes, sort of. I mean what exactly happens when someone calls into Capitol? Do you ask them who they are or do you put them straight through to whoever they want?'

'First we ask them who they are, then we put them through.'

'And do you keep records?' Paddy asked with transparent lightness.

Monica chewed invisible gum and eyed him for a moment. 'Do you want to see 'em?' she asked. A lesser telephonist might have demurred on the grounds that it was more than her job was worth, but not Monica.

'Yes, I would. Please.'

'You hang on here and I'll fetch the note-pads,' she said and was gone. She had the kind of walk that suggested she was being pulled forward by her nipples.

Paddy went to the bar to refill their glasses. He watched a young Jamaican remorselessly bombarding a space invader – was fascinated by the skill and yet sympathised with the poor creature being monotonously exploded on the screen. Wasn't he, too, an alien being repelled? But by whom? And why?

'Here we are then,' said Monica as she returned beaming with conspiracy. 'Cheers.'

'Cheers.' Their glasses touched.

'I got Lorraine's book as well. Between us we cover all twenty lines. Now how far do you want to go back?' she asked, producing two fat spiral pads.

'From Wednesday afternoon,' Paddy told her.

The Everly Brothers crooned from the juke-box as Monica shuffled back through the pages of the last three days. 'Here we go, Wednesday,' she said, flattening a page. They were sitting close together and Paddy could smell the fresh, sweet scent that Monica had borrowed especially. 'There's nothing much I don't know about most of them.' She saw herself as Madonna and let the smoke from her cigarette balloon out in front of her before sucking it in again voluptuously, like a lotus-eater.

Each call, it seemed, was carefully logged. Firstly the time was noted, then the extension or the initials of the person they wanted, followed by the name of the caller himself. In the event of no reply the operator took the caller's number or a brief message to be passed on to the office in question.

Paddy noted down the details of all the calls that concerned Sir Toby together with any additional information that Monica could volunteer. By the time he finished the list was long and varied.

'What's this Ganymede mean?' Paddy asked. The cryptic message for Sir Toby had been recorded three times from an unnamed caller.

'I dunno. Bloke just said to tell him that – nothing else,' Monica answered.

Paddy's appetite for sleuthing was whetted. As from Thursday there was a mass of calls for the chairman of Capitol from Heime, Matthew and himself most of which had N/A for not available noted against them.

'One last favour?' Paddy asked as they were leaving. 'I want Sir Toby's home number.' Monica gave it to him from memory and they walked round to the car-park. The rain had stopped but orange dampness hung round the street lamps.

'Any time you want any help – let me know,' she said, flattening her spiked hair as she strapped on a helmet.

'Thanks, thanks a lot. Would you buy your dad a bottle of Glenmorangie for me?' Paddy slipped three tenners into her pocket. He sensed that the list she had given him would yield dividends.

'I'll be your mole,' Monica winked and started up her moped. Very Madonna.

10 In the guest wing of the Cass ranch Fernando's woebegone literary adviser was, as ever, wrestling with the tired remnants of his moral sense. It was a running battle – matter over mind. Irving Barstow had showered at length, letting the fierce, hot jets ablute his body as best they could. For it was ablution he sought. He washed and rinsed and washed again between his legs, holding up his weary penis to the full force of the water as if to drown it.

Now he was standing in front of the mirror inspecting his nakedness; he was the judge viewing himself in the dock. The gloss of wetness flattered the unfirm texture of his flesh but it was clear that the years had been playing Grandmother's Footsteps on him. His nipples were slipping slyly away and his knees and shanks looked shockingly like his father's. He studied, too, his genitals hanging mauve from a grey-flecked bush – they were the culprits. They had urged him yet again to spend the night searching out his own lost youth in the sleek haunches of the Mexican boy.

Irving contemplated his image with remorse – the moral hindsight that is the morning's penalty for a night's enchantment. His libido and his intellect were old sparring partners. Even the tenderness had been a lie. He felt no love for Chico, had merely wanted to rob him of his bloom; to siphon it off like some elixir for his own use.

A sense of panic gripped poor Irving. His nakedness was fuelling its own rebuke. He was a failure – a middle-aged failure, a middle-aged failure with a flaccid body and no morals. He dried and dressed himself with haste. From somewhere he would find resolve; he would return to England, to sanity, to Radio Three, to hard work, even.

Irving breakfasted alone in the shade; Chico brought him orange juice and strong coffee.

'Good morning, Mr Barstow, sir,' he said. No trace of guilt, hardly any of recognition. Irving reminded himself that the promises made in a bedroom seldom run any risk of being redeemed. Perhaps after all the little Mexican had only been seeking to please; certainly the orange juice was fresh. Chico's sole ambition, Irving had gathered, was to become an

American and Fernando was generously negotiating the sponsorship.

The thrill of the arrival of the London *Times*, Irving considered, was always in direct proportion to the distance it had travelled and this morning he set about the airmail edition with verve. A small paragraph with the headline 'G. P. Conran Film to Fold' caught his attention. He read about Capitol TV's withdrawal from *Stratagems and Spoils* and Paddy's determination to persevere. This was the cataclysm he had been waiting for.

Irving reread the article and found conclusions leap-frogging to the forefront of his mind. There was a smell of treachery here. It was instantly clear to him that Fernando Cass and that creep, Lefrak, were involved in some low deal to hijack the English production.

His thoughts bubbled with indignation laced with a feeble patriotism. He was quite an admirer of Mr Brummel whom he had once had occasion to review during a brief spell as critic on the *New Statesman*.

This was the final straw that broke the back of Irving's lassitude; he felt overcome with righteousness and accordingly went off in search of his employer.

In the Cass gymnasium colourless disco music filled the air adding injury to the stark chrome that festooned the room. Fernando was lying flat on a bench pumping pulleys to the hideous rhythm. He was in oblivion, a straining trance. His body was uppermost in his mind and a sheen of sweat covered him. Irving watched in fascination for a while then cleared his throat, to no avail.

'I'd like a word with you, Fernando,' he shouted. There was a loud crash as piles of weights thundered to their base point and Fernando opened his eyes in a startled fashion. He looked like a man in mid-orgasm.

'What?'

'I'd like a word with you,' Irving approached. The very sight of the fevered exercise had made Irving hot himself. It occurred to him that he had not chosen a good moment. 'But there is a tide in the affairs of men,' he told himself, 'which, taken at the flood, leads on to fortune.' Or not, as the case may be. He was past the point of no return.

'Now?'

'Er, yes.' Irving was in the headmaster's study in short

trousers. Fernando sat up, sweat eddied down his torso.
'What is it?'

– What the hell is it? Irving wondered. A crisis of
conscience? A flurry of rebellion from the pit of his stomach?
He was on a high diving board and the pool beneath was
suddenly empty.

'I'm leaving.'

Pause.

'I'm leaving for good.'

Fernando stared at Irving without expression.
Expressionlessness was one of his fortes – for years film
directors had been coaxing him towards the minimum
reaction. 'Don't just do something, stand there,' was the
axiom. Let the audience do the work.

'You're leaving,' Fernando repeated.

'Yes.'

'Handing in your notice.'

'Yes.' Irving's armpits were moist. His intellect, his logic
and his bottle had all fled.

'I see.' The star nodded and then laboriously resumed his
position on the plinth. Irving felt foolish and wished he had
premeditated the scene, or was in some way able to forestall
this cool manoeuvre.

'Aren't you going to ask me why?' Irving asked. He was
still holding the copy of *The Times*.

Cass was pleased to sense an animosity in his gym and sat
up again with languid patience. 'OK, why?' He was spoiling
for a fight.

Irving suddenly loathed the man with a force that sent
adrenalin fizzing through his veins like electricity. His
Adam's apple was a ballcock in his throat and his heart
thumped. Irving was no stranger to the symptoms of funk.
He had been a coward since childhood but now, in this airless
muscle laboratory, a gust of bravura came upon him. He had
lived far too long haunted by *l'esprit de l'escalier*, he would
for once speak his mind spontaneously. Perhaps. The music
suddenly stopped and the silence compounded his confusion.

'Well, Irving?' The pause had become an issue in itself.
'Why are you leaving?'

'Personal reasons,' said Irving with a weak smile. The
sudden idea that Fernando might punch him in the face had
tipped the balance in favour of the soft option. He turned and
walked to the door.

The anticlimax nettled Cass; he felt deprived. 'So long then, faggot-face,' he shouted.

Irving stopped in the doorway, his foot on the *escalier*. 'Actually I'm leaving because you're a cheat, a bully, a thief and a fucking appalling actor.' Irving put down his copy of *The Times* as proof and left.

An hour later as Irving went to load his car he found a wad of torn up paper under the windscreen wiper – Chico's application for US citizenship.

Lady Anthea Goddard secretly loathed bridge and had a dread of partnering her husband that dated back to the early days of their marriage. In those days her overbidding would provoke Toby to a certain brutality in bed later. She had never been that keen on sexual intercourse either and had mercifully been spared the horror of childbirth.

Tonight it was Sir Toby who was playing erratically. Their friends, the Coopers from Onslow Square, were a shaming three rubbers up. There must be something on his mind, Anthea thought, something bothering him. And goodness me, there was.

The Filipino maid came in to announce a 'terrorfoam' call, urgent, for Sir Toby. He excused himself and took his tumbler of malt whisky to the study.

'Hallo,' he challenged.

'Sir Toby?' an oily voice enquired.

'Yes.' The cigar in his mouth was wet and comforting.

'My name is Cavendish, Hugo Cavendish of the *Sunday* ...

'I'm not talking to the bloody press.'

'. . . *Globe*. I think you'd be foolish not to.'

'Especially not at my home at this time of night ... What do you want?' Sir Toby's curiosity had overcome his indignation. Normally he reacted to pressure grumpily but his confidence had suffered something of a *bouleversement* in the last few days and he found himself being uncertain and tentative.

'Well we were very sad to hear that Capitol TV have decided to withdraw the finance for *Stratagems and Spoils*.'

'Oh yes.' He matched solicitude with sarcasm.

'I get the feeling that something of a mystery surrounds the exact circumstances ...'

'No, not at all.' He felt trapped. This was the territory of the press department surely. 'It was a Board decision to withdraw – perfectly simple and straightforward.'

'Isn't that rather drastic action to take?' The question oozed reason.

'Films frequently have to be cancelled for various reasons. It's regrettable, of course, but there it is.' Sir Toby was looking out of the window without seeing the familiar lamplit view of Cadogan Square.

'What reasons would they be?'

'They're confidential.'

'Well, there are a number of theories being circulated in Fleet Street.'

'That's not my concern.' Actually it was. Sir Toby's cigar had gone out and he was now comfortless.

'There is speculation that Capitol has hit a financial crisis. What would be your comment on that?'

'Nonsense, utter nonsense.'

'That's what I thought, Sir Toby.' The voice of Hugo agreed, but the softening technique seemed to butter no parsnips with Sir Toby. So he went on. 'Then we have to consider the rumour of a rival production . . .'

'I know nothing about any such thing. This is nothing more than gossip.' He could see but was unable to reach a box of matches on the bookshelf. For Sir Toby this was the very definition of stress.

'Paddy Brummel says he knows of an American interest, and the feeling is that it is not unconnected with Capitol's withdrawal of funds.'

'Rubbish,' he lied. How he had come to be embroiled in this wretched intrigue was a puzzle. He had led an industrious and creative life; he held honorary posts and was kind when he had the time. Knighthoods aren't that easy to come by.

'You are saying that you know nothing about any such plan?' pressed the journalist.

'Yes absolutely.' He was a man on quicksand. 'That is exactly what I'm saying.'

'In view of the circumstances, you don't feel you owe Fledgling Productions at least an explanation?'

'The only explanation that I am obliged to make is to my shareholders.' He was pleased to have mentioned that.

'Could you tell me what you think of Mr Brummel's attempt to persevere with the film on his own?'

'That's his business.' In other circumstances Sir Toby might have admired the actor's determination.

'So you deny there's any personal vendetta between you?'

'Yes.'

'And there's no question that you stand to make any personal gain?'

'That is enough, Mr Cavendish.' Sir Toby Goddard had a fleeting image of himself standing in the dock with dignity, an innocent victim of circumstances beyond his control . . . 'And I suggest that you consult very carefully with your legal department before going into print with any of your wild allegations.'

'We certainly will, Sir Toby – however, there are still a number of questions that remain unanswered so we will be continuing our investigations, with or without your co-operation.' There was a slim glint of metal in his tone.

'Good night Mr Cavendish.' Sir Toby was curt.

'Good night.' Was there a smirk in his voice?

Sir Toby at last relit his corona cigar and contemplated his predicament before picking up the telephone and dialling. He complained at length about his predicament and received little sympathy from the other end of the line. He gave instructions in the tone of a martyred man and hung up. He was blind to the truth, that he was hoist by his own greedy petard. But he knew for sure he was in a hell of a mess. The mess of man who attempts to line his pockets privately with public money. The line of least resistance had led him to a maximum involvement in the whole sordid business. In all he was a very disgruntled tycoon.

When Sir Toby returned to the bridge table he was relieved to find he was dummy.

11 Cradling his car telephone, Paddy grinned to himself in the darkness, the grin of a man who has killed two birds with a single stone. He was pleased with his impersonation of the unwitting Hugo Cavendish; firstly it had undoubtedly rattled Sir Toby and secondly it might serve to put a temporary spanner in the *Globe*'s work. A permanent delay to their story of his personal life would be even better.

Paddy dialled again, a local number.

'Hallo,' Jemma answered.

'It's me, Paddy. I thought I might look in for a drink.'

'Sure. Where are you?'

'Outside your front door.'

'Idiot.' She hung up and a moment later the front door opened. 'Come in.'

The house was warm and there was a smell of recent frying of fish fingers. Jemma's hair was wet and her script was open by the fire. Paddy gave her the flat carrier bag he was holding.

'Another present?' she beamed. 'What is going on here?'

A good question. She laughed as she saw what it was, a new recording of Vivaldi's 'Four Seasons'. She thanked him with a kiss and Paddy had a brief smell of her – warm and soapy. They both wished Kelly wasn't sound asleep upstairs, her presence would have eased the self-consciousness that had taken them unawares. Jemma poured him a drink and he told her what he had been doing – even repeated his impersonation of Hugo Cavendish which she enjoyed. She was simply an ally, a jolly useful ally, Paddy told himself. The truth was in no hurry.

Jemma studied the list of telephone calls that Monica had supplied while Paddy called Matthew at home as arranged. He had apparently drawn a blank having spent all afternoon trying to trace any American interest in their film. Matthew had, however, managed to speak to one of the members of the Board at Capitol TV and it seemed that Sir Toby had personally swung the vote in favour of withdrawing their funding on the grounds that the film was no bloody good and quite unmarketable. How curious.

'Also, apparently, the press have been on to my Uncle Toby,' Matthew said, his mouth sounded full as always.

'Oh really?' My, my, doesn't news travel fast?

'Yeah. Someone at the *Globe*. I've just had Heime on the phone – apparently the old boy is pretty vexed, demanding injunctions and so forth.'

'Good.' Paddy's moment for confession of authorship had passed before he could grasp it. On consideration, it might be no bad thing to keep it secret.

'It might help bring things to a head – force his hand.'

'Let's hope. Where are you calling from?'

Paddy told him.

'Oh yeah. Well have a good weekend.' They disconnected.

Jemma was thumbing through a dictionary and the sweet flute of James Galway was leading the Summer movement of Vivaldi. Actually she could have done with a new needle too.

'Ganymede,' she announced. '"A cupbearer, potboy; the beautiful youth who succeeded Hebe as cupbearer to Zeus" – not much help is it?'

'I can't say I know any cupbearers. Probably the name of a company.'

'Pretty cryptic all the same,' she reckoned. Paddy's mind was on the plight in which Hugo Cavendish would find himself the next day.

'I see our friend Ron Griffin is here on the list. What do you make of that?'

'I don't know. It would be interesting to find out. I shouldn't imagine he's called Toady for nothing.' But what toadying could he be up to for Sir Toby?

For the second successive evening a Mrs Goodall speciality was left to waste in Paddy's kitchen as he watched Jemma scrambling eggs in hers. Her bare feet moved deftly on the quarry tiles and she was naked under her silk dressing-gown. Paddy wanted to touch her, stroke her. It was an abstract desire that he knew his body would not endorse. On three occasions he had tried to fly in the face of his miserable penance. He had taken girls to bed in a bluff bid to exorcise his impotence, like an optimistic bankrupt bouncing cheques. The embarrassment of it was appalling. His fumbling excuses had been accepted with such patience by his partners, lying bewildered in the dark – all undressed with nowhere to go. He saw it as a punishment to fit his crime and

81

thought it best to leave his beastly affliction unchallenged. His cocksure days were over – Hannah had taken them.

Paddy felt a fraud, though, masquerading his attraction to Jemma as comradeship. It never crossed his mind that she understood. They talked easily during supper in front of the fire, like old friends. They were simply fellow sleuths on a case. Nothing more. Just friends. They took turns to probe each other's past, then played backgammon. As Jemma leant forward to make her move, Paddy could see her right breast – very friendly.

Driving home, Paddy began to wonder if his obsession with the film was foolish. Was it really that important? The doubt came from nowhere and loitered in his mind. Surely there would be other films to do . . . and what about his life, that other suspended activity? Perhaps he should apply himself to that instead. And then there was Jemma; Jemma with the warm green eyes who kept beating him at backgammon. The outlook suddenly seemed less bleak. This upturn in his spirits was on a short lease.

Flimsy clouds ambled across a fullish moon and in the yard of Paddy's farm the wind moaned and banged about the barns. He locked the car and moved towards the house.

To any 'B' movie fan a crunch of gravel speaks volumes. And so it did for Paddy. Before he could turn, the single crunch became a stampede as two dark figures lunged towards him. Paddy tried to run, turned, tripped and fell. Now they were above him, black silhouettes wielding cudgels against the sky – their frenzied breath whitened by the cold moon.

This is surely the moment when the director calls, 'Cut', he thought in panic. This is where the stunt man is substituted for the painful bits in the wide-angle shot. This was no movie. A boot swung hard into his ribs and a heavy stick thudded into his shoulder. I'm an actor – mind my face, for Christ's sake, mind my face. Spontaneous pain ricocheted through his body, huge blows pounded into him. He must do something. Act. Do nothing. He pitched forward on to the ground – motionless. Quite still. Stay still. Doggo.

'Come on. Let's get out of here.'

'Yeah.' The booted foot stormed a farewell into his side. Don't move. Don't blink. Warm blood dribbled from his mouth. At last they left. Crunch. Crunch. Crunch. Don't move.

A minute or a decade later Paddy opened his eyes and the moon exploded. Its triple image was a burning white light in his head. He lay still letting eager tentacles of pain race into uncharted zones. And this surely was the proper moment for the director to reinstall the hero for his dishevelled close-up shot.

Violence was not to Lefrak's taste. It carried an unrefined and untidy association. He was confident that if he had been dealing direct with this wretched Brummel character he could have achieved his goal by subtler means. Certainly the situation was urgent and as Marty had seen fit to introduce force what did he care?

'We've got to get this show on the road, Marty – that's all that matters.' It was lunchtime and Lewis was eating a low calorie yoghurt in his office at Mediavision.

'It's looking good, Lewis.' It was early evening in New York and Marty was smoking a low-tar cigarette. 'It's all going to be OK – it's all going to be OK.' He used repetition as an aid to credibility. 'We're right on target.' He expressed more confidence than he possessed. His English ally had reported to him that a brief visit had been paid to Paddy Brummel at his country home and as a result continued filming would now be out of the question. To Marty the sword was no less mighty than the pen.

'I want it tied up, OK?' Lefrak's impatience echoed from the West Coast. 'It's all taking too long.'

'We're on schedule. No sweat. Stay cool, buddy.'

Marty Clanger was a man who hedged his bets – he lived on slices of other people's action. He operated in the shadow, he was a scavenger, a crook of all trades. To his mind his old buddy from Chicago was already in too deep. It was just a film for God's sake.

'Sure thing. Call me tomorrow. Ciao.'

Lefrak brooded over his decaffeinated coffee. Next door Nancy was landscaping her left eyebrow when the plucking of a wayward hair was interrupted by a telephone call from Fernando Cass.

The affable superstar and the budding producer greeted each other like old friends.

'You got the letters?' Lewis asked.

'Yeah, yeah – I sent them on to my attorney. I appreciate that, it was good of you.' As agreed Lewis had composed and sent off a back-dated correspondence that would vindicate Fernando and leave Bud Schwartz full square in the firing line for the wrath of jilted Frank Hoffman. Hollywood has no fury like a producer scorned.

'I was calling about the movie,' said Cass changing tone slightly. 'I hadn't realised there was a production of *Stratagems and Spoils* already in motion.' The accusation was thinly veiled.

'Yeah. In London I think.' Keep it casual, Lefrak told himself. 'A shoestring outfit shooting in black and white, would you believe, with no name.' Lewis laughed to further demean the enterprise – a mirthless sound. 'I told Schwartz about it – it's no big deal.'

'Is that right? You told Schwartz? The sonofabitch never mentioned it.'

'I'm sorry.'

'It's not your fault . . . But the thing is that it has come to my notice that this show in England has been busted, folded.' Cass was rattled, not so much by Irving Barstow's peevish departure as by the article in *The Times* that he had left behind. The imputation had been at once obvious and unpalatable. His erstwhile acolyte had clearly cast him in the role of villain, and God knows who else might follow suit. Guilt Cass could handle but misplaced guilt was another can of worms. It provoked a genuine indignation.

'So I heard.' Lefrak loaded his voice with insignificance.

'It struck me as something of a coincidence, one production folding – another being set up.' Fernando's comment was, in fact, a question. Lefrak was hunched earnestly over his desk to conjure up sincerity. The ground he was on was far from solid.

'Busted or not it's no threat. Either way it was a two-bit piece of nothing. I mean what we're talking about is the big league, you know, grown-up movies, huh?' Lefrak could hear no sound from the other end. The star knew how to judge a pause.

'Yeah,' he said finally.

'You know what I'm saying?'

'Yeah.' Fernando was offering Lefrak his doubt to be dismantled.

'For Christ's sake – you don't think I had it fixed up do you?'

'I don't give a goddamn,' Cass answered. 'The thing is, I don't want to know about it, right? You produce – I act.'

'Hey, Fernando, look it's all legit, OK, straight up. On the line . . .'

'Yeah, yeah.' Cass dismissed the need for honesty. For him the real issue was keeping his nose clean. The truth was just a by-product.

'FERNANDO CASS IN DODGY DEAL INQUIRY' was devoutly to be avoided. 'I just don't want to get tangled up in any of your shit, right?'

'Right.'

They hung up. Lefrak sat back in his chair. He had underestimated the man. He should have known better than to imagine Cass had scruples.

12 The church bells of St Bartolph peeled out over Finchbury and left their bright sounds hanging in the mist. 'Come to church, good Christians all.'

From outside his house Paddy could hear the summons clearly, its gaiety undiminished across the fields. Had he, in fact, been a Christian he might at that moment have chid his God on the subject of suffering. Movement of any kind was painful but getting into the car and reversing out of the garage was unspeakable.

His ribs were tightly bound to staunch the pain but his neck and head ached freely. As he headed west on his weekly visit to the nursing home he was mightily glad of the power steering.

After his assailants had left, Paddy had lain on the ground absorbing its coldness in the light of the triplicate moon. In the distance he had heard a diesel-powered car drive off, its silencer severely failing. He had crawled into the house and sunk himself into a hot bath where he lay drinking whisky for some time, the pain subsiding with his power to reason. With packs of frozen peas he had tried to control the swelling bruises on his face without success. His right eye was the colour of a stormy sunset. Generally his skin seemed not to fit – was either too tight or loose, like a glove on the wrong hand. It was as though all this pain had been dormant in him all his life and was now melting into reality.

Doctor Foster had come from Thame to examine him and proclaimed no bones broken, no organ ruptured. His body would survive but what she thought of his mind for refusing to go to either hospital or the police was another matter. She bound him and dosed him and promised to call back. Mrs Goodall had rallied round and spent the previous day plying him with broth and glucose. Her continuous chatter had mercifully been lost on Paddy whose mind was on a pendulum swinging in and out of oblivion.

It was Paddy's intention to listen to the omnibus edition of *The Archers* during the drive to Hungerford, but his concentration was not on Ambridge. His thoughts were unruly, he was by turn confused, determined, puzzled and scared by the assembled facts in his mind. They didn't add up or they did, too well.

Beyond the veil of mist there was a pale hint of sunshine which the daffodils would welcome and the roads were Sunday-morning empty. He thought of Hannah and the pointless journey he was making. For whose benefit was it – his or hers? When his car telephone bleeped he couldn't think what it was. Incoming calls were such a rarity. All the previous day Mrs Goodall had told callers that Paddy was playing golf and was not expected back. Paddy could not rationalise this nonchalance except as a safety measure. He pulled into the side of the road and answered.

'Paddy Brummel?' The confidential voice of Hugo Cavendish was shredded with static. He excused himself profusely for bypassing Paddy's ex-directory status; he sounded humble indeed as if some great weight had been dropped on him from above.

'I've been having a little difficulty,' he said.

'Oh dear.' Good. 'In what way?' Paddy asked.

'About my article on you. Capitol TV are trying to stop it – all kinds of threats to my editor and so on. Very fishy. Talk of injunctions and things.'

'Very odd,' agreed Paddy.

'You don't know anything about this?'

'Certainly not. A deal is a deal,' answered Paddy studying his mauve eye in the driving mirror.

'They seem to have the idea I've got something on them, something to do with their investment policy. Their film funding and so on.'

'And have you?'

'No of course not. I told you it's a personal story – human interest – I'm doing, not a finance investigation. The point is my editor has been forced to give them the right to censor the article. The power of veto. Bloody nerve.'

'I don't quite see how I can help,' Paddy regretted.

'Well being warned off always rather intrigues me, on the principle of no-smoke-without-fire . . . so I was wondering if we could bring our next meeting forward so that I can look into this cancellation of your film. Somehow I seem to have stirred up something of a hornet's nest. I want to know what's going on.'

'Sure,' said Paddy, wondering whether Hugo's curiosity would, in fact, turn out to be a bonus. They fixed a rendezvous and he drove on.

The two huge cedar trees which dominated the lawn in front of the nursing home looked overwhelmed with an ancient sadness. Their heavy branches swooped low over the grass with the grace of limbo dancers. Even the house itself, forlornly Georgian, seemed to have sacrificed its life-force to the inhabitants. Perhaps over the years the patients had sapped its vitality in a last attempt to retrieve their own.

As always Sister Wordsworth shone with starch and Christian cleanliness. Her optimism defied the gloom of her environment and she greeted Paddy, as always, with great warmth and a puzzled disbelief that his injuries had been caused by 'a little fall'.

'I'd rather Hannah didn't see me like this,' Paddy said, 'it might upset her.' The truth was she probably would not notice.

'Very well, Mr Brummel,' she answered, privately considering that such animation in her patient would be no bad thing. 'I'll not turn the overhead light on and you can sit with your back to the window.'

'How is she?' Paddy asked. They were sitting in her office. Strip lighting took away any reality the room could offer.

'Much the same. Sometimes I get the impression she's just not trying, she's that despondent. The physio gets quite exasperated with her at times and she can be very picky with her food.' Twice a week Paddy sent a hamper of Hannah's favourite things: smoked salmon, Camembert, Kiwi fruit, Gentleman's Relish, Bath Olivers, game soup, and marron glacé. Flowers, music. Anything to please her, woo her back from her abyss.

The corridors smelt of polish and the floor was unblemished. The sensible shoes of Sister Wordsworth squeaked ahead, and Paddy followed trying to conceal his limp with an air of meditation.

Paddy need not have worried that Hannah would see his bruises. Her sky-blue eyes were out the window trailing the clouds in a trance that brooked no interruption.

Sister Wordsworth moved a chair for him, angled it to conceal his face as best she could and left.

'Hi,' Paddy said and kissed her brow. Not a flicker from his wife. He was invisible, like a ghost. He made conversation with himself with a weak belief that she was listening. Just as an actor has to simulate a telephone call by making himself hear the replies on the other end of the line, Paddy had learnt to trade questions and answers with himself in a charade that never seemed to quite find its mark.

Over the months Paddy had developed a fluency at the game; could chat on for hours undaunted by Hannah's cool disinterest. Today he felt awkward though, stilted like a suspect with a dodgy alibi. He wanted to tell his wife what had been happening to him, to transmit to her some of the energy and excitement he had been feeling. He wanted to tell her about the onslaught of events around him, about his resilience, about the gamble he was taking, about his new companion. But he didn't, and the gulf between them seemed to stretch out.

Paddy had brought her a large bottle of Chanel No. 5 and as he leant to dab it on her passive neck, the old guilt revisited him. It was anger and love mixed together; an awful frustration at this mask of deadness. He looked down at her smooth fair skin and hair and remembered clearly for an instant how free and fluid their lovemaking had been. He wondered if he could not simply love her back to life, could hear for a moment the familiar cry of her pleasure, the gentle gasp of disbelief and enjoyment. And not for the first time he experienced an ugly urge to violate her.

He bent and kissed her forehead. Not a flicker.

He put on her favourite Billy Joel tape and plucked the dead heads from the winter jasmine by the window. Its faint smell had long ago stopped struggling against the disinfectant. Hannah lay quite still and Paddy felt a horrible desolation for them both.

'The magnolia is beginning to bud ... Perhaps I should have pruned it ... I'll have to look it up somewhere, in that lovely book Prue gave us ... Some things you have to prune in the autumn ... and others in the spring ... I can never remember which ... and of course neither can Mrs Goodall ...' Paddy stroked her hand, her skin was white as white and her pulse was slow like a sleeping child's. Sometimes it appeared that Hannah withheld her symptoms from him deliberately to make things harder; to thwart his sympathy by giving it no point of focus. Her withdrawal from the world seemed wilful – like a giant sulk that had taken root.

The tape finished and there was a deep silence. Paddy tried not to think of Jemma. Her green eyes – laughing, worried, curious – alive. He felt guilty at the thought, and then angry at the guilt. Suddenly the room was too warm and quiet for him and Paddy was impatient to leave. He went to stand up but a small pressure from Hannah's hand stopped him. Her lips moved briefly without a sound. Painfully Paddy leant closer. The new scent had warmed on her and again he felt confused with memories of long lovemaking on summer afternoons. Was she always going to be his final lover he wondered. Again she went to speak, paused, blinked, sucked in air and whispered, 'Careful.'

The pronouncement was flat and ambiguous. Paddy wanted desperately to capture the moment for analysis but the meaning had already flown beyond his reach. Only much later did it strike him that it had had the ring of a fey warning.

Hannah shifted her head and for an instant Paddy was caught in the gaze of her blue eyes as they skimmed past him on their way back to the clouds. Not a flicker.

Paddy left the room with the near panic of claustrophobia. He filled the Volvo with the sound of Mahler and set out for home. He drove too fast trying to shake off the contagion of antiseptic gloom.

As Paddy drove up his drive the clouds had dispersed and watery sunlight had broken through giving everything a clean, sharp look. In the undergrowth spring seemed coiled and ready to be sprung.

His spirits soared at the sight of Jemma's Morris standing green and empty in the yard. It wasn't that he had forgotten she was coming, he had simply learnt to resist anticipation, that short-lived pleasure that rides before a storm. What kind of game was he playing with himself he wondered as he hooted his horn.

Kelly ran from the barn. 'Look! Eggs!' Her hands were full of them and her face was beaming toothlessly. Paddy levered himself out of the car as Jemma appeared. She was wearing jeans and a rough coat, clean green boots too, longing to be muddied. It felt like longer since he had seen her as she kissed him hallo.

'You look ghastly,' she said, stroking his hair like a child. He had grossly understated the extent of his injuries on the telephone the night before; his upper lip was swollen but still stiff.

'You look great. Great,' said Paddy. She seemed prettier. 'And so do you.' As he bent to kiss Kelly the pain in his ribs was like a stab. They walked slowly round the garden, a tour of inspection. Kelly picked daffodils with too short stems and Paddy told Jemma the details of his attack.

'For Christ's sake why not call the police?' She asked the time-honoured question very reasonably.

'I don't see the point. And I don't want anyone to know.'
'Why?'

Paddy thought a moment and then tapped his nose and said, 'To rattle the enemy, rattle the blighters.' The truth was, he didn't know.

'These guys are the bad guys, Paddy, they mean business.' Her wide brow was grooved with concern; concern for him, she was his ally.

'So do I,' he said. Gregory Peck couldn't have said it better. They agreed not to discuss the film any further for the moment. 'There's some champagne in the fridge.'

'Lovely,' she grinned. They were standing under the magnolia tree, Hannah's favourite. It's ivory petals were half open.

'Do you know anything about them?'
'Yes. What is it? A Grandiflora?'
'Er . . . Yes,' answered Paddy. 'I was wondering when to prune it.'

'You shouldn't. They don't like it,' she answered, scrutinising a severed branch from Hannah's last purge. 'You need to put some bone meal in the soil.'

Paddy had not had a visitor in his house since long ago and had forgotten what a personal matter it was. He felt self-conscious at what it might reveal about him; or rather not him – Hannah, for the rooms were so much part of her, her flare, her colours, her ideas. Notions of territory and loyalty filled his mind and he felt a sudden sadness at the thought of the place being sold. He wished Jemma would stop enthusing about his wife's taste.

'I didn't know you've got a baby,' Kelly said. She had been exploring upstairs and found Camilla's room with its evidence of her brief life still intact.

'I haven't. Not any more.'
'Oh, where is it then?'
'Her name was Camilla. And I'm afraid she died.'

'Babies don't die.' Kelly was confident of that, seemed almost indignant. Death was for hamsters, goldfish, grandparents. There was no question of the distant bell tolling for the likes of her, thank you very much.

'Sometimes they do, my darling,' Jemma interceded. 'Very seldom.'

Kelly sucked her Coke. 'Poor mummies.'

'And daddies,' suggested Paddy.

'Oh yes.' She acknowledged the lesser breed. 'You said you had a dog.'

'I do.'

'Where is it?'

'Fitzgerald is probably upstairs hiding – she's very old and grumpy and hates visitors I'm afraid.' For Kelly the excursion was losing its thrall. She skipped off to freak the cats.

'Sorry about that,' said Jemma.

'No problem,' Paddy answered, and for the second time that week felt better for having his sadness aired.

Mrs Goodall had decided that Paddy's plan to picnic was a good thing despite his injuries and had accordingly left a huge pile of provender. They ate round a fire in the clearing of a nearby wood. The weather was warm and nothing needed cooking, but Paddy insisted on a fire. He liked bonfires; his early fantasies were bedded in the wholesome world of *Swallows and Amazons*. In the lighting of this one he was forced by his injuries to play an executive role while mother and daughter foraged and kindled. Paddy watched them bending to their task and was amused to see that their denimed bottoms were pretty identical.

When they finished eating Kelly went to build a bracken house while they lay back staring into the leafless trees and drinking Chablis.

Was it only four days since they had met? What were they doing here, playing out this tableau of family life? Paddy took refuge in the belief that he was the innocent victim of events – a passenger without responsibility for his destination. Now was the only moment that counted. Before and after weren't part of it. Now was good, with the smell of the bonfire and Jemma talking. It was like a wartime romance, Paddy thought, where people felt free to help themselves to a little life before death.

They strolled and talked and talked and strolled. They fed a horse and picked primroses. Kelly sat on a gate and watched with astonishment as a sheep, with nonchalant ease, gave birth to a lamb. Her perceptions were having a busy day with life and death. After tea it rained – proper sploshing rain that floods gutters and pounds windows. Paddy and Jemma read the papers and Kelly watched television with her thumb in her mouth. Like a family.

With very heavy rain the bonnet of a Morris can leak and if the bonnet leaks the distributor can get wet, and if the distributor gets wet the car won't start, and if the car won't start the passengers can't leave. And so it was that yet again Jemma's Morris played a major role in the design of things. It was perfectly obvious that they would simply have to spend the night and travel up together the next morning. Kelly was the only one of them though to show her pleasure openly.

Jemma cooked kedgeree and Paddy read out crossword clues. Upstairs Kelly dreamed about having a pony. They drank too much and made each other laugh. Paddy giggled a foppish hissing sound to save his ribs from hurting. Later they fell quiet like players in a stalemate. Berlioz sounded lofty and fine on Paddy's CD player as they each watched the same flames licking upwards from the fire. Where do we go from here, was their common thought.

'I've got a toothbrush you can borrow,' Paddy said, the perfect host.

'Thank you,' said Jemma, the polite guest.

Paddy levered himself to his feet. 'You may need a hot water bottle in the spare room.' His heart was pounding with cowardice.

'I thought perhaps I'd sleep with you,' she said without looking at him. Hers was pounding with bravado. They were both icy cool of course. 'Seeing as you're *hors de combat*, as it were.'

'Um, fine,' he said. With such an alibi he could hardly feel challenged and anyway the hot water bottle was leaky.

'Shall I make us both a hot drink?' she asked.

'Yes please.'

They sat in the big brass bed and drank their Horlicks with the formality of fellow travellers on a train. Jemma had a T-shirt on and they both wore their underpants. On the mantelpiece was a photograph of Hannah, smiling in a peaked cap, which they both wished wasn't there.

'I am very glad you're here,' Paddy said lying bandaged and prostrate in the darkness.

'So am I.'

'I can't move I'm afraid . . .'

'I know.'

'So why don't you kiss me,' Paddy suggested. And she did. Under the bed Fitzgerald let out a silent but deadly fart.

When she arrived for work the next morning Mrs Goodall was delighted with the evidence she found about the house. It was untidy and empty, food had been eaten and beds slept in. A green car had been even left behind. Perhaps Paddy was at last coming out of himself, she thought. High time too, poor man.

The eaters and sleepers had left early and were driving towards London and the gaudy dawn breaking beyond it. The car was stuffed with daffodils and the three of them were lightheaded with an unaccountable optimism. They sang silly songs and at Jemma's house they had a second breakfast and waited for the mother's help.

In the make-up chair Sally gently managed to improve the colour, if not the contours, of Paddy's face. His story was that he had fallen off a horse and he watched everyone keenly for signs of disbelief. To his faithful dresser he told the truth and FQ was duly scandalised by what he heard. Would he like an aspirin? A valium? Vitamins? A massage?

'No thank you.' He didn't want to be rubbed up the right way. 'I want you to do me a favour,' Paddy asked, as FQ eased him into a shirt. FQ nodded, he was admiring the tight bandaging. It gave his master the look of a matador. 'I'd like you to go round the studio car-park and make a list of all the diesel-powered cars – then I want you to check their exhaust pipes and let me know about any that are faulty or loose.'

'Right you are, Boss.' FQ was thrilled to be playing Watson to Paddy's Holmes and hurried off.

Henry Gorringe showed only slight disbelief at Paddy's story and had no trouble arranging his camera angles to disguise the bruising. The scene was a dimly lit encounter between Blandford and his ex-wife, a brittle exchange of views. Jemma wore a dark blue silk dressing-gown and played the dialogue with languid irritation, her eyes as cold as ice until the camera cut.

They had hardly spoken since the night before and were glad of the safety they found in their scripted lines. As themselves they didn't know how to proceed, or how the story would end. The ground rules of the old game had become unfamiliar to them both, and they didn't know what to say.

Their kiss the night before had been long and gentle, an unambitious minuet rather than a tango. Paddy had lain prone like a horizontal sentry, only their mouths were touching in the old how-do-you-do. Jemma had relaxed and felt a warm thawing in the pit of her belly. Not so Paddy. He lay like a starving man with no appetite.

For Paddy the day had an unreality like the aftermath of anaesthetic. During takes the pain seemed to subside as though it was not part of Blandford's character. The problem of the murderous bastards who were trying to hijack his film was not uppermost in Paddy's mind. Jemma was.

The time was fast approaching when an explanation was due; not because she sought one, quite the reverse, but he realised the truth was what she deserved. The only problem was putting it in words – it was somehow beyond articulating. Paddy remembered the prep. school honour in owing up and wished it was only a new boy's tuck he had stolen now.

'I'm very happy you know,' Jemma said. She had sat beside him in his quiet corner behind the set. Paddy was staring at the crossword but he hadn't a clue what to say. 'I'm very happy the way things are,' she went on. 'You don't have to explain anything or promise anything or . . . anything heavy like that . . . that's all.' She grinned to lighten things and Paddy just looked at her. She was lovely and kind. 'Isn't it "nosy"?' she said pointing at the crossword. 'Curious about Cyrano? . . . nosy.' Intelligent too.

'Yes, of course,' he said, and put it in.

Over lunch Heime had nothing to report and was generally less inclined than most to believe the origin of Paddy's wounds. He scrutinised and probed with paternal concern and Paddy felt callow for not telling him the truth. Why should he withhold it from Heime for God's sake? What kind of paranoia was it that excluded your oldest friend?

During a mid-afternoon lull in proceedings FQ appeared to announce dejectedly that he'd had no luck in his search;

further bad news came when Jemma reminded him that her contribution on the film was all but finished. Paddy felt tired and confused and fell to wondering if the price of the whole damn enterprise was too high and painful. Was this his darkest hour? Dawn was certainly long overdue,

'I think I've done it,' Matthew Goddard grinned. His teeth were a snow-white notice board of glad tidings. Paddy had been summoned to the production office at the end of the day's work. He ached all over and his senses were dull with analgesic.

'We're going to be OK for Christ's sake,' Matthew was shouting. Paddy was keen to show a reaction but couldn't find one, he just stood dumbly like a boxer taking the count.

'You've got the money,' he said at last.

'Yeah. Good as. Isn't it great?' Matthew cackled with excitement and rushed to hug Paddy. Pain and the good news fizzed through him in a joint sensation. 'Ah-ha-ah,' he grunted.

'Oh God! Yeah. I'm sorry, you fell off a horse, right?'

'Yes ... it's OK. Don't worry. Tell me about it. Where's Heime? Let's have a drink.'

'He's joining us later.' Matthew drenched ice cubes with vodka. 'Here's to our saviour.' They swigged with the glee of victors.

'Who is he? And what's the deal?' Paddy asked trying to take in this reprieve.

Matthew explained.

Noel Pettifer had made his fortune in property development and had over the last ten years been applying himself and his wealth to more artistic endeavours. He had recently taken to investing in theatre and film production and was always keen to be involved in new ventures. Matthew had spent the day with him, had shown him the rushes, the script and the budget and had at last won from him a commitment to bail them out of their difficulties. They were all due to meet later at the Garrick. Cocktails tonight, contracts tomorrow.

As Paddy and Matthew went upstairs to meet their benefactor the Garrick Club's subtle power to hold the chaos of the twentieth century at bay seemed to restrict their mood of end-of-term ebullience.

That someone is exquisitely well dressed should not at first be apparent – it should be a slow realisation. And so it was with Noel Pettifer. Paddy was straight away impressed with the effortless warmth of his greeting but it wasn't for a while that he recognised the unmistakenly fine cut of his charcoal-grey double-breasted Hassler and McBride suit. Altogether Noel had the healthy look of a first-class traveller, tanned and assured. His face was pleasantly creased – not so the jacket.

Heime rang to say he thought he had the flu and would they excuse him as he was going to bed. Champagne arrived and the three of them wasted little time masking their enthusiasm for the business in hand.

'I've always been such a fan of Conran's – of yours too, of course.' Noel toasted Paddy with a grin. 'I was just appalled though at what they did with *Alleluia Jeremiah* – ghastly. Actually, in my opinion, the movies have never done justice to his books. *Stratagems and Spoils* is such a good story . . . so rich. I'm really thrilled that it looks as if we'll be able to work out a way of getting it finished. I think it looks terrific, what you've shot so far, it's going to be great. Great.'

Noel had the easy good manners and charm of a man whose privacy is fathoms deep. His voice was soft but he spoke with a measured precision that carried an implication of great certainty. He was a man in charge.

Paddy and he discussed the merits of the book in some depth while Matthew threw peanuts down his throat. Books were not his bag. Paddy had expected someone more in the financial mould, shrewd and mediocre and was delighted to find Noel so literate.

It was a spring evening and the three of them decided to walk round to Soho for dinner. Paddy's aches were quite abated with the energy from this new upturn in events and his mind was flooded with rosy thoughts. He would call the estate agents in Thame and take the house off the market; he would go to the *Sunday Globe* and the mashed potato people and retrieve his privacy. He would take his head out of the sand and face the world unblinkered. Jemma would be there, she would understand, she would . . . Paddy checked himself. He remembered how volatile happy endings could be.

They drank Vouvray with their Dover Sole and kümmel with their coffee, a jolly, harmonious evening. Paddy's only regret was that Heime was not there. The celebration would have done him good, restored him to his happier self. The past week seemed to have sapped him of his usual vigour.

Money, it seemed, was no object to Noel Pettifer; his concern was only for the quality of the film. Certainly he wanted a return on his investment but had the confidence not to be too eager for it. In his opinion the film would be a success of the slow-building, rather than the overnight, variety. An artistic triumph, he thought, that would do well at Cannes or possibly even as an Oscar contender . . . Steady. Steady.

'We'll tie up the detailed contract tomorrow,' Matthew said. Candlelight refracted in the wetness of his eyes momentarily giving him the wicked look of a temptress. 'Noel has got some creative accountancy to work out, isn't that right?' Noel nodded. 'Well Fledgling Productions will do all they can to help, won't they Paddy?'

'Of course,' grinned Paddy. To him creative accountancy was a contradiction in itself, presumably it meant cooking the books to give Noel some tax advantage. What did Paddy care, the film was all that mattered and why shouldn't the benefactor benefit?

'As far as I'm concerned Capitol's loss is my gain.' Noel smiled his easy smile and raised his glass. 'To *The Merchant of Venice*.'

'Why's that?' asked Matthew.

'For giving us the title – it's where it comes from. Stratagems and Spoils,' Noel explained.

'Oh yes, of course,' said Matthew before breaking a branch of celery with his teeth.

Noel had half closed his eyes and in a thick, quiet voice quoted: 'The man that hath no music in himself, nor is not mov'd with concord of sweet sounds, is fit for treasons, stratagems and spoils . . .'

Paddy found himself completing the speech: 'The motions of his spirit are dull as night, and his affections dark as Erebus: let no such man be trusted.'

The next morning on her doorstep Jemma was surprised to find a magnum of champagne among the milk bottles. The note with it said, 'Didn't want to disturb you. Wonderful news. Can you please come to a celebration lunch at the

studio? Love P. – PS Tell Kelly to look under the hydrangea.'
Tied round the giant tube of Smarties was a rough cartoon of
a Morris Minor winking at a fat little girl with no front teeth.

Having taken her daughter to school, Jemma lay in the
bath and pondered. Outside a blackbird sang and sunlight
flooded the house with great cubic rays of dust. She felt
excited with unspecified expectation. Paddy's invitation had
saved her from that feeling of anticlimax that an actor has
when a job ends. For without his *alter ego* to escape into, the
actor is forced back into the quiet waters of reality. The
mundane world has a brutal way of repossessing its players.

She soaped herself lazily and had the idea that her body
had been in hibernation. She studied her breasts as they
shifted idly in the water. The silver white dials round her
nipples were a legacy of Kelly's suckling. They were firm and
well shaped breasts but not since the birth had Jemma
properly regained that pride in them or herself that she had
had before.

Jemma had never been ashamed of the gentle narcissism
that is the linchpin of a young girl's sexuality but now she
missed it.

The business of procreation, she ruminated, had taken its
toll on her sensibilities and pushed any notion of pleasure
very much into second place. As Kelly was being born, she
remembered that the timeless hurricanes of pain had seemed
like retribution for all the enjoyment she had ever had.

Why hadn't her husband been able to understand this new
ambivalence in her, this change in the status of her body?
The brief squirting spasm that had periodically sated Dennis
only compounded her discontentment and had left her feeling
beached and lonely. Fucking wasn't what she had wanted.
She wanted courting. She wanted gentleness. Oh, she wanted
gentleness. And she wanted it from Paddy.

As Jemma had lain beside him in his bed she had realised
that it was not just his ribs that were restricting him. He had
kissed her with the sad resolve of someone about to leave on
a long journey – a platform kiss, with no chance of going
anywhere. She longed to say she understood, or it didn't
matter, but she knew it could be fatal.

Given time she could be his cure, and he hers. Whatever
the barrier was she had an idea they were on the same side of
it.

'I've had God knows how many impotent men in my life,' Jemma's girlfriend, Hattie, had told her on the telephone. 'It's just a question of keeping cool, darling . . . As my mother used to say, a watched pot never boils.' Screech of laughter.

13 The studio bar was crowded and noisy with euphoria. Betty wavered between her mother-earth and her nymphette approach. A good time was being had by all. *Stratagems and Spoils* was saved and celebrations were well under way. In the corner Paddy and Jemma shared a bowl of crisps. She was wearing a yellow silk dress and her hair shone like ebony. He told her the good news and longed to stroke her. Everything was tickety-boo.

Earlier Heime and Matthew and Paddy had sat round a table with Noel Pettifer and his accountant. Coffee cups and contracts were strewn about and through the slatted blinds sunlight sliced the blue smoke of Matthew's Gauloise while he explained. 'It seems that the best way for Noel to structure this investment, the most expedient anyway, is for him quite simply to take us over. He will buy Fledgling Productions from us lock, stock and barrel.'

'Is that necessary? Is it the only way?' Heime had asked gravely, his hands clasped in front of him.

'Apparently the best way to maximise the tax advantages in a rescue operation of this nature is to take over the company rather than simply subsidise it.' Noel had spoken with the casual air of a doctor giving a diagnosis. Beside him a pallid accountant had concurred with a nod.

Paddy had not paid much attention. He looked alert but his mind was elsewhere, like during algebra at school. The jargon was beyond him but it all felt right. The truth was he didn't really care who was paying the piper as long as the tune was intact. Contracts had been signed and the announcement of the rescue had been greeted with a huge cheer on the studio floor.

Heime made his way across to the bar to join Paddy and Jemma. He had the modest look of a man who is back in control after a crisis.

'You've just about finished with us then?' he asked her.

'I am afraid so – apart from the funeral scene in Munich,' Jemma replied.

Heime looked at each of them and then smiled questioningly as if he had suddenly realised there was more between them than the empty bowl of crisps.

'Well, I'm delighted,' he said. 'Your performance is excellent, I couldn't be more pleased with it.' It was a champagne-powered compliment, but heartfelt. Jemma thanked him. Heime turned to Paddy, and keeping his eyes down he said, 'And thank you, dear boy, for my lovely present.' Paddy had sent round a new recording of the Brandenburg Concerti on compact disc. It had been intended partly as a celebration offering and partly to seal the rift that the crisis seemed to have put between them. The rigid little Spaniard smiled an awkward smile that left a lot unsaid and Paddy felt a sharp pang of filial affection. They had a lot in common after all, apart from shyness. Before leaving them Heime patted Paddy's arm and said, 'You're not so bad, either.'

A moment later FQ approached with the unsubtle stealth of a ballet dancer. He brought with him the first of two items of information that Paddy was to receive before leaving the party.

'I thought it might interest you to know,' FQ began, holding his champagne glass in front of his mouth like a microphone, 'that our friend, Mr Toady kiss-my-arse Griffin, has just had a brand new exhaust pipe fitted to his car.'

'Is that right?' said Paddy.

'Yes, and' FQ sipped his drink to tantalise, 'it's a Peugeot 305' . . . sip, 'diesel-powered' . . . sip. 'And he was off sick all day yesterday.' FQ played his royal flush with a beam.

'Well done – thanks a lot. That's very interesting,' said Paddy. Although he was not entirely surprised he found the news shocking. FQ was Mata Hari now and glided off gracefully to fill his glass.

'For God's sake, you must go to the police,' Jemma said firmly. She was standing close to Paddy and smelt of primroses.

'Have dinner with me tonight.'

'How lovely,' she said.

'I'll take you to Le Caprice.' He never did. They were interrupted by an urgent message to call Paddy's hapless biographer, Hugo Cavendish, at the *Globe*: the second item of information.

'Something very interesting,' he announced. His voice was like salad dressing, oily yet tart.

'Oh?' Paddy's curiosity was cool.

'I thought the best way to begin the investigation into your little fracas with Capitol would be to suss out the other original contenders for the film rights of *Stratagems and Spoils*.'

'How?' Across the bar Jemma was listening intently to Henry Gorringe. Her head was on one side and her weight on one hip. In her silk dress she was a willowy yellow 'S'. Concentrate. 'How did you manage that?'

'Let's just say I had a very useful if liquid lunch with an assistant of Conran's literary agent.'

'And?'

'Well, as you know there was quite a lot of interest in the rights when the book first came out. As a matter of fact it's still quite a sore point how you came to get them ... anyway it seems there was one particularly persistent bidder in the race; a British-based company operating on behalf of some Americans. They seemed willing to pay pretty well anything.'

'Who were they?' Paddy was straining to hear above the noise.

'Ah well, that's what is curious.' Hugo knew how to whet an appetite. 'There was a certain amount of mystery as to their identity – a lot of "on behalf of my client" and "I am instructed by the interested parties" etcetera. That kind of thing. But whoever it was was working from the offices of Zeus Productions who have premises in Islington.' Hugo paused, inviting Paddy to egg him on.

'Well who are they?' Paddy obliged.

'They've gone into liquidation. Folded. Gone.' False end of story.

'Very odd.'

'The only interesting thing that I could find in the register of companies,' Hugo sprang his surprise climax with glee, 'was the name of one of the original directors of Zeus who resigned eighteen months ago ... Sir Toby Goddard.'

It was a surprise and instantly not a surprise. It was obvious.

'The bastard,' Paddy whispered.

'I tell you, mate, his balls are really in the mangle. I'm going to blow him sky high ... And Christ knows what else we'll find in the woodwork.' Hugo chuckled like a gourmet before eating. 'Just leave it with me and keep schtum OK?'

'OK.' Paddy told him about the rescue deal that had been arranged and they agreed to meet in two days time. Jemma was laughing at something Noel Pettifer had said, and for a second their eyes locked across the room. Paddy longed to be alone with her again.

'I'm telling you, mate,' Hugo said before hanging up, 'when I explode this little bombshell on the world it's going to be big – fucking enormous. You ain't seen nothing yet.' He was right. Neither of them had yet.

In the excitement of the film's reprieve Paddy had forgotten the injustice and injury he had suffered but suddenly all this damning evidence against his malefactors rekindled his indignation and his curiosity.

Who was Sir Toby working for? And why? Would whoever it was now back off or was the film still under threat? Christ. Or would Toady and his friend come visiting again? And on whose orders? Who was it who had tried to bribe him? The complexity of the conspiracy against him suddenly seemed too dense for Paddy's comprehension. One thing was certain; someone, somewhere had very much wanted the rights to the film and had gone to a lot of trouble to try and get them – the question was, would they stop now?

Without the moon behind him Toady Griffin did not look menacing at all. Paddy studied his visitor in the dressing-room doorway. He had eyes that were constantly moving as though his brain was in turmoil (it was), and his chin gave the impression that its maker had run out of material or time or both. It was a weak face – more of a gerbil than a toad. Paddy allowed the silence to swell between them, diminishing what was left of Toady's confidence. He had done a production of *The Homecoming* in Salisbury and had learnt from Pinter the sinister value of his famous pauses. They could speak volumes.

'You wanted to see me Mr Brummel?' Toady asked at last. His voice was loud with shallow confidence.

'Yes,' Paddy answered with quiet deliberation that made the question look stupid. 'Shut the door. Sit down,' he said. Was it an invitation or an order? Toady accepted or obeyed.

Paddy limped over and turned the lock on the door. It was quite an unnecessary thing to do and Paddy inwardly criticised himself for this gesture of fatuous theatricality – it was hammy.

'Your dresser said you wanted to see me. Wanted to ask me a favour.'

Paddy felt a disturbing pleasure at Toady's obvious anxiety. This was revenge, not sadism, he assured himself.

'Yes,' he said. 'I want you to do me a favour.' Harold Pinter to a T. Paddy paused again. 'I want you to help me,' he spoke genially.

'How? In what way?' Toady asked eagerly. Perhaps after all the star simply had an electrical problem he wanted help with. Perhaps not.

'I am puzzled,' Paddy began warmly, an iceberg drifting in tropical waters. 'I am puzzled why a little fucker like you should come down to my home and beat me up.' Paddy raised his eyebrows as if offering somebody soda in a whisky.

'How do you mean?'

'Who sent you?'

'I don't know what you're talking about.'

'And why?'

They studied each other timelessly. Paddy was holding his stout walking stick – weighing it in his hand with an implicit menace.

'Have a drink, Toady,' he said, and poured the gerbil a brandy.

'You can't prove anything,' said Toady, the drink burning his throat.

'Don't bet on it,' smiled Paddy.

'You said you wanted a favour.' Toady felt a little braver.

'Yes ... I don't want to hit you do you see ... I hate hurting people.' This was good news. 'I would like you to help me control myself from any act of violence.'

'Certainly.' Toady was quick to see the wisdom of compliance.

'We needn't involve the police in this you know.' Paddy poured himself a vodka and watched his guest in the mirror. 'It was Sir Toby who sent you, wasn't it?' No reply. Paddy drank. No reply. The stick sang through the air, crashed on to the table in front of Toady, hawthorn on formica. Paddy shouted, 'Wasn't it?' Very un-Pinter. Toady nodded.

'Why?'

Toady shrugged.

'For money?'

Toady nodded. 'He wanted the film stopped,' Toady sighed.

'So he paid you to beat me up?'

Toady drained his glass. 'I'm sick and tired of it,' Toady whined. 'Do this, do that, do that or else, the bastard ... He knows I've done time you see; he knows I haven't any bloody choice.'

Toady's remorse did nothing for Paddy – he unlocked the door.

'Hand in your notice tomorrow morning,' Paddy said as he switched off the tape recorder. 'I never want to see you again.'

Toady left.

So if Sir Toby was pulling Toady's strings, who was pulling Sir Toby's?

FQ always travelled home on the top deck of the bus, not for the scenic virtues, simply for a smoke; a sweet, butch Marlboro anonymously enjoyed among his fellow commuters. Today, however, he was a troubled man; a man focusing on the tricky point at which the perimeters of two loyalties overlap.

On the one hand he had a longstanding affection and deep respect for his employer – the clever, generous, inaccessible Paddy Brummel. On the other he owed an allegiance to his twilight fraternity, the gay world which guards its secret with the zeal of Freemasonry.

FQ thought long and hard as he journeyed through the suburban dusk. By the time he reached his home he had decided to keep his mouth shut. As things were turning out, it would do no harm to leave the skeletons in the cupboard and the gays in the closet. He closed his front door and a friendly voice shouted, 'Dinner's in the oven, luv.'

14 Capitol TV Studios were familiar territory to Paddy – even in the dark. He had worked there on and off for six years and knew well the layout and the rat-runs. Fred, the security chief, was an old friend, and after a brief chat Paddy left him happily studying the image of Florence Nightingale on the back of a £10 note as he slipped into the main studio.

An empty stage is a skeleton. With nothing but the dimmest light the scenery is the merest bones of a story. The flesh goes home at night, leaving the whole charade without purpose or dimension. There is a noise, too, that is not unghostly – entire rooms suspended from the rafters creak restlessly like abandoned ships. Paddy made his way through a magnificent portico to a non-existent hall. He passed stairways that led to nowhere and tiptoed along a vast horizon of crumpled canvas. At one point he tripped and fell against a plastic pillar that supported nothing. As he weaved his way to the emergency exit that led to the admin. block beyond, the universal smell of sisal brought back to Paddy memories of the theatre and a life long ago.

The echo of his footsteps raced ahead of him up the service stairs as he climbed wearily to the executive offices on the ninth floor. Paddy's ribs ached and he began to wonder if his courage and energy would match his curiosity in this expedition. A kind of reckless lunacy seemed to be upon him and his bladder was bursting with terror. From the wrong side he prised open a one way door and split his fingernail. He longed for a penknife, the childhood ally that primed conkers and scratched your initials on the desk.

The offices were in darkness lit only from the orange overspill from the city below. Paddy zigzagged through a maze of desks, the untidy tombs of long-fled secretaries. Sir Toby Goddard's office was partitioned off in a corner position. The door to his inner sanctum was substantial – but unlocked.

Inside Paddy stood still awhile, his heart pounding with achievement and terror. The room was sparsely furnished and dominated by a large desk. The high-back swivel chair behind it was silhouetted against St Paul's Cathedral across the river. On the opposite wall was a drinks cabinet. Paddy's priorities were clear; he took a hefty swig of blue label Smirnoff from his malefactor's bottle and then settled down to search through his desk.

What purpose would it serve, this rifling through his enemy's effects, Paddy wondered. None, was the answer, but as Oscar Wilde warns, 'A man cannot be too careful in his choice of enemies.' Paddy was getting to know the essence of the man. A picture was emerging: his background and his business style; his priorities and his proclivities, were all part of it. It was the picture of a respectable television producer, a successful man, well organised, knighted and wealthy. A man, one would imagine, who had no need to use bribery and fraud to get his way; a man in whose desk Paddy was hardly likely to find the smallest scrap of dirty linen.

Under a small pool of light Paddy watched his trembling hands leafing through diaries and correspondence. They were hands he knew only too well. He had been watching them at different forms of mischief for years: stealing sweets, cribbing exams, gluing things, signing married names in hotel registers. It wasn't fear of being caught that made them tremble now, it was this scrutiny of an unwitting man that gave him the uneasy excitement of a Peeping Tom.

In the movies Paddy would have soon discovered a secret panel or a piece of blotting paper crammed with the mirror image of code names. In the movies there would be the chime of a distant clock or a chord of music to keep the suspense alive. But this was not the movies and he found nothing. The room was sterile and empty.

Paddy paced the office in the half darkness soaking up its ethos; he didn't want to go but he had no reason to stay. He took another swig of vodka from the bottle and went back to the desk.

As he sat again his foot struck the waste-paper basket and he eagerly grasped it up. Again it yielded nothing – the harmless memos of legitimate business, used tissues, and an empty packet of Rothmans. From nostalgia for his old addiction, he opened the packet of his former brand. There inside was a screwed up piece of paper. He took it to the light with the careful hand of a prospector . . . A cablegram, pure gold. 'Goddard. Capitol TV London. As agreed Ganymede withdrawn. Clanger.'

This was what he had come for. Paddy had no idea what it meant but knew immediately and for sure that his find was significant. It was the link he had been looking for, a link between whom or what? His mind was tumbling through a labyrinth of information. Slow down. Keep cool ... Take another swig.

Ganymede, the cupbearer ... to Zeus? ... Ganymede ... Clanger ... Clanger. Where had Paddy seen the name before? ... dropped a clanger ... banger ... come on ... of course. It was on Monica's list of Sir Toby's callers, Clanger from New York. Ganymede withdrawn. Withdrawn ... What did that mean? Removed, deflected, silenced perhaps. Paddy took another swig from the bottle.

'Isn't that rather uncouth?'

Sir Toby was standing in the doorway, his voice was quiet but the sound exploded in the air as it synchronised with the light that now filled the room. Paddy was blinded and the vodka tore at his throat like sand ... this was far too like it was in the movies.

To stalk his victim Sir Toby had moved with unaccustomed stealth, and he now stood smugly panting in his dinner-jacket. Paddy was speechless. He wanted to say something frivolous like, 'Fancy seeing you,' but whispered 'Hallo' instead.

'Perhaps you'd like some ice and a glass,' offered Sir Toby, in the tone of a host.

'No thanks,' Paddy croaked. This wasn't a cocktail party, it was an ambush.

The two men sat down across the desk from each other. They had known each other for some years and had always exchanged platitudes, lunches, Christmas cards, etc. As a breed, Sir Toby had little time for actors. He considered them vain and stupid, a necessary evil in the grand scheme of television production.

'I wasn't expecting you,' said Paddy stupidly.

'Obviously not. The security man did well to reach me – I was at a preview theatre in Soho.' Indeed Fred was now downstairs admiring the portrait of William Shakespeare which adorns the back of a £50 note – sheer poetry.

'Perhaps you would be so good as to tell me what you are doing here?' Sir Toby's voice was oily with paternal menace.

'I was looking for something.' Paddy felt classically

disadvantaged: the poacher with a brace of pheasants over his shoulder.

'What?' Sir Toby was preparing a cigar for his wily lips. Paddy could think of no answer, his throat was filled with a throbbing lump of chalk. 'What was it you were looking for Mr Brummel?'

'I wanted to know why you cancelled *Stratagems and Spoils* – I want to find out what it is you stand to gain by halting production.'

'And what did you find?'

'Nothing.' Paddy crossed his legs, not so much from nonchalance, more to ease his aching bladder.

'Nor will you.' Sir Toby sucked his cigar to life and blew out the match with blue breath. 'You must feel rather foolish Mr Brummel.' He emphasised the 'Mr' to remind Paddy of his superior status. 'You've wasted your time.'

'I don't think so, Sir Toby,' Paddy answered taking a side-swipe at the title. It was, he reminded himself, a knighthood bestowed for outstanding service to the entertainment industry. Huh. 'Sooner or later you'll be exposed as a crook. A crook who cheated his own company, his friends, his nephew even for personal gain. For greed.' Paddy spoke in a tone that flattered rather than insulted.

Sir Toby pondered awhile, swinging gently to and fro in his swivel chair. The floodlit dome of St Paul's bobbed from left to right behind his head like an elusive skullcap. 'The trouble with you,' he said slowly, 'is that you're so bloody arrogant.'

'Oh, yes?' Paddy did not agree with the diagnosis.

'It never crossed your mind that your precious film was no damn good.'

'The film is great.'

'Unmarketable.'

'Not according to Heime.'

'We'll see.' Sir Toby grinned smugly.

'Anyway it's going ahead. We've found new backing.'

'Noel Pettifer.'

'Exactly.'

Sir Toby continued rocking but their eyes stayed locked like formation dancers.

'Give me the tape,' he ordered quietly.

'What tape?' Paddy knew what tape.

'The tape you made this evening of a conversation with Mr Griffin.'

Doesn't news travel fast, thought Paddy. 'You mean your pet thug?' he said.

'Just give it to me.' Sir Toby's eyes had the unthinking stare of a corpse.

'I haven't got it.' It was in his pocket.

'Give it to me.' From nowhere Sir Toby produced a small revolver, his fat fingers enveloped it like a toy. It wasn't a toy. This was a proper grown-up villain, for God's sake, not some bumbling rascal. A dozen pigeons were trying to fly out of Paddy's stomach; he wanted to laugh it was that serious.

'Give it to me.' There was a ghastly patience in the command.

Paddy put his hand in his pocket to fetch the cassette and felt briefly the crumpled cablegram. At least he had that. It was some comfort. He was sure Hugo Cavendish would be able to decipher it; all was not lost. The tape spun across the leather surface of the desk between them.

'Thank you,' Sir Toby smiled coldly. On the far wall was a framed photograph of him smiling the same smile as he shook hands with Princess Margaret. 'You broke a rib or two at the weekend, I gather.' He put the revolver into a neat flat box and returned it to his pocket. 'You should be careful. It might have been your neck.'

Paddy swallowed dryly. 'Is that a threat?'

'Oh, yes,' said Sir Toby and let out a roar of laughter shrill and hollow from a mouth full of gold. It was a sound of madness. Was the man mad? Paddy wondered, and the idea chilled him with a new panic. A psychopath would be a very different kettle of fish. 'Yes, I think you should take it as a threat.' The laughter stopped abruptly and Sir Toby said coldly, 'Keep your nose out of my business.'

In the deserted car-park they parted company cordially like gentlemen after a game of squash. Paddy watched the Rolls Royce pull out into the street and at last began a long, sweet pee.

'You slept in Mummy's bed, didn't you?' Kelly's question froze the muesli in Paddy's mouth. To lie or not to lie. 'I saw you,' she said.

'Yes.' He opted for the truth. Her wide eyes seemed to give him no choice. Jemma was still upstairs and they were having breakfast in the kitchen. Kelly's hair was tightly pony-tailed and her face. shone like a fruit.

'Was it nice?' Kelly crunched her cereal loudly. Paddy wished he had had an early call at the studio instead of the late one that allowed him to be part of this inquisition.

'Yeah. Well I was tired . . . it was cosy, nice and cosy.' That was certainly the truth.

Paddy had arrived late still fizzing from his interview with Sir Toby. Jemma had scrambled eggs for him. They had called the Clanger number in New York without success and spent some time puzzling over the cable. 'As agreed Ganymede withdrawn. Clanger.'

It had troubled Jemma. 'He just doesn't seem the bribable type,' she had said. Upstairs in her bedroom, on her marital bed, Jemma had rubbed Paddy's aching shoulders with oil and they had fallen asleep loosely entwined like lovers; but not quite, for their affection was still unconsummated and undiscussed.

Paddy had slept soundly, unaware that in his empty home the telephone was ringing unanswered in the night.

'Does that mean you love Mummy?' asked Kelly, as if it might simply be another legend of the grown-up world. Paddy studied her for a moment. The muesli was sawdust in his mouth.

'Yes, I suppose it does.' It was news to him too. For a moment he felt trapped at having his feelings housed in words. Perhaps it really was that simple.

As a child Paddy's mother had often rebuked him for his emotional constriction and photograph albums bore witness to a po-faced little boy. 'Smile for God's sake,' she had shouted at him, frowning on the Ferris wheel. And when he was fourteen she had sobbed at him, 'Don't be afraid to cry, my darling,' as they stood by his father's coffin. He smiled at Kelly and fleetingly envied her lack of complication. He had never been as free as her.

'And you too, of course.' He kissed her cheek and she grinned toothlessly. A week ago none of this had begun, he thought.

Jemma sang as she came downstairs. Her face was shining too, like her daughter's. Paddy imagined for a moment that he had in reality made love to her and it was the impotence that was part of a dream. He watched her make coffee and felt a sudden sadness that sex should be such a centrifugal force between two people. He resented nature's sly monopoly of people's affection for one another. Weren't there other equally binding commodities to be shared . . . music, a joke . . . *The Times* crossword?

Jemma opened the window, 'Looks like a lovely day.' It was, so far.

Driving to work Paddy listened to Sibelius and ran through his lines. He was full of optimism and caffeine.

'Good morning, Colette.' He was collecting his key from reception.

'Oh, Mr Brummel, isn't it awful?'

'What?' he said knowing it was bad.

'You haven't heard?'

'What, for God's sake?'

'Mr Chadwick is dead.'

'What?' He meant how.

'It was on the news.' Colette was out of her depth; false eyelashes had overwhelmed her eyelids. 'He killed himself.'

Paddy wanted to punch her in the mouth. 'Thank you,' he said looking at his watch. Eight-fifty-five. He took his key and went to his dressing-room. He turned on the radio and set the percolator. Listening to the shipping forecast he felt weightless like a moonwalker. On Dogger Bank. Oh, Heime. He leant against the double glazing and watched the gulls dipping over the river as he heard that his good friend, Heime Chadwick, the producer of many popular television series including *The Declancey Inheritance* had been found dead in his flat in Highgate. Some sleeping pills had been taken away for analysis and a police spokesman had said that foul play was not suspected.

The coffee percolated. A speedboat raced silently up-river. Paddy was desperate to unscramble the information and produce some feeling. Like a computer inadequately programmed, he couldn't find any. Sentiment not known – insufficient data – repeat, no known sentiment. Sorrow would come later, he supposed, late at night or on the Chilterns. It would take time. For a moment he just felt bewildered. Paddy hoped his friend had not lost dignity in dying; he was a tidy, dignified man for whom a self-determined death seemed quite extraordinary. The coffee tasted bitter in Paddy's mouth. There was a quiet knock on the door and FQ came in wearing a vermilion cashmere sweater.

'Isn't it ghastly?' he said quietly.

'Yes,' said Paddy without turning. His old meanness, the reluctance to share or show emotion was taking hold.

'They tried to call you. You must have left.'

'Yes.'

'It's too awful.' FQ's gravity provoked a flippancy in Paddy.

'Yes,' he said, 'poor old Heime.'

He's obviously sadder than he seems, thought FQ. He had so nearly worn a dark-blue jersey and for the hundredth time that morning wished to God he had.

'What's going to happen?' Paddy asked.

'Piers in the press office wants to know if you could face a few minutes with the reporters. A brief statement. They're in main reception.'

'Sure. Then what?'

'There's a company meeting in the production office in half an hour.' FQ turned to go. He had a horrible feeling that he had made a wrong decision the night before sitting on the 37 bus. Paddy halted him.

'Was there a note? Did Heime leave a letter?'

'I don't know,' FQ replied.

'I'll be down in a minute.' Paddy shaved slowly, not looking himself in the eye.

There were twenty-five or so journalists waiting in the lobby of the studio. Piers silenced the barrage of questions and introduced Paddy on behalf of Fledgling Productions. Paddy stood with his hands in his pockets, eyes down.

'I am not answering questions,' he said. The flashing bulbs enraged him and he felt a loathing for the eager faces in front of him. 'I just want to say how sad we all are at the death of Heime Chadwick. He was a wise and honest and generous man. An excellent producer, and a good friend to many of us here.' He paused. Was he sounding too stiff? At the back of the crowd he caught sight of Hugo Cavendish standing with his arms folded looking calm and expressionless.

'We will all miss him, very much. And send our deepest condolences to his family. That is all.' Again there was the baying of the tabloids, they wanted more – a break in the voice, a subtle tear. Paddy felt dizzy and enclosed, wanted to escape, wanted to get to Jemma. For God's sake what was going on?

In the corridor a man with a note-pad approached. 'Mr Brummel could I trouble you for a moment?'

114

'No.' Paddy walked on.

'I'd like to ask you some questions.'

'I said no questions.'

'I know.'

'I have no answers. I have nothing to say to the press.' Paddy carried on walking.

'I'm not the press. I'm the police.'

'Oh.' Paddy stopped walking.

'Detective Inspector Robbins.' The little man fumbled for an ID card which showed a photograph of a younger and happier face than the bearer. Paddy sympathised, he was used to being confronted with ancient photographs of himself.

'Come with me,' he said and led him to his dressing-room.

Robbins held his mug of coffee with both hands and looked out at the river. It was compulsive viewing for him like everyone else, and certainly easier than looking his wife's heart-throb in the eye.

'I'm sure the last thing you want at this point is to answer questions, Mr Brummel.'

'Not at all,' Paddy lied.

'A most distressing thing to happen.'

'Yes.'

'Just a few routine questions.'

'Fire away.'

'Er, yes.' Robbins seemed nonplussed – he had been predisposed to find the star disagreeable.

'Had you known Mr Chadwick long?'

'About eight years.'

'As an employer?'

'And a friend, he was a close friend.' Paddy recollected the awkward distance between them over lunch two days before and a complex kaleidoscope of ideas tumbled through his mind.

'And when did you last see him?'

'Yesterday – we had a party.' It came to Paddy that if Heime had left no explanation it wasn't for him to help expose one. 'A party to celebrate.'

'How did Mr Chadwick seem?'

'Perfectly normal.'

'Quite cheerful?'

'He wasn't a cheerful man,' Paddy said and was immediately contradicted by a memory of Heime laughing – a rare, robust, gurgling noise full of Spanish gusto.

'I'm told that this production you are working on has not been without certain difficulties lately – something of a financial crisis, I understand.'

'Yes.'

'But satisfactorily resolved now?' It was barely a question.

'Yes. That was what we were celebrating.'

'Nevertheless he had been under quite some pressure I suppose.'

'Yes, obviously. We all have.'

'But as it has turned out all right there doesn't seem to be cause enough for him to take his life.'

Paddy shrugged. In the back of his mind minute memories were awakening doubts.

'So professionally speaking there's nothing we could call attributable. What about the personal side?' Robbins was as casual as a policeman's boot with his change of tack.

'I wouldn't know.' Paddy tried to deter this trespass.

'You were his close friend.'

'Yes. But he was a private man – his private life was not my business.' It was true that Paddy knew little in that respect, but he felt a fleeting curiosity.

'He was unmarried?'

'Yes.'

'Single.'

'Yes.'

'He was half Spanish I believe.' The policeman loaded the nationality with significance.

'Yes,' Paddy answered as he watched a tug labouring up the river and had his first taste of remorse. He did not want to be drawn into the territory of Heime's private life.

'Apparently he was a homosexual.'

Silence. Stay silent.

'Well?' Robbins persevered.

'Well what?' Paddy's insolence was poorly hidden.

'Mr Chadwick was a homosexual,' repeated the unhappy copper.

'That's a statement is it, Inspector?'

'Yes.'

'Not a question?'

'No.'

'Then no answer is required is it?' Paddy's reasoning was bland.

116

'No.' Robbins felt outwitted by this old trick and his neck flushed with annoyance. He took a deep breath, the way his wife suggested, to relieve tension. 'I quite understand, Mr Brummel, that this is a very delicate subject, but within the context of Mr Chadwick's private life we may possibly find some clue to the mystery of his death.'

'Of course,' Paddy relented. He poured them both more coffee. 'What I'm saying is that if he was gay he certainly wasn't one of the screaming, rampant variety. He was a very discreet, private man ... and whatever his proclivities they won't help you find a motive.'

'Possibly not.' Robbins was not convinced. The gay world was a closed book to him, although he had once been fumbled by a sergeant in the locker room.

'He loved opera,' Paddy said, and even as he spoke he realised that the information was extraneous.

'Is that so?' answered Robbins. The deceased's psyche was beyond him. He was no fan of the opera either.

'He lived alone,' Paddy explained.

'So I gather.'

'It would be foolish to think of it as a case of *cherchez l'homme.*'

Robbins smiled like a man of the world – he knew wit when he saw it. 'We shall see,' he said. Everything about the little detective had a downward slant – his eyes, his moustache, his shoulders, his tone of voice.

Paddy turned away and watched the silver-black clouds jostling to escape over the skyline.

On reflection it was perfectly possible that Heime had died from a broken heart, Paddy supposed. History was littered with much less likely people who had fallen victim to that great trip-wire of sex. With the rawness of his own sensibilities in that regard, Paddy sympathised. He resolved to do nothing to help Robbins hang the tag of turpitude round his friend's neck.

'Mr Chadwick was in good health was he?'

'Yes. A bit tired, I suppose. We all are.' Paddy remembered how pale Heime had been during the last week.

'Well,' said Robbins in the tone that concludes fruitless interviews. 'We must suppose he had his reasons.'

'Yes,' said Paddy. 'There'll be an inquest won't there?'

'Sometime in the next week or two.'

Robbins rose and with a hesitation that Paddy recognised only too well, asked if he might have an autograph for his wife.

'What's her name?' Paddy took a photograph from his dressing-table.

'Shirley,' Robbins proclaimed with pride, and his downward face smiled briefly with gratitude as Paddy signed his name.

'Can I ask you what time Heime died?' Paddy wanted to know.

'About midnight it's thought.'

Robbins was landscaping his trilby in the doorway. 'We'll know more after the PM.' The two men eyed each other for a moment.

'Who found him?' Paddy asked.

'We did. We received a phone call.'

'From him?'

'No.'

'Then whom?'

'Ah,' Robbins half smiled, 'that's what we'd like to know. It was an anonymous call ... a gentleman, said he was a friend.' There was no need for the fractional stress on friend – the point was made. Robbins left.

On his own again Paddy felt the first vestige of sadness in his solar plexus, the familiar symptom of an old ailment. He was puzzled too, more puzzled than Robbins because he knew so much more ... Things were stinking rotten in the state of Denmark.

15 Lewis Lefrak had been out late at a witless fondue party in Malibu and he was now brooding alone in the jacuzzi. He was an emperor: in his left hand was a glass of vodka and orange, in his right was his penis: he'd got the whole world in his hands. His mind was bright with cocaine, the sweet snort of success.

This was it, the life he had always wanted. Certainly the jets of water were a thrill but what really turned him on was the feeling of triumph. He was a winner in the dog-eat-dog world – *Stratagems and Spoils* was going to make him the hottest goddam producer in Hollywood. His small cock was hard with self-esteem, a love that he would consummate later in his black silk sheets.

Above the wail of the Beach Boys, the telephone rang. Lefrak doused the music and answered. He heard the hiss and click of satellites and oceans and knew it must be England.

'Hello ... Yes.' He listened. 'Christ. Christ Almighty.' Lefrak had never met Heime Chadwick but the news of his death came as a shock indeed. No remorse did he feel, just an impulse for self-preservation. Were his tracks covered? He understood the power of innuendo; and was keen to keep his act clean.

'Was there a note?' he asked, then listened.

'Good. Well done ... then there's no problem. Jesus, I guess some people are just bad losers, eh?' He laughed heartlessly with the compassion of a boa constrictor. This suicide was a cheap manoeuvre that he would not allow to impede him. Condensation ran down his high window and in the clear night sky above, the stars looked blurred. There must be some advantage to be taken ...

'So they'll need a new producer on the show?' Lewis said slowly. His implication whizzed through the universe and was met with a chuckle in England. 'It's too good an opportunity to miss ... I mean what's to lose? Let's go for it.' Wasn't all fair in love and movies? It would simply streamline his enterprise in the long run. Poor old Heime.

'Go for it Buddy. I'll call Clanger. Be in touch. Ciao.' He hung up. Lewis had a lot to do, the pace of things was hotting up. The Beach Boys sang out again but his erection had vanished with the excitement.

Thoughts were treadmilling around Paddy's mind like in the death throes of a bad dream. His hands shook the way they did on first nights, as he went to dial Jemma's number. He had a sharp memory of Heime's face across the canteen table only days ago, sad and uneasy. Had his eyes perhaps concealed a secret cry for help? With hindsight Paddy could see that Heime's tiredness might well have been desolation.

Jemma's number was engaged. He wondered if he could have saved his friend; he blamed himself for not having seen the germ of this voluntary death taking hold. He dialled again. Why was there always so much left unsaid?

'I know,' Jemma said before he could tell her the news. 'Matthew rang after you left. I'm sorry. You must be devastated.'

'Yeah.'

'Would you like me to come over?'

'No.' Paddy looked in the mirror and saw his father's face, hollow and pale, the same stubborn self-constraint. Say something, he told himself, say 'I love you' or 'I can't cope' or 'fuck the whole stinking, shitting world.'

'He left no note,' he said.

'Was it pills?' she asked.

'Yes.'

'Maybe he meant to.'

'What?'

'Leave a note . . .'

'Yeah. It's certainly odd.'

'Poor Heime. It was all too much for him.'

There was a lull in their staccato exchange.

'Did you know he was gay?' he asked.

'Yeah, of course . . . didn't you?'

'Yes, of course, but . . .' But what? It never seemed to matter, wasn't relevant.

'Is it to do with why . . . I mean was that the reason?' Jemma's voice was faint.

'God knows. Maybe. I wouldn't think so.' There had to be a better reason. What better reason, Paddy wondered. And who was it that had called the police. 'It's what they seem to think.'

120

Jemma was sitting at her kitchen table, Paddy's cup and bowl were still in front of her but the day had changed complexion since he left.

'Dennis rang,' she told him. 'My husband ... he's been investigating.' Jemma waited for some encouragement to go on. It did not come. This wasn't the moment perhaps but she went on, 'He's been looking into Capitol TV, the royalties and overseas sales.'

Paddy remembered the greedy little man hell-bent on revolution, and wondered what the connection was.

'I told him about Zeus, the production company that Sir Toby has been using,' Jemma reminded him.

'Oh yes.' Hugo Cavendish's gleeful revelation came back to Paddy.

'It seems there were two other directors that we didn't know about ... Marty Clanger from New York.'

This was no big surprise. Paddy still had the crumpled cablegram ... 'As agreed Ganymede withdrawn. Clanger.' An American link was inevitable, wasn't it? Time for a British war of independence.

'And who else?' he asked.

'Henry Gorringe.'

'Henry ...'

'Yeah.'

'Henry Gorringe. I don't believe it.' Paddy sat down. This was a big surprise. 'I don't believe it.' He felt dizzy.

'It's true.'

This wasn't paranoia, this was everybody plotting against him. This was real. Henry, his friend, and Sir Toby, his enemy, had been scheming with this faceless American to rob him of the rights of *Stratagems and Spoils*. They had nearly bankrupted him and had sent men with sticks to beat him up. They had failed a year ago by fair means and were now still pursuing their purpose with fouler ones.

'Hallo,' Jemma's voice interrupted his comprehending.

'Sorry,' he said. 'I was just thinking ... Heime must have known, must have found out about Henry ...' Paddy suddenly understood that this news on its own could have been the final straw for Heime. This was the treachery that had sent his friend to a do-it-yourself death. A horrible rage throbbed in Paddy's veins, a rage that was in fact diverted grief.

'Also . . .' Jemma was saying, 'it strikes me we've had it arse-about-face, this involvement of Sir Toby. He wasn't being bribed, he wasn't seeking to make money. It was protection he was after. He was being blackmailed. Think about it.'

Paddy thought about it. 'Zeus Productions . . . Ganymede. Ganymede the cupbearer who changed allegiance. What else could the message have meant. "As agreed Ganymede withdrawn. Clanger."' Paddy thought some more.

'Sir Toby doesn't need money,' Jemma went on. 'He's got plenty and it's perfectly safe. It's his respectability he's frightened to lose. He's being blackmailed, I'll bet you.'

It was a bet Paddy wouldn't take. 'You're right,' he said at last. 'You must be right.' He was pacing back and forth, the telephone was a leash restricting him. Heime, the innocent bystander caught in the crossfire, as Sir Toby struggled to appease his blackmailer, Marty Clanger. Paddy wanted time to think, to digest these new unsavoury morsels.

'I'll see you later.'

'Sure, fine.'

Paddy wanted to say more, something affectionate, or grateful, or just not ice-cold.

'I think you're terrific,' he managed.

'Thank you.' She knew the compliment was not meant to sound reluctant.

'Bye.'

'Bye.'

Separately they hated the telephone for a moment. At least face to face there is a certain ambiguity to hide behind; the telephone, though, creates a horrible need for things to be explicit.

Like a visitor to the sick-bay FQ had wafted in; his head was bowed and his eyes down; a balletic kind of sadness that concealed his real emotions, including a nauseating fear that left the taste of bile in his throat.

'They're waiting for you in Heime's . . . in the production office.'

'Are you OK?' asked Paddy as he went to leave. His dresser's face was flaky white as though all the colour had drained into the vermilion polo neck. FQ nodded a lie.

The production room was crowded and thick with the

cigarette smoke that hung trapped in the solemn air. Sad faces studied blank note-pads. What was there to write? Obituaries, letters of condolence . . . Paddy longed to be alone walking his favourite path through beech woods.

'Paddy, we've had the *Fergus Llewellyn Show* on the telephone.' Piers Ramsay was being the Girl Guide triumphant in crisis. 'They want to know if you could perhaps do a small bit on Heime, tonight?'

'No.' Paddy's spontaneous reply sounded rude. He relented. 'Perhaps another time.'

Across the room Paddy met the dark gaze of Matthew Goddard. He sat very still with the light behind him, not eating for once, not joking, quite different. Without expression, they stared at each other, both of them diminished by their friend's death.

Voices were planning a memorial service, hymns for God's sake. Paddy shut his eyes to keep in his anger. Who the hell was it who had called the police, he wondered? A picture of Heime came to him from nowhere; not the alert, elegant Heime but a sprawled, gormless, dead one.

Henry Gorringe was watching clouds abstractedly the way fishermen do. Paddy imagined holding him by the throat and demanding to know about his involvement in the rival bid for *Stratagems and Spoils*. The anger was warm inside his head despite a saner voice urging him to give the benefit of the doubt.

'What about filming?' Paddy's voice demanded. To hell with funerals – he wanted to escape into fiction where death is just another stunt. His question was followed by a silence that suggested disapproval.

Noel cleared his throat. 'I'm afraid we'll have to suspend for a while,' he said.

'How long?' asked Paddy.

'A few days.' Noel was wearing a dark-blue suit and a black tie already. Perhaps he kept a spare in his attaché case, Paddy thought, just in case of an unscheduled death during the day.

Noel ran his finger down the crease of his trouser, 'We have a lot to sort out. It's not easy. Also we have to find a new producer if we are going to carry on.' He spoke delicately but the truth was plain.

'I see,' said Paddy.

'Any ideas?' said Matthew.

'Well, I've had a telex from a chap by the name of . . .' He scanned his Asprey's memo pad . . . 'Lefrak. Lewis Lefrak.' The hideous name rang no bell around the room. 'An American, apparently, seems keen. I'll check him out . . .'

After the meeting Paddy stalked Henry Gorringe down several passages, caught him at a swing-door.

'Have you got a moment?'

'Sure.'

'Er . . .' Paddy suddenly realised his enormous admiration for this man whom he was about to indict. He hoped Henry would deny the accusation of treachery, in fact almost withdrew it for fear that he wouldn't. They walked on, out of step.

'It's just that I hadn't realised you were involved with Zeus Productions.' Paddy presented it as a casual statement not a question, out of kindness.

'Hadn't you?' Henry asked.

'No.' Paddy expected a show of indignation at least. 'Nor that they had tried some time ago to buy the film rights of *Stratagems and Spoils*, you and Sir Toby and this man Clanger in New York.'

Henry stopped walking and they stood with the corridor between them, square on like boxers before the first jab. There was no look of shame in Henry's face, only a kind of disappointment.

'You must think I'm an arsehole?'

Henry could be ingenuous. Behind him on the wall was a photograph of Sylvia Syms as a nurse, smiling wanly.

Paddy shrugged slightly, the wind was out of his sails. 'I was curious,' he said.

'It was a complete cock-up,' Henry sighed, 'a bunch of morons. Yes, I was a partner. They thought I'd lend some kind of credibility to the project. I didn't pay anything . . . anyway I resigned.'

'When they failed to do the deal?' asked Paddy. Close behind his head was Dirk Bogarde in a balaclava quizzically gazing into the middle distance. Henry nodded. 'Why the secrecy?'

Henry considered a moment. In the background typewriters chattered and telephones rang. Henry shook his head, he didn't know, he just felt hoisted on his neighbour's petard.

'What about Heime?' Paddy asked. 'Did he know?'

'Yes. He found out ... maybe he knew all along but he called me last week to say ...'

'What?' Paddy tried to be gentle.

'Not to tell you.' Henry would not look him in the eye. Dirk Bogarde didn't seem to care.

'Not to tell me ... why?'

Henry paused. 'He said it wasn't important but it might cause bad feeling. He said you might not understand.' True. 'It might spoil our relationship – yours and mine.' He was looking down at his red and green sneakers. 'I suppose it has.'

'Yeah.' Paddy could see no point in lying. It was time for being candid.

'The truth is, I don't get offered that much decent work,' Henry spoke quietly, 'crap mostly. I just wanted to make this film. I have done ever since I first read it.'

'Me too,' said Paddy.

'I never wanted to get caught up in all this shit – I just wanted to make the film, that's all.'

Paddy's capacity for believing people had taken a beating lately.

'I'm sorry,' said Henry Gorringe. It was an apology for misjudgement not treachery. Paddy nodded. The question of Henry's veracity was best left 'on hold' for the present. Allies were getting thin on the ground.

'Let's have a drink,' Paddy said. They walked off towards the bar leaving Dirk and Sylvia smouldering into each other's walls.

16 As an interim measure the ex-literary adviser of the great Fernando Cass had fled from the star's ranch south to Los Angeles and was now holed up in downtown Hollywood. Irving's appetite for revenge was growing fast in the moist heat of his motel room. The noise of the air-conditioning drove him mad so he had chosen to sweat in silence. Feeling trapped and spiteful he paced back and forth to keep the stucco walls from closing in. He was fighting a losing battle with his worse self; soon he would surrender and pick up the telephone. His loathing of Fernando Cass made him feel quite dizzy.

Peevishness was Irving's most bourgeois failing. He was forever flouncing out of things on the spur of the moment; bedrooms, jobs, parties. It couldn't be helped, he told himself. It was entirely biochemical; so, wasn't he entitled to a little self-pity? He gazed out of the window of his hacienda-style cabin.

Outside a young man stood on the diving-board of the pool, hesitating as if reluctant to disturb the water. Irving admired the infinite blackness of his skin in the sunlight and shared the diver's indecision. The telephone was waiting patiently for him.

Irving was going to cook the film star's goose. With his inside information there was ample scope for revenge. Cheating on a cheat wasn't really cheating, he told himself. At last the black man dived deliciously into the water – ebony into azure. Irving watched his sleek motion with keen interest. His hormones were taking him off on another mystery tour.

Irving stared at the telephone. The heat was getting worse. So, too, was his hatred of Fernando Cass. He saw it as his duty to expose the star's devious double-dealing and protect the British interest. As a literary man he owed it to G.P. Conran. He dialled the number of International Famous Artists and was soon talking to Bud Schwartz. The worried agent was no stranger to low diplomacy and they arranged to meet that evening for a cocktail in Beverly Hills – the happy hour.

Replacing the telephone Irving felt unburdened and

happier than he had done for a while. It wasn't spite, it was patriotism, he told himself. Meanwhile he opened his french window in answer to a nagging little desire. A short time later Herbert, still dripping wet, was standing in his room sipping a Coca Cola. The real thing.

Dennis swung the tea-bag from his mug to the swing-bin and scalding water landed on his foot. Would he never learn? The pain made him resent the woman in his bed; she seemed to have aged overnight, almost disintegrated. He guarded the privacy of his mornings zealously and longed for girls to vanish promptly after copulation.

'Sugar?' he asked.

'Two,' she answered, spread-eagled under the lion's share of the maroon duvet. There was about her a ghastly look of permanence. Dennis had begun regretting the whole episode in mid-coitus the night before. The two of them had somehow confused their political accord with sexual desire – workers must unite.

'I was thinking,' she said, her breasts looked slack and incapable of thought, 'about those bastards at Capitol and Northern TV.'

They had met at a rally of aggrieved actors to debate the question of overseas royalties. They had shared the euphoria of injustice and a lot of home-made cider, heady stuff. And now here they were drinking tea together in his bed in Herne Hill.

'Who is this guy,' she continued, 'this American who handles all the US sales?'

'At Transworld Telly?'

'Yeah.'

Dennis thought, 'Something to do with bells. Ringer. Chimes. Dropped a . . . Clanger, I think, Marty Clanger. He's the man in New York who does it all.'

'The sole agent?'

'Yeah.'

'And all the books are quite in order?'

'Yeah – they're not stupid these pigs.'

'This Clanger sells British programmes to all the American TV stations?'

'Yeah.'

'At a price that's too low. The question is not why, but how? I mean it's obvious that there's a rip-off going on. We've just got to find out how they manage it.' She slurped her tea pensively.

'Right.' Dennis wondered if this pursuit of his *bête noire* was merely a ploy she was using to stir him.

'Supposing,' she mused, staring at the clogged cornice round the ceiling, 'supposing then what this Clanger guy does is not to sell them directly?'

'What do you mean?' Dennis was forced to ask.

'I've heard of it before,' she said. Her street wisdom had been honed through years of touring in children's theatre. 'They cook the books by selling to a middleman who sells on to the main outlet.'

The noise of the traffic outside had the aggravated tone of ordinary people going to work. Dennis pondered.

'You mean if this Clanger was selling to a middleman we wouldn't necessarily know about it,' he said.

'Exactly. He probably sells them at a deliberately low price to a guy who then makes a fucking great mark-up when he sells them on.'

'Then they split the profit.' Dennis was keen to mask his commercial naïvety but she had a point. 'All the sales records would be perfectly in order and it's us poor bastards, the actual workers who get screwed.' He scratched his ginger beard ferociously.

'You've been wasting your time checking on things this end,' she proclaimed. 'If you ask me Clanger is the man in the hot seat.' There were small nuggets of sleep in the corners of her eyes.

'You may be right,' Dennis said. He simply couldn't remember her name.

Dennis lay back on his pillow, his anger at the world had a new target in Marty Clanger. With Paddy Brummel's help he'd trounce those greedy pigs at Transworld Telly and get Sir Toby up before the tribunal, cut off his head, cut off his assets. Equality. Fraternity. Against his thigh what's-her-name's shin bristled with revolutionary stubble and he felt a surge of Marxism in his loins. Today was his day for supplementary benefit. The world was not so bad. He put down his empty cup and slipped his hand between the legs of this clever woman, the source of his intelligence.

Later, as she was brutally straddling him, he got it: her name was Tracey Louise.

Paddy meanwhile had slipped out of the studios and was driving west along the Embankment. He had no destination, only a desire not to arrive. Angled rain slashed his windscreen and the east wind sharpened the city skyline.

There was a frantic carousel of questions chasing answers in his brain, round and round. Paddy filled the car with Bach and let the lofty sounds soothe him as he drove towards the motorway. In time he came to feel lightheaded with the music. Perhaps you didn't need to be depressed or stressed or broke or even broken-hearted to kill yourself. Maybe all you need is that giddy explosion of defiance that demands to be cut loose and fly across mortality. Like the music.

Over lunch Marty Clanger had learnt some information of an impending collapse of a small furnishing business in Ohio. It was information he was hurrying back to his office to make use of. Like the carrion crow, Marty lived off the carcasses of his fellow men.

It was one of those crisp days when New York seems suspended from its strips of sky and the streets smoulder with the steam of some deep boiling point underneath the city. WALK. DON'T WALK. Marty felt good. He was the hunter homeward bound. He strode into the sharp wind coming off the Hudson River with his chin up, about him lesser New Yorkers walked slowly, stooped forward like furious gargoyles.

The tricky events surrounding the acquisition of the rights to *Stratagems and Spoils* had taken a turn for the better, he reckoned, with the fortuitous death of Heime Chadwick. Marty had been impressed to learn that his old buddy, Lewis Lefrak, had deftly manoeuvred himself into the dead man's shoes. What a flair the guy had for finding the gold lamé lining.

Marty's office was like a tomb, oak-panelled and double glazed for thorough silence. In a cone of bright light, his agile fingers danced over the calculator while his voice purred finance down the telephone with the gentle intensity of witchcraft.

By four o'clock Marty had recouped the cost of the lunch a

thousand fold and Kwik-Fit Furnishings of Ohio had had their bones picked clean.

'There's a call from London, England.' The secretary had been told not to disturb him.

'Who is it?'

'The guy wouldn't say.'

'What's he want?'

'Says it's urgent, Mr Clanger, very forceful.' The secretary's voice would have you believe she was slim and attractive. Wrong.

'Put him through.' Marty was disturbed.

'Good afternoon, Mr Clanger,' a British voice bade him.

'Good afternoon,' he answered. 'Who is this?'

'It's about Ganymede.' In the silence the Atlantic shifted gently on the airwaves.

'Oh,' Marty could be cryptic too. 'Who are you?'

'I want to ask you some questions. My name is . . . Turpin, Richard Turpin.'

'Hi. What is all this?'

'About *Stratagems and Spoils*, the movie,' the voice said.

'I know nothing about it.'

'I think you do.'

'Look, what is this? Who are you?' Marty's patience was going.

'This is part of an investigation here in Britain into the blackmail and suicide of Heime Chadwick.'

'I don't know anything about that, Mr Turpin.' Marty sounded flaccidly defensive.

'Call me Dick,' said Mr Turpin.

'What?'

'Dick. Call me Dick. I'm trying to help you, Marty.'

Marty obeyed and heard the stupid monosyllable echo down the line.

'Dick.'

'You could be in a lot of trouble, Marty.'

'Oh yeah,' Marty tried sarcasm.

'What?' It was wasted.

'Oh, yeah, I said, oh, yeah.'

'Don't get fucking lippy with me, Clanger, or I'll fucking explode you.' Mr Turpin's voice was quiet but firm like someone used to authority or animals.

'What do you want?'

130

'Answers, Marty, I want answers.' There was something mocking in Dick Turpin's voice.

'OK.' Marty was irked.

'I want to know about Transworld Telly Sales – you are an employee of that company?'

'Yes.'

'Employed by Mr Chadwick and Sir Toby Goddard?'

'Yes.'

'You took your orders from them?'

'Yes.'

'It was a company used to misappropriate funds, the residual fees due to artists who appeared in the programmes that you were responsible for selling in the US.'

'Is that right?' Marty swivelled his chair. The office window had barely a few square inches of sky to its credit. Marty gazed up at the high blueness to the left of Lexington Avenue and felt mildly trapped, a vestige of indigestion or some such. Nothing to worry about, he told himself, he had allies in LA and London who could fix things or carry the can. 'What are you asking me Mr Turpin?'

'Dick.'

'Dick.'

'Details. I want to know the details.'

'There's nothing illegal. The business was above board, all the transactions were fair and honest . . .'

'Rubbish. Don't get smart with me, Marty, or I'm going to put you in the shit. Do you understand, Mr Clanger, the shit. You'll go to jail. Do I make myself clear?'

Mr Turpin certainly did. The caller made himself very clear. He commanded respect in Mr Clanger. A respect that was in fact fear.

'Yes. OK,' said Marty with subdued petulance. 'What do you want?'

'I want the names of all the companies you do business with, every single one together with a list of their directors. OK?'

'OK,' said Clanger. The trouble with being a middleman, reflected Marty, was that you got caught in the middle, in the crossfire. 'I'll telex it to you,' he stalled, 'tomorrow.'

'Don't be stupid, Clanger. I want it now, do you hear?'

'What about me?' asked Clanger. It was a plea for mercy.

'You tell me what I want to know and I'll do my best to leave you out of it, all right?' Mr Turpin was in control.

'Sure,' said Clanger doubtfully. 'Hold on for a while then.' For a bird of prey he was suddenly quite vulnerable.

On the other end of the line Paddy Brummel said, 'I will'. His audience was seated round Jemma's kitchen table much impressed. Paddy cupped his hand over the mouthpiece.

'I'm sorry about your phone bill,' he said, 'but I didn't want to give him a chance to check things out with Sir Toby or anybody else.' Dennis nodded, it wasn't his to pay and Jemma shrugged.

'Yes, Marty, I'm still here. I'm listening.' He listened a great deal and made five pages of notes. He had copious lists of companies with all their directors – the names were seldom simple or Anglo-Saxon and some were unpronounceably Polish. Among them though were the two Paddy was after – he wasn't shocked or surprised, just rather sad. It seemed that Tracey Louise's hunch was right.

'You've been most helpful, Marty, most helpful.'

'Now you stick to the deal and keep me out of this, OK, Dick?'

'You bet,' said Paddy.

'Say, where can I reach you?' Marty was thinking of revenge more than correspondence.

'You can't.'

'Who the fuck are you anyway?'

'No more questions from you, Mr Clanger.' Dick Turpin hung up. There was much laughing in Jemma's kitchen, as they shared the dangerous belief that the joke was on the enemy.

FQ was travelling by cab today; he couldn't face the bus. His nerves were in a terrible state. Not since he had given up the thrilling perils of rough trade had he tasted so clearly the sour flavour of panic in his throat. In fact wasn't that why he had given up the thrilling perils of rough trade – the fear?

To unlearn the secret that he held was FQ's devoutest wish. He knew that to hold it was a liability that certain other people would guard with his life. As he rode home to Clapham FQ was a very frightened homosexual.

Detective Inspector Robbins would have had more success with his interrogation of FQ had he heeded Granny's adage that 'you get more flies with honey than with vinegar'.

'You all seem to know each other's business, you people,' Robbins had announced.

'People?' FQ enquired. What was he: a freemason, a black, a stamp collector?

'Queers. Er, gays. What I'm saying is ... I reckon you might have some idea who it was called us about Mr Chadwick's death, maybe even from his flat.' FQ had shaken his head. 'Heime Chadwick had a friend perhaps?' Robbins persisted. FQ shrugged. 'A bum boy?' Nothing. 'I just wonder who it was?'

'I've told you, Constable, he wasn't my type.' FQ had retaliated with fake bravado. 'I tell you I haven't the foggiest notion who the hell it was,' he lied.

Who the hell it was had that afternoon cornered FQ in the laundry room. Had stood close and threatened him with a garlic-scented whisper, 'Keep your mouth shut or you're dead.'

As the taxi crawled across Clapham Common, FQ shuddered. He tried to imagine himself being stoic like Ingrid Bergman but he knew he was caught between the devil and the deep blue sea and could barely muster an Audrey Hepburn.

Irving Barstow looked down at his reflection in the glass-top table. His freckled skin looked shiny like plastic and from narrow eyes his own meanness stared back up at him. He stirred his Bloody Mary and felt giddy almost as he watched it swirling like liquid marble in its huge glass. Across the table Bud Schwartz ate olives with a speed that wasn't hunger. They neither of them spoke.

Sure they were on common ground; they shared a splenetic appetite to be avenged on Fernando Cass. In the corner the piano man played Rogers and Hart ... 'The lovely loving and the hateful hates ...'

'You say you have proof,' said Bud, jettisoning a stone, 'proof that the correspondence between Cass and Lefrak was backdated.'

'Yeah, for sure. He hadn't even read *Stratagems and Spoils* till two weeks ago. I tell you.' Irving sipped his drink.

'I knew it.' Well, he did now.

'Of course.'

'The son of a bitch.'

'Exactly.'

'The son of a bitch,' Bud repeated. For the last few days he had been helplessly trapped in a legal out-of-the-frying-pan-into-the-fire situation. On the one hand Frank Hoffman was seeking to prosecute him for breach of contract over Fernando's withdrawal from the *Life Sanction* deal; and on the other his megastar client had fired him and was suing him for mismanagement. Individually these suits posed no serious threat but combined they would ensure that the arse of Bud Schwartz was destined to be busted.

The glad tidings brought by this pale and wistful Englishman altered things. The buck had not stopped at Bud's lap after all; it had merely paused. There was now a chance that it could be passed to Fernando Cass where it belonged. Frank Hoffman was a valuable friend and Bud knew that, whatever the outcome, litigation would do nothing to enhance their relationship. A direct contest between Hoffman and Cass would leave him in the clear. Bud chuckled, an evil bronchial rumbling.

'Would you testify?' he asked.

Irving eyed him over the bloody rim of his glass. 'At a price,' he said tartishly.

'Of course,' Bud nodded. Here was a Brit who was even nastier than he looked. They raised their glasses — 'Fernando'.

17 Nancy watched with spaniel eyes as Lewis Lefrak paced back and forth. She knew her idol's confusion would soon transform into a splendid anger. She anticipated the fearsome torrent of his abuse — relished it shamefully. Lefrak's temper was the substance of her richest fantasies. He was a tiger, she a kitten.

Lefrak was indeed confused. Things were not going according to plan. Some British wise-ass had got the idea that Marty Clanger had been fiddling the books and was being blackmailed. The wise-ass had further reckoned that the price involved was the film rights of *Stratagems and Spoils*. For the time being the bonus of Heime Chadwick's suicide was proving to be a bummer.

On reflection this wise-ass had a pretty good grasp of things. Lewis was disturbed not just by what he might have discovered but by his very identity.

'Who the fuck is Dick Turpin?' he had enquired.

'An eighteenth-century highwayman with a horse called Black Bess,' had come the answer and not at all did it lighten Lefrak's darkness.

Even if Marty Clanger was in trouble, he reckoned, the good news was that his own name had so far remained untainted; so much so that he had been invited to become the new producer of *Stratagems and Spoils* in London. He had accepted without delay. The means justified the ends even if they were a little frayed.

Like a conjuror Lefrak had been busy snatching balls out of the air. In record time he had completed contracts with Fernando Cass, the director, the financiers, the distributors and the studio. His trick was nearly ready to be presented. He had one hell of a film up his sleeve.

'I'm going to London,' Lewis announced calmly. 'Book me a flight.'

'Sure, honey.' Nancy felt cheated. Where was the explosion?

Lewis, as a boy, had liked the story of the Trojan horse; the enigmatic booby trap appealed to him. He liked the idea of disgorging an ambush from an unexpected gift and that's what he would do in London. He'd show Paddy Brummel a thing or two.

'I'm going to knock the shit out of those guys,' Lefrak declared with the grit of Charlton Heston. It was time to shoot from the hip and get on with things. He wasn't afraid of any motherfuckin' highwaymen, no sir, nor their black horse neither. He'd be hanged if he was.

Fernando Cass was London-bound too, to promote *Life Sanction II*. He was not a good traveller; he did so unhopefully with a dread of arriving. He supervised his packing with a heavy heart. Travelling light was an art he had long ago abandoned. Why risk exposing oneself to all those possible deprivations when there was a certain cachet in having excessive baggage? The destination was irrelevant, his theory was take the lot just in case: videos, hi-fis, computers, dumb-bells, herb-racks, medicine ... even a few clothes; anything to cushion him from the rigours of ten days at the Savoy Hotel.

In point of fact, he would have tolerated a little hardship in this instance. Fernando was becoming increasingly obsessed with *Stratagems and Spoils*. He had a gut feeling that Eliot Blandford was going to be a great role for him – a winner. He had the optimism of a man in love. If there were obstacles, Lewis Lefrak would remove them – to hell with ethics and finesse. If the whole thing failed and Lefrak was caught with his pants down, Fernando had always got *Life Sanction III* and good old Frank Hoffman to fall back on. 'LOYAL CASS OPTS OUT OF FILM FIASCO.'

The finer things of life had never been vital to the well-being of Hugo Cavendish. And so it was that the tired reporter was watching *Dynasty* and eating a toasted cheese sandwich when the telephone rang. The international operator invited him to accept a call collect from: 'Irving Barstow! Long time no hear, old mate,' Hugo enthused, remote-controlling Joan Collins to silence.

Irving Barstow and Hugo had been colleagues on the *Globe* for a time in Art and Gossip respectively. They had had little in common except a thirst for gin which they had occasionally slaked together in the Cock and Bull. They were not friends; good taste was a chasm between them.

They quickly established that they were both in good health; that it was cold in London and warm in LA, and that the elections in both countries were imminent. Hugo, on whose bill this smalltalk would be reflected, was curious to know the reason for Irving's call.

'So what can I do for you, Irving? What's up?' he asked. On his TV screen Joan pouted mutely and shrugged her red sequinned shoulders.

'I've been working for Fernando Cass, you know,' Irving began.

Hugo didn't know. 'Oh yes,' he said.

This had better be good, he thought. He listened as the information was spewed forth. It was good, very good indeed. There was a story here. Clichés to wrap it in danced through Hugo's head. He made notes . . . already he had ideas; there was a deal to be done. For once he was in a key position and would grab the opportunity with both hands.

When Hugo finished it was past Joan Collins's bedtime and his toasted cheese sandwich had gone cold. With a happy grin on his face he sat and brooded on his scoop.

For his part, Irving Barstow slept soundly that night, his conscience blissfully unclean.

Net curtains concealed curious eyes on either side of the street where Jemma lived. Outside her very door a huge black limousine with its similarly huge black liveried chauffeur had been waiting for some time. Rumour had it that Paddy Brummel was in her house and Capitol TV had announced earlier in the afternoon that the heart-throb of *The Declancey Inheritance* was to be that evening's live guest on the *Fergus Llewellyn Show* . . . oh the glamour of it all!

The spectators were at last rewarded with a brief glimpse of the tall, blond actor, in the flesh. Stooped against the rain he scuttled from the house into the leathery haven of the car. 'Fancy him wearing jeans.' 'He's taller than I thought.' 'Older.' 'I never watched him.'

Jemma had eventually decided not to go with him. Kelly needed bathing and they would watch him together on television. Paddy was happy to be on his own; he needed his wits about him at the studio. Fur, and maybe bullets, would be flying.

'For God's sake keep cool – stay cool,' she had urged him as he left.

But armed with the mass of detailed information which they had gleaned in the last few days, Paddy wasn't listening. 'I'm going to blow the whole bloody lot of them sky high,' he had grinned.

There was, for Paddy, a neat irony in the idea of exploding Sir Toby Goddard's can of worms right on his own doorstep; live and raw in front of twelve million viewers. Paddy was off to beard the lion in his den. Capitol TV would be hosting their own prosecution – trial by telly. Why not?

Paddy was tired but he felt sharp, like a man on his way to a duel. Dennis, Matthew, Jemma and he had sat up through the night piecing the evidence together and then wondering what to do with it. The information levered out of Marty Clanger had taken some digesting. They had spent hours painstakingly checking and cross-referring. Jemma's telephone had been hot with transatlantic sleuthing. In the end, from whichever way they looked, the picture was clear. The fraud was manifest. They knew every detail. They knew everything.

For Dennis it was a red-letter day beyond his wildest Marxist dreams. The system was even rottener than he had hoped, and his capitalist bosses even greedier. With grubby zeal he predicted that this would be the final nail in the coffin of privately owned TV stations. It was heady stuff for Dennis; so, too, was the Glenfiddich on the kitchen table. Jemma had been practical, methodical and as impartial as possible – a shopkeeper who had found a sales girl with her fingers in the till. Paddy, in the end, had just been sad to find that his dead friend, Heime, had had feet of clay after all.

Matthew had joined them later looking pale and tense. He had been frantically chasing around trying to keep the film alive. They had bombarded him with the details of their detective work like gleeful dogs with old bones. Matthew had been appalled. He had hated the idea of a showdown on the *Fergus Llewellyn Show*. 'What's the point? Why don't we leave all that to the police and just get on with making the film?' Sir Toby was his uncle, they told themselves, so perhaps Matthew's blood was thicker than they had reckoned.

Matthew had good news though, they now had a new producer for *Stratagems and Spoils* – a bright young American whiz-kid, Lewis Lefrak. 'He sounds terrific. Very on the ball. Very keen. Great fan of Conran and of yours, Paddy. Noel had him checked out and we seem to be in a go situation. He should arrive in the next few days.'

Paddy sat back, glad of the glass partition that cut off any chance of communication. At forty-two he resented the time he had wasted on pointless conversation, he had become a miser with his energy; it was gold and he had better use for it. He was feeling dangerous and invincible cocooned in his smooth car. This was a crusade. Maybe he couldn't clear Heime's name but he would certainly sully Sir Toby's. That was the target. The surprises he was planning to spring were like a time bomb ticking away in his gut, and he had to remind himself what a dangerous force self-righteousness could be.

Malcolm DeFreitas had been the producer of the *Fergus Llewellyn Show* for three years and even by his standards today had been hectic. He was no stranger to stress; he had a knack of creating it and suffering from it simultaneously. At the end of the day he had job satisfaction and valium.

That morning Paddy Brummel (you're kidding!) had telephoned to say he had changed his mind and would like to be a guest on the *Fergus Llewellyn Show*.

'Er, when?'

'Tonight.'

'Er, tonight?'

'Yes.'

'Er, sure, fine, terrific.' Christ ... he couldn't refuse. This was a chance not to be missed. There was nothing unusual in a last minute change of plans; he could handle it. There was nothing unusual in the delicate rescheduling of other guests; he could handle it. What was unusual was his summons to the top floor for special instructions from Sir Toby. Could he handle it?

Paddy watched out of the car window; ordinary people hurrying wetly home from their ordinary jobs. He thought of what lay ahead.

'Whatever you do,' Dennis had instructed, 'don't hector, don't accuse. Ask questions, don't demand, suggest.' Suggest. Suggest.

Jemma had advised, 'Stay cool. Be subtle.' He'd be subtle all right, with four aces up his sleeve he couldn't lose.

The texture of the road changed beneath the wheels. The huge car had swung into a cobbled side street. Paddy looked out at the terrace of derelict houses on his left and the yawning arches of the railway above to his right. It was obviously a short-cut to avoid the traffic. Obviously the driver knew what he was doing. Obviously. Ahead Paddy could see nothing beyond a high brick wall . . . a cul-de-sac.

A faint taste of panic welled up Paddy's windpipe. The car slowed down. Stopped. He pushed the button to lower the glass partition. It didn't move.

'What's going on?' Paddy shouted banging on the window. The chauffeur didn't even turn his head. His hairline and his collar were parallel lines that didn't flinch. 'What the hell is going on?' No reply. The street was horribly empty. Where had all the ordinary people gone?

A shadow stretched along Paddy's line of vision, a spectral shape angular and slowly menacing. Paddy froze. The gas lamp was eclipsed as the shadow advanced until there was nothing but a huge silhouette edged in sickly yellow. This cul-de-sac could be a dead end.

The door beside Paddy opened. The light inside the car blinded him momentarily; he cowered away in the far corner blinking. Who was this? Was he dreaming?

'Good evening, Mr Brummel.' The voice was familiar, oily and polite. Paddy said nothing. His tongue was slack and his throat dry. The fat visitor climbed in beside Paddy filling the car with the smell of cologne, cigar and threat.

'Hi,' said Paddy. His pulse was in frantic syncopation. 'What is going on?' Even if he sounded casual, who was he fooling? The door slammed shut.

In the glow of the cigar Paddy could see Sir Toby's grin. 'We keep meeting in the oddest places.' The TV mogul's tone was genial.

'Yeah.' Paddy said as if he believed in the coincidence. For a moment they studied each other in the half-light.

'I have this feeling that you don't like me, Paddy.' There was no point in answering. 'I've got an idea that you're out to get me. Hmm? To persecute me? Screw me up? Am I right, Mr Brummel?'

Paddy pondered the question in the darkness; his brain was reeling with the onslaught of adrenalin.

'Yes,' he answered.

'Why?' asked Sir Toby with a nanny's patience. Time passed, rain purred on the roof.

'Because . . .' Paddy began, 'you are a swindler, a fraud, a crook . . . and a bully.'

Paddy's fluency was on the mend. Death had lost its sting and he steamed on dizzily. 'You're a cheat. An embezzling, vicious, self-seeking, fat toad.' He paused in the darkness; the fat toad nodded with the indulgence of a doting parent.

'I see.'

What did you have to do to insult this man? Paddy wanted Sir Toby to lose his cool so that they would be on an equal footing.

'Tell me, what do you know?' asked the visitor kindly.

'A lot.'

'What?' insisted Sir Toby.

'Everything Ganymede knows.'

Paddy heard a slight sigh, an exhalation of breath from his inquisitor that he could not quite construe. Was it exasperation? Defeat? Amusement?

'You've been profiteering,' Paddy went on, 'misappropriating Capitol TV's export earnings. Your company, Transworld Telly Sales, rigs the sales of programmes across the US by selling to a middleman, Screen Scene Inc. who sells them on at double the price. The royalties and tax in the UK are based on a false and deliberately low price. The same system works in reverse for the programmes you import for Capitol. Screen Scene sells to Transworld Telly who sell to Capitol at double the original price. Nothing illegal in that – standard business practice, sharp but not actually crooked – until you find that the directors of Transworld Telly Sales are also covert partners in Screen Scene Inc., Marty Clanger, Heime and you.'

'You have been busy, haven't you?' Sir Toby patronised like a playschool teacher.

'But it went wrong. Someone found you out, blackmailed you – not for money. What they wanted was *Stratagems and Spoils*. In exchange you had to close down our production, you had to break Fledgling Productions . . . Poor Heime, it can't have been easy for him. Faced with the choice of having his dishonesty revealed, or betraying his friends, he took his life. But not you, no bloody fear, you'd sell anybody down the river to save your skin. So you set about doing your level best to screw us up.'

Sir Toby let out a mirthless giggle and the gaslight flashed yellow on his teeth. The hatred between them fizzed in the darkness.

'Poor Heime, a good man.' The toad shook his head ruefully as though good was bad.

'He was honest . . . honourable . . .'

Paddy was going to say more but changed his mind. No part of his bereavement would he share with Sir Toby.

'Foolish.' The word came on a breath of smoke, spiteful but true. Paddy had to agree, how else could Heime have become embroiled in such an enterprise unless by foolishness.

'So,' Sir Toby resumed, 'you think you've been very clever?'

Paddy nodded, 'And thorough and lucky.'

'But you don't know who it is?'

'Who?' Paddy was wrong-footed. 'Who what is?'

'Ganymede.' There was a grin in his voice. 'You don't know who it is?'

This was true. The identity of the blackmailer had not seemed important; they had uncovered his secret, that's what mattered. Paddy's mission was to expose it, live on Capitol TV . . . They had been so hellbent on spiking the enemy's gun they hadn't looked to see who it was with his finger on the trigger. So who indeed was Ganymede – the wily cupbearer? Paddy still wasn't sure it mattered.

'No, I don't,' he confessed.

'Heime thought you did.'

Interesting. So how come Sir Toby had heard what Heime had thought that Paddy knew? They must have spoken . . . When? Had it been to Sir Toby that the wretched Heime had made his final appeal? Could it have been Sir Toby who had called the police with the tip-off? It was a chilling idea.

Paddy had called the weary Detective Inspector Robbins that morning to ask if there was any new information and drew a blank. The police view remained that it was the suicide of a lovesick poof who had been under a lot of strain.

Paddy could feel Sir Toby's eyes studying his profile.

'It doesn't matter,' he said but a doubt remained unleashed.

'We'll see.' Later Paddy regretted missing the cryptic challenge in Sir Toby's tone. 'What are you going to do?' he asked with casual politesse.

142

'I'm going to bust you,' Paddy answered.

'On the *Fergus Llewellyn Show*?'

'Yes.'

'I thought so.'

Why had he thought so? Paddy wondered, hoping desperately he had not underestimated his adversary.

'Hardly discreet,' Sir Toby reproached gently.

'Tough shit. I've got the information.'

'Yes, I think you have,' he answered quietly in the darkness.

'I've got questions to ask, questions you'll find hard to answer. You're in trouble.' Paddy had the confidence of the boy who has done his homework. He had forgotten it never pays to be smug on the school bus.

'You could have gone to the police,' Sir Toby said.

This was true. And like millions before him Paddy had no answer. Live on television, he knew there could be no hushing-up, no deflection, no fudging of the truth. 'We'll look into your allegations in due course' wasn't good enough. He was going to make his case loud and clear. Unretractable. He didn't care if it was vindictive, that's the nature of revenge.

'It won't matter in the end.' Sir Toby flicked his Dunhill lighter and its even flame flared between them. For an instant their eyes locked unflinching like gladiators – to the death. The fat man sucked on his cigar and in the darkness it glowed like a rosebud as its stench filled the car. 'Why do you suppose I'm here?' he asked with his infuriating patience.

A good question and one that had been jockeying for attention in Paddy's busy brain for some time. Why was he there? To try and stop him Paddy supposed.

'To try and stop me, I suppose,' Paddy said.

'Exactly.' The rosebud nodded.

'You can't,' said Paddy. No sign of the neat little revolver, yet. Perhaps Sir Toby was contemplating bribery; the cheque book for him must surely rate mightier than the sword. Even if he had been forewarned, Paddy reckoned Sir Toby wasn't necessarily forearmed. He reckoned wrong.

'It would be pointless to restrain me physically,' he said, 'there are others who have all the information.'

In the rear-view mirror Paddy caught a fleeting glimpse of the driver's eyes, ice cold and keen like lychees in chocolate.

'Of course,' acknowledged the rotund smoker.

Paddy was quickly losing the feeling that he was one step ahead. Perhaps he was even one behind. Foreboding churned in his stomach.

'So?' Paddy wanted some conclusion. The interview had suddenly taken on a timelessness.

The rosebud pulsed redly for a moment and subdued.

'Your wife has been moved.'

'What?' Paddy had heard perfectly well. He needed breathing space. Take a breath. Swallow hard.

'Your wife has been moved to another nursing home.'

'Where?'

'She's perfectly safe and comfortable.'

'You bastard.' Paddy was giddy with fear and loathing. Small hairs were being plucked out all over his body. Breathe, come on, breathe. In. Out. Think. Come on let's get the picture straight: Hannah has been abducted to ensure a discreet silence from me. Right. So what options do I have? None. There are no options. The sound of the rain seemed louder. The driver blinked languidly in the darkness; he didn't give a damn it seemed.

'What do you want me to do?' Paddy enquired.

'I want you to be sensible. Do you understand? Agreeable.' Nanny was to be obeyed.

'Perhaps I should pass on the *Fergus Llewellyn Show*? Cancel?'

'Oh no.' The voice was full of fat relish. 'I particularly want you to do the *Fergus Llewellyn Show*.'

'What do you want me to say?' Paddy had got the measure of defeat.

'Very little.' Sir Toby let out his falsetto laugh, shrill and loony in the fug. 'Very little ... You're not a stupid man.'

You could have fooled Paddy.

'Now then,' said Sir Toby brightly, 'it would never do for you to be late.'

The fat man levered himself out of the car. He stood for a moment on the pavement unhurried by the rain. What an impermeable man. Leaning back towards Paddy he unleashed another screen of smoke.

'Just think before you speak,' he warned.

'What about Hannah?' Paddy was oddly desperate for his enemy not to go.

'I'll be in touch.' Rain hissed on his cigar.

'If you hurt her in any way ...' Paddy realised that threatening this man was pissing into the wind but couldn't stop himself. 'I'll kill you. I'll kill you,' he promised twice with five-star sincerity.

Sir Toby grinned and the door slammed solidly between them.

18 'Tonight from Capitol. Live in London. The *Fergus Llewellyn Show*.' The warm glee of the announcement was followed by the familiar fanfare.

Twelve million viewers watched Fergus Llewellyn spring on to the stage with a well rehearsed spontaneity. He had, after all, been voted TV personality of the year by the readers of the *Globe*. Three times.

Paddy was standing backstage on a rostrum ready to make his entrance. The studio audience were laughing keenly at Fergus's jokes – they had been well primed. For Paddy, reality had long since flown the coop. Max Factor and Smirnoff had been applied and he now had the sharp focus of a man facing death.

As it happened, Paddy had not arrived late at the studio (how cleverly these things are planned). Fergus Llewellyn had greeted him in the make-up room with the courtesy of a busy surgeon.

'It's great to have you on the show,' he had said. 'We'll have plenty of time. Twenty minutes. So we can talk about pretty well anything, anything you like ... your film, Heime Chadwick ... I like to keep things very low key. OK?'

Had there been a canny glint in his eye or was it just mascara? Paddy had been surprised to find that this most famous of household faces belonged to a man altogether shorter and less Welsh than he would have his public believe.

'Sure,' Paddy had answered. The four aces he had had up his sleeve now looked pitifully like a low pair.

From a corner of the make-up room he had found a moment to call the nursing home. 'I thought a change of scene was a good idea, if a little sudden,' the ever amiable Sister Wordsworth had said. This confirmation that Hannah had been abducted dashed his wild hope that Sir Toby was bluffing. On Paddy's instruction apparently two men and a nurse had arrived to collect the patient.

'She didn't seem to mind?' Paddy enquired. He couldn't very well ask who had taken her or where.

'Oh, no,' said Sister Wordsworth. 'No, she didn't seem to mind.' She had watched the private ambulance, like a long white hearse, sweep past the cedar trees and out the gates at a far from funereal speed. 'You might have given us a bit more warning,' she said. The truth was she felt a slight relief at the departure. Hannah was not an easy patient, nor one to heal herself.

'And the people who came for her . . .?' Paddy asked.

'Perfectly charming. Efficient. Said you were looking forward to having her nearer to home.'

'Did they?' Paddy was running out of coins for the phone-box. 'I'd like to come and see you later . . . about nine o'clock.'

'All right. I'm on duty all night.' The puzzled nurse had hung up in time to see the *Fergus Llewellyn Show* which was just beginning.

'And now for my special guest this evening . . .' Fergus had finished his witty monologue in a gale of hyped laughter.

Paddy was on the high diving-board again. Don't look down. Don't think of Hannah. Think of Hannah. His introduction was far from simple. Fergus Llewellyn's eulogy was longwinded and oblique. Paddy breathed deeply, around him technicians picked their teeth. Cool, he told himself, stay sharp. He was a gambler with stakes he couldn't afford.

'Will you please welcome Paddy Brummel.' There was a chord of music, applause and Paddy's legs were walking him forward into the light. Fergus Llewellyn was shaking his hand, guiding him to a chair.

Fergus was listening to the whispered instructions of Malcolm DeFreitas on the minute earpiece that was concealed in his right ear. He resented this umbilical cord to his producer and was always pleading to have it severed. He was ready to go solo.

'Take it easy to begin with,' Malcolm was saying, 'soften him up, OK?'

Fergus smiled hugely into his close-up camera. 'It's good to have you on the show.'

'Thank you,' said Paddy. His teeth were dry like old bones in his mouth.

Kelly, with her hair newly washed, was sprawled on the floor in front of the television, good and close. The new man in her life was on her screen. Further back her mother sipped wine, tense with the inability to help or understand. The interview was going nowhere, softly marking time. Later Jemma was unable to pinpoint the moment she realised something was seriously amiss. Paddy seemed to be concentrating in the way a man with a migraine does ... Where was the showdown? Come on Paddy, ask the questions.

Jemma sat forward like her daughter to improve her view. And what was it she detected in Fergus Llewellyn's eyes? Mischief? No, it was mischief with a hint of sadism. Her heart was thudding with the powerless horror of someone watching an accident about to happen. On screen the two participants were discussing G.P. Conran.

'*Stratagems and Spoils* must mean a great deal to you?' The Welshman's make-up was like a veneer of plastic.

'Yes,' Paddy nodded.

The trap was sprung.

'So this evening's announcement must have come as quite a blow then?' There was spite in the question beneath its innocence.

The camera advanced towards Paddy with the stealth of a cobra. His face filled the screen. Jemma held her breath and watched him struggle to mask his confusion. What were they talking about? What announcement?

In the production box in front of a bank of television monitors Malcolm sat like a winning spider. His net was full. The fight was on. 'We've got him,' he whispered in Fergus's ear.

Paddy remained impassive. Not so his pulse.

With a huge glass of gin in his hand Hugo Cavendish winced at his TV screen. Since his conversation with Irving Barstow he had tried to reach Paddy, to warn him. He had rung his cottage and his agent and his car again and again without success. In his work he was accustomed to people being unobtainable; he was a born pariah. He winced not in the manner of I-could-have-told-you-so but with the real sympathy of a fellow loser. 'Paddy,' he wanted to say, 'beware Fernando Cass.'

Paddy half smiled and his eyebrows asked the question, 'What announcement?' before he spoke it.

Fergus Llewellyn showed surprise. 'You haven't heard?'

'No.'

'You've been dropped.'

'Attaboy. Go for it,' Malcolm urged quietly in his ear.

'Fernando Cass is going to take over your part,' said Fergus Llewellyn.

'You bastards.' Jemma was on her feet.

Paddy laughed. It was all part of a crazy dream, the only question was when exactly had it begun? This morning? Yesterday? Last week . . . at birth? 'No, I hadn't heard that,' he said.

Fergus Llewellyn showed embarrassment. 'Well, I'm sorry,' he said. 'I thought you would have been informed.' The studio audience were silent with tension. What a bullfight this was. Paddy shook his head. 'Noel Pettifer announced it this afternoon . . .' Fergus Llewellyn was in his stride. 'He said it had been agreed with your new producer, Lewis Lefrak, to reshoot the film in colour with Fernando Cass.'

This wasn't a dream. This was a booby trap. The camera waited in front of its victim for a reaction, a sigh, an oath, a scream, a tear. It got nothing. The great metal cyclops did not intimidate Paddy; he could outwit it any day, that was his job. In his head he could hear the high-pitched giggle of Sir Toby Goddard. 'Just think before you speak,' he had said. Twelve million viewers wondered what was going on. Anger bubbled in Paddy's head. He would think before he spoke all right. Time whizzed by. Prime time at that, Malcolm bit his nail. Silence is not so golden on a chat show.

Paddy smiled and spoke, 'I'm sure Fernando will be marvellous in the part. I wish him good luck.' He sounded as if he meant it. Sincerity is just another trick of the trade.

In the production box Malcolm lent forward perplexed, where was the explosion of indignation he had anticipated? This bland turning of the other cheek was the last thing he wanted.

Jemma was crouched in front of her television, outraged and bewildered. Tell them, Paddy, for God's sake. Ask the questions. Go on . . .

'In your position,' Fergus was not going to let Paddy take his defeat lying down, 'I would look upon this as something of a kick in the teeth.'

Paddy nodded in understanding of his inquisitor's shortcoming. 'It's just a film,' he said. A bead of sweat ran down his temple, the camera lapped it up.

'All the same, one that must have meant a lot to you.' Fergus wanted tears before bedtime.

'Oh yes. But easy come, easy go. I'm sure that an actor of Mr Cass's calibre will do it more than justice, especially in colour.'

The audience let out its breath, not quite a snigger. Paddy checked himself. This hamming up the losing-with-good-grace could be dangerous. He thought of Hannah pale and empty-eyed. Her last whispered word suddenly came to him: 'Careful . . .' Oh yes, my darling, I'll be careful.

Jemma wondered if he had been drugged. He had the catatonic look of a man in shock – his eyes seemed to be scanning a horizon that wasn't there.

'So now your film career has taken this, shall we say, knock, can we perhaps expect to see you back in *The Declancey Inheritance* here at Capitol?' Fergus's question was sickly with solicitude.

'I don't know. I haven't heard of any such plan,' said Paddy. 'Perhaps you have?' The point was gently scored.

'There is no truth then,' persisted the inquisitor, 'in the rumour of a rift between yourself and the management here at Capitol?'

It was Paddy's turn to show amazement. 'Good heavens no, nothing could be further from the truth. Sir Toby Goddard and I are old friends.' Malcolm had the stunned look of the man who has lost his shirt on a certain winner but he knew better than to say a word to his fellow loser in the hot seat. Fergus Llewellyn felt betrayed and foolish like a sharpshooter firing blanks at a sitting target. Later, for sure he would take his loader to task, his forehead was bubbling with sweat under the make-up. Paddy stared at it like a wound. Perhaps the Welshman would melt away completely, into a pool of cosmetic slime. 'In fact,' Paddy went on, wrenching himself from the science fiction, 'I had a most pleasant meeting with him only this afternoon.'

Paddy's message was expressly for Jemma's benefit. She received it clearly.

Fergus Llewellyn had the disappointed look of a fight promoter whose star bout ends in a round one knockout. Behind the camera the floor manager signalled that the show was running short. Seven minutes to go.

'Any plans for the future?' he asked his guest.

'Yes,' said Paddy with a ponderous finality. He, too, had seen the signal and would do nothing to help.

Malcolm was sweating too. He had never seen the genial Fergus so rattled . . . He wished to God he had not been forced to cancel Christopher Cazenove – that would have been a piece of cake. 'Stretch it. Stretch it. Pad it out,' he whispered into the furious ear of the Welshman.

In desperation Fergus sallied into the unsafe waters of questions in the personal category. He felt cheated by his researchers and vengeful. The idea of improvising for six and a half more minutes was appalling.

'It's well known of course that your personal life has recently been beset with tragedy,' he began. A wiser man would have heeded the look in Paddy's eyes. 'How have you come through all that, as a person?'

Viewers from the Northern Isles to Cornwall winced. The entire studio was under pressure – not a dry armpit in the house. Jemma bit her lip. Malcolm's arteries were suddenly brittle. Paddy held his silence. The pause was the time of a grenade in flight.

'Good question, Fergus,' said Paddy eventually with an evil sincerity. The nation sighed. 'And the answer is yes.'

'Yes?' queried the host.

'Yes, I did come through it as a person.' Not a parrot or a turnip.

'Oh I see.' The Welshman was manifestly foolish.

Paddy looked at his watch with a languor that made the studio audience laugh uneasily. He felt a brief moment of elation. Surely he had honoured his side of the agreement with Sir Toby ... Hannah would be safe. Safe but where?

Despite the wrath of his superiors Fergus Llewellyn was wrapping up the show five minutes early. 'Carry on. Carry on,' begged Malcolm to no avail. They could fill the time with Dutch greyhound results for all he cared. Discretion was the long overdue part of valour.

'Anyway, we wish you well, Paddy, and it's been a pleasure having you on the show.'

'Has it really?' said Paddy with sweet surprise. The audience laughter expanded into applause that lasted long enough for Paddy to bow graciously and escape to the sanctuary of backstage.

If it was drama and conflict that Capitol had wanted that evening they should have had the cameras in Fergus Llewellyn's dressing-room after the transmission. In the field of expletives new ground was broken.

Paddy meanwhile had slipped out of the studio and, having retrieved his car, was soon on the M4 heading west to find his wife. He played no music and let the high speed soothe him.

It would have been wiser for Paddy to make a plan of action but he wasn't in the mood for methodical thinking, he just had to get to Hannah. And to that end the trail must begin at the nursing home with Sister Wordsworth. Nothing else mattered, he told himself, not Heime, the film, the crooked dealings, the blackmail, even Jemma. All he could think of was his wife. She was his responsibility, his dependant, his child, his albatross, his past, his cross . . . his fault. They were inextricably wedded no matter what. There was no price he wouldn't pay to save her. In Paddy's mind a divine reckoning was being wreaked.

The picture that Paddy had of his wife – pale and light years away in melancholy, had been more like death than he realised. Perhaps it had suited him to see her like that, perhaps it made things easier. But now suddenly before him was his original Hannah – healthy, funny, active, sweet, frantic, sexy. If he could find her now he felt he had the power to revive her, to regenerate her life force with his. They would live together simply ever after. Maybe even happily. They would learn to share the sadness of their daughter's death . . . and have another baby maybe. This, at any rate, was the substance of the deal that Paddy was striking with the gods as he sped down the motorway . . . Just let her be all right.

Into none of this did Paddy dare let sneak a thought of Jemma – it was a confusion he couldn't cope with. The previous night they had hugged each other in the dark. No T-shirt. He had felt the warmth of her breasts against his chest. Her nipples had brushed his as her body rocked softly with its simple invitation. Surely the gods would make allowances . . . Just let Hannah be all right.

Paddy had the window down. The rain had stopped and the night air whistled in, clean and sharp. For the second time that week he told himself *Stratagems and Spoils* didn't matter. It really didn't matter. The price had got too high. As he had said to the eager Fergus Llewellyn, it was just a film after all. He suddenly felt oafish at having cared so much; it had been foolish to imagine that he could outsmart the establishment and turn up trumps with an Oscar-winning black and white masterpiece. Very foolish – foolhardy too. Paddy made no bones about it, he was levelling with the gods. He had been thoroughly beaten, outwitted and betrayed. But just let Hannah be all right.

No more filming for Paddy. No cameras, no technology, no wheeler-dealing, no Toby Goddard. 'Do you hear me, gods, no more greed or gloss or vanity or ambition . . .' Paddy found the gods were striking a hard bargain. He promised he would return to his other first love, the theatre, where the sweet business of story-telling is at its simplest: actors and audience in that spontaneous nightly affinity . . . Shakespeare or Chekhov or Wilde. Surely the gods would sanction the classics. Paddy glanced into the driving mirror and his mother's eyes looked back at him . . . In the evenings he would go to the theatre and he would spend the days gardening. He would not prune the magnolia and he would feed the earth with bone meal. He would stay at home and look after Hannah . . . OK, you gods?

From memory Paddy dialled Sir Toby's private telephone number on his car phone and again got no reply. Panic churned in his stomach. He had kept his side of the bargain, been the epitome of submissiveness on the ghastly *Fergus Llewellyn Show*. On the other hand, it suddenly struck him, what reason did he have to suppose Sir Toby would honour his promise? Wouldn't he hold on to Hannah just in case?

Standing in Hannah's room Paddy could feel no evidence of her – each of his senses scurried forth and came home empty-handed. As with all vacated rooms, this one had ruthlessly reclaimed its anonymity . . . Was his nose imagining it or was there a whiff of jasmine in the sterile air? Certainly nothing else. All the room had to say was 'Next patient please'.

In the corridor Paddy's footsteps echoed in the massive silence, a silence that seemed to push downwards from the high ceilings. Sister Wordsworth offered him a drink. His hands were trembling, she noticed, and his eyes had a kind of panic in them, the panic of a bystander whose role is undefined.

Paddy eyed Sister Wordsworth across the desk – her skin had the soft look of purity. 'It's very complicated,' he announced in answer to the unasked question.

'Oh,' she said calmly, her curiosity had never killed the cat.

'You understand this is all strictly confidential,' he went on.

'Of course,' she said with only a little apprehension.

'It was not me who authorised Hannah's removal – she has been abducted.' Paddy spoke quietly with his eyes down.

Faced with gushing haemorrhages Sister Wordsworth was trained to stand her ground unflinching, cardiac arrest she could take in her stride. Death, too, in its ugliest manifestations she could handle, but in terms of losing a patient, abduction had a ghastly novelty. Paddy told her the details as best he could, improbable though they were.

'I see,' said Sister Wordsworth. What merit might she find in a vodka herself she wondered. This news made sense – it explained the pale pinched look on Paddy's face and the lacklustre, not to say dull, performance he had given on the chat show earlier. 'We'll have to find her then,' she said simply once Paddy had put her in the picture. Her panic was well hidden under the nurse's cap.

Of the two men and the nurse who had come to collect Hannah, Sister Wordsworth's memory was scant. They had seemed competent if brisk. Hannah naturally had not shown any concern. The car had been a light-coloured Citroën, possibly. The nurse, blonde ... possibly; one of the men was plump ... possibly. 'And there was a thyroidal look to the taller man ... bulging eyes.'

What the Sister lacked in powers of observation she made up for with a sturdy belief in the fine-tooth comb. Between them they spent the next two hours telephoning all the private ambulance services and nursing homes within an ever-increasing radius – nothing. Not a trace of any abductors. With a horrible fear it occurred to Paddy there was no reason to suppose that the three abductors were anything but common or garden thugs: Plump. Blonde. And Thyroidal.

Paddy was restless to be gone; he felt smothered by the ethos of the place. Sister Wordsworth urged him not to go, she didn't like the look of him. She tried without success to persuade him to take soup or sleep. She had a growing scepticism about his abstracted state of mind. Sister Wordsworth could be a cynic at heart despite her calling.

On the motorway again, Paddy felt free to let his unruly thoughts run ahead of him along the central reservation. He was trapped in a dream that was running out of control. He was weakening, wanted desperately to call Jemma. For God's sake he owed her an explanation, an apology, a goodbye. He was even holding the car phone in his hand on the brink of reneging on his deal with the gods, when it rang.

154

Paddy jumped – the gods were certainly on their toes.

'Paddy?'

'Yes,' he confessed.

'It's me, Hugo.' The tone was dramatic. With each encounter with the man Paddy felt a mounting irritation, inexplicable like an allergy. He pulled into the slow lane.

'I've had trouble getting you,' Hugo said. It was true, Paddy had chosen to ignore his messages.

'It's late,' he said without apology.

'Where are you?'

'Does it matter?' Paddy replied. He might have said he was passing the Windsor turn-off where the castle was sharp against the night sky.

'I must talk to you. I've been investigating – I've got a lot to tell you ... about the movie ...'

'It doesn't matter. Nothing matters ... the film doesn't matter.'

Hugo was well accustomed to people not liking him – had almost learnt to sympathise with them. He didn't like himself that much either. He was a patient man though, and his instincts were better than people guessed. Hugo had sensed that Paddy's acceptance of defeat on the *Fergus Llewellyn Show* was far from voluntary. Someone had him by the balls.

'Someone's putting the pressure on, right?' he asked.

'Listen, it's over,' Paddy told him. 'Finished. Just let it drop will you?'

'They won't harm your wife.' It was an arrow fired in the air but Hugo knew that it had found the mark by the silence of its impact. Paddy didn't answer for a quarter of a mile.

'How do you know?' he asked, eager to believe it.

'They just won't, believe me.' Hugo sounded convincing and kind. It was not in his nature to carp or he might have mentioned that if Paddy had been decent enough to return his many calls he could have saved himself the humiliation on the *Fergus Llewellyn Show*. Instead he asked, 'What have you discovered? ... About Capitol TV?'

'I can't tell you.' Paddy was driving behind a huge lorry. In his headlamps was a message in large letters, 'KEEP YOUR FAMILY SAFE WITH DETTOL'. It would take more than disinfectant.

'I won't use it. Trust me.'

155

Paddy felt suddenly tired and lonely, he needed someone to talk to. *Faute de mieux*, he told Hugo everything that he had been barred from telling twelve million viewers on the *Fergus Llewellyn Show*. He told him every detail of the Transworld Telly swindle.

Hugo was utterly unsurprised. In return he told Paddy what he had learned from his old colleague, Irving Barstow. Paddy was utterly surprised.

'You mean this Lewis Lefrak is Clanger's partner?' he asked.

'Yes.'

'All along?'

'Yes.'

'Christ, and Noel Pettifer didn't know?'

'No.'

'What?' Yes and no can be so unspecific. Paddy wanted clarification.

'Noel knew,' said Hugo.

'He knew?'

'Yes.'

'Christ. Noel knew what he was hiring – knew who Lefrak was?'

'Yes.'

'You mean it was all planned?' The Trojan horse was clear to see.

'Yes.' Hugo's patience was endless.

'Clanger, Lefrak and Noel all together . . . all in it?' Paddy knew he must be sounding stupid and didn't care. 'All of them?'

'Yes. Afraid so.'

'But Noel is . . .' The word 'friend' eluded Paddy. So did 'completely trustworthy,' etc. 'For God's sake it was Heime who recommended him . . . Oh, I see.' Paddy was only travelling at 30 mph but he had to slow down to take in this information. He understood it all (he thought). The recommendation of Lefrak was the blackmailer's price that Heime had been forced to pay . . . Poor Heime. Poor silly Heime.

'Hallo?' The silence had been too long for Hugo.

'I'm here,' Paddy said. He was miles away. 'You're quite sure?'

'As eggs.'

'So – they've got the rights. *Stratagems* is theirs. They've fucking well got it at last. And they're fucking welcome to it.' In front of the viewing millions Paddy had been honour-bound to be the boy scout, sharing his toys with the enemy and being gracious in defeat, but in the privacy of his own car he felt entitled to a little spleen. 'They're fucking welcome.'

'I have a plan,' Hugo said.

'No, that's it. All over. I don't want to hear it . . .'

'Listen . . .'

'They've got Hannah. They've got my wife . . . There's nothing to be done.' Paddy meant to sound kinder.

'I understand,' said Hugo. 'If there's anything I can do, let me know.'

Paddy wasn't listening, his mind was somersaulting through space.

'Anything, OK? I'll give you my address: 37 Totteridge Crescent, Islington. There's always a key by the dead geranium.'

'Thanks,' said Paddy. He rang off and sped on towards London. The world he lived in was too clever for him.

'I don't think Paddy likes being on television, Mummy.' Kelly had hit the nail on the head. 'Will they let him out of it soon so he can come home?'

It was a question that troubled both of them in proportion to their ages. Paddy was much on their minds during the ritual bedtime, and not even Roald Dahl at his most gruesome could properly distract them. As the evening had worn on, Jemma had felt in turn worried, threatened, hurt, and angry. She eventually went to bed and with the telephone beside her she fell into an unsatisfactory sleep.

As always in her dreams she was shrivelled back into childhood, marooned in the knee-high world of deaf grown-ups. This time she was at ballet class and all around her were television producers grinning and spinning. Gigantic in their midst was Sir Toby Goddard all in green, pirouetting towards her with a dead baby in his arms.

Having reached London Paddy's resolve was weakening and his subconscious was leading him to Jemma's house in Battersea. But like an alcoholic with the glass poised upon

157

his lip, Paddy checked himself. This was no time to go courting. The one ally a man does not need in the rescue of a wife is a girlfriend. The gods can be quite picky about that kind of thing.

Parked on the Albert Bridge Paddy stared at the river swirling darkly beneath him and took stock. On the debit side, he had lost his wife, his job, his friend, his investment and a lot of face. On the credit side, not a lot . . . Certainly he had nothing much left to lose. Had he known how urgently Jemma needed rescuing from her sleep he might not have turned his car towards Holland Park. But as it was he was mindful of the gods and not a little tired as he headed north for his old basement flat. It was the neglected love-nest where Hannah and he had at first been lovers and then newly-weds and from where, more recently, Hannah's reason had decamped. A backlog of junk mail splayed out behind the front door and the unused air smelt of an old potpourri. Paddy switched on lights, heating, the radio and kettle, the life support system of an empty home. He needed to marshal his new thoughts and keep the older ones at bay.

The vodka bottle on the dresser caught his eye, beckoned him, but Paddy stood his ground. He would be strong and not drink, he put the bottle in the fridge – out of mind. He wanted to write things down, put them in columns and number them to make them make sense. He went to the bedroom to fetch a note-pad.

The flashing light from the answering machine startled him in the half-light. He couldn't, in fact, remember leaving it on. So few people knew the number and those that did could always reach him at the farm or studio.

Paddy sat on the edge of the bed and pressed the message report button. The buzzing and whining and a click were followed by a pause and then the clear soft voice of Heime Chadwick.

Three times Paddy rewound and listened to the message and then without hesitation he went to the fridge.

19

Matthew answered the door in a sky-blue bathrobe. He was tousled and surprised.

'Christ, Paddy it's you. Are you OK? Where the hell have you been? Come in. Come in . . .'

'I'm sorry it's so late . . .' Paddy followed him upstairs to the sitting-room.

Without asking Matthew poured a hefty vodka for his guest and a whisky for himself. In silence he lit a Gauloise and sucked in its blue cloud with a force that made Paddy dizzy with envy.

'Where have you been?'

'Around . . .'

'For Christ's sake. You should have called me. I've been going crazy.'

'I'm sorry. I was a bit distracted.' Paddy felt the vodka scorching down his chest.

'God I felt for you. Fergus Llewellyn is such a runt . . . it was ghastly to watch.'

'It wasn't much fun to do.'

'I tried to warn you.' Matthew half smiled.

'About Lefrak's announcement?'

'Yeah.' Matthew nodded. 'You had left Jemma's by the time I heard and then the studio said you were running late. I left a message.'

'I never got it.'

'Obviously.' Matthew was curled into a huge armchair, his feet tucked under him. Paddy took it as a mark of sympathy that for once he wasn't eating.

'Thanks anyway.'

'What a pisser.' Matthew could say that again. 'What a pisser.'

'There's nothing to be done,' Paddy said flatly.

'Noel is appalled.'

'Is he?' Odd.

'We'll fight it.'

'No.'

'Who is this arsehole Lefrak – he can't fucking well do this. He can't.'

'Leave it. It doesn't matter.'

'Fernando Cass for Christ's sake.' Matthew exhaled a funnel of grey smoke in distaste. 'We'll fix the bastards.'

'No,' Paddy raised his voice, and their eyes met. That morning at Jemma's house they had grinned at each other with confidence, the confidence of David going after Goliath with his trusty sling. They weren't grinning now. The Philistines had rather turned the tables.

'They've taken Hannah,' Paddy said.

'What?' Matthew whispered. 'Who?'

'My wife.'

'No, who's taken her?'

'Your uncle.'

'Oh my God.' Matthew turned away. Paddy told him the details. 'No wonder you were subdued on the show. I thought it was the news of the film.' Matthew was motionless, the colour had gone from his face, even the blue of his eyes seemed opalescent.

'That's not all,' said Paddy. 'That's not why I came.' From his Barbour pocket he produced a tape recorder. There was a flash of apprehension and curiosity in Matthew's face. Paddy pressed the 'play' button. 'Listen to this,' he said. The sound quality was far from pure and the contents were no threat to driven snow either.

'Paddy? Er . . .' Heime's voice. 'Hallo. I wanted to talk to you . . . to reach you before . . . privately. I hate these damn things. I wish I could say call me back.' Here there was a splutter of some kind, a cough or maybe a little laugh. 'Actually it's probably better like this . . . I've never been very good at goodbyes. The official letter which I've written gives a full explanation with what should be enough detail to ensure retribution . . . or revenge rather. In fact I don't really care what happens to Toby and the Transworld Telly lot . . . my hatred for Noel Pettifer knows no bounds. It is a white-hot loathing . . . I should have known all along that you were too bright not to find out about my Ganymede . . . my poisonous, cheating little cupbearer.' Heime paused as if to regain his self-control. When he resumed there was a monotone in his voice that bleached out sentiment. 'Not quite the Zeus I thought I was. Achilles more likely, with my heel on my sleeve. What a fool I've been, what a silly, bloody, doting fool.' Matthew drained his glass. 'Hey-ho, I digress. It all began so innocently the business with Clanger and Toby

... No, not innocently, but on a very small scale. Crafty more than criminal. It started out as a tax dodge or so I was told. But of course it snowballed ... I had no idea how tangled the web would get ... It's somehow become impossible to withdraw, until now that is.

'Believe me the pressure has been pretty unbearable. As incurable diseases go, blackmail takes some beating.' Heime sighed, an exhalation of breath that bore with it a tired bitterness. 'So what do I feel? ... Trapped ... lonely ... betrayed? Yes. Certainly a little sad at being driven out of the world with my tail so pathetically between my legs. Er ... I hated lying to you. I've tried telling myself I had no choice. Anyway it's only on your account that I feel any real shame.' Heime spoke faster now as if to save himself from faltering. He was on thin ice. 'I have enormous respect for you ... and, ... affection, too ... So please don't just remember this last horrid débâcle ... there were good times as well. Do try and ignore my filthy linen as they drag it out ... as drag it out they will. I've left you whatever money I have ... should be around £200,000 after death duties. It's not meant to buy me a pardon, just to say ... I'm sorry.' His voice was a whisper. 'Bye.'

Paddy switched the machine off. Matthew was standing with both hands on the mantelpiece staring into an arrangement of dried acacia in the grate. His shoulders shook gently like an idling motor and his unslippered feet made Paddy feel uneasy. He had no consolation to offer.

Here was Matthew sad and unchimerical – almost unrecognisable. It was a surprise to Paddy that he knew this man so little. He liked him and trusted him the way one does a stranger, more on the basis of instinct than knowledge.

Matthew blew his nose. 'So who do you think Ganymede is?' he asked.

'Noel.'

'Noel?'

'Obviously,' said Paddy.

Matthew turned slowly, a deep puzzlement in his eyes. They stared at each other across the room – fellow fall guys in a duff stunt.

'We were completely taken in,' Paddy said.

'Yeah. What a bastard. What a bastard, and what fools we've been. Bloody fools.'

161

'The question is,' Paddy began, 'where the hell is the suicide note?'

'Of course.' It was rare for Matthew to appear slow-witted. 'The letter.'

'It's been stolen.'

'Of course.'

'Stolen by whoever telephoned the police about Heime's death,' Paddy explained. 'Who would want to preserve such evidence against himself?'

'Christ. Yes, of course.' Matthew went to refill his glass. 'Ganymede ... what a crock of shit. I mean it's not easy to get hold of, is it?' He paced back and forth for concentration – his legs were brown and sinewy. 'Have you told the police?'

'No, I came straight here with the tape ... from my flat.'

'Good. I want to hear it again.'

While Matthew listened again to the final words of the man who had been their mentor, Paddy went to take a pee.

It was a bathroom of marble and mirrors in which Paddy caught glimpses of his recurring profile, an endless chorus line of himself holding his cock. Much later he would have to force himself to dredge from his subconscious something disquieting that had lodged there during that uneventful urination.

In the sitting-room Matthew was back in dried-acacia-contemplation. 'What can we do?' he asked simply. His abdication of leadership struck Paddy as significant.

'Nothing while they've got Hannah.' An idea sprang up in Paddy's mind. 'Your uncle has a country house somewhere, doesn't he?'

'Er, yes. Why?'

'Where?'

'Sussex.'

'I want to check it out ... Hannah could be there. Give me the address.'

'Not now for God's sake.'

'Maybe not.' He was planning to go alone.

Paddy was soon driving south through the sprawl of Streatham. The night was endless ahead of him. He was full of a crazy energy; not the real thing but the phony hybrid that is born of recycled tiredness. There was no question he could outwit the enemy and beat them at their own game. He had surprise and darkness on his side. And right too. All he lacked in the enterprise was premeditation. He was blind to the danger of feeling lucky and brave, the cold light of day was still a long way off.

Paddy's mind was full of rescue plans. Perhaps he would be able simply to steal his wife back. Or failing that he could bribe her captors, he had at his disposal quite a large sum of money, with Heime's legacy a small fortune. Poor Heime. Paddy suddenly regretted leaving the tape with Matthew. He wanted to hear it again now as he sped over the Downs under a ragged moon.

Creeping through the rhododendrons Paddy consoled himself that if he was caught he might be reunited with Hannah in captivity. He shivered with the dampness that the leaves thrust at him. He had played the scene before; many were the cameras he had pursued through moonlit undergrowth. It was, he found, true to life that twigs snapped too loudly and the crunch of gravel could deafen.

The house stood white and squarely Georgian against the black hill behind it. Several lights were on and no dog barked. Hidden by a scanty beech hedge, Paddy advanced in the time-honoured, half-crouching position.

Optimistic though Paddy had been that his visit to Sir Toby's country house would be fruitful, he was quite unprepared for the shock of success. As he rounded the stable block there, clearly before him in the light from a high sash window, was the boot-end of a white Citroën Estate sticking out of the garage. Armed with this positive evidence Paddy fooled himself that he had already felt Hannah's proximity intuitively.

Paddy lingered behind the rainwater tank and studied the house across the courtyard. His father had been a military man whose second most hackneyed dictum was 'Make a plan. Make a plan, boy, and stick to it.' His first had been 'Sleep on it.' Paddy could see the wisdom of both but chose to ignore them. He was going to play it by ear – he still felt lucky.

The only lights on the ground floor were at the back of the house. Paddy stood well back and then edged slowly into the line of vision. Standing in the lee of an outhouse, he had the advantage of the darkness but his heart thumped against his bruised ribs. He froze.

Through the uncurtained window he could see into the kitchen. Sitting round a table were the team Sister Wordsworth had described, soundlessly celebrating. The bottle of whisky in their midst had long since abandoned hope of a reunion with its cork. The plump man and the blonde woman rocked in silent laugher and the third man thumped the table with delight then threw back his head. For an instant Paddy glimpsed the huge eyes bulging at the ceiling.

A wiser man might have withdrawn at this point to consider how best to proceed. Not Paddy. Like a gambler on a winning streak he couldn't leave. Hannah was near at hand, he had to stay.

The laughter in the kitchen seemed unending as it spun round the trio at the table. Abduction was clearly a big joke. Paddy watched patiently, 'Make a plan, boy'.

Suddenly the party froze. The laughers were statues with the mirth congealing on their faces. Their heads were cocked for listening and they instantly looked gormless with concentration. The woman held up her hand like a conductor. Had a telephone rung? A dog barked? A prisoner screamed? Perhaps they had just heard the frantic thudding of Paddy's heart.

Charting the origin of their interruption, three pairs of eyes looked up to scan the ceiling. Directly above them Paddy could see a curtained window partly open with a dim light.

Thyroidal shook his head; they were mistaken, all was well, on with the fun. As the revelling resumed, Paddy withdrew further into the darkness. He felt his way round to the back of the shed. With laborious stealth he stepped up on to a grain bin and from there he levered himself inch by inch on to the roof. He was now almost level with the window above the kitchen. Paddy had no doubt it was Hannah's room.

Cupping his hands over his mouth Paddy let out the soft call of an owl. He waited. And hooted. And waited. She must hear. Surely in the dark recesses of her mind their old call sign would strike a chord. Again he repeated the eerie sound, and somewhere in the shed beneath a rat took heed and fled.

In the kitchen the whisky bottle was on its last lap and the mood was mellowing. Paddy hooted again, the sound was hollow in the damp air – he raised the volume of his call with an unowlish urgency that echoed dully in the yard.

Hannah's answer was electric. A scream that tore the night open. A sore, bellowing rasp that erupted from the gut and scorched the throat in its release. It was a searing cry of torment that exploded from the house and ricocheted into the hill behind Paddy.

The jolly drinkers were on their feet struggling for their jackets and sobriety as they ran out of the room.

Above, the curtains were ripped open and there stood Hannah howling Paddy's name into the darkness. 'Paaaddy.' Her arms outstretched, a pathetic silhouette in a hospital nightdress.

Paddy waved in panic. Be quiet. Stay calm, my darling. I'm here. I'm real. Sshh for God's sake. But Hannah was beyond hoping for reality in her nightmare. She was quite blind to the flesh and bone of her husband on the roof of the potting shed. It didn't strike him until later that this was the first glimmer of animation he had seen in her for three years. Paddy waved in vain like a castaway at a ship that's sailed on by.

The door of Hannah's room flew open and the merry threesome rushed in. Their prisoner cringed as they advanced. The blonde now wore a white coat and in her hand she held a kidney bowl. The chilling chromium was like a weapon in her hand. Thyroidal took hold of Hannah by the arms while the plump man drew the curtains shutting off Paddy's view.

'Stop. Stop. Don't touch her. You bastards.' He was shouting against the pitiful descant of his wife's screaming. 'Don't hurt her you fucking bastards.' He was standing helpless and numb on top of the shed. 'I'll kill you. I'll kill you fucking bastards.' His voice was hoarse with impotent rage. Rage at himself for not having a plan. Rage at his father for being right. Why hadn't he gone to the police for God's sake? What crazy whim had led him to believe he could ever win? Hadn't he yet learned that he was perpetually destined for the losing position? He carried on shouting madly.

The curtains of Hannah's room were torn open again and Thyroidal was standing there peering stupidly into the darkness. The blonde was dismantling her syringe and Hannah was out of sight as her screaming ebbed to a moan and died.

'Hannah. Hannah.' He yelled across the yard. The blood was roaring in his ears. He wanted to shout: I've come to save you, everything is OK. But the truth was he had let her down again and the plump man was now in view, for some reason pointing his arm through the open window towards Paddy. A shot rang out. The whistling explosion multiplied back and forth among the trees across the valley. Dogs barked. Paddy stood defeated and breathless wishing to God the bullet had not missed him. 'Should have made a plan .. Retreat. Retreat.'

Paddy was running flat out, and pathetically slow it seemed. His leather shoes exploded into the gravel with each stride and his legs turned to liquid. Nothing orderly in this retreat. As a boy, running had made him feel dizzy and free; now he just felt sick.

The car was right out of the driveway and a hundred yards along. The ignition key was somehow swollen, and Paddy had to use two shaking hands to get it in. He stalled, began again and was at last away – North. South. East. West. It didn't matter. With the windows down Paddy gulped in the black air and could hardly hold it in his lungs for long enough to service his pounding heart. In the mirror, nothing. No . . . a light. Two lights. Christ. Two lights hovering with indecision. Would they turn left or right? Paddy drove in darkness channelled by the high hedgerows either side. The headlamps behind him arched away in the opposite direction. It had been a while since Paddy had won an even money bet.

The raging panic in Paddy's chest had subsided and he longed to smoke a cigarette. He had not a faint idea of where he was going as he raced along the warren of narrow lanes. The road signs were invisible and the moon was useless, dodging about. Paddy drove on in the darkness as best he could. Still nothing in the mirror – all clear.

Ahead, faintly and then stronger, were two great columns of light swinging back and forth with every bend in the road. By turn each hedge was thrown into silhouete. This couldn't be right, meeting your pursuers head on.

The oncoming car was straight ahead, glaring and furious. In spontaneous self-defence, Paddy flicked his lights full up and blasted his horn. There was a desperate yelling of tyres as the two vehicles slewed together, followed by the mighty crunch of chassis meeting and the rain of broken glass.

Across the plateau of the abutted bonnets, Paddy was face to face with his opponents. The relics of their combined headlamps threw up a pale glow like a campfire between them.

The huge eyes of the driver were bulging forth, hellbent on escaping from his head, it seemed. This close encounter with his wife's malefactor was as shocking to Paddy as the sight of his passenger. There, shrouded in a sly malevolence, was the horrid visage of Toady Griffin. With their fenders and their eyes locked both parties contemplated the basic impasse they had reached. The moon had vanished and there was a deep silence. This was no time to exchange insurance details, Paddy turned the ignition key and the engine sprang uninjured back to life and gently he shifted into reverse.

Like a courtier bowing out of the monarch's chamber, Paddy withdrew. Toady and Thyroidal sat impassively behind the crooked grin of their radiator as the gap between the two cars widened.

The reverse reflexes needed for driving backwards are tricky at the best of times but in the dark on an unfamiliar narrow lane, Paddy found it nearly impossible. The car lurched and swerved and his neck ached with the over-the-shoulder driving. Amazingly the other car stood still. Please God let there be a turning point soon . . . a gate, a drive, anything to escape the confines of these damn hedges.

The sign post saying Climford West 1½ and Climford Bottom 2, had not been more welcome since its reinstallation at the end of World War II. There it was, dear sweet Climford. Paddy reversed past the turning, changed gear and shot forward down it. For three hundred yards there was a merciful blackness in Paddy's mirror. The Volvo seemed none the worse for its ramparting and Paddy guessed that the enemy Citroën was incapacitated, with any luck.

No such luck – a solitary beam swung into view several bends away behind him but clearly in pursuit. Paddy put his foot down and the car surged forward. Climford West was not a metropolis that supported anything more than six houses and a letter-box. Paddy pumped his horn in a frantic call for help but he doubted that the local citizens would heed him, let alone telephone the police.

Half a mile separated the two cars as they sped around the

foothills of the Downs. The lanes were a labyrinth. Three times they raced through Climford Bottom. This was the stuff of nightmares – the old panic of the maze. Paddy was desperate to be on the motorway where there were lights and other cars and maybe even safety.

Several times they passed over the elusive motorway and under it. All the time the single beam of the Citroën was like a relentless cyclops behind him. At last Paddy glided round, twice round, a roundabout where huge blue signs offered him the M23, Brighton to the left, London to the right.

Prompted by a crazy fear that beyond Brighton he might be driven into the English Channel, he chose London and raced up the northbound slip road. Never had he been so pleased to see traffic.

The Citroën remained full square in his rear-view mirror as they cruised in convoy up the middle lane of the motorway. Without the need for rally driving, Paddy was able to take a moment for orientation. He was suffering chronological disorder – time and events and north and south were haywire in his head. Where was he going? Wasn't dawn due? What was the range of a revolver? Would a bullet go through the headrest? What orders did Thyroidal have? Who gave them? And who was guarding Hannah? Paddy felt alone and confused, reckless and terrified at the same time.

It was only three-thirty, still three hours to daybreak. The petrol gauge was just under the half-full mark and from the look of things Paddy reckoned his trackers were happy to play a waiting game. It would be a race to the empty tank.

Roughly speaking Paddy had eighty miles left to run. To run where? To whom? What could he do? Paranoia had so run amok with his common sense that even the police seemed a dangerous option. At best they would never believe him. He had no proof, no witnesses. 'Please, sir, the bad guys who want to stop me acting in my film have taken my wife hostage.' 'Very good, sir, we'll file a report in the morning.' All in all Paddy had no faith in the short arm of the law.

Perhaps the answer was to surrender to his pursuers. Appeal to their better natures, surely they must have them. That's what he would do – pull in and beg the crooks for mercy. A hard shoulder to cry on . . . No, no, no, in captivity what use was he? If he gave himself up what negotiating power would he have? None. What negotiating power did he have as it was? None. At large though he could maybe call their bluff or gather reinforcements. The US cavalry were long overdue.

'Make a plan, boy. Make a bloody plan.' It's too late for that, Dad, I'm on my own. I'll manage somehow. How? On impulse he picked up the car phone and dialled a Chelsea number.

'Yes,' Sir Toby answered quickly, as if he had been expecting a call. 'Who is it?'

'Paddy Brummel.'

Sir Toby's silence had a talk-of-the-devil tone to it. 'Where are you?' he asked.

'Half a mile ahead of your two thugs in the Citroën.' Paddy could see their silhouette in his mirror. 'Listen, I've found Hannah.'

'I know.' Sir Toby sounded irritated.

'I know where she is. Let her go now. Let's stop this. I won't say anything.' Paddy sounded like a weedy boy scout. 'The whole thing is getting out of hand ... You and Noel and Clanger just go ahead, do what you want; I don't care as long as Hannah is safe. Let her go. Please. Now. OK?'

Peace in our time. Fat chance. Sir Toby's answer came without hesitation. 'No.'

'Why not?'

'I told you earlier, Mr Brummel. She would be perfectly safe as long as you were sensible.' The line was spattered with static.

'I am being sensible,' Paddy shouted. It wasn't true, he was being utterly crazy, petulant, indecisive, floundering naïvely way out of his depth in murky waters. 'What do you want me to do?'

'Stay away. Keep quiet. Don't try to find her again. Don't do anything.' Was there an edge of panic in Sir Toby's voice?

'Where is she?'

'She's already been moved.'

'Where to?'

'Just do as I say and nobody will get hurt.' Sir Toby sounded sincere.

'Why are your thugs chasing me? Tell them to leave me alone.'

'I can't. They have their orders.'

'What fucking orders?' Paddy was sick of being one jump behind.

'Use your common sense, Mr Brummel. Use your common sense.'

'Go to fucking hell.' Paddy disconnected. For a moment he felt like crying, he was losing track of the situation like a tired child. Ideas flew past him going too fast to get hold of. Behind him his trackers kept their distance. What were their orders, he asked himself, although the answer was obvious. What was forty-two from three score years and ten, he wondered.

Anger throbbed in Paddy's throat and his shoulders ached with tension. Below him on either side of the road a thin mist hung over the fields like low clouds. Paddy was flying. Behind him the Citroën kept its distance implacably.

Where the hell should he go? Home? No, although there was some argument for dying on familiar ground. Escape was still a better plan. At the speed he was going he had forty miles or forty minutes to think of a destination. He sensed the Citroën could easily outdistance him – his enemy's patience spoke of a full tank. There was no doubt – Paddy was being run to earth.

The traffic on the motorway was thinner now. Who were these other drivers anyway? Drunks and adulterers skulking back to their home county? Certainly samaritanism from them was out of the question.

Paddy dialled Matthew's number. Engaged. Engaged at four in the morning? America maybe, or off the hook. A gap between two tankers sprang up beside an exit road. On impulse Paddy swerved between them at the last minute and raced off the motorway. No dice. His one-eyed predator was with him all the way. They skidded round the interchange and rejoined the motorway together.

Matthew's number was still engaged. Acid was burning Paddy's throat. 'Make a plan, boy.' He dialled another number telling himself he had no choice. The gods would forgive him.

Jemma's voice was wide awake with the shock of being woken. Her nightmare at least was over.

'Just listen,' Paddy began.

'Where . . . What . . .?'

'I'll tell you later. Just listen.' His tone was rude with urgency and Jemma staunched her curiosity and indignation and anxiety and listened. She had no time to write down what he said.

'I'll be there,' she said when Paddy finished. This was no time for her to lose confidence in her navigation or her Morris. She sat for a moment paralysed . . . she'd never make it. Then suddenly her mind was sharp with the vigour of emergency.

With none of the haste and all the speed her grandmother had nagged about, she got herself together and within five minutes she was out of the house urging her sluggish Morris westward. The back seat was stacked with the fruits of her efficiency as per Paddy's instruction. Jemma's only worry was leaving Kelly – she would sleep for another three hours for sure and by then . . .

London was enjoying its quietest hour. Jemma was hunched over the steering wheel like a jockey in the final furlong. The gearbox grumbled as she zigzagged west on the familiar rat-run to the BBC and then the motorway beyond. The law of averages seemed to be cheating her of green lights, so she jumped a red or two to redress the balance. She was short of time. She shivered with the cold or fear or both.

The Morris was now on the motorway and the foot of the driver was on the floor. This was a car for gentle Sunday outings whose speedometer was wavering now in the uncharted region at 65 mph – no picnic. Jemma glimpsed herself in the mirror, wide-eyed and ghoulish in the feeble light of her dashboard. Twenty miles in twenty minutes, she'd never make it.

Paddy was on the M25, the magnificent London orbital highway. He was driving clockwise against the clock with Thyroidal relentlessly in the middle of his rear-view sighting, the roar of tyres in his ears. Paddy had regretted embroiling Jemma almost immediately – her car was dodgy, she'd never make the rendezvous. What chance did they have anyway, a couple of play actors?

Without the courtesy of signalling, Paddy forked left onto the M40 Westbound towards Oxford. Toady and Thyroidal were sure to follow. They did. Ten miles to go, less than ten minutes . . . Would she be there? Please be there.

Clouds of her warm breath mushroomed in the air as Jemma scrambled out of the car. Was this the right place? Christ, it had to be. Her sense of direction and punctuality had never known such pressure. She had no time in hand, three maybe four minutes. Jemma rushed about her business without any real hope of success. Luckily the narrow lane was deserted; a passerby would think her crazy. She was crazy.

Over the last few miles Paddy reduced his speed, stalling for time and giving his hunters a scent of victory. His petrol gauge was on the emptier side of empty. He had no margin for error. Also he realised he had no way of knowing if Jemma had made it.

Jemma's pulse was racing with the fear of failure. In the distance three headlights were approaching closely bunched. How three? Stay calm, she told herself. Paddy's orders were obeyed. She told herself. Paddy's orders were obeyed. She was ready for action and quivering like a jelly.

The Cyclops Citroën was close on Paddy's heels, its beam below his line of vision now. He could see the outline of two skulls eagerly tracking him up the slow incline of the road. Paddy slid the driver's seat back as far as it would go and with a sharp tug tested his safety belt. If his scheme was to work he needed all the advantage of surprise he could get. He ran through in his mind the sequence of what he had to do. Speed would be vital. Less than a mile to go. What a laxative danger is.

The Volvo and the Citroën advanced in tandem to the crest of the hill where the motorway cuts through high chalk on either side. Paddy knew it well. The escarpment was spanned by a minor road above. 'I've made a plan, Dad . . .'

Paddy slowed down further, the beaten victim, outrun at last, ready for the kill. He braked and indicated he was pulling in. It was his token of surrender in the chase. The Volvo stopped plumb at the apex of the hill. Well judged, Paddy, keep at it. The Citroën came to a halt close behind him.

At an angle he could only guess Paddy tilted his mirror down, then doused his lights. So did his followers. Darkness. Paddy ducked his head to the left throwing himself across the passenger seat. The engine was idling gently. Not so his pulse. Paddy looked up into the rear-view mirror. He had got the angle right for there were the enemy clearly in his view. 'Not yet. Not yet,' he told himself, and for two lots of held breath he waited.

The doors of the car behind began to open. NOW! Paddy sat up, pulled the gear lever into reverse and stamped on the

172

accelerator. The Volvo shot backwards and for the second time that night made contact with the front end of the enemy Citroën.

Paddy felt a savage punch across his chest as the safety belt held him firm. In a flash he released himself from it and was throwing himself out of the passenger door. With a single backward glance Paddy got a fleeting picture of Toady and Thyroidal sprawled half out of their car, the picture of bloody-nosed stupefaction.

Racing for the embankment Paddy yelled with all his strength and faith, 'NOW!'

From the bridge above Jemma obeyed. She gave a mighty push. And from below she heard the explosion of a bull's-eye as her sack of empty bottles hit the Citroën full square on the roof. Perhaps Paddy's luck was changing.

More by fluke than good judgement Jemma followed her success with the rest of her improvised barrage. With trembling hands she let rip three pounds of flour (wholemeal of course), a potted fern, a present from Dennis's mother, an economy-size box of detergent, a huge jar of chutney, another of Cooper's rough-cut marmalade, a bag of potatoes, a giant pot of floor polish and a dozen tins of soup (mostly Kelly's favourite Tomato) which she dropped individually and with great accuracy. She had got her eye in now.

Paddy had taken a good run at the escarpment. He knew the bombardment could not last for long and soon the bullets would start to fly. The climb was a lot steeper than he had imagined and as he scrambled frantically upwards, the ground raced from under him in a torrent of scree. On all fours he clawed at the ground begging it to hold. Tufts of grass were fickle handholds and his leather-soled shoes could find no purchase. One step forward – three back. The missiles from the bridge had stopped and Toady and Thyroidal were shouting below him.

A pistol shot rang out and echoed back and forth across the motorway. Paddy wondered if he had been hit – surely he would notice. Knowing his luck he'd cop the first bullet in the bumhole even in the pitch dark.

'Come on,' Jemma shouted with impatience. She had no understanding of his plight. 'Come on.' Another shot rang out and Paddy waited for a pain to slice through him. It didn't. Again he tried to advance, again he was dragged back by the undercurrent. He was barely treading water and sweat was running down his face.

Not before time Jemma grasped Paddy's problem. With a car like hers the most vital piece of equipment was a tow rope and she rushed to get it. Paddy grabbed the life-line as another shot whizzed into the night. Jemma had no time to make her end fast and had to brace herself against the parapet to take his weight. Slowly Paddy pulled himself towards her straining silhouette and was never gladder to see the first hint of dawn behind her.

A volley of shots spattered into the chalk above Paddy's head. Thyroidal's aim was getting better. Paddy froze. Never again would he think stunt men were overpaid. On the motorway a pantechnicon hove into view chugging up the hill. Its headlamps revealed two cars conjoined on the hard shoulder amid an assortment of groceries. Also two men standing nonchalantly nearby – no sign of a gun.

Paddy struggled to take advantage of this temporary inhibition of the enemy's fire power. Ten yards to go. His hands were raw, his whole body ached and a terrible weakness washed over him.

'Come on, Paddy.' Jemma's voice was ludicrously near and yet so far away. Yes. Yes. I'm coming. Or dying. He inched forward.

The gorge was in darkness again now, the moment of respite was gone as the throb of the diesel receded. Another three shots rang out losing themselves in their own echo. One of them seemed oddly linked to a stab of warmth somewhere in Paddy's thigh. He swung loose at the end of his rope for a moment, stunned not by the pain of his wound but by the realisation of it. His flesh had been breached. 'I've been shot,' he said like a child that's lost its first tooth. 'I've been shot.'

From above no word of sympathy, just a groan as Jemma held his dead weight and then strained to winch him up. Slowly. Slowly Paddy came into reach. She grabbed his hair. He grabbed her wrist. She grabbed his hands. He grabbed her shoulders, and as the two last shots were fired Paddy fell over the parapet and the pair of them lay gasping together in a heap, out of range.

20 As the mighty 747 slumped down towards Heathrow, Lefrak looked out of his window. Beside him Fernando Cass had slept soundly all the way, his face ageing horribly without the benefit of consciousness.

Shrouded in a foggy haze Slough was not at its loveliest. England was very much as Lewis expected. However, had the aircraft banked the other way he might have been impressed by the first rays of a glorious dawn over Windor Castle.

Lefrak was pleased that they were travelling together on this his first visit to Great Britain, but without his grandiose companion he might have dropped his cool and allowed himself a thrill. The country that gave you Hitchcock, Lean, Chaplin, the Beatles and James Bond couldn't be all bad.

'I tell you it's a dreary goddam shit-hole,' said Cass having retrieved his lost youth with orange juice and an electric razor. Here was a man who viewed the world through turd-coloured glasses.

'It sure ain't Hawaii,' conjoined Lefrak. 'We just got to get our act together and then get the fuck out.' This simple view of things was due for some radical revision.

In the immigration and customs hall Lewis was amazed by the accent of the staff. Michael Caine had not invented it after all.

The principal talent of an airport photographer is running backwards with his cameras at work. Unblemished by dehydration like other mortals, celebrities stride off planes with gusto, their toupees and smiles raring to go, and their eyes fixed in the middle distance. They seem unstoppable. They would have the world believe that this intrusion of the press had angered them.

'It's great to be back.' Fernando grinned a twelve-tooth salute. 'Am I an Anglophile or what?' This was good humour. The *Life Sanction* movies were popular in the UK and Cass was keen not only to please his fans but also to appease the tetchy side of Frank Hoffman. In a cesspit Fernando could always come up smelling of Dior.

'Is the latest *Sanction* film as violent as the first?' a bearded reporter asked.

'You bet,' Cass quipped.

'Are you looking forward to the Gala on Tuesday?' a second beard enquired.

'I can't wait. It's a great movie.' Cass had seen it too often already.

'How do you feel about *Stratagems and Spoils*?' asked a reporter with only a moustache.

'I'm not here to talk about that. One thing at a time is my motto.' It wasn't. If anything, it was, 'I'm all right Jack.' Lewis had briefed him well on the journey and he knew the subject was a minefield.

'Is it true,' persisted the moustache, 'that you've been brought in to save the film?'

'I don't know about that,' said Cass.

'How do you feel about stepping into another actor's role?'

'No comment.'

'Would you say Paddy Brummel was a good actor?'

'I've never heard of him.'

'Are you the right casting for this project?' asked a reporter with no beard or moustache. 'I mean wouldn't you say *Stratagems and Spoils* is a pretty English kind of story?'

Lewis Lefrak hid himself behind the star's entourage, the situation called out for a low profile and dark glasses. Fernando Cass could handle it; he wasn't known as the 'Quote Kid' for nothing.

'That's a racist question, Mister.' Fernando could be as satirical as the next megastar.

A reporter with no hair at all who had had three large brandies with Hugo Cavendish the night before, stepped forward, his face shining with hangover and asked, 'I was wondering, Mr Cass, if you had anything to say with regard to the rumour that *Stratagems and Spoils* has been hijacked by the Americans; that the rights have been acquired by foul play and by bully-boy tactics, by fraud and by blackmail even?'

The pack of media people, hairy or not, around Cass were all at once still and quiet. There was a pause and the bareheaded journalist asked with charm, 'Had you not heard?' And for his curiosity received for an instant the full power of the star's icy glare.

Fernando's anger hovered on the brink of a huge headline: 'CASS IN AIRPORT BRAWL.' Where the hell was Lefrak?

The rat. He shrugged. 'No I hadn't heard that. It's not my business. I'm just an actor. I play parts. I do my job.' Fernando spoke quietly with the simple sincerity that he had used so effectively in *Duel at Dusk*. He prepared to leave. '*Life Sanction*, gentlemen, is what we're here about. And I want to tell you it makes *Rambo* look like the *Wizard of Oz*. Now if you'll excuse . . .'

Flash. Flash. Flash. Grin. Grin. Grin. And the party was over. The paparazzi had better fish to fry; Jane Birkin in Terminal Two.

Safely upholstered and downcast Fernando stared out of the window of his Rolls Royce. A PR man with technicolor spectacles was explaining a schedule of publicity and Lefrak was apologising for his intransigence in the arrival hall. Fernando was listening to neither, his mind was elsewhere.

With something that he did not recognise as compassion, Fernando was wondering about Paddy Brummel. Who was this other actor with whom he shared a common ambition; this obsession with the role of Eliot Blandford. As with a rival in a love affair, Fernando felt a sympathy for the other fool. Wasn't he, too, just an actor? An artist like himself, being jerked around by puppeteers?

All this went through the mind of Fernando Cass quite quickly as he frowned at Hounslow out of the window. Dawn without a sunrise was a washout, he was California dreaming. He was all right, Jack, wasn't he? Hounslow frowned back.

Jemma and Paddy ate bacon and eggs in his kitchen. Outside the roosters were crowing at last; it had been a long night.

'How are you feeling?' she asked again.

'OK,' Paddy nodded. 'Thanks.' The sweetness of his tea reminded him that he was supposedly in shock. The calmness he felt was perhaps illusory. Not so the burning in his thigh.

It had not been a long drive from the scene of bombardment from the bridge. In her role of heroine Jemma had even remembered to bring vodka for the wounded. Paddy had poured some of it into the hole in his thigh which hurt like hell, and the rest into the one in his face which hadn't hurt at all.

As they had wended their way home across the Chilterns

Paddy told her of the night's events. Then without much coherence he tried to tell her why it was he had not been in touch. The explanation seemed to confuse him more than it did her. Jemma easily understood the making of deals with gods. She, too, was an old hand at bargaining with fate. She appreciated that when he had telephoned her for help he had had no choice (a matter of life or death) but break his contract. She understood it all. Would the gods?

Paddy had stood naked and shaking in front of Jemma as she dressed his wound. He had never felt more vulnerable. As the TCP exploded in the tissue of his leg he had noticed that on the nape of her neck she had a small birthmark the shape of Cyprus.

The first thing Jemma had done on arriving was to arrange for her disgruntled ex-husband to go round and collect Kelly. Life had been so quiet a week ago. She looked pale and her eyes were huge and liquid. 'What are you going to do?' she asked.

'Exactly,' Paddy answered. A number of options were circling in his brain but the clear favourite prompted him to limp across to the telephone and dial Matthew's number. Too bad if it woke him – Matthew was the ally they needed. He would know what to do, he could handle it all.

'Hallo. 224 2081.'

Paddy hung up, wrong number. Dialled again. Ring-ring.

'Hallo.' Matthew's voice was quiet but awake.

'It's me,' Paddy announced.

'Are you OK ... Paddy what's up?'

Paddy told him what was up and Matthew said 'Christ' intermittently.

'Why the hell didn't you call me?' asked Matthew.

'I tried.'

'Where are you now?'

'At home. The farm.'

'With Jemma?' Matthew sounded in control.

'Yes. What the hell do you think I should do?' Paddy asked.

'Don't do anything. Just stay there. I'll be with you in forty minutes. Everything is going to be OK. Just stay put, OK?'

'OK. Thanks.' Paddy hung up. Good old young Matthew. What a pal. He was filled with relief at the idea of handing over control to Matthew. Matthew was a born winner.

Paddy stared out of the kitchen window. Diagonal sunbeams

were splintering through the broken timbers of the barn. Why did he feel so alien looking at this familiar view? Perhaps he had seen it all in a previous incarnation. Like a sneeze that won't quite come, an urgent thought was eluding him hovering on the outskirts of his consciousness. A premonition was it? Or a recognition? Or a memory? Paddy shuddered. Whatever it was it had a nasty smell.

'Hallo 224 2081.' 224 2081 ... 224 2081 ... Was not a wrong number. 224 2081 was Matthew's number all right. 224 2081 – nothing wrong with that ... attishoo ... it was the voice that was wrong.

Paddy did not move. A frozen moment of awareness was melting in his mind. A picture was coming into focus ... Don't force it. Gently does it. Somewhere in the tangled sewing-basket of his brain a memory was emerging ... A memory of what? Come on. Come on ... A mirror. Yes, yes. Something in a mirror. A room of infinite mirrors. Yes, yes. A bathroom. The bathroom at Matthew's house. That's it – that's where, now what is it? What is it specifically that's so urgently summoning up this recollection. Come on. Concentrate ... Paddy was peeing, surrounded on all sides by reflected multiples of himself, peeing among a whole line of peeing clones. Yes. Yes. It was nearly there ... Over his shoulder, behind him, in the mirror ... on the back of the bathroom door. Yes. Yes. A shirt had hung ... that wasn't it ... The tie. Yes. Yes. Pale pink and green. That was it. The Garrick Club tie ... The wrong voice on the telephone. The wrong tie on the hook. The voice and tie of Noel Pettifer. Noel in Matthew's flat? ... Noel and Matthew.

Paddy's eyes were half closed as if peering at something through a fog. His mouth was moving in unison with the unshaped chaos in his head. God, how slow-witted he had been. The full plot was now becoming clear. The truth was avalanching towards him, bowling through the boundaries of his wildest paranoia. The shock was of his own making; he had ignored all the warning signals.

'Matthew is Ganymede,' Paddy said quietly to the patient Jemma.

Heime's voice came to Paddy as he stared on out of the window ... 'I should have known all along that you were too bright not to find out about my Ganymede.' The taped message rang in his ears. 'My poisonous, cheating little cupbearer.' Matthew Goddard. Matthew whom poor Heime had loved. Little wonder that '. . . my hatred for Noel Pettifer knows no bounds. It is a white-hot loathing . . .'

Paddy had not been bright enough to find out about Ganymede. He had blundered forward with his understanding at half-cock. A clever little know-all who knew nothing. Paddy felt ashamed. The suicide was after all a matter of the heart. Heime had been in the losing corner of an all-male triangle. It wasn't the substance of the blackmail that had driven him to his death; it was the blackmailer himself. His own Ganymede who had jilted and betrayed him.

Across the farmyard strolled a fat cock pheasant, his coat shining in the feeble sunlight. Paddy leaned against the window pane; in his head new understanding was tumbling downstairs in front of his eyes. Had Matthew intended from the outset to exploit his lover or had Noel Pettifer seduced him to that purpose at some later point? For how long had they all been led blindly up the garden path?

What a stupid damn fool Paddy had been. Hadn't he, too, fallen under the whiz-kid's sway, been dazzled with the others by his blue-eyed optimism? 'Christ,' he said out loud. 'It was him.'

Jemma had been pacing round the kitchen reaching conclusions too. Which one was this that Paddy had got to. 'What?' she asked.

'He must have the original letter, the official suicide note. It must have been addresed to him. It must have been Matthew who called the police.'

'And you left the tape with him. Your one?' she asked.

'Yes.' A horrible chill ran through Paddy's body. This new ruthless Matthew was an enemy. An enemy whose real loyalty lay with Clanger, Pettifer, Sir Toby, Lefrak and Fernando Cass. Who could Paddy turn to? Allies were getting scarce. He turned to Jemma.

'We've got to get out of here,' he said. 'Matthew is already on his way.' He needed time to juggle all this new information into sense. On the one hand he had the advantage of Matthew not knowing his secret was out, on the other he was powerless to do anything while his wife was still prisoner. In five minutes they were back in the Morris bumping down the drive.

'I tell you he fucking well knows, he's found out. Why else would he have gone like this?' Matthew was on the telephone in Paddy's kitchen.

'Calm down. For God's sake – how can he know?' Noel tried to placate his hot-headed cupbearer. 'He'll come back. Maybe he's gone to the doctor.'

'I still don't fucking like it,' Matthew answered. 'I don't like it.' If his secret was out it was high time. No longer could he play the double-agent with a foot in both camps. This wasn't just a skirmish in the movie-star wars, this was a full-blown criminal business and even for him the stakes were getting dangerously high.

'Look, dear boy, just come home and we'll sort it out. He'll ring. You're his friend. It's all OK.' Noel was trying to present the voice of cool reason as he sat at home in his green silk dressing-gown. 'He can't do anything anyway – not while Hannah is still with us.'

'I tell you he's dangerous, Noel, he's crazy,' Matthew said. On the wall where he was standing was a photograph of Hannah. The caption read: *'Romeo and Juliet* Regent's Park 1982,' and there she was laughing brilliantly in a sky-blue Elizabethan dress. 'We've got to find him – we've got to shut him up.' His new hatred for Paddy was mushrooming frantically. He hated his self-righteousness, his persistence and his honesty.

'Come home and we'll sort it out with Toby,' Noel soothed. 'Come home, dear boy.'

'OK,' said Matthew after a while. He was trying not to look the photograph of Hannah in the eye. 'I'll see you later.' But there were demons dancing in his head.

Sir Toby seldom smoked a cigar before lunch but today he made an exception and lit a massive corona as he sat in the back of his Rolls Royce. It was little comfort to him. From all quarters he was receiving news of things in disarray. Trapped as he was in the slow traffic along the Embankment even the dismal river on his right was overtaking him.

On his car telephone he had just been talking to the fretful Toady Griffin who had, it seemed, broken his collar-bone and was in a mood of spiteful vengeance. Never before, Sir Toby reflected, in the annals of criminal conflict had a can of tomato soup been cited as an offensive weapon. He was now listening to Noel Pettifer on the line in a state of anxiety. 'I tell you Toby, it's all getting out of hand,' was his understatement of the situation.

'Paddy Brummel is a damn nuisance,' said Toby. As he sucked in the first lungful of smoke, the impact on his throat and head was fabulous. 'I'm sure he won't have gone to ground for long. He'll turn up. He'll call me. He has no choice. Then we'll do a deal. Pay him off. Release the girl . . . We'll work it out. Whatever. Where's that nephew of mine got to?'

'I've no idea,' answered Noel. 'He should have been back two hours ago.' He kept silent his own worst suspicions. 'I'll see you at the Savoy then,' he concluded. They were due to have a drink to welcome Lewis Lefrak and Fernando Cass before lunch. A Buck's Fizz would soon put things right.

The two gentlemen sitting in the Ford Escort outside Paddy's London flat reading tabloid newspapers looked as conspicuous as film extras in a B-movie. 'Don't stop. Drive on,' Paddy said.

Jemma obeyed. There was no good reason for the men to be there at eight-thirty in the morning and certainly a bad one.

'Where to?' asked Jemma.

'Your place won't be any better.'

Paddy's leg was throbbing as his mind searched round for a destination. They needed a bolt-hole somewhere to regroup, rethink and retake the initiative if possible.

'Let's go to the police,' Jemma suggested as though the idea was a novelty. She was tired and tense and the whole thing seemed all wrong to her. Wasn't it the bad guys who were supposed to be on the run?

'No.' Paddy was unequivocal.

For everybody round them it was Friday morning – just Friday morning. People's problems included what joint to buy for Sunday and when to visit the in-laws. There could be nobody else in the whole of High Street Kensington trying to think of somewhere not to get shot. Paddy was on his own.

Passing the news vendor outside the station Paddy glimpsed a bill board: *The Globe* . . . Hugo Cavendish . . . Hugo Blessed Cavendish. What was his address? . . . Where did he say the key was? . . . Was it number 37? Was it under a dead geranium?

It was. It was.

Hugo was not there. With the soft tread of fugitives they entered his home. A much pleasanter house than Paddy had dared to imagine – light and clean and not untasteful. Safe anyway. The most amazing item the maisonette contained was a letter on the kitchen table addressed to Paddy Brummel.

Not believing in the preordination of events, Paddy opened it eagerly.

'Dear Paddy,' it scrawled. 'I thought I'd leave you a note just in case you should decide to drop in for whatever reason – sorry not to be here, I've got a rather hectic day. Hectic, in some part, on your account. I'll explain when I see you. I don't for one minute imagine that you are here from anything but lack of choice but welcome anyway – you must need a place to lie low. We are dealing with a most unsavoury bunch of crooks and you must be under quite some pressure.

'Please make yourself at home. In the food line I'm afraid I'm a freezer-to-microwave man but there's a fair selection. There's white wine in the fridge and the rest in the sitting-room. The sheets in the top bedroom are clean. And the water should be hot. Use the phone as you wish but I suggest you don't answer. I'll call you later. Two lots of three rings will be me. If not I'll see you this evening. It might be best to park a few streets away. Till later – Hugo.'

'I still think he's a creep,' said Jemma, steadfast in her dislike.

'PS – Welcome to Jemma too, if she's there.'

'He is not to be trusted,' said Jemma heaping coffee into the creep's percolator.

'We have no choice,' said Paddy who was suddenly tired to the point of dizziness. It was hopeless doing anything until he had slept. And sleep he did, like a man under anaesthetic in the spare room of his gutter press biographer, his saviour Hugo Cavendish.

On the radio downstairs Jemma heard a disc jockey announcing, 'The arrival this morning of that all-American hunk of corn-beef – Fernando Cass, the unthinking woman's crumpet who is here for the Gala on Tuesday of his latest film

Life Sanction II which boasts the bloodiest climax of all time
. . . violence . . . Listeners, do we need it? Your calls please on
239 . . .'

Jemma shook her head. A bloody climax was not what we
needed.

The all-American hunk of corn-beef was holding court in his
suite at the Savoy. With his cowboy-booted feet on a
reproduction Louis XV footstool and his head thrown back in
goldplated laughter, he seemed happy enough. The people
round him were chic and intellectual, such qualities as he
normally only glimpsed in back issues of *Time* and *Vogue*.
Here they were in the flesh – the flesh of his new partners
and producers.

Lewis Lefrak and Noel Pettifer were chuckling and
toasting themselves with Buck's Fizz and Sir Toby was the
epitome of the avuncular empire-building Brit. Champagne
was bubbling in their veins and optimism was running amok;
there was talk of billion dollar deals and Oscars . . .

'Eliot Blandford is a role you were born to play,' vouched
Sir Toby.

'I feel that, too, Sir Toby,' said Cass. The knighthood
confused him. Military rank he understood (he had even
played a general once) but this man's title was somehow
unspecific. Was he of the garter, or the round table? Or was it
a lampoon like Duke Ellington or Count Basie? For sure the
guy had power; Fernando could spot the cold quality of it in
his eyes.

'If you don't get a nomination at least,' said Noel swizzling
his champagne, 'I'll eat my hat.' His caviare trilby no doubt.

'Now what is all this shit I was put through at the airport?'
asked Fernando sweetly. 'Are you guys on the level?'

Lewis nodded seriously and looked to Sir Toby. Sir Toby
nodded seriously and looked to Noel Pettifer. Noel did some
serious nodding and was hugely relieved when the door
opened to admit Matthew. With increasing curiosity the two
older men observed that there was about him an air of shifty
exuberance. 'Hi,' he beamed. 'Sorry I'm late.'

'This is my nephew, Matthew – Fernando Cass.'

'I'm so pleased to meet you,' said Matthew shaking the
star's huge hand. Is the guy a prince or duke, Cass wondered.
To him he looked like a Hollywood toy-boy – Dallas fodder.

'We were just celebrating,' said Noel handing his friend some champagne.

'Right,' said Matthew. He raised his glass. 'To us, to you, Fernando. To *Stratagems and Spoils* – Welcome.'

'I was just enquiring about this story that came my way that you guys got hold of this project by foul play, by bully-boy tactics, by fraud and by blackmail?' Fernando's recall of the bald reporter's words was perfect.

It was Matthew's turn to nod seriously. He did so quite a bit, then said, 'Well, it sure as hell wasn't handed to us on a plate.'

The boy was brilliant under pressure. They all grinned.

'As you know there has been a British production of this film which we have been involved in,' Sir Toby began slowly. 'I don't want to sound disloyal – I mean I dare say that we are as responsible as the others . . . but this film was . . . it was a turkey, what can I tell you?' Sir Toby was a linguist to boot. 'It was cheap looking rubbish . . . I mean black and white. And the man playing the lead . . .' Sir Toby clicked his fingers to make Matthew volunteer:

'Paddy Brummel.'

'Paddy Brummel.' Sir Toby shook his head, 'Tell them.'

'Ghastly.'

'Awful.'

'Dull.'

'Appalling.'

'We had no choice,' said Matthew. 'We stopped production.'

'We then decided to mount a rescue operation,' said Uncle Toby. 'It wasn't easy. That's why we teamed up with Lewis here and Noel . . . We had work to do.'

Words like 'rescue' and 'team up' found their mark. Cass was a spoon-fed baby at heart.

'We decided to start all over again,' said the young member of the Goddard duo. 'We had to reschedule, rebudget, reshoot, recast.'

'It was damn hard . . . nobody likes being ruthless.' Sir Toby took up the tale. 'Of course there was going to be some bad blood, some ill feeling and wild accusations,' he paused to mark his regret, 'but I didn't get where I've got by being namby-pamby with people's feelings.'

'Anyway,' said his nephew, 'all that is behind us. We just want to get on with the job of making this movie. Making it good, Fernando. Making it with you . . .' Counsel for the defence was concluded.

In the field of bullshit this was grade 'A' material and it silenced Cass at a stroke. The honesty of these gentle folk was abundantly clear and so impressed was Fernando that he actually put his feet to the ground and stood up.

'That's all I wanted to hear,' he said, shaking hands all round. Matthew poured a palmful of peanuts into his face. Noel smiled and Lewis Lefrak closed his mouth at last.

On with the party. Buck's Fizz and flattery. Production details were discussed – schedules and casting gone over. With a magnificent sleight of hand Sir Toby even managed to banish Cass's intention of having Candida Pink in the role of Eliot Blandford's ex-wife. Hadn't he heard somewhere that Jemma Culver had been perfect casting. From Heime was it? 'It would undermine too much of Eliot's natural authority,' he said. 'It could detract from his intrinsic sympathy.'

'You could be right,' said Cass. He had, in the heat of the moment, perhaps overlooked intrinsic sympathy.

Before the visitors left, they were all agreed on the need for keeping their venture in low profile. 'I mean you're here on Frank Hoffman's tab,' said Noel. 'And if we start shooting off about *Stratagems* he's not likely to be too pleased. We don't want to get up Frank's nose do we?' They none of them did.

Having smoothed the feathers of the American actor, Noel and the Goddards were anxious to get on with plucking those of the British one. They left Fernando to his work-out schedule and withdrew to a corner of the bar downstairs.

With terrible misgiving the two older men noted that there was a wicked excitement in the blue of Matthew's eyes, the tell-tale glint of cocaine. 'Where the hell have you been?' they asked with one voice.

'Everything is under control,' Matthew said. 'Everything is under control.' In his pocket was the tape of Heime's final words which were still churning in the residue of his conscience. Toby and Noel watched their protégé swallow a large brandy in a single gulp and listened to their hopes of a quiet life fly out the window as Matthew told them what he had been doing.

'I am sorry Bernard Havers is unable to take your call at

present,' lied the recorded voice of FQ. 'Please leave your name and number after the little bleep and I'll get back to you as soon as poss. . .'

FQ was busy in the kitchen making chilli for his friend. As his Ansaphone went into action he froze. Any movement might give away his presence; breathing can be fatal in hide-and-seek. He was sick of being sought, wanted no more phonecalls and certainly no more visitors, thank you. His mouth fell open and his wooden spoon dripped on the tiles as the caller spoke, 'It's Paddy.' It was his master's voice. 'I want to talk to . . . Bernard . . . I'll try again later.'

FQ pounced on the apparatus. 'I'm here, I'm here. Hold on,' he shouted down the telephone. The machine brooked no interruption (when you're out you're out). 'Paddy, Paddy, wait,' shouted the little man struggling against the Ansaphone's power of veto.

'It's OK. I'm here,' Paddy told him down a clear line at last. 'Are you OK?'

'Yeah.' He didn't sound it. 'You?'

'Yeah.' Neither did he.

'Actually I'm not,' FQ confessed.

'No, me neither,' Paddy followed suit.

They had a lot in common, it turned out. They were both lying low in fear of the same enemy. Slowly by turns they put each other in the picture. FQ wished more than ever that he had been braver, less loyal to his own and come clean sooner.

Paddy told him about the taped farewell from Heime.

'Did you know?' he asked.

'What?' FQ knew what.

'About Noel and Matthew?'

In the silence FQ's breathing mingled with the static in a wheeze.

'Yes,' he said.

'I see.' Paddy tried to imagine the dilemma he had been in, which horn to protect. 'I see.'

'No you don't. You don't see at all,' FQ was nearly shouting. His floodgates were opening and Paddy knew not to prompt him. 'The bastard . . . the stinking effing bastard . . . The lying cheating bitch . . .' FQ took a breath. 'You see, he was my friend. Noel and I were friends . . .'

'Christ,' whispered Paddy . . . FQ and Noel were friends were they? Friends indeed. Paddy wondered what real friendship the two of them had shared, if any.

'I see,' he said. His own stupidity seemed to know no bounds.

'Oh yes. We'd been together for nearly two years ... Everything was fine, until Mr Kiss-my-arse, Mr I'm-the-nephew-of-the-boss, Mr Matthew fuck-you, fucking Goddard came snaking in on things ... the bastard ...' FQ's boil was well and truly lanced. 'There was nothing I could do, nothing. He just wormed his way in under my nose and took him. He's so gullible, Noel, a real sucker for a pretty face ... What could I do? I just sat and watched it all happen ... the little runt. I'd like to kill him ...' Paddy let him run on. 'I was just passed over like an old heap of laundry ... Thank you, Mr Pettifer. Excuse me while I go back to the wardrobe department, Mr Pettifer. Me? Bitter, Mr Pettifer? Why thank you, Mr Pettifer, two thousand pounds to keep my mouth shut. I felt like something that's fallen off the back of a lorry driver.' The joke was bitter, this was the pus flooding out. 'Of course, Mr Pettifer. Well fuck him –who does he think I am? Nothing but a frock queen ... a brainless twit of a dresser.' Paddy listened to the age-old pain of an abandoned lover and silently begged him not to cry. Stay angry FQ. 'You just stay in the wardrobe, Frock Queen, where you belong and keep your mouth shut.'

There was a long pause. FQ's poison was all out.

'Why didn't you tell me?' Paddy asked gently.

'I couldn't,' FQ answered simply. 'I would have. I wanted to ... You don't know. I wish I had.' The truth of what he said was clear. 'And then after Heime passed away they threatened me – said they'd hurt me if I told you or the police or anyone about anything. So I didn't ... I was frightened ... so I thought, yes it was probably best to let sleeping dogs lie, and I've got a new friend anyway, at the moment ... I'm ever so sorry. I really am.'

'It's OK.'

'I mean, I know what you've been through and everything ... I've been so worried, and nervous, I'm no good at lying, I mean I was shaking like a jelly with that horrid policeman ... it's all so awful ...'

'It's OK, really.'

'I'd have done anything to save you, Paddy, but I daren't – I thought everything would be all right. I had no idea it would end up like this. I mean Noel is no crook – shady perhaps but not criminal. I tell you it's those fucking Goddards . . . Poor Hannah and poor you, your leg and the film and everything and that horrible Fergus Llewellyn. . .'

'It's OK.'

'He was a dear man, Heime,' said FQ showing compassion for the other loser in the love quadrangle. 'Is there anything I can do to help?'

'Er, I need a doctor. A very discreet doctor,' said Paddy, 'for my leg.'

FQ had the telephone number of an old alcoholic who fitted the bill perfectly, Doctor Ernest Tidmouth.

'Thanks,' said Paddy.

'You know, er . . .' FQ spoke quietly, 'I hope this doesn't mean . . . you won't hold it against me?'

'No, of course not.'

'You see . . . I wouldn't want you to think . . . I mean we're still OK aren't we? I respect you, Paddy, a great deal.' He would have said love but thought the word might cause alarm.

'Everything is going to be fine,' Paddy assured him. 'What are you working on?'

'The boring old Gala on Tuesday at the Regal – all starch and sequins and that dreary Fernando Cass. Give me a bit of drama any time.'

When they hung up FQ found his chilli had rather congealed but there was a load off his chest.

21 The doctor arrived sometime in the mid-afternoon. The whites of his eyes were the amber of a drinker and his breath spoke of a medic who had been buying, not doing, his rounds. Paddy's wound was superficial and clean apparently but Ernest Tidmouth recommended hospitalisation to check it out. 'There could be fragments of clothing caught in it.' Paddy assured him that he would go the next day, and was given a tetanus and a tranquilliser, a dressing for his thigh and a dressing down for his foolhardiness. The doctor left at last with a fist full of money for his discretion, two hundred pounds' worth of whisky vouchers.

Paddy lay in the alien bed at the top of this alien house overcome with a feeble depression. Thoughts rushed past him like the fragments of a dream, he was quite unable to grasp them. Again and again Hannah's face appeared before him crying for help that he was powerless to give. There she was tumbling through space or sinking in the quicksand and he could do nothing except lie trembling and sweating in the dark. 'I'm sorry, darling, I've let you down again.' The only reality for Paddy was the warm throb of his bullet hole.

Two lots of three rings. Hugo? Just in case, Jemma answered the telephone downstairs in a Cockney accent.

'Ullo. Who is it please?'

She had got rave reviews as a maid in a farce once – Hugo was unconvinced.

'Is that you, Jemma?'

She admitted it was.

'How's Paddy? Is he there?' he asked. Jemma saw no reason to keep the full story from him; he was, after all, their host. Hugo listened.

'Right,' he said. 'You just stay put there. I'll be home in about three hours and we'll sort things out. Everything is going to be OK.' Jemma was glad of his optimism. 'Tell Paddy I'm on my way to a private meeting with a man called Frank Hoffman, the producer of the *Life Sanction* films . . . could be interesting.' Hugo chuckled and they hung up. He really wasn't so bad, she thought, and they were in no position to be selective about their allies.

Jemma had spent the day nursing, shopping, arranging. They were under siege. Her house in Battersea was being watched and Dennis had decided to evacuate Kelly to an aunt in the country. Jemma found she had a flair for being a fugitive, it was like being snowed in away from school. With your best friend, but jolly scary.

Upstairs she found Paddy staring at the ceiling with the vacant look of a man in a coma.

'We've got to do something,' he said sipping the tea she had brought. He could scarcely believe that their salvation lay with Hugo Cavendish. Times were hard.

Like soldiers on the eve of battle, Paddy and Jemma were silent for a while and fell to staring at each other in the gloaming. They could work out what was to be done later; meanwhile they just looked at one another, on and on. Neither of them had the answers – even the question wasn't clear.

Jemma poured oil on his back and shoulders and her fingers ploughed softly up and down his spine. Paddy was flying free on valium. On his face, a faraway smile was half lost in the pillow. His flesh was yielding to her hands and his mind was not far behind.

For Jemma, too, the massage was therapeutic. With the skin of this man running through her fingers like silk, she felt safe and in control. In every part of her a persistent new desire was taking hold, unfamiliar and urgent. She knew that soon they would be lovers and everything would be all right. There would be no pressure, no faking, no more of her usual loneliness at being stranded in the hurly-burly. With Paddy there would be none of the fear of heights that always held her back.

The way sweet-natured people do, Jemma always blamed herself for this perennial missing of the boat. For the most part the pleasure she displayed in bed was a flattery from host to guest – an imitation of passion that she didn't quite believe in herself. With Paddy she could be real, he somehow already knew the secret of her.

For his part Paddy was in a whimsy state of tranquillised panic. Jemma's hands were making him giddy. The blood was hurrying in his veins to the rhythm of her movement. With every second the situation became simpler; he wanted her. The past and future were being rubbed out and now was all that counted. Take a chance he told himself. His impotence was flying out the window – the fear of falling on his sword was gone even if the cause was not.

Jemma took off her clothes, with the lovely calmness of someone losing control, and Paddy watched in the orange light from the street below. She looked like a ghost coming across the room.

They lay side by side to save Paddy's wound. They kissed for ever with their legs entwined and their eyes open. They felt each other's pulse and breathed each other's air. They stroked each other with trembling, gentle hands. The heat of her belly was irresistible. Sunrise in the desert as he entered her. They lay quite still clinging to each other at last. For a long time they neither moved nor hardly breathed like people waiting for an explosion. And the gods looked on frowning with anger.

If love is really gratitude for pleasure, they fell asleep later in each other's debt.

The Phantom of the Opera is the hottest ticket in town and the black market price of seats is horribly high. Not that it was the cost of the evening that dismayed Sir Toby, it was the sight of his guests sleeping soundly beside him. Fernando looked old and hewn in granite and Lewis like a rat. Jet lag and culture can be a soporific combination.

Having spent an ostentatiously busy day, Sir Toby and his nephew thoroughly enjoyed the show, it was noted, and clapped loudly at the end. Their alibi was set.

Smiling was not a habit of Frank Hoffman, rarely were his teeth ever exposed in felicity. Glimpses of them were readily available as they ravaged nut cutlets and the like, but seldom if ever were they seen in the traditional expression of happiness. Across the table Hugo Cavendish was unaware of the privilege but sensed that he had struck gold with his proposal.

The dour vegetarian had listened with the stillness of Buddha to the grubby journalist. He liked what he heard, he liked it a lot; there was something symmetrical and vicious about it which is why he smiled.

'I like it, Hugo, I like it,' Frank proclaimed. 'I'll do it. You know it's kind of . . .' He nearly risked the word ironical. 'Neat.'

'I thought you'd go for it,' said Hugo. He was drinking orange juice out of deference to his host. 'To neat,' he toasted.

'To neat,' Frank concurred. 'Say, what's in this for you?'

'Er, we all need exclusives from time to time and I owe a friend a favour,' Hugo answered.

'Right,' said Frank and he smiled again at the thought of how his old adversary, Bud Schwartz, would take this new manoeuvre. In their long game this would surely count as nothing less than checkmate.

'Great. Let's do it. I'll leave the details to you,' said Frank, for surely Hugo was to be trusted as a fellow Christian.

'My pleasure, Frank,' said Hugo sincerely. 'It'll be in the papers tomorrow.'

Driving home Hugo felt clever and happy (smug by any other name). He had outwitted the big bad world and found a brilliant silver lining to Paddy's cloud. But the news he heard on the car radio as he drove home soon changed all that.

In Hugo's kitchen the new lovers were drinking champagne. Paddy watched as Jemma fixed sardines on toast. Later and for ever Paddy would remember inch by inch the happiness he had woken up with, the foolish certainty that everything would be all right. The memory was held fast like the seconds before an accident.

The gods pick their moments well for the wiping of smiles from faces, especially from the faces of those who have reneged on deals.

The television by the fridge had not been demanding much of their attention; who needs the world news when you have just made love? Who cares about economic growth and bilateral *détente* when there's champagne and sardines in the offing? Then what was it that caught the ear? Or eye, was it? And made Jemma go cold and turn up the volume with a trembling hand.

'Police in Oxfordshire are anxious to question the actor Paddy Brummel following the discovery of his wife's body at their farmhouse near Thame. A police spokesman said this evening that there was some evidence of a struggle and they were setting up a murder enquiry. Mrs Hannah Brummel was apparently abducted from a nursing home near Hungerford yesterday evening, on the instructions of her husband. Here's a report from Joanne Arkley . . .'

There on the screen was Joanne Arkley standing outside Paddy's house underneath the magnolia tree. The courtyard behind her was busy with policemen and vehicles.

Paddy stood shaking in front of the television.

'This was the couple's dream home,' Ms Arkley was announcing grimly. 'Here in picturesque rural Oxfordshire they gave the appearance of being the couple who had everything going for them. Money, success, happiness. Then two years ago tragedy struck; their baby daughter, Camilla, died of the mysterious cot death . . .'

A black and white photograph of a couple who had everything going for them appeared on the screen. The man was smiling and the woman gazed at the baby in her arms . . . a christening.

'Since then, Mrs Brummel has spent most of her time in a nursing home suffering from acute depression.' A picture of the familiar Georgian sanatorium appeared, in colour this time with its cedars and gloom. 'According to Sister Wordsworth, the matron in charge, Paddy Brummel had turned up late last night behaving somewhat strangely and apparently denying his earlier instruction to release his wife. She is quoted as saying the actor seemed dazed and distracted.'

Jemma stood beside Paddy, tears were running down her face with sadness and disbelief. Paddy was dry-eyed.

'Recently,' continued the reporter under the magnolia buds, 'Paddy Brummel has had a number of disappointments with his career and yesterday on the *Fergus Llewellyn Show* he gave what a spokesman at Capitol TV described as a lack-lustre performance . . .'

Paddy was suddenly staring at himself on the screen. The yesterday and the today him, face to face. Was it really him standing dumbfounded in a strange kitchen in North London? Fergus Llewellyn was asking him about all the sadness of his life and the look on Paddy's face as he listened impassively reminded him of an old photograph of his mother.

'How did you come through all that, as a person?' the inquisitor asked.

'Yes,' Paddy had answered like a sleepwalker.

'Er . . . what?'

'I came through it as a person.' Paddy's answers looked silly now, not enigmatic at all.

Joanne Arkley went on. 'A police spokesman told me this afternoon that they were worried that Mr Brummel might himself have suffered some kind of breakdown.' Paddy could understand the concern. 'He has left no indication of his whereabouts and his damaged car was found abandoned not far from his home. The police believe he may be with the actress Jemma Culver . . .'

An old photograph of Jemma with long hair and no smile appeared briefly.

'Meanwhile the search for the missing actor continues. This is Joanne Arkley for *News at Ten* in Oxfordshire.'

The smell of burning sardines filled the air. For the gods, the reckoning was done; all square.

'You'd be crazy to hand yourself in. Crazy.' Hugo spoke urgently to the back of Paddy's head. 'The case against you is bound to be rock solid and you'd be powerless to dispute it. At the same time you have no evidence against the Goddards, not a shred. Matthew must have destroyed Heime's suicide letter and you also left him the Ansaphone tape.'

'He's right,' said Jemma, pale as skimmed milk.

'As for the fraud,' Hugo went on, 'the Transworld Telly business and all that, they will have had plenty of time to cover their tracks. We're up shit creek without a paddle.' He could offer no solution, no comfort, only platitudes and more whisky.

Paddy stared out over North London. In his mind Hannah's being dead and the process of her dying were separate aspects of the same event. The outrage and the sadness were old travelling companions but his wife's actual killing was something else.

It was two o'clock in the morning, just a day since he had seen Hannah's face at the window of Sir Toby's house in Sussex. Twenty-four hours since he had heard her frantic scream and run away. How many hours ago was it he wondered, since he had first met her ... quite a few. A collage of their times together spun through his head like the end credits of a short film.

The only picture of Hannah that Paddy could hold was the unblinking gaze of her vacant eyes. Where were the happy ones? They would not be summoned. So there she was racing away from him, free from the life she had not been living anyway. Her anguish was over. For a moment Paddy had a notion of his wife and his daughter being reunited; two angels in a blaze of sunlight, as Botticelli would have it. The shock of finding that he really wasn't sad almost made him cry. Perhaps his anguish was over too.

The matter of his wife's murder on the other hand, left Paddy feeling a coldness that was more than just an icy calm – he stared out over the empty streets and wondered what to do about it.

'We'll work something out,' Paddy said.

Since Hugo had arrived they had drunk much sweet tea and whisky and talked in circles with their eyes not meeting. Paddy had not dared to look at Jemma, had not wanted to explore how she might be feeling, but now quite suddenly her misery came winging through the air at him. Paddy turned and held her in his arms for a while, without speaking.

One of the few things Detective Inspector Robbins did really well at home was sleep. Never mind his mediocrity at gardening and DIY, in the sleeping field he was champion. And so it was that at three in the morning it took Shirley, his wife, a lot of shouting and even his corgi barking to rouse him. The drowsy policeman trotted to the hall telephone with mounting dread.

'Detective Inspector Robbins,' he announced as if on duty in his Viyella pyjamas.

'Paddy Brummel here,' came the reply.

Was it a joke? It wasn't a joke. Robbins swallowed hard and stood stupidly to attention. 'Hallo,' he said.

'Hallo,' said Paddy. 'I'm sorry to call you so late.'

'It's quite all right.'

'It's about my wife's death.'

'Ah ... yes ... I'm sorry ... Where are you?'

'Never mind ... I just wanted to tell you that I didn't kill her ...'

'I see ... er ...' The detective was distracted by his wife standing on the stairs listening for the bad news. 'Actually it's not my case ... the best thing is for you to make a statement.'

'That's what I'm doing,' said Paddy. 'I've decided not to hand myself in to the police for the moment. I am completely sane and quite harmless. OK? That's all.'

'Right.' This was most irregular.

'The case against me must look pretty convincing?' Paddy asked.

Harold's fellow officers would not believe a word of this in the morning. He cleared his throat, the downwardness of his face plumbed new depths. 'Er, yes. It does look fairly substantial,' he found himself saying. The evidence, in fact, looked overwhelming. 'How did you get my home number?' he asked.

'Never mind,' said Paddy. There was nobody Hugo could not reach. 'I wonder ... could you tell me ... how my wife died ... Please?'

Even as he spoke it, Harold knew that a phrase about proper procedure was a mistake. When Paddy shouted, 'Oh for God's sake,' he quickly relented.

'There was a minimal amount of bruising,' he said, 'for a strangulation.'

'Not much of a struggle then?'

'No. Not much.'

'Isn't that odd?' Paddy asked.

'Well ... this is unconfirmed as yet, but there is evidence that she was under pretty heavy sedation.'

'So it would have been quite quick.' Paddy clenched his teeth. He wanted to see Hannah's final moments as brief and unpanicked but knew it wasn't likely.

'Yes,' answered Robbins without conviction.

'Has it been established that she died at our house?'

'I couldn't say,' said Robbins. 'Look why don't you come in and have a chat with us, hm? Sort things out.'

'No thanks ... Well I'm sorry to disturb you. I'll be in touch before long. Don't worry, I'm not at all unhinged. Goodbye.'

'Goodbye.' Click.

Not for the first time the poor man kicked himself for not being quicker witted.

Shirley made them both a cup of tea. She looked horribly

old these days and smelled of sleep. To her, it was perfectly obvious and understandable that her heart-throb was innocent.

'Don't be so damned stupid, woman, people don't get "fitted up" in real life,' he told her, but as he tried to get back to sleep it struck him that the evidence against the actor did look suspiciously solid.

There was nothing about the well-muffled man limping home with his girlfriend to arouse suspicion in the night owls of Finsbury Park. Saturday night is a time when lovers and drunks can dawdle all they like, even in an icy wind.

Sleep was out of the question for Paddy, he had felt restless and enclosed. Shut up in a house was not his idea of being on the run. He had urgently wanted to be outside thinking and walking. Hugo had resisted the idea as dangerous even under cover of darkness, so Jemma had offered to accompany him. For safety's sake.

They walked in silence for a long time.

Paddy would rather have been on the Chilterns where he could let his thoughts go as far as they liked uninterrupted. In the rhythm of his stride he began to find comfort. The wind cut into his face; and his mind was sharp with new perception.

Where was the ferocious sorrow he had felt at his daughter's death? It wasn't there. Paddy wasn't feeling sorrow, and slowly it dawned on him that it was because the Hannah he loved had really died two years ago. The recent blank-eyed Hannah was just a relic; a ghost that had, at last, been laid. This wasn't the beginning of his mourning – it was the end.

Where was the fear he had expected? The good guys had joined forces with the bad guys against him. He was wanted for a murder that he couldn't disprove. Shouldn't he be in a panic? Calmly he sensed the answer was within his grasp. The only problem that preoccupied him was himself.

As he walked it became clearer and clearer to Paddy that he was not the victim of the circumstances round him. He was the cause of them. At the heart of this whole nightmare was his own blighted personality – his own bloody sang-froid. What right had he to go through life fouling things up with

198

his meanness of spirit? Was it possible that he had himself fallen prisoner to his own self-containment? Where had it all started?

The only child of a cold war marriage Paddy had quickly learnt the dangers of loving. Aloof and bookish at school, 'not a team boy, no house spirit'. He had been tagged a loner, but what he had felt was lonely. Friendship was ice too thin for Paddy to risk. Even as a young lover his appeal and his failing had always been a coldness.

Paddy reviewed himself with the distance of a stranger. It struck him as odd that only as an actor was he able to let himself go; why should he need the licence of being someone else to express emotion? Why couldn't he cry with misery, shout with rage, tremble with fear and laugh, too, like everybody else?

Normally Paddy avoided introspection, blamed his shortcomings on genetics or the fluke of his rising sign. 'I am what I am,' he had lied like the rest of us. But now he was beginning to see things differently. Was it such a big deal not saying what you felt?

Limping down Shoreditch he realised beyond doubt that all his defects were home-grown. The time had come to end his isolation – there was no purpose in it and he had no right to make an island of himself. The remedy was simple – all he had to do was speak; shape into words all the bogies in his head and tell them to his companion. It was that simple – once he had put his own house in order everything else would be all right.

'We had been filming in Kent, the garden of a stately house. Working late, 23 August, two years ago. Two and a half.' Paddy had not spoken for more than an hour, his lips felt brittle and unwilling. 'It had been very hot and dry. And suddenly we had this thunderstorm, a real downpour. It was the evening and we were waiting to do this scene in the garden. Not a difficult scene, quite short . . . and we were sitting in this summer house running the dialogue – a kind of pagoda; it was me and Meredith Hanbury, Meredith Hanbury.' Paddy repeated the name as though it was a special formula.

'A good actress. The rain was like a monsoon. And then afterwards as the light faded there was a smell of pine and moss and night-scented stock . . .' Jemma got the scent, if not the picture. She sensed that the memory that was being unfurled was somehow vital.

'And we started talking, not about the scene, about . . . God knows. Meredith just talked and she seemed extraordinarily happy. I mean, I hardly knew her but I could see this happiness about her. Not just a flash of it because of the rain, or the film, or whatever but something overall – she was generally content. Lightheaded or lighthearted, I don't know.' In silence they both wondered what these symptoms were.

Flurries of takeaway litter raced past them in the empty streets, and gathered round shop doorways. Piles of black plastic bags gleamed in the shadows like a Zulu ambush. Jemma was almost too cold to speak and anyway it was better not to.

'Anyway we eventually did the scene . . . strolling through this garden together. It was quite good . . . gentle. Twilight and a sort of faint mist coming off the lawn, you know the kind of thing.' Jemma had seen it. In what now felt like a previous lifetime she had watched the pair of them ambling along the gravel paths. A very good scene.

Paddy went on: 'Hannah was still breastfeeding Camilla at the time. Pretty well non-stop. I loved watching the two of them dozing and sucking – always to music, Mendelssohn mostly. And in the afternoons rocking together in the hammock. In the middle of the night, at dawn . . .'

Paddy's breath was fleetingly orange in the street light. They were lost, a long way from home, 'Sometimes I used the flat, just to get some sleep when I was working late or early . . . Anyway we had finished this scene and Meredith needed a lift back to London. I said was she hungry . . . and we went to Pomegranates. There was no reason to drink champagne . . . and it was soon obvious that we were going to go to bed together – I mean, she was very attractive . . . calm and wicked and carefree and she had this happiness about her.'

Paddy spoke his words flatly so that they barely sketched the story he was telling. Jemma was suddenly sick of being saintly and wanted to protest but kept her silence. On and on they walked.

'I didn't see it as being unfaithful – it was nothing to do with Hannah, it was just an adventure a . . . nothing important, just spontaneous and harmless . . .' Paddy's mitigating circumstances were cutting no ice with either of them. He had nothing new to say on the way in which ships manage to pass in the night. This was an explanation – not an apology. Not to Jemma anyway.

'So we drank more champagne,' Paddy continued, 'and we were sort of laughing the way you do. And we went back to the flat. It was a hot night – airless and humid – and in the middle of fucking her, right in the middle, Hannah walked in.' The shock of telling it stopped Paddy in his tracks as it had before. His eyes were focused inwards on the replay in his head. He stood still staring at the pavement, or was it his wife?

'Suddenly all the lights were on. She had let herself in and she was just standing there in the doorway . . . Poor Hannah. She was wearing a bleached kind of pinafore with an old coat of mine over her shoulders. She looked so pale, awfully pale, white almost, like her dress and her hair was . . . uncombed. She just stood there. None of us spoke or even moved. We had nothing on . . . we were uncovered because of the heat and . . . it was awful. Awful. Then I noticed that she had something in her hand . . . Camilla's yellow crocheted shawl and I knew. I knew. And she looked right at me and she said, "I just came to tell you that your daughter is dead. Camilla died in her sleep."'

Paddy seemed out of breath like a man who has run up a hill. His face had the look of a dumbfounded spectator. 'I was just lying there all naked with Meredith beside me. I couldn't speak. And then Hannah said, 'I never want to see you again,' and she left. I heard the door slam. The police from Thame had brought her with a nurse, she hadn't wanted to tell me on the telephone you see. And that was the last time I saw her as she properly was; properly alive. She's been pretty well dead since then really . . . So I've felt all those things . . . guilt and misery and . . . whatever for quite some time, do you see?'

Two sympathies vied in Jemma's head. One for the demented mother and one for the demented father. She couldn't arbitrate, didn't they both deserve her pity for having been party to such horror. She said nothing. She just put her arms around him and held him against her, implacable as a corpse. Paddy was staring ahead of him at the beginning of dawn – a blurred pink through his tears.

22 What with no fog, fresh orange juice and a perfect shower this was altogether not the England of Fernando's worst fears. In fact the Savoy breakfast, the shining of the sun and the gliding of the river at its own sweet will all served to put the superstar in a good mood.

From the Sunday papers strewn about his dining-room Fernando got the impression that he was, for the moment, topical. There were plenty of photographs of him and interviews, even in the grown-up papers. Also two news items with which his name was linked.

The lesser story was only a paragraph with the headline 'Sanction Sale'. Fernando was puzzled more than alarmed to read that the peevish Frank Hoffman had sold his controlling interest in the *Life Sanction* movies to an undisclosed buyer. Bud Schwartz would have the answers. Meanwhile he put it down as a face-saving manoeuvre from his old employer.

The tabloid headlines were mostly concerned with the story of the hunt for Paddy Brummel who had apparently murdered his wife. One of the reasons for this tragedy it seemed was the distressed state of the actor's mind. This was due in part, they surmised, to the fact that he had been sacked from his beloved project, *Stratagems and Spoils* and replaced by the American superstar, Fernando Cass.

By an amazing happenstance, the *Sunday Globe* was able to boast that on its centre pages it was carrying an in-depth interview with the wanted actor conducted by their own number one reporter Hugo Cavendish.

Under the headline, 'The Tragedy of Paddy's Personal Inheritance', Fernando found himself staring at a life-size portrait of his English adversary. It was not the mean, aggressive face he had expected; worse still it was younger and better looking than he had imagined. The picture looked unposed and showed a man not given to vanity or deceit. Blonde and saturnine, there was about him a lack of pretension, a world-weariness that gave an impression of candour and even warmth. Fernando regretted seeing it, he disliked his rival better without a face.

More still did he regret reading Hugo Cavendish's article.

The last thing Fernando wanted to feel for Mr Brummel was sympathy, but here was the story of a simple, private, literary man, like himself, whose talent as an actor dwarfed the work he did. A man whose success had been a two-edged sword denying him the chance to fly, a man who believed unfalteringly in his current commitment to *Stratagems and Spoils*.

Swallowing hard Cass read the details of all the misfortune that Paddy's company, Fledgling, had suffered at the hands of Capitol TV. Sir Toby Goddard, it was clear between the lines, had been, at best, heavy-handed in his management of Lefrak's take-over.

As if these professional problems were not enough, Hugo's article went on to reveal the shock and misery of Paddy's family bereavement. In touching terms the journalist described the anguish of cot-deaths and invited readers to support the charity that was seeking to eradicate the mystery of it.

Before leaving the hotel Fernando arranged for a cheque for $5000 to be sent to The Foundation for the Study of Infant Deaths, 15 Belgrave Square, London, SW1. He had, after all, a kind spot in his heart and an infallible instinct for PR: GENEROUS CASS SENDS HUNTED RIVAL A BONUS FOR CHARITY.

Paddy and Jemma had slept the deep sleep of people whose minds welcome the escape from consciousness and whose feet have spent the night walking the London streets. No dreams infested Paddy's sleep; he was spared that mischievous rewinding of the clock that can beguile the newly bereaved. Through the fog of waking, all the news of the day before was quick to stalk him down and reinhabit his mind. It took Paddy some time to muster the courage to get up and go downstairs.

In the kitchen Jemma was writing in a note-pad. The table was strewn with all the Sunday papers and from every angle photographs of Paddy were smiling and frowning back at him. They greeted each other formally, these fellow fugitives, in the cold light of day. Neither of them were quite sure of the new ground they were on.

'How are you?' asked Paddy.

'Fine,' Jemma answered. She looked grey and listless. 'How's your leg?'

'Fine,' Paddy answered. He, too, looked grey. 'Hugo's gone out. He'll be back this afternoon. Read that.' Jemma passed Paddy a copy of the *Globe* folded open at the headline 'The Tragedy of Paddy's Personal Inheritance'.

Paddy would have preferred not to read it but there was an element of command in Jemma's tone. The *Globe* had, after all, paid him a fortune to print the story; the least he could do was look it over.

Reluctantly Paddy began to read the dismal account of his own life. Hugo's prose was surprisingly subdued, and yet again Paddy found he had underestimated his host and benefactor. The facts and the quotes he used were all accurate and the sentiment was minimal. All in all this was not the sensational sob-and-tell saga that Paddy had dreaded.

On the subject of Camilla's sudden death, Hugo wrote with a touching simplicity and compassion, and appealed for funds to unravel the mystery of cot-deaths. It was the final paragraph of the article that took Paddy's breath away.

'"I don't mind talking about Camilla's death," Paddy told me in conclusion. "Because I know that between us; you with your finest prose and me with whatever eloquence could not grasp one small fraction of 1 per cent of what it is like to hold your dead baby in your arms." Paddy Brummel is the father of Camilla Elizabeth who is just one of the 1,200 babies who die each year and I am the father of Joshua Michael who was another. I have to say Paddy is right, neither him with his eloquence nor me with my finest prose can begin to describe how it feels.'

There was no reason for Paddy to blame himself for not having liked Hugo, for not having recognised this common bond, but he did. Lately he had lost confidence in his judgement of people and nothing surprised him. Friends and foes were becoming interchangeable. Form an opinion of someone and then reverse it, was his new maxim. Paddy drank his coffee in silence for some time.

'Well,' he said eventually, 'what's to do?' They weren't holiday-makers planning an excursion.

All the vitality was gone from Jemma's face – the enormity of their predicament had sunk in overnight. She doodled with some spilled muesli on the table, not looking at him.

'I think I must go,' she said. 'I can't see that I'm any use to you here. I'm going to the police.'

'What?'

'I think the expression is . . . giving myself up. It won't affect you. I won't tell them anything . . . where you are or anything.'

'It's OK.' It was like a gentle thud in the solar plexus.

'There's my mother, you see, and . . . Kelly.'

'Of course.'

'I'm sorry.'

'It's OK.' Paddy was suddenly appalled at the selfish way in which he had conscripted Jemma into his nightmare. What she had said made sense, it just took him unawares. He lent across and touched her face; he wanted to say sorry, and thank you, and don't go. 'It's the best thing to do,' he said.

'I'm not very good at being on the run. I'm sorry.'

'It's OK,' repeated Paddy. In all the newspapers there was evidence to the contrary. 'It's OK,' he grinned. 'All I need is a day and I'll be with you. Perhaps they'll give us adjoining cells.'

An hour later, in dark glasses and a scarf she was gone. They had said goodbye in the bedroom the way lovers do with the tender brutality that is intended to be indelible.

From the window Paddy watched her walk down the street. His debt to her was beyond repayment, she had uncrippled his body and unlocked his mind. And what had he done for her? Nothing that he knew of, until he read the letter she had been writing on the note-pad at the kitchen table.

With caffeine and Jemma's letter revving up his brain Paddy paced about the house. There was no point in remaining at large if he couldn't put the time to good use. What was he to do? The solution was out of view but within reach. Whatever it was he was impatient for it.

The evidence against him was solid, Detective Inspector Robbins had confirmed that, and if it wasn't why else would the Goddards risk their safety. He was guilty until proved otherwise . . . Prove otherwise. Come on . . . How? Think. Think. Think. Concentrate.

'I am innocent. I am innocent,' Paddy said out loud. Prove it. Think laterally. Turn the problem on its head . . . if you're not guilty, someone else is. Don't defend – attack. Prove someone else guilty.

What evidence would there be available to him, Paddy wondered, evidence that would point the finger squarely at the enemy. He was not in a good position for freelance sleuthing. What chance did he have of finding any of the time-honoured clues; the fingerprint, the forensic chance in a million, the blotting paper, the ashes of a note in the grate ... ?

On the lunchtime news it was announced that Jemma Culver had given herself up to the police. Apparently she had no idea where Paddy was. (He was staring at her photograph on the screen longing to be with her.) A spokesman for the police was saying, 'Miss Culver is helping us with our enquiries.' Not a lot, he hoped.

With renewed urgency Paddy roamed the house searching his mind for the answer and longing for nightfall so he could go outside again.

For sure the Goddards and Noel Pettifer must have destroyed any evidence against them. What was there then? What had Heime said on the tape? 'The official letter which I've written gives a full explanation with what should be enough detail to ensure retribution ... or revenge rather ...' What had Matthew done with the lethal document? Where was it now? Eradicated of course, but how? In the dustbin, down the loo, in the grate ... burnt, shredded ... Where? At Heime's flat? In the street? At Matthew's? What would it look like, this vital letter? Imagine it. Concentrate. Paddy was quivering on the brink of a chasm ... See Heime's letter. See it ... Now he was falling freely ... See the letter. He was getting close. Imagine Heime's writing. See his handwriting. POW ... Paddy landed on his feet ... Heime's handwriting . . .

At last Paddy had a tip, an outside chance to put his money on. Long odds.

With snooker on his TV screen and a huge gin in his hand Hugo found the worries of the day receding. He didn't hear the Porsche pull up outside his house. The cue ball oozed across the baize and nudged the pink into a pocket, just so.

The doorbell rang.

Hugo started. It couldn't be Paddy back so soon and wasn't he going to ring anyway from his destination? A nest of reds exploded around the table.

Putting his eye to the spy-hole Hugo felt the vanished tension quickly flowing back. Horrid to see was a fish-eye view of Matthew Goddard chewing gum; he was flanked by two beefy-looking profiles. The door bell rang again. Matthew was chewing with alarming vigour. Hugo couldn't move. Level with his crotch the flap of the letter-box flew up.

'Is that you, Hugo Cavendish? Open the fucking door.'

'No.' His genitals weren't used to being spoken to like that.

'Open the fucking door or we'll smash in the window.'

Hugo thought for a moment. Then with trembling hands he opened the fucking door. The unfriendly two surged in. Their search of the house was uncouth and without method.

'What do you want?' Hugo asked.

'That was a nice piece in the paper today . . . about Paddy Brummel.' Uninvited Matthew was pouring vodka into three tumblers. He had read the touching biography in the *Sunday Globe* and taken an outside bet on the bond between the bereaved fathers. The two henchmen seemed awkward, undecided on their status – were they guests or intruders? One was black with narrow eyes, the other white with eyes like fruit bulging from their sockets. They stood either end of the sofa as still as opposing chess pieces. Pawns.

'Yes. Good. I'm glad you liked it,' answered Hugo; his eyes scanned the room for tell-tale signs of Paddy. On the television the black ricocheted off three cushions and missed its goal.

'Where is Paddy Brummel?'

'I don't know.'

'You do.'

'I don't.'

'You do.'

'He's not here.'

Hugo felt the supersonic explosion of pain in his groin before Matthew's foot left the ground. He was lifted in the air by the impact and fell to the floor dizzy and disbelieving of the pain reaching through his body, its range and depth and ferocity. Through clenched teeth Hugo shouted illiterate obscenities.

Matthew's face was suddenly close to him on the floor. 'Where is Paddy?' he whispered urgently like a lover. His breath was warm with garlic and white wine.

'I don't know.'

'Tell me where he is?' Matthew's eyes were the cold blue of a Persian cat.

'I can't,' said Hugo. His whole carcass was full of molten lava from the earthquake in his crotch. The throb of it was crashing in his ears and flooding his mind. 'Mustn't tell, mustn't tell,' he told himself. Over Matthew's shoulder the two other faces were feasting on his agony. 'Fuck off,' he screamed.

At once his face stung with new pain as Matthew's hand smacked into his cheek. Left. Right. Left. Right. Forehand. Backhand. Matthew had straddled him and was shouting, 'Tell me. Tell me. Tell me,' like a child in a tantrum.

The small pebbles in Hugo's mouth were the capped teeth that had cost him so much. The pain was still claiming new territory as it funnelled up through his body; there was warm blood filling up his throat and nostrils and crimson stars speckled his vision. In a state of giddy unawareness it seemed to Hugo that his testicles were bleeding in his mouth.

For a moment Hugo heard the gentle collision of billiard balls from the game he had been watching a million years ago.

'Tell me where Paddy is you stupid little man,' screeched Matthew.

'No, I won't, you fucking bastard.'

Hugo was punch drunk and longing for the oblivion that was on its way. The last thing he remembered was Matthew's hand grasping him by the hair and yanking up his head. For a moment he caught the steel in Matthew's eyes and smelt the garlic on his breath and wondered what was going to happen next. Wasn't it nearly over, please? Yes, yes, his head was being thrust backwards, racing through space with his mind trailing behind. He expected to hear the thud on his pine floorboards but he didn't. Blackout. Snookered.

23 Fumbling with imaginary keys Paddy had slipped past a leaving inmate of Heime's apartment block. He had taken the lift to the fourth floor and was now standing at his old friend's front door.

In films the ease with which a monkey wrench breaches a solid door had often worried Paddy. Not so now, in the quietness of that corridor, he was glad of it. The locks and wood yielded eagerly and in a moment he was inside leaning against the other side of the door.

Paddy stood stock still in the silence, the silence of a crematorium. His nose was full of nostalgia in the darkness. Lavender and french polish brought back Heime to a T. If it hadn't been for his racing pulse this might have been the moment for a spot of mourning, but his eyes, like his mouth, were dry.

Whether or not the drinks tray was subject to probate, with gloved hands Paddy poured himself a vodka and toasted his absent friend before settling at the desk.

Inanimate electrical things had a history of showing passive resistance to Paddy. Like sullen sales girls they rendered their services to him with unmasked reluctance. Heime's Amstrad word processor was going to be uphill work . . . Power On, dumbo.

Under the dim light Paddy scrolled back and forth without a proper system to his search. The green glow of the screen threw up all manner of memory – scripts, letters, accounts, memos, travel plans . . . under what heading would a methodical man file his suicide note? On what floppy disk would Paddy find the vital letter?

Paddy was too tense for proper concentration, and computers, even more than sales girls, balk at impatience or the cutting of corners. With mounting frustration he found himself retreading his earlier tracks . . . come on, come on.

The telephone rang, the sound of an injured creature that startled Paddy in his work. He didn't move. Three rings and then it stopped. Paddy waited for the count of twelve. It rang again and stopped.

'Yes,' he said the next time round.

'It's me.' Only just, it was Hugo. His voice was hoarse and distant.

'Are you OK?' Of course he wasn't.

'They came ...'

'Who?' Paddy didn't want to hear the answer.

'Matthew ... and two friends ...'

'Christ.'

'One black. One white.'

'Frog eyes?'

'Yeah ... they ... they ...'

'What did you tell them?' Paddy's concern was blatantly selfish.

'Nothing ... but the diagrams I drew on how to work the Amstrad have gone ... from the kitchen table.'

'Christ.'

'They must be on their way ... if they've got any brains ...'

'Since when?' Paddy's pulse rate was back in overdrive.

'I don't know.' Hugo sounded on the verge of sleep.

'What did they do to you?' Paddy asked. 'Did they hurt you?'

'A bit.' Hugo whispered like a hero.

'Bastards.'

'Balls ...'

'That's the spirit,' said Paddy.

'Paddy ... just get the hell out of there ... those men are horrid.' Hugo put down the telephone and sank back to the kitchen floor ... 'It is a far better thing I have just done.' His face was turning crisp with blood and he was dizzy with the pain, so much so that oblivion became elusive.

With no idea what length of grace he had, Paddy had no doubt that time was against him. His trembling hands pocketed the floppy disks and filled a plastic bag with other items pilfered from around the flat. To any underdog in the game of cat and mouse, leaving by the door you entered can be a cardinal error. He bolted the front door from inside as best he could and climbed quietly out of the window on to the fire escape.

Just in time. For the second time that night the front door of the late Heime Chadwick was opened without benefit of key. Just as Paddy had done an hour earlier Matthew now stood with a wrench in his hand, alone, stock still in the dark, and let the place revisit him. With an old familiarity he felt for the light switch and cursed when it failed him. The mouse had thought to turn the power off at the mains leaving this cat in the dark. Striking book matches Matthew found a torch, and by its light discovered that the flat was empty. The Amstrad was still warm and the floppy disks were missing. Paddy had gone and taken with him the proof he needed.

For years Matthew had cultivated his cool; its importance reached back to the high-chair. His laid-back charm was so finely honed that it was second nature to him. But now standing in his ex-lover's study the vicious rage of his first nature was reborn, gone was his easy-goingness. He growled with anger and frustration and his right arm still holding the lethal jemmy soared through the air and crashed into the blameless word processor. The micro-wizardry crumbled like melba toast. Not so user-friendly. 'I'll kill him. I'll kill the bastard. I'll kill him. I'll kill him.'

He stood quivering with indecision for a moment and then with the speed of furious inspiration Matthew connected the draught on his legs with the kitchen window and the fire escape . . . and he was there. The night air was dangerous in his nose. Out there was the mouse he was going to kill. 'Paddy Brummel,' he challenged the darkness with the name and it came back dully unanswered.

Without a backward glance Matthew swung himself out on to the metal rungs to the left of the window. Agile with adrenalin he climbed quickly downwards still clutching the terrible wrench.

What small sound was it or perhaps instinct that stopped Matthew in his tracks, made him look up and see Paddy above. Ten rungs separated them. Matthew felt stupid at being outwitted by such an elementary trick. Had he paused to think he might have realised that by retreating he could have met his enemy on level ground. The front of the building was covered, Paddy would have been trapped; but Matthew did not pause to think, he advanced.

'For Christ's sake, Paddy, give me those fucking disks,' he snarled.

'No,' Paddy answered. Three rungs between them now. A lot of anger too.

A fleeting glint of metal in the darkness was followed by a mighty clang as the wrench hit the ladder between Paddy's feet. A near thing. He retreated upwards.

Matthew advanced and swung again at Paddy's legs.

Another miss, another clash of wrench on rung and Paddy withdrew again. They were still three floors up.

In the madness of the moment Paddy valued the evidence in his pocket above his life. Almost. How, he wondered, could he preserve the vital floppy disks from the murderer beneath him? By preserving himself.

Again the jemmy arced through the air. Again it missed. Again the dull clank rang out. This time Paddy stamped his foot on to the evil hook as it made contact with the metal. With his weapon trapped Matthew was powerless. 'Fuck you,' he said between clenched teeth. He glared furiously up at Paddy. 'Give me those disks.' His need for them was obvious. In his pocket he had the tape recording of Heime's final words but in his head he held the memory of the final letter itself. The vitriolic suicide note was still vivid in Matthew's mind as was the sadness on the face of his dead friend nearby. 'For God's sake, Paddy, give me the disk,' he asked more simply. He had destroyed the letter of course, had thoroughly cremated the evidence against him and was now desperate to do likewise with the possibility of its reincarnation. He had been foolish to overlook the retentive capability of the word processor.

From his superior position ten feet above Paddy studied his young partner. In the light of what he now knew Matthew's charm seemed so evidently transparent. What, he asked himself, had blinded him to the true nature of the boy? Why had he not seen him for what he was: a greedy, vicious, scheming opportunist. Had he really not seen a flaw in his hail-fellow-well-met veneer? Had he not had an uneasy suspicion about his true sexuality? Paddy pondered his adversary.

'Ganymede,' he said at last. He spoke it as an accusation and Matthew shifted his gaze and saw the ground a long way beneath him. In the pale light his hair was the colour of a raven.

'Oh, Paddy ... I can explain,' he said. 'Why not come inside?'

'No,' Paddy answered without hesitating. His foot still held the jemmy immobile. For an instant Paddy was Peter Pan victorious with Captain Hook's evil hand trapped on the gunwale.

'For Christ's sake.' There was something worse than the fear of crocodiles in Matthew's voice.

'No.' The rungs were ice-cold in Paddy's hands. Yet again he found himself unready for the situation. In no way had he prepared himself for a moment of reckoning. If he had it certainly would not have been like this – he preferred his confrontations horizontal, not vertical. Either way, he supposed this was it – the show-down.

'What is it you want, Paddy? What are you after?' Matthew asked in the tone of a doctor.

It was a telling question and Paddy gave it some thought. 'I want . . .' he was going to say justice but honesty got the better of him. 'Revenge,' he said.

'For what?'

'For Hannah . . . for Heime . . . for Conran . . . for me. I want to see you rot in hell.'

'And what fucking good will it do?'

'None.'

'Let's talk. Let's do a deal.'

'No.'

There they were trapped together between the pavement and the sky. The pause between them was a hostile stalemate.

'You killed Hannah, didn't you?' Paddy knew for certain even as he asked.

Matthew did not answer. He could do nothing to staunch the unwelcome memories of the event. The pictures in his head were a hideous kaleidoscope. There was a man strangling a woman, the woman at first comatose and then frantic as she realised what was happening to her. Her body was writhing and her face was startled as though she had glimpsed death and didn't want it. He saw the man too, relentlessly gripping at her neck. He was frenzied and breathless and quite beyond the point of no return. This picture was less clear, blurred in fact, as he refused to allow himself to be part of it.

'You strangled my wife.' Paddy repeated the accusation.

'That's not the way the police see it,' Matthew answered.

'Maybe. But I'll prove it was you.'

'Not if you're dead.'

'I don't care. You killed her.' Paddy was shouting. 'Didn't you?' The question echoed into the darkness as they stared at each other in silent hatred.

'She was half dead already for God's sake. Half dead. A

213

fucking vegetable, you know that.' Matthew's voice was slow and vicious. 'You know that, don't you Paddy, because it was your fault. It was you who sent her crazy wasn't it? It was you. It was you not the death of your precious baby that drove her barmy ...'

Paddy was speechless. Behind Matthew the ground was getting closer. It wasn't only vertigo that was making Paddy giddy and sick.

'I know all about you. The Holier-Than-Fucking-Thou Brummel.' Matthew went on, sensing his advantage. 'Caught with your pants down weren't you? Eh? Screwing a bit on the side weren't you? A scrubber. That's what did it. She caught you, didn't she?'

Behind Matthew the ground was receding. Paddy tasted a sweet acid in his throat.

'You bastard,' was all he could say.

'Oh yes. We all saw the poor grief-stricken Paddy Brummel.' Matthew had no mercy in him. 'The darling of the goggle-box who revelled in the nation's sympathy ... Poor Paddy. His daughter dead and his wife demented with her psychotic depression ... Poor Paddy. Poor stupid, drunken Paddy with his obsession about his stupid fucking film. Paddy Brummel the has-been who can't get it up any more ... who can't even fuck women nowadays ...'

'You bastard,' Paddy roared. He was shaking with terror and cold and sorrow.

Suddenly from beneath his foot Matthew pulled the jemmy free. For an instant it gleamed in the night air before it struck the ladder between Paddy's legs. The vibration of it stung their hands as they gripped the metal for dear life. Paddy retreated upwards. Matthew followed.

Holding the rung at his waist level with both hands Paddy waited for another strike from below. Again it missed but as it struck Paddy let himself drop to arm's length. The jolt was electric as his shoulders took the impact of his weight. He kicked out wildly, made contact, heard a grunt and then an instant later the welcome sound of the jemmy hitting the ground below.

Matthew's hands were suddenly clutching at Paddy's ankles, pulling him, imploring him to the ground. His arms were giving in, his fingers too. His head was spinning. Hold on. His feet fought loose and flayed the air like a frantic

214

swimmer searching for a footing. At last he found a rung. Paddy clung to the ladder like a boa constrictor.

'You bastard,' Matthew rasped from far too near. 'You fucking shit.'

Paddy had no breath for vitriol; scarcely enough for living. He looked down between his feet. Matthew was holding on with one hand while from his pocket he was struggling to produce something; something small and black like coal. A revolver.

With any less hate in him Paddy might have hesitated but spontaneously he raised his foot and stamped with all his might on the knuckles of the man below.

As the heel of Paddy's shoe shattered his left hand Matthew knew somehow that he was near death. It is not simply for those who are awaiting him that the grim reaper appears unmistakable at the door. Somehow Matthew's grip had gone. Somehow the fingers of his right hand were locked in the trigger-guard of the revolver which, in turn, was somehow caught up in the threshold of his pocket. A split second would have saved him but there's no suspending gravity. Paddy had somehow timed it right.

Matthew knew nothing more than a rush of cold air. With the speed of dreams the sky was zooming away from him. And somehow he was dead.

From Paddy's bird's-eye view the fumbling and the teetering and the fall itself looked slow and absurd. As the pavement raced up behind him the look on Matthew's face was one of tired amazement. His soft exclamation was one of disappointment more than horror. Only in his blue, blue eyes was there a faint query, as though his life was just so much unfinished business.

Not any sound-track of any special effect by any stunt man in any film ever captured for Paddy the true noise of a man landing on concrete from three floors up. The real thing was a crunching splat that made Paddy feel sick.

Oh so slowly, for his limbs were liquid, Paddy climbed on down the ladder. There was about his armpits the smell of crushed dandelions as he hung at full length from the final rung. He dropped to the ground and stumbled against some dustbins. In the dimmest light Paddy leant against the wall, trembling and retching and not daring to look.

Five feet from him was the body of his late partner. Paddy

approached it with the delicate steps of someone on ice. Never had he seen Matthew so still before. Later he wished to God that he had had the stamina to close the unfocused eyes of this man who had been his friend. As it was he had trouble removing the revolver from reluctant fingers.

For a moment Paddy looked down at the fractured pile of skin and bone with a hollow feeling of waste. Whatever Matthew had made of his life he had been a new-born baby once. He told himself this was no time for sentimental reflection. It's not often the mouse kills the cat. Somewhere near at hand Thyroidal and his friends would be lurking. With what stealth he could manage Paddy limped round to the front of the block. And there sure enough, across the road was a huge dark shape leaning against Hugo's Volkswagen that was to have been Paddy's getaway car.

The night was cold but dry as Paddy set off on foot for God knew where, north maybe. To allay suspicion he assumed the gait of a man who has missed his last bus home from the pub. It was not one of his better performances but there wasn't much of an audience.

Paddy's options were limited. He could not return to Hugo's house, Goddard's henchmen would be on duty there and at Jemma's the police were sure to be on surveillance. After due thought Paddy changed direction and began to walk south. 'I've made another plan, Dad.'

Jemma was in the deepest of sleeps, dreamless and timeless like a short-term death. She had taken two pills to send her there. After four hours with the police she was a tired but innocent murderer's moll. She had repeatedly assured them that Paddy would soon be turning himself in and they had repeatedly assured her that his help with their enquiries would be much appreciated. As interrogation it had gone gently round in circles.

The ringing of her telephone was incomprehensible in the depth of her sleep and Jemma's hand had picked up the receiver before her brain knew what was happening.

'It's me,' Paddy announced. 'Don't say anything, please, I've got to see you. It's important.' Jemma's brain was surfacing fast. 'Are you listening?'

'Yes,' she answered. Paddy gave her no chance to warn him that her phone was tapped, and her house watched.

'In the King's Road just before you get to the Duke of York's Barracks, almost opposite Peter Jones, there are four telephone boxes. I'll call you in the left-hand one in twenty minutes OK?'

'OK but . . .'

'Bring the usual.' Paddy was gone.

For a moment Jemma wavered. The plan was doomed, she knew that, but perhaps it was time this crazy course of events was concluded one way or another. She was dressed and ready to go in five minutes. Her car was parked round the back of the block. Without turning on the hall lights she let herself out the front door.

For the benefit of the two unmarked policemen in their plain clothes car she affected to saunter off down the street. Whoever went for a saunter at three o'clock on a cold March morning? The actress in her was walking an invisible dog. The faithful Morris was none the worse for its fine-tooth combing from the forensic department, they had done their best to leave the piles of mess on the back seat as they had found it. Bless them.

Jemma had gone less than a mile when she realised she was being followed. How could she have imagined otherwise? It didn't matter; receiving a telephone call is not a spectator sport. They kept their distance for the short drive over the river to Sloane Square.

The two unremarkable cars pulled up ten feet apart on the double yellow lines at the top of the King's Road. Jemma had three minutes to spare. The whole area was probably crawling with undercover people and devices but Jemma supposed they would not have had time to install bugging or tracing equipment. Apart from being nervous she was curious to know what Paddy had to tell her. Something urgent and practical.

Jemma got out of her car. So did the two policemen. They greeted each other cordially like neighbours in a bus queue.

'You obviously know why I'm here,' said Jemma.

'Yes,' said Detective Sergeant Protheroe modestly. 'Yes we do. And my superiors have told me, Miss Culver, to ask you to urge Mr Brummel to give himself up. If he's not guilty he has nothing to fear . . . we'll soon sort it out, eh?' All three of them were rubbing their hands with cold and awkwardness.

'I'll tell him,' said Jemma. In her coat pocket was the bottle of vodka as requested. What was she to do with it? Pour it down the receiver? She wandered towards the appointed booth. And there stuck on the wall above the telephone box was a folded bit of paper addressed to Jemma. It read: 'Too risky, changed my mind, sorry. Go home. Love Paddy. PS Please marry me.'

'Very romantic, I should say,' said Protheroe foolishly. What HQ would make of it was another matter. The whole excursion was a waste of time it seemed, and they were quick to bid each other goodnight. They returned in convoy to Battersea.

As she headed back across the Albert Bridge Jemma was relieved that Paddy had aborted the enterprise. She was puzzled, too, at how he had managed to leave his billet-doux. Or was it a billet-don't?

'Jemma, it's me, Paddy,' a voice whispered.

Jemma slammed on the brakes. 'Paddy?'

'Drive on. Drive on. Are they behind you, the police?'

They were, closer than ever. Jemma drove on speechless with surprise and horror and delight. 'How the hell . . .'

'You should learn to fasten your side windows,' Paddy was speaking from somewhere behind the handbrake. 'Christ, I'm uncomfortable, sorry about all that wild goose chase. I had to talk to you. Also give you something.'

Jemma slipped her left hand behind the driver's seat and held Paddy's briefly.

'Did you bring the vodka?' he asked from beneath the pile of coats and rugs. 'You're marvellous. Thanks,' he said when she passed it to him.

It was a short distance to Jemma's house and the roads were clear. Paddy had no time to be anything but succinct in his explanation; so much so that Matthew's death sounded almost incidental. The crucial thing was the floppy information that might or might not put the culpability of things where it belonged.

'The discs are here on the back seat OK?' said Paddy. 'Hugo will know what to do with them. I'll call you later, around midday, for news, all right?'

'OK.' Jemma was used to her role of second-in-command. These adventures that Paddy summoned her to in the night were becoming commonplace. They were nearly at her home.

'Park round the back again, or I'll never be able to get away,' Paddy said.

218

'Where are you going to?' Jemma enquired.

'I don't know. I'll let you know somehow . . . send my love to Kelly. And thanks.'

The police watched Jemma park in the exact space she had left twenty minutes earlier. Before locking her door she leant back in the car to retrieve her handbag. 'What was that PS on your note supposed to mean?'

'It was by way of being a proposal,' said the pile of jumble. 'Will you marry me?'

'I should think so,' she answered, 'anything for a quiet night's sleep.' So saying Jemma locked her fiancé in the Morris and left.

Fernando Cass passed the night in much more comfort than his British rival. The blonde actress he had taken to bed with him had whispered that most popular of all post-coital questions, 'Can you call me a taxi?' and had left the superstar to a sound and solitary sleep.

The feelings of harmony and youthful vigour with which Fernando awoke on the Monday morning were short-lived. Over breakfast Lefrak brought to his attention a story in one of the tabloid papers. Under the heading 'Cass for the chop?' it read, 'There is mounting curiosity over the identity of the new producer of the smash hit *Life Sanction* films. Following the announcement that Frank Hoffman has sold his controlling interest in the project, there are rumours that Fernando Cass himself might be due for the chop. Already several names have been put forward as replacements. Dubbed "the fastest pensioner in the West", Cass is in London for tomorrow's Gala Première of the latest blood-bath movie. Amid stories of rifts and feuds and skullduggery in showbiz circles, the star is apparently planning to take over the lead role in *Stratagems and Spoils*, an idea described by Paddy Brummel recently as being about as thrilling as asking a kitchen chair to play Hamlet. Has the time come to trade in his holster for a truss? The star was not available for comment.'

The fruit juice in Fernando's mouth was suddenly acid. 'Bullshit,' was his verdict. 'It's a crock of bullshit.'

Lefrak stayed silent the way obvious targets know they should. The smell of his aftershave was horribly pungent in the air.

'Nobody, no fucking body is taking over the *Sanction* movies,' Cass declared. 'It's a load of bullshit. Horseshit. Crap.' No matter from which particular faeces the story was composed, it rankled the star, and he spent a long time brooding in the looking-glass. Was he making a fool of himself? His image in the mirror seemed to share his concern.

24 Jemma found Hugo in poor shape. His face was swollen and mauve like plums. Dressed in a large kimono he waddled pitifully towards her.

'Champagne,' he said. 'How lovely.'

'A present from Paddy and me.'

'A whole case. You're so kind.'

Hugo was lisping badly with his new deficiency in the dental department. Jemma told him of her meeting with Paddy the night before. He had heard on the news about Matthew Goddard's death and the true details came as no surprise. His heart didn't exactly ache although the rest of him certainly did.

They took the floppy disks into his study where the vivid green screen did nothing to sooth the raw feeling behind Hugo's eyes. With swift fingers that knew their business, he soon found the disk they wanted and drew out all manner of detail about Heime's life: his dates, his bills, his projects, his loves, his inoculations, his tax, his chiropody, his business . . . his life. It was unclean work even for a popular journalist, this rummaging through a dead man's things.

Outside Hugo's house at opposite ends of the street were two pairs of onlookers; one on either side of the law. Both of them were wondering what business it was that drew the two people inside together.

While Hugo scanned the information Jemma cleared up in the kitchen – the floor was still bloody from the night before.

'Bingo,' shouted Hugo.

Leaning over his shoulder Jemma read what was appearing on the screen. Coming to light at last was the letter of explanation that Heime had written to the world to justify his departure from it.

It was a letter packed with damning detail. It listed chapter and verse, it gave dates and reference numbers, it decoded Swiss bank accounts, it left no stone unturned, or uncast.

As evidence of fraud and mismanagement and embezzlement and blackmail, it was irrefutably bad news for Sir Toby and Matthew (God rest his soul) Goddard, Noel Pettifer, Marty Clanger, Lewis Lefrak, Uncle Tom Cobbley and all. Heime had even recorded that Matthew and his uncle had discussed abducting Hannah as a means of restraining Paddy's objections.

By so much did this letter exceed their wildest hopes that Jemma and Hugo did not hesitate in opening a bottle of champagne.

They raised their glasses in silence. Hugo was toasting the best scoop of his career while Jemma drank quietly to the innocence of her lover. Was this the beginning of the happy ending?

Some days later when the security staff at the Regal Cinema, Leicester Square were quizzed by their superiors and, in due course, the police, nobody had a clear memory of that Monday afternoon.

The staff were reminded that it was the last day of the long-running James Bond film, a wet afternoon which had brought a small attendance to the matinée. They were urged to cast their minds back and search their memories. To no avail, not one of them had any recollection of anybody resembling Paddy Brummel entering the cinema. Not even little Wendy, the Jamaican usherette could say how it was that the most wanted man in Britain had entered her cinema. (She was a girl of principle; £50 she sent to Oxfam, and the other half of Paddy's present she put towards her bottom drawer.) To the police it would remain a mystery how he got there.

At the first showing the film made little impression on Paddy. He just sat enjoying the warmth and safety of the Royal Circle. If the villains on the screen had chosen to open rather than break windows and had used silencers on their guns, Paddy might have had a better doze.

Since leaving Jemma's car Paddy had kept on the move. From the pile of oddments on the back seat he had taken with him a knitted cloche hat and a long purple scarf which had served as a scant disguise without doing much to keep out the cold. The dawn had been a long time coming. Paddy had plodded towards it numb with tiredness almost wishing to be caught. He breakfasted from vending machines and longed for a toothbrush. Never again would he see the romantic side of being a tramp.

In his hurried departure from Heime's flat the most useful item Paddy had taken with him was the mobile telephone. During the second showing of the film he withdrew with it to the lavatories. Jemma's line was tapped of course, so he dialled his other ally. Hugo Cavendish had to shout as the battery was beginning to fade and Paddy could only just hear the good news that the floppy disks had yielded fruits beyond their expectation.

In an urgent whisper Paddy told him what he was going to do and what he needed. Hugo took notes; despite his discomfort he was eager to oblige. It had been a while since he had made a friend.

'Oh, by the way,' he lisped, 'I had a call from the secretary of the Foundation for the Study of Infant Deaths and apparently money is pouring in . . . over £10,000. Isn't that great?'

When they disconnected Paddy sat in the dim lavatory for a long time. His parents, his wife, his daughter and his partners were dead. He was a new man starting again, the past had to be left behind. Not since his first term at boarding-school had he blubbed in the loo.

In accordance with Paddy's instructions Hugo called Jemma out of the blue and had invited her to see the Bond movie with him. On her bugged telephone she had been slow on the uptake of his oddly insistent invitation but was ready on time. As they arrived at the Regal Cinema for the late afternoon performance, men high up on scaffolding were dismantling the huge 'Timothy' of Dalton's neon billing.

In their handy Panda car two policemen waited patiently for Jemma to come out while in his beige mackintosh Toady Griffin kept vigil too. Overhead the starlings were squealing in the gloaming.

The cinema was fuller now and Paddy was relieved to have his allies either side of him in the back row. In the reflected glory of the screen he saw that Jemma looked terrific – tense and bright. Hugo was pitifully lopsided.

Eagerly Paddy took the sheaf of papers and the toothbrush that Hugo had brought and made his way to the loo. Both items were mightily satisfactory.

In whispered tones the three of them conferred. On the screen James Bond was a shining example to them all, sardonic and brave, commissioning cocktails in the face of mortal danger. Bullets and kicks in the groin hardly touched him. What a man. Quite untroubled by cowardice or impotence or grief.

The three confederates were eventually agreed on the principle that going with a bang was better than a whimper. The question was not whether their plan was spectacular, it was simply whether it could possibly work? Jemma had brought provisions: a fresh battery for the Vodaphone, a change of shirt and shoes, a flask of soup and a bottle of vodka. She was better than Miss Moneypenny and 'Q' put together. It was a long time since either Paddy or Jemma had kissed in the back of a cinema. They had both forgotten how uncomfortable it was, and envied James Bond the luxury of his fairy-tale embrace as the end credits rolled.

As Hugo limped out of the cinema with Jemma on his arm, the men in the scaffolding had finished their work. The hoarding would now read: 'Fernando Cass in *Life Sanction II*. A new dimension in violence and revenge to chill your blood.' They didn't need their blood chilling, thank you.

Twice more the indefatigable Bond was dispatched on his now familiar mission while Paddy dozed in his seat. A little before the end of the final performance he slipped from his seat and as the audience filed out he was crouched inches from them in a cleaning cupboard under the emergency stairs.

The footsteps and the clatter soon subsided and the silence settled in. Paddy waited. Time became distorted in the blackness, seconds and minutes got ideas above their station and felt like hours. Paddy had nothing to measure them against except his own discomfort. At last from outside he heard the heavy-booted tread of a security man and then the clink of chains as the fire doors were padlocked for the night.

Leaving a more than ample safety margin Paddy crept forth into the corridor. His knees were locked at right angles and his eyes ached from reaching into nothing. He turned on the torch and let its feeble light explode the hefty darkness. With slow stealth he toured the building to possess it and to check he was alone. He was alone all right.

As he stood in the auditorium low watt bulbs gave out an eerie gloom, light years away a police siren wailed above the London buzz and reminded Paddy of his isolation. He picked his way through the debris of confectionery, walked up and down the aisles taking in the smells that crowds leave behind. He was looking for ghosts and found none – the place was too dead for spirits.

In some theatres the teasing of the wind can shift old backcloths in their mooring and give a hint of haunting. The echo of bygone drama is all too ready for the fancying. But this was just a cinema, where the atmosphere is simply a trick of the light through celluloid that leaves the premises intact when the plug is pulled. Paddy returned to his old seat in the circle, drank the chicken soup and toasted the darkness with the vodka. He was in control.

After his picnic Paddy went to explore the stage area. He crawled under the heavy pleated curtain on to the narrow stage and groped his way along the curve of the screen. Behind it was a shallow gap and then the outside wall – this was the unvisited hinterland of the cinema full of rubbish and dust. There were damaged seats and old posters – all the magic of show business.

Up the left-hand wall ran an iron ladder, and by the light of his torch Paddy saw that it led to a kind of crow's nest thirty feet above the stage. It was a platform about the size of a decent desk, the sort of dusty awkward place that does not invite inspection. It was just what Paddy wanted.

Before returning to his seat Paddy stood for a moment on the stage. And then, the way actors do in strange theatres, he tested the acoustics. 'How now brown cow?' he whispered into the darkness and the sound came back dead. 'For God's sake, let us sit upon the ground and tell sad stories of the death of kings . . .' Richard II's lament fell on absent ears – no trace of a ghost to help it on its way.

Dimly Paddy could see the empty seats in front of him. Tomorrow they would be filled with the glittering patrons of Fernando Cass's 'new dimension in violence'. What an evening it might be.

FQ was not asleep but the ringing of his bedside telephone surprised him from his book. 'Hallo,' he answered cautiously.

'It's me,' said Paddy's voice. The line was crackling and faint. FQ swung his feet to the floor to absorb the shock.

'Well you're in a bit of a pickle aren't you, mate?' he said in the manner of John Mills in a black and white war film. 'Are you OK?'

'I'm fine.'

'Where are you?' FQ regretted asking the question that was on the nation's lips.

'It doesn't matter.' Paddy was back in the Royal Circle.

'I am sorry about Hannah.'

'I didn't kill her . . .'

'Don't be daft . . .' FQ had glimpsed more than anyone the obsolete love Paddy had for his wife. Too private to voice were his thoughts about Matthew Goddard's death.

Paddy swigged vodka from the bottle Jemma had brought and felt it sting his gums. 'Are you still doing the première at the Regal tomorrow?'

'Yes.'

'With Fergus Llewellyn?'

'Yes.'

'Live?'

'Yes.'

'Did you go to the production meeting? The briefing?' Paddy asked.

'Yes. Endless.'

'Tell me about it . . . Every last detail. Absolutely everything about the rig-up and the schedule . . . every last detail.'

'Hang on, I'll fetch the bumf.' With trembling legs FQ padded to the kitchen and then read out the information. Paddy listened in silence, willing his memory to take it all in.

'And what time will you get there?' he asked when FQ had finished.

'About four. Apart from attending to God himself I've got to be there to help doll up the celebrity programme sellers. You never know when the odd button might fly and you know what sequins are like . . . What have you got in mind?'

Paddy told him.

'I see,' said FQ in the gentle tone of a samaritan, for this was certain suicide. 'I see, and is there anything I can do?' He prayed there wasn't. There was. 'You don't want much do you?' FQ went quite moist in his powder-blue night-shirt as Paddy gave him the details of his requirements. This was a role he didn't care for. Playing Watson to Paddy's Sherlock Holmes was one thing but Digby to his Dan Dare was something else.

'OK. Sure. I'll do it,' FQ said. There was no one he would

rather die for. They disconnected. 'Be butch, Bernie, be butch,' FQ told himself as he reached for the valium.

In the stalls below Paddy could hear mice scavenging popcorn; sleep was elusive but he did his best to relax his body and empty his mind. When dawn came it was not with birdsong and pink light, rather just an upping of the far away tempo of the traffic. Paddy squinted through the foyer doors and saw a greyish morning in Leicester Square. It was the time of day when the garden belonged to its proper residents – tramps and pigeons.

In cold water Paddy washed and shaved. He breakfasted on fruit and biscuits and longed for daylight and a copy of *The Times*. According to Wendy, the cleaners and staff would arrive at nine by which time he would have to be decamped from his Royal Circle base. Before withdrawing he made a telephone call.

If a policeman's lot is not a happy one, neither is his wife's, especially when her home has become a key location in a major murder hunt. In fact, so fractious had Mrs Robbins become with all the aggravation, that her husband had contrived to leave early for work that Tuesday morning. The idea of a quiet bacon and egg in the canteen almost put a smile on his downcast face.

And so it was that Mrs Robbins found herself, a housewife in a housecoat doing the housework, alone in the house and despondent when the telephone rang.

'Is that you, Shirley?' Paddy asked.

'Yes.' She sounded uncertain of her own identity but not of her caller's.

'Shirley Robbins?'

'Yes. Yes it is.' Shirley was doubly amazed. Her name had never sounded so nice. 'My husband's not here,' she announced.

'Never mind.'

'Where are you?' If only she had been in a Patricia Highsmith book she would have asked more subtly.

'I'm fine thanks,' answered Paddy deliberately. 'And you?'

The telephone tappers and later the entire wardroom at

the police station had trouble believing their ears as the dialogue continued. 'Actually I've got a bit of trouble with my sciatica.' Shirley was determined not to get in a fluster.

'Shirley, I'm going to give myself up.'

'Pardon?' Shirley's neck was pinkening fast, she could feel it.

'I'm going to give myself up.'

'Oh ... er ... right ... Good idea.' The fluster was fully fledged. 'I'll tell my husband ... that's the police ... er, right away.' She didn't need to.

'Thanks. If you could tell him I'll be turning up at the Regal this evening for the première of *Life Sanction II*. That's in Leicester Square, OK?'

'Yes.'

'Are you OK?' He really seemed to care.

'Er ... yes, fine.' She didn't sound it.

'Well ... have a nice day.'

How could she after this. 'You too,' she said. 'Thanks.'

'Bye then.'

'Bye ...' Shirley's neck was the colour of geraniums.

From high up in his backstage bolt-hole Paddy could hear the cackle of cleaners above the drone of the Hoovers. Later he was scared witless as the enormous curtains opened and the mighty beam of the projector ricocheted a brilliant white light off the screen beneath him.

As the projectionist focused and checked his equipment, Paddy was treated to a sneak preview of *Life Sanction II*. From his oblique angle the screen was filled with hurly-burly flickerings while the amplifiers told an everyday story of screeching tyres and gunfire. At one point Fernando's voice growled the immortal line, 'Let's get out of here,' and Paddy felt a fresh conviction that Cass was not the man to supplant him in *Stratagems and Spoils*.

After a time the technicians from Capitol TV arrived to prepare the cinema for the live *Fergus Llewellyn Show*. Paddy listened to the noises of people about their business; he longed to stretch himself and breathe air that wasn't weary with years of imprisonment behind the silver screen.

For no good reason Paddy fell to wondering if his father would approve of what he was doing. Probably not; to throw caution to the wind and rush in shooting from the hip was not his nature. Or was it? Paddy could picture the austere face of his father. 'Oh, Dad, if only you weren't dead, perhaps we'd be friends by now.' In the dust and darkness the past looked suddenly rosy.

Shortly after four o'clock the cinema went quiet again – the work-force had broken for tea. Slowly, a rung at a time, Paddy began the long descent from his cramped eyrie. 'Please FQ, don't let me down.' With his wounded leg aching horribly he reached stage level. His torch carefully shielded, he edged forward towards the designated spot. 'Please, please, FQ.'

Stashed in the corner, in the hollow of the proscenium arch itself, was a black plastic bag. Paddy carried it to the darker recess behind the screen and probed the contents with his fingers. 'God Bless FQ.' Inside was all he had asked for, plus a note which read, 'Thought you might like today's *Times*. I know you like to do the crossword when you're hanging about backstage. Also some aftershave. Yours ever, FQ. PS Take care.'

Paddy smiled in the dark. The equipment itself looked simple enough but there was no way of testing it. There would be no dress rehearsal – this was a one-shot chance. Paddy changed into the dinner-jacket, a perfect fit. Without a mirror he had trouble with the bow-tie, and the aftershave was quite out of the question.

Back on his narrow platform Paddy drank the hot coffee from FQ's flask. Although he glanced at the crossword his mind was filled with other problems. A paragraph on the front page came to Paddy's attention.

By the dim light of his torch he read: 'Police now believe that Matthew Goddard, who fell to his death from a fire escape on Sunday night, had broken into the apartment of his late partner, Heime Chadwick. There was evidence of a break-in but police sources are unable to find a motive. They are continuing their enquiries and as yet foul play has not been ruled out.' Paddy sat in the dark repeating the words 'foul play' to himself until they lost their meaning.

25 As a result of Paddy's telephone call to the flustered Mrs Robbins, the crowd gathering outside the Regal was peppered with policemen, plain clothes and otherwise. The citizens had come to catch a glimpse of Fernando Cass but the constabulary had a different star in mind.

Round the corner at the other end of the massive cabling which ran like an umbilical cord from the belly of the Regal, was the mobile video scanner emblazoned with the Capitol TV logo. Inside it was Malcolm DeFreitas finishing off preparations for the evening's show. He was glad to be on location and well pleased to have a guest of Cass's calibre on the show. In his stomach lurked an unexplained tension.

Again and again Malcolm had rerun the Paddy Brummel interview from the previous week to see if his conscience was clear. He had been charged with sadism in letting Fergus Llewellyn exert such hostile pressure on the actor and was keen to find vindication. Surely there had been a glint of madness in Paddy's eyes; predestiny at least, or drugs. Anyway Malcolm had been following orders from upstairs and the proof of the pudding was in the ratings.

In the make-up van Fergus Llewellyn was having a deep tan applied to his face; he had no intention of being outbronzed by Fernando Cass. He was looking forward to the première (not the film itself, God forbid); he liked the challenge of a live event. The spontaneity and the danger were his life's blood – he saw himself as a matador alone in the arena. He smiled at himself in the mirror. 'Attaboy.' It was unlike him to be nervous.

Noel Pettifer entered the Regal like a sleepwalker flanked by Lewis Lefrak and Sir Toby. His eyes and tuxedo looked hollow. Until Sunday he had understood the need to keep secret his love for Matthew but now with an ache of sadness in his solar plexus he wanted to shout himself hoarse with it. He wanted to set the record straight or wind the clock back. He wanted the world to take note that he had loved this black-haired, bright-eyed boy, this clever, witty, always chewing boy, this plotting, and amoral, and now dead boy.

When Noel remembered the pleasure of his Ganymede his eyes and throat stung with salt, for he sensed that Matthew would be his last taste of youth, his last delight. Old age was swamping his bones.

'It's what Matthew would have wanted,' Sir Toby had said to persuade Noel to come. 'We're not giving up now,' he had declared. Toby's bravado was shallower than it seemed; inside him was a desperate energy urging him to settle his nephew's account. Like an old Tibetan warrior he knew his time was nearly up, he wasn't really fighting to win anymore.

Lewis Lefrak was sensitive to the strain in his companions as they took their seats, and kept silent. His face was grave but his brain was dancing with cocaine. He longed to be back in Hollywood where making movies was easy and people didn't keep dying all over the place.

The *Sunday Globe*'s trusty correspondent walked in slowly to disguise the soreness of the glands between his legs. On his arm Jemma looked pale and concentrated like someone before a race. Her heart thudded horribly; this wasn't a dress rehearsal, this was a gala première.

The cinema was garlanded with flowers which provided meagre camouflage for the cameras around the auditorium. The technicians from Capitol TV were camouflaged too, in dinner-jackets long past their prime. Like the starlings in the twilight outside the chatter in the Regal was high pitched with much flapping of brightly feathered wings. In a corner of the foyer FQ pushed another valium down his bone-dry throat.

Perched in his filthy lair Paddy listened to the sounds below. Who did he think he was – the phantom of the opera? Wasn't this the actor's nightmare? The old horror of being centre stage with no lines to speak, no props to hold, no friends, no prompt, no costume, no escape. The audience watch patiently like relatives round the sick-bed as the actor freezes, melts and dies. Paddy swigged vodka from the bottle and let it lay waste in his throat; this was no nightmare, this was really happening.

On the small, blurred screen of FQ's Sony Watchman Paddy watched the opening of the *Fergus Llewellyn Show* and for the second time in a week he felt his stomach churn as the signature tune blared out.

'Tonight. Live from the Regal Cinema, Leicester Square ... The *Fergus Llewellyn Show*.' The audience applauded. Projected on the big screen in front of them the face of the Welshman loomed large, his smile was a yard wide. Fergus was sitting in the back of a limousine. His huge bow-tie had the too-good-to-be-true look of a phony. It suited him well. 'Here we are in London's glittering West End, the heartland of British showbiz.'

Paddy could hear the oily lilt amplified from all around.

'Tonight my special guest will be a true megastar in Hollywood's constellation, the one and only Fernando Cass ... Meanwhile here we are arriving at the première of his latest film *Life Sanction II* at the Regal Cinema in Leicester Square.'

The car was pulling up. Spot on cue. The bodywork shone inky black in the bright lights for a second before Fergus emerged. From high up the camera showed the red carpet like a scar running through the cheering crowd. Behind the barricades people waved and shouted, flashlights spangled the air. The bow-tie was having its finest hour. Fergus waved. Fergus smiled. Fergus bowed.

Suddenly on his ear-piece Fergus heard the voice of Malcolm, 'That's enough, move on. It's going great.' Paddy heard it too and smiled with relief. FQ had served him well; the equipment was working perfectly.

Obediently Fergus followed his command and moved forward. In fact, he kept so close to the hand-held camera retreating in front of him that his face on the screen looked grotesquely convex, the eyes angling back and the nose reaching forward like a burrowing mole.

The manager of the cinema greeted Fergus stiffly like an unhappy butler and together they crossed the foyer and entered the back of the stalls. The cinema screen went blank for now the image of the man himself was flesh and blood strutting down the aisle to the dais. Applause. Applause.

Both Fergus and Paddy heard a whisper in their ear, 'Great, great. It looks terrific,' Malcolm was saying. 'No hurry. Shake a few hands if you want. Great.' Fergus needed no encouragement to make body contact with his public, for the camera he would kiss anything. He actually leant across Hugo Cavendish to touch a lady to Jemma's right. On his small screen Paddy watched and chastised himself for feeling, for a moment, a little in control.

On the dais Fergus raised his hand commanding the clapping to cease. And it was so. With well schooled charm he welcomed the audience and especially thanked an interminable list of people. Fergus's confidence had all the unstoppability of a tidal wave. He seemed to trust his personality the way a dandy does a good suit. Cockily he brandished his Welshness like a well used season ticket.

'So now before we meet the star and the producer of the film, let's take a look at a clip from their earlier film, the first *Life Sanction*.' The lights dimmed and the screen was at once frantic with activity.

One of the principal advantages of showing clips on a live show is that it gives those involved a moment of respite, a breathing space.

'Looking good. That was great,' said Malcolm from his cramped control room round the corner. 'We're running ahead, we've got plenty of time – there's no hurry.' Fergus nodded into the close-up camera and Malcolm smiled back at the ten images of the Welshman on the monitors in front of him. 'Keep it hard with Cass ... The morality of violence etc., OK?' Fergus nodded again. 'Put on a bit of pressure ... Remember he's hot at the moment ... vulnerable.' Fergus raised his thumb to the camera and grinned. Message understood. Paddy's pulse was racing like any other eavesdropper's.

The clip had under a minute to run. On Paddy's pocket screen Fernando Cass was taking aim with a revolver, double-handed. Paddy was praying to FQ, 'Don't let me down,' he almost whispered.

One minute to go. FQ was in two minds. To do it or not to do it? He was hovering behind one of the camera crews just below the dais. There was nothing he wouldn't do for his beloved Paddy Brummel: cook, sew, wash, garden. Anything. But this demand on his courage was beyond him, almost. 'For me, FQ, please, FQ, Dear FQ, Do it, FQ, Go, FQ, Do it, FQ, Now.' Paddy shut his eyes.

'Just a mo,' said FQ to the floor manager. 'His jacket looks a fright.' No one thought to stop him. With small steps FQ ran forward up on to the podium to attend to Fergus's jacket. It was his job. With thirty seconds left before the show was live again, a make-up girl was dabbing the Welshman's brow with eau de cologne.

'Excuse I,' said FQ waving a clothes brush. 'I'd just better give you a teensy sprucing up, all right?'

'All right,' said Fergus. He wasn't butch enough himself to be nice to gays. 'Hurry up.'

'Twenty seconds,' shouted the floor manager.

Jemma was clenching Hugo's hand and she had to force herself to breathe deeply as she watched FQ fussing round the evening's host. 'God bless FQ.'

Paddy had no idea what was happening.

FQ dusted off dandruff that was not there and straightened Fergus's straight tie. Then with shaking hands he ran his fingers round the back of the Welshman's cummerbund as if to adjust it. And there, yes, there it was; the radio transmitter from which the wire ran up Fergus's back into the barely visible earpiece.

FQ knew exactly what he had to do. He had practised blindfold over and over again. In rehearsal the vital sleight of hand had not been hampered by shaking fingers. Time was against him now, Fergus Llewellyn was getting restless.

'Ten seconds.'

There are three channels on which pocket transmitters can operate. A, B, or C. To alter the channel is a simple matter of shifting a tiny switch. Both parties simply have to synchronise which they are using. In this case Malcolm and Fergus (also Paddy) had been communicating on C.

In a flash of inspiration FQ deliberately trod on Fergus's foot and in the brief moment of hiatus FQ's thumb shifted channel from C to A.

'Whoops, I am sorry, love,' said the humble dresser.

Fergus heard a sharp crackling in his ear.

So did Paddy as he too switched to channel A.

'There you are, pet, right as rain,' said FQ, and scuttled off. The clip of *Life Sanction II* was nearly over. On the huge screen blood was spewing from an old man's neck.

'Five. Four. Three. Two. One,' counted the floor manager '. . . And cue.'

The lights came up. The screen went blank.

'Fierce stuff,' announced Fergus as he reappeared on the nation's screens. The glittering audience applauded.

'Hi,' said a new voice deep in Fergus's ear. 'This is Paddy Brummel here and I want you to do as I say. If you don't I'll shoot you. Straight away. Through the head. OK? As a signal I want you to stroke your nose if you understand me.'

Way back in the 70s when Fergus had tripped on LSD he had survived the horrors by holding on to the knowledge that the truth was no longer the truth but a chemical hybrid. No such comfort now. This was real, as sure as eggs is eggs. It was unmistakably and inexplicably the voice of Paddy Brummel in his ear.

The applause was beginning to subside.

How did a bullet feel going through your head? Fergus wondered. Which way would it be going? Where the hell was this murderous, lunatic actor? Ahead? Behind? Above? Below? With a quivering finger he stroked his nose several times quite unnaturally. 'Don't shoot, don't shoot. I promise to obey,' was his silent message.

Holding the tiny television close in front of his face Paddy was relieved and excited to receive the signal of capitulation. It might just work.

'And now,' said Fergus, 'it is my great pleasure to introduce my first guest this evening, the man himself, the star who has kept hearts and box-office tills throbbing for more than a quarter of a century ... Please welcome Fernando Cass.'

To an observant viewer Fergus Llewellyn was imperceptibly less laid back; his voice was rasping a fraction and his blink rate had quickened.

Malcolm in the control room imagined that his protégé's transmitter had failed. He was not unduly worried, Fergus was a trapeze artist who didn't need a safety net. It never crossed his mind to switch channel.

Jemma could feel cold sweat coursing down her back into the velvet seat; her knuckles and neck ached with tension.

One of the cameras had panned across the stalls to the central doors through which the one and only Fernando Cass now ambled. He looked magnificent, bronzed and amiable and not unintelligent.

At £50 a ticket the applause is always stupendous and as the star walked down the aisle he brought the generous patrons to their feet. Some rose because they were devoted fans, some because they wanted to assess his height, and some because everyone else had.

Off camera for a moment Fergus took the opportunity to survey the packed cinema for signs of his enemy. No enemy could he see. No Lee Van Cleef skulking in the corner, no balaclavaed paramilitaries with machine-guns . . . where the hell was Paddy Brummel?

'Remember just do as I say, all right?' Paddy's voice struck fresh terror deep in Fergus's earhole. 'I'll tell you what to say.'

Fernando stepped on to the podium, shook the hand of his host then turned and bowed to his public. It was the deep bow of an artist humbled by such appreciation.

In his spider's hole Paddy had no time to savour what he had in his net, he was too busy listening to Fergus's opening questions and Fernando's polite answers. It was trite stuff for the most part. 'Ask him,' said Paddy picking his moment, 'if this new film is going to be as mindlessly violent as the first.'

Fergus Llewellyn felt sick like someone on a helter-skelter.

'Er, now Fernando,' he said, 'turning to this new *Life Sanction* film, can you tell me . . .' his throat was clenched sandpaper.

'Ask it, exactly,' Paddy urged.

'. . . I was wondering if this new film is . . . perhaps . . .' Fergus attempted a disclaiming kind of smile at the patient Cass. 'I mean . . . is this film as mindlessly violent as the first one?' He finished the question quickly.

Except for Jemma and Hugo the entire audience felt the first warm prickle of embarrassment. Malcolm leant forward; were his monitors deceiving him or had young Llewellyn lost his delicate touch?

Fernando felt the confusion of a man who has just been ambushed. Had this unfriendly question really come from this friendly man? From the audience 1,500 anxious faces and five anxious cameras watched for his reaction. If in doubt, smile, he thought, and smiled.

'Well, Fergus, we're certainly not talking Walt Disney,' he said. 'It's an action movie, you know, but it's got a lot of heart too.'

Fergus nodded, he was trying to listen to Paddy simultaneously. His ears were unaccustomed to this dual function – a dilemma in stereo.

'Right,' he said, 'so you wouldn't agree with the idea that films like this are . . .' Fergus's forehead was bubbling with sweat, 'an insult to people's intelligence, a waste of time and money.'

The mouths of Sir Toby, Noel Pettifer and Lewis Lefrak

fell open like a barber shop trio. The mouths of Jemma and Hugo controlled a grin. The mouth of Malcolm sucked on the wrong end of a filter tip cigarette.

Frank Hoffman, who was standing at the back waiting his turn to be interviewed, felt a surge of indignation; it was after all his time and money that had been wasted on the mindless violence in question. On reflection though, it was good to see the star who had betrayed him put on the spot.

'Are you putting me on?' asked Fernando slowly.

'No,' said Paddy.

'Er . . . No,' said Fergus.

'I don't believe this,' said Cass. 'I mean, this is a Gala Première, right? And you're giving me a bad time, huh?'

'So it would seem,' smiled Fergus. His puppeteer was briefing him again. 'Let's move on a moment, Fernando, to your plans for the future. Is it true that you'll be doing the last G. P. Conran novel – a film of *Stratagems and Spoils*?'

'Yeah. That's what we're planning. It's going to be terrific.' Fernando was still not sure of his ground.

'What role will you be playing?' asked Fergus Llewellyn. His heart was thumping with the fear of dying.

'I play a guy called Eliot Blandford.'

'A character who is supposed to be a thirty-eight-year-old British intelligence officer, a quiet and proud man.'

Fernando hadn't analysed the character in great depth yet but answered, 'Yes, I guess so.'

'Do you think as a fifty-eight-year-old cowboy you're quite right for the part?' Fergus dared not look his victim in the eye.

'Pardon me,' said Cass. He wanted to drop a bomb on the United Kingdom.

'Are you not completely wrong for the role of Eliot Blandford?' said Fergus. 'Completely miscast?'

Not thirty feet away Paddy warned himself not to go too far.

'I don't believe this,' said Fernando, echoing the sentiment of the entire assembly.

'One way or another the whole project seems to be mysterious and controversial. Perhaps Lewis Lefrak, the producer, would care to come up here . . . and answer some questions . . . Lewis Lefrak,' Fergus called.

'What in the name of fuck is going on?' moaned Malcolm.

Cameras were already scanning the stalls for the unscheduled guest.

'What is this arsehole doing, huh? I've been set up,' complained Lewis sinking low in his seat. Sir Toby shrugged his ignorance although he had a shadowy suspicion.

'Come on up here,' urged Fergus. 'Lewis Lefrak.' He called the name as if it had won a raffle.

Lefrak had no choice. Reluctantly he rose to his feet. The cameras swooped in on him tracking his progress to the stage. The audience applauded apprehensively. What was all this? Were they in a cinema or a courtroom? After this the film itself was bound to be an anticlimax.

Up in the confines of his nest Paddy peered at the tiny screen and saw for the first time his adversary striding towards the stage in a dazzling white tuxedo.

'Will you walk into my parlour, said the spider to the fly.'

At the back of the stalls Frank Hoffman was relieved to have been bypassed in favour of this upstart who had usurped his star. He supposed this was all part of the elaborate scheme that Hugo Cavendish had arranged in order to bring Cass to heel.

'Welcome, Lewis. Nice to have you on the show,' Fergus was saying. In his ear Paddy was planting a long question.

Fernando was glad of the company; he had never enjoyed a chat show so little and was tired of being alone in the firing line. Lefrak was the cavalry at last.

In stupefaction Malcolm sucked on the right end of his Rothman's and wondered if this was an April Fool or whether the Welshman had flipped his lid. In any event what would it do for the ratings?

'This is an unexpected pleasure,' said Lefrak. His smile looked more like an escape bid by his teeth. 'I thought you guys were supposed to be talking about *Life Sanction II* which I have to tell you is terrific . . .'

'It's a heap of garbage,' said Paddy into the microphone.

'. . . I've seen it already in the States and I have to tell you . . .'

'Say it,' ordered Paddy.

'. . . that it is one terrific film.' Lefrak was speaking with the sincerity of a PR spokesman. 'Sure it's violent but it has humour . . .'

'It's a heap of garbage,' said the dripping Fergus Llewellyn without conviction.

'Pardon me?' said Lewis who had heard.

'It is a heap of garbage,' repeated the chat show host.

An audience always likes to know what is expected of it. Like a good dinner guest it doesn't want to be caught drinking from the finger bowl. Was this a joke? Should we laugh? From the upper circle a small group decided 'yes', and soon the laughter spread throughout the building and was in turn relayed to the viewing millions. It is a joke so we laugh. It is satirical so we clap.

By the time the applause subsided Fergus had been thoroughly briefed by his controller.

'Let's talk about you and Mediavision and *Stratagems and Spoils*, and how exactly it is that you have come by the film rights,' suggested Fergus. He was feeling more optimistic about his prospects now; he was obeying orders and didn't deserve to die.

'Er ... OK,' said Lefrak modestly.

'Now you've got a number of partners,' began Fergus. 'Marty Cranner in New York ...'

'Clanger,' hissed Paddy. 'Clanger. Not Cranner for God's sake.'

'... I mean Clanger.' Fergus corrected himself adroitly but Malcolm had spotted the clue. 'Marty Clanger in New York,' Fergus continued, 'and Noel Pettifer here in London ... And who else. There's someone else. Who is it?'

'No one.'

'No one' was sitting expressionless in his seat. He was as cold as ice yet sweat poured down his furrowed brow. Sir Toby wasn't frightened of death any more, it was no big price to pay. Somehow he knew the moment of it wasn't far off and he didn't mind.

'Come on,' said Fergus, 'who was your other partner? What's his name?'

The audience had now decided to do hushed silence. In a whisper that Orson Welles would have been proud of Lefrak announced Sir Toby's name.

'Sir Toby Goddard, Chairman of Capitol TV,' Fergus sounded surprised.

The audience did some murmuring.

Malcolm was curiously beginning to enjoy the proceedings in the way a man whose parachute has failed enjoys the view.

'Find Sir Toby,' he instructed camera 4. 'Hold on him.'

With the speed of a terrier the camera unearthed its quarry and the monitor screen was filled with Sir Toby's troubled face. Troubled, it would have you believe, not so much by the matter in hand as by some altogether weightier problem like the economic crisis or the famine in the third world.

'Sir Toby, perhaps you would care to join us,' Fergus relayed the invitation. 'You, too, Mr Pettifer.'

'I would not,' answered the television mogul with the clear tone of a man who knew his mind. 'Nor me,' said Noel Pettifer quietly.

With shaking fingers Malcolm fumbled with the transmitter. His communication with Fergus had been on channel C. On impulse he now shifted the switch to B. Nothing. And then to A. He held his breath and listened dumbfounded for a moment. He was free-falling through a stormy sky. The shock that filled him as he realised what was happening was nothing compared to the shock of recognising whose voice it was hijacking his show.

In the distance Paddy could hear the wail of a siren. He hoped it was the police closing in.

It was. Barely an hour earlier the vital evidence had been delivered by courier to the detectives in charge of the case. They had been quick to check the authenticity of Heime's official suicide note as well as all the carefully documented corroboration. The link between Mediavision and Transworld Telly Sales was abundantly clear as a motive for what had been happening. A covering note from the elusive Paddy Brummel invited the constabulary to the Regal Cinema, Leicester Square where *Life Sanction II* was the forthcoming attraction, among others.

Fergus Llewellyn was floundering, his ear-piece had gone silent and he was desperate for a prompt. He was a puppet with its strings cut loose. 'Tell me about ... tell me about film-making,' he asked in desperation. As Lefrak began to reply Fergus wasn't listening, for in his other ear he heard a click and then:

'Is that you? Paddy Brummel?' Malcolm DeFreitas's question was an outraged whisper.

'Hallo, sailor, indeed it is.'

'What the hell are you doing?'

'Sorting out one or two problems,' Paddy answered.

'Get off the air,' hissed Malcolm.

'No.'

'I'll call the police.'

'They're on their way.'

'I'll stop the show,' said Malcolm in the tone of a spoilsport.

'Don't,' said Paddy with a cold force. 'Don't do that.'

A shiver ran up Malcolm's spine. Fergus's too. Lefrak had finished speaking and the two of them were now staring at each other with the uncertainty of two people about to dance. In both Fergus's ears there was the kind of silence that takes gunfire to break.

The audience looked on and held its breath. Cameras edged forward for a closer look at the unease of the three men on the podium. Behind them the huge screen quivered. Its taut surface erupted like still water with a skimming stone, as behind it Paddy groped his way towards the light.

Fernando, Lewis and Fergus were frozen like pantomime villains in a tableau. They didn't need the time-honoured cry, 'He's behind you,' as Paddy emerged into the light. He somehow contrived to appear like a triumphant opera star summoned by an adoring public for an encore. He blinked and smiled and raised his arms and bowed deeply. The audience did the polite thing and clapped its clammy hands.

Paddy walked across the stage with the panache of a master gatecrasher. Apart from a scuff or two, his dinner-jacket looked immaculate. With an outstretched hand he greeted the open-mouthed trio.

'How do you do?' He pumped Fernando's hand. It was wet and cold like so much offal. 'I've so wanted to meet you. My name is Paddy Brummel.'

'Oh, yes. Hi,' Fernando answered. He had been convincingly bewildered on his own *This is Your Life* but he was now in a whole new dimension of bewilderment. 'Glad to know you.'

'Are you really,' replied Paddy lightly. The audience suppressed a laugh. He turned to the other American. 'And you must be Lewis Lefrak.' He pronounced the name with distasteful relish.

'Yes. I guess so,' answered Lefrak; he would rather have been Rudolf Hess.

Paddy turned to Fergus Llewellyn with huge bonhomie, 'Good to see you again so soon, Fergus, great show.'

'Thanks ... Welcome,' mumbled the deposed host wondering where the gun was hidden.

'Now then,' Paddy was addressing Lefrak again. 'Let's talk about *Stratagems and Spoils* shall we?'

'I don't see the point . . .' began Lefrak.

'Don't you? The point is you're the little runt who thinks he now owns the rights to it.'

Lewis faced a problem. Either 'Yes' he had the rights, or 'No' he was not a runt. He said, 'What's it to you?'

'Quite a lot,' said Paddy. 'Perhaps you'd tell us how you came by those rights?'

'It was a perfectly straightforward deal.' Lefrak raised his eyebrows and shoulders as if they were connected hydraulically. He was expressing innocence but in his throat there was a sharp sting of acid. 'It's surely of no particular interest.'

'It was not straightforward,' Paddy interrupted with his first note of anger. 'And it is of particular interest to me . . . because to get those rights you have cheated, robbed, blackmailed and murdered.'

The audience was suddenly a prim congregation – had the vicar belched?

'What is this?' asked Lefrak attempting indignation.

'That's a very serious allegation,' croaked Fergus Llewellyn who could not recall the last time he had been to Mass. I'll go on Sunday, he promised his poor-weather God.

'You're darn right it is,' answered Paddy.

'Perhaps we had better take a commercial break,' suggested the Welshman.

'No,' said Paddy.

'No,' echoed Malcolm in his other ear. 'We can't.' Two detectives had just entered the scanner and were appraising the delicate situation anxiously. Neither of them had appeared on live television before.

'OK,' said Fergus. 'We won't take a break.' Paddy nodded his thanks. 'So? . . .'

The audience was now a jury. Paddy pondered a moment in the manner of prosecuting counsels.

'For three years now, Mr Lefrak,' he began, 'you have been fraudulently trading in imported British television programmes. Your partners in this swindle were two directors of Transworld Telly Sales – Sir Toby Goddard and Heime Chadwick . . .'

'This is outrageous . . .' Lefrak expostulated.

'Be quiet,' said Paddy. 'It was no big deal – a simple fraud. But when you failed in your bid to gain the rights to *Stratagems and Spoils* by orthodox means it gave you the opportunity to persuade your British partners to somehow fix things for you. You blackmailed them. Under orders from your side-kick Marty Clanger they were forced to set about sabotaging the existing production – my production of the film. They began by withdrawing the finance and when I resisted they had me beaten up. Poor Heime Chadwick had no stomach for your tactics and chose an honourable withdrawal by taking his own life . . .' Lefrak had the glazed look of a martyr and his skin was the colour of duck's eggs. 'Matthew Goddard managed to destroy Heime's suicide letter and Noel Pettifer was brought in to help kill off the film in order that Mr Fernando Cass could take over the leading role. My role. One for which he is about as suited as Kermit is to play King Lear.'

Fernando's arteries were humming with bad vibrations. The audience was laughing at him, his head was spinning and he wanted to sink his teeth into Paddy's nose.

'Who gives a damn,' he shrugged. 'It's just a movie for God's sake.'

'No. It's not just a bloody movie. *Life Sanction* is just a bloody movie – a mindless, shapeless, tasteless pile of crude, ham-fisted violence, but *Stratagems and Spoils* is the last novel of one of our great writers and it deserved to be made properly as a film.' Paddy was in control.

'Just who do you think you are, some two-bit punk talking to me this way? I'm an actor like you. I do as I please, OK?' The gleam in Fernando Cass's eyes was like a cactus after rain.

'Not with my film you don't.' The politeness in Paddy's voice was chilling.

Jemma's knuckles were clenched white in Hugo's.

'Your film my ass.' Fernando could feel the blood racing warmly around his skull.

'Steady, steady.' Paddy spoke to him as he would a shying horse. 'I've got an idea – a proposal I want to put to you.'

'Oh,' was all Fernando could manage.

'It's very simple,' Paddy reassured him. 'I want to make sure I get the rights to *Stratagems and Spoils* back. I want to finish filming it myself. Exclusively. Are you with me?'

Fernando nodded.

'You see, if someone takes something of yours and won't give it back you have two choices; either you retake it by force, or you take something of theirs in the hope of doing an exchange. Are you with me?'

Fernando nodded. He was with Paddy all right. This was a rule of law his father and brothers had taught him years ago in Athens.

'Now unlike your friend,' Paddy went on, 'I don't like violence. So I have managed to put myself in a position to make you an offer, an offer you would be foolish to refuse.'

'Oh yeah, what is that?'

The two actors were facing each other squarely.

'I'm offering you a deal.'

'A deal?' Cass growled. 'What kind of a deal wise-ass?'

'I will tell you Mr Cass.'

The audience was on the edge of its seat. The police in the production van were agog at the negotiations. Lefrak felt oddly seasick and in the ears of Fergus Llewellyn a pulse was beating like an army boot.

'I am all ears, punk,' challenged Fernando.

'You should not be so rude you know, Mr Cass. I could be the producer of your next film.'

'Oh yeah,' said Fernando.

'Yes,' said Paddy. 'You see, I have recently acquired, legally acquired, the rights to the *Life Sanction* project.'

In the back of the stalls Frank Hoffman grinned, almost chuckled at the neatness of the way things were turning out.

'You ... you.' Fernando was incoherent.

'Yes,' said Paddy patiently, 'so perhaps you can guess at the deal I have in mind.'

Fernando's brain was spinning with rage and confusion.

Paddy went on, 'You see, you've got my film and I've got yours.'

'You've bought the rights to *Life Sanction*?' Fernando asked, his voice thick with slow-wittedness.

'Yes.'

'From Frank Hoffman?'

'Yes.'

Fernando pondered long and hard. From time to time he nodded like a man doing arithmetic. The audience were doing rapt attention. Eventually his mouth curled into a

smile which broadened into a chuckle which became in turn
a great bellow of magnificent laughter that went on and on.
To all and sundry there was no doubting the sincerity of his
amusement.

It was Paddy now who stood open-mouthed as the huge
American actor advanced and enveloped him in an embrace
which squeezed the wind out of him. The audience
applauded. Was this the end or just the interval, they
wondered.

'You son of a gun,' roared Cass, 'you goddam son of a gun.'

'Do we have a deal?' asked Paddy, as Cass held his face in
two hands.

'I guess so,' laughed Cass, 'I guess so.'

He turned to Lefrak who did not seem to have got the joke
at all.

'It's just a goddam movie isn't it?'

'Yeah,' gulped Lewis.

The two actors shook hands. They were simply fellow
artists.

Fergus Llewellyn cleared his throat. Paddy turned to him
with the smile gone from his face. 'We could have discussed
all this last week when I was on your show but the Goddards
had abducted my wife and were holding her hostage to make
me keep quiet. My hands were tied. I'm sorry it was such a
dull show.' Paddy was certainly making amends now. Fergus
smiled weakly. The audience were giving a deathly hush: Act
II was looking very interesting already. 'However as you can
see I don't feel so restrained now. Because she's dead.
Murdered. Not by me as they would have you believe. She
was murdered by his nephew . . .' In the tradition of all good
QC's Paddy had kept his theatrical powder dry but as he said
the name he pointed unequivocally into the auditorium at Sir
Toby. 'She was killed by Matthew Goddard. Isn't that right,
Sir Toby?'

The audience were now a spellbound jury, their faces were
beaded in sweat that glistened like their jewels.

'It's a pack of bloody lies,' Sir Toby was on his feet speaking
in a deep breathless growl. 'This is disgraceful. A pack of
bloody lies — you haven't got one shred of evidence.'

Camera 4 had swung round and zoomed in to catch the
knighted mogul in close up. The viewing public would see his
face filling their screens, it was as pale and shiny as new
putty.

'Good evening, Sir Toby,' said Paddy. 'I'm afraid you're wrong. I've got exact and irrefutable evidence. In fact I've got the very letter Heime Chadwick wrote before he died. The police, I believe, now have copies.'

They certainly did. All round the Regal Cinema police were in readiness. The detective in charge was in the scanner van glued to the bank of screens. There was clearly no point in making a move until the show was over. Paddy Brummel had things well in hand. This was live television at its most compulsive.

Fernando Cass forced himself to breathe through his nose and did his utmost to register a bewilderment he didn't altogether feel. 'STAR DUPED BY MURDERING MOVIE MOGULS' was the best he could hope for. Lewis was going to seek refuge in the fifth amendment.

Jemma and Hugo gripped each other's hand like the parents of a tightrope walker who is making his début, without a safety net.

'It was, as you know, a very detailed letter,' continued Paddy. 'Written on a word processor. You nephew destroyed the original print-out but he overlooked the floppy disk from which we took copies.'

'You bastard,' roared Sir Toby.

'It was that disk that he was trying to retrieve when he fell to his death. He was trying to destroy the evidence.' Paddy was shouting into the auditorium. 'The evidence against you and your bunch of great fat greedy crooks.'

Sir Toby took in his penultimate breath and moaned, 'No, no, no, no, no.' His heart was finished and his last breath was only good for the whispering of 'Dear God' before he died.

It was not until later that the trembling operator of camera 4 reflected how appropriate it was that Capitol TV's chairman should be the station's first live death on television.

At last the audience screamed. The police surged in and ten million viewers had only a brief glimpse of Paddy Brummel grinning dumbly like the surprise winner of an Oscar, before their screens went blank.

GEORGIA HAMPTON
Desire

* IVAN ST PETERS – a brilliant and
  devastatingly handsome Russian sculptor,
  possessed and tormented by his own genius and
  irresistible to every woman who crosses his
  path . . .

* MAISIE GREEN – Ivan's muse and inspiration
  who thinks she loves him until she is jilted for
  another . . .

* EMMA BLACKSTONE – heiress and the
  perfect Boston blue-stocking, prepared to
  sacrifice everything to win the man she
  desires . . .

* JULIAN SLADE – Ivan's influential and
  unscrupulous art dealer and Emma's ex-fiancé
  whose revenge threatens to destroy everything
  Ivan has lived for . . .

New York is the world of *Desire*. A world where
art and money are traded for love in the bohemian
fifties and sixties. A world where love ignores all
restraints and inhibitions and grabs you by the
soul.

SARAH DUNANT

Snow Storms
In A Hot Climate

'Full of drug smuggling, murder and revenge ...
thoroughly enjoyable and reminded me of Patricia
Highsmith at her best.'

Paul Theroux

'Snow is cocaine and when Maria goes to New
York to meet her old girl friend Elly she finds her
deeply involved with a cocaine dealer. She is
living in luxury, love and fear – can Maria get her
out? A long struggle ensues, with the snow trail
leading to California, London, Paris and Scotland.
It's not whodunnit but who's telling the most lies
that's the key to this complex, well-written story.'

Mail on Sunday

'Excellent ... tart on the tongue and satisfying to
the intellectual tastes.'

Literary Review

'A powerful account of two women's friendship
torn apart by the love affair one of them has with
an insufferable man.'

New Statesman

'High in suspense, intelligence and entertainment.'

New Society

JOAN JULIET BUCK

Daughter of the Swan

Florence's world is elegant and claustrophobic. Her life in Paris, with her antique-dealer father, is regularly punctuated with trips to London, to her charismatic Aunt Julia. But when Julia is killed, Florence is devastated. In her anguish, she consults a clairvoyant, who tells her she is soon to encounter the love of her life. And then she meets Felix.

Flawlessly handsome yet enigmatic. Felix may indeed be Florence's romantic destiny. But their relationship is only the beginning of a dark, haunting, sensual journey, a fairy-tale spell of transcendent longing and frozen passion from which Florence must ultimately be released.

'Totally absorbing on all levels. Buck is a fantastic story-teller.'

Gail Godwin

'A moody, atmospheric tale of a woman's obsessive love – it's good and it gets better.'

New York Times

'Joan Buck writes like a Colette with savvy. She creates a *demi-monde* of sophisticated innocence that is so intoxicating that you don't want to leave it.'

Emily Prager

A Selected List of Fiction Available from Mandarin

☐	7493 1352 8	**The Queen and I**	Sue Townsend	£4.99
☐	7493 0540 1	**The Liar**	Stephen Fry	£4.99
☐	7493 1132 0	**Arrivals and Departures**	Lesley Thomas	£4.99
☐	7493 0381 6	**Loves and Journeys of Revolving Jones**	Leslie Thomas	£4.99
☐	7493 0942 3	**Silence of the Lambs**	Thomas Harris	£4.99
☐	7493 0946 6	**The Godfather**	Mario Puzo	£4.99
☐	7493 1561 X	**Fear of Flying**	Erica Jong	£4.99
☐	7493 1221 1	**The Power of One**	Bryce Courtney	£4.99
☐	7493 0576 2	**Tandia**	Bryce Courtney	£5.99
☐	7493 0563 0	**Kill the Lights**	Simon Williams	£4.99
☐	7493 1319 6	**Air and Angels**	Susan Hill	£4.99
☐	7493 1477 X	**The Name of the Rose**	Umberto Eco	£4.99
☐	7493 0896 6	**The Stand-in**	Deborah Moggach	£4.99
☐	7493 0581 9	**Daddy's Girls**	Zoe Fairbairns	£4.99